BLOOD B

DEATH ON THE PITCH

EXTRA TIME

**JOSH REYNOLDS • ROBBIE MacNIVEN • ANDY HALL
MATT FORBECK • GRAEME LYON • ALEC WORLEY
DAVID ANNANDALE • GAV THORPE
DAVID GUYMER • GUY HALEY • ROBERT RATH**

BLACK LIBRARY

A BLACK LIBRARY PUBLICATION

Death on the Pitch first published in 2018.
'Dismember the Titans' first published in *Inferno! Volume 3* in 2019.
This edition published in Great Britain in 2020 by
Black Library,
Games Workshop Ltd.,
Willow Road,
Nottingham, NG7 2WS, UK.

10 9 8 7 6 5 4 3 2 1

Produced by Games Workshop in Nottingham.
Front cover illustration by Filipe Pagliuso.
Back cover illustration Karl Kopinski.

See Black Library on the internet at

blacklibrary.com

Find out more about Games Workshop
and the worlds of Warhammer at

games-workshop.com

Printed and bound by CPI Group (UK) Ltd, Croydon, CR0 4YY

'Hi there, sports fans, and welcome to the Blood
Bowl for tonight's contest. You join us here with
a capacity crowd, packed with members of every
race from across the known world, all howling like
banshees in anticipation of tonight's game. Oh, and
yes, there are some banshees... Well, kick-off is in
about two pages' time, so we've just got time to go
over to your commentator for tonight, Jim Johnson,
for a recap on the rules of the game before battle
commences. Good evening, Jim!'

'Thank you, Bob! Well, good evening and
boy, are you folks in for some great sporting
entertainment. First of all though, for those of
you at home who are unfamiliar with the rules,
here's how the game is played.

'Blood Bowl is an epic conflict between two teams
of heavily armed and quite insane warriors. Players
pass, throw and run with the ball, attempting to
get it to the other end of the field – the end zone.
Of course, the other team must try and stop them,
and recover the ball for their side. If a team gets the
ball over the line into the opponents' end zone it's
called a touchdown; the team that scores the most
touchdowns by the end of the match wins the game.
Of course, it's not always as simple as that...'

CONTENTS

MANGLERS NEVER LOSE

JOSH REYNOLDS

It was the night before game day, and Marius Hertz, star player for the number-five-ranked Middenplatz Manglers, was dead. Not dead to the world, or even dead to rights. Just plain dead. Proper dead. Ready for the deep six in the bone yard, food-for-ghouls, dead. The ex-Blitzer lay on his bed, naked save for some artfully arranged pillows. Two flat-chested, whey-faced elvish cheerleaders sat nearby, determinedly not looking at the corpse. Neither of them wore any clothes either, which wasn't surprising.

'Are you sure he's dead, Doc?' Tyros Bundt, the Manglers' coach, asked, staring down at the body. 'Maybe he's just sleeping.' Bundt was a former Blitzer, growing round in middle age, once-solid muscles going to fat. After a certain point it was all downhill, and he'd decided to enjoy the trip. He felt he'd earned it. Few Blood Bowl players survived long enough to retire, let alone get fat. Marius certainly hadn't.

'He's purple,' the doktor said. It was that sort of keen

diagnosis that had earned Doc Morgrim a position as the Manglers' team doktor. He was a thickset dwarf, covered in scars and tattoos beneath his greasy smock. His hair and beard had been stiffened with bear fat and dyed in Manglers' colours, giving him the look of someone who'd wound up on the wrong end of a lightning bolt in a dyers guild.

Morgrim poked the body with a blunt finger. 'Which, as any dwarf will tell you, is not a proper colour.'

'Maybe that's his natural hue,' Bundt said. 'My old da turned blue one time. Granted, it was cold that winter, but he never complained.'

'Marius was poisoned,' Morgrim countered, firmly.

'He didn't drink that much, surely.' Marius had been celebrating in his usual fashion. Bundt picked up a bottle and sniffed it. He gagged. It smelled like potatoes and old socks. But then, Marius hadn't cared about smell, or taste, only that it got him good and snookered. A simple sort of soul, their Marius. Simply foul.

'His insides look like porridge,' Morgrim said, opening Marius' mouth and tilting his head so Bundt could see down his throat. It wasn't pretty in there. It did look like porridge, though, albeit with lumpy bits in.

'Maybe–'

'No, it's not supposed to look like that. Someone poisoned him. Or several someones. I've detected traces of four different poisons in this mess.' Morgrim swept out a hand, indicating the trashed room. 'The coloration is due to a combination of bloat-toad venom and bile-dragon spew, the leaking and… general melting is from some Lustrian concoction – and that smell that's coming out of his pores? That's Lahmian Rhapsody, or I'm a beardling.'

Bundt goggled at him. 'Four?'

'Four.'

'That's quite a few.'

'Three more than is entirely necessary, in my experience.'

'Maybe they'll counteract each other?' Bundt asked, hopefully. He glanced at the cheerleaders. Neither would meet his gaze. The Manglers had lost star players before, but usually due to game-related mishaps. But it wouldn't have been the first time a team's rivals tried to tip the odds with a bit of extracurricular homicide. All was fair in love and Blood Bowl, especially with a tournament on the line.

Morgrim frowned and let Marius flop back down onto the bed. 'Only in the sense that they're making him dissolve.' He wiped his hands on his smock.

'Can't you prescribe something?'

Morgrim peered at the body, doing a quick calculation. 'A bucket.'

'But the game is in three hours!'

The Manglers were set to face the Haakenstadt Screechers in the final game of the DeathHex Doom Bowl. The Screechers were a vicious bunch of vermin – literally. Half the starting line were skaven, and the other half wore vaguely rat-themed gear, in the name of team spirit.

'We could… paint the bucket in team colours?' Morgrim said, with a shrug.

Bundt frowned. 'Would that work?'

'No,' Morgrim said.

'You're not helping,' Bundt said. With Marius down, they were one player short of eleven. The semi-finals had been rough on the benchwarmers, and the Manglers had lost a lot of players over the course of the tournament. And now Marius… It was as if the gods were out to get him. Bundt shook his head. Without Marius, they'd have to forfeit. 'There's got to be something you can do.'

'I'm a doktor, not a necromancer.'

Bundt snapped his fingers. 'Yes!'

'No.' Morgrim shook his head. 'That won't work. The sponsors…' The Manglers had the misfortune to be sponsored by Errantry Illustrated, the Magazine of Chivalric Virtues. Their gold spent as well as anyone else's, but it came with strings attached. Namely, the morals clause in the sponsorship contract. No lying, cheating or stealing – off the field, anyway – and certainly no drunken shenanigans with elf cheerleaders. If word of this got out, the sponsorship would be pulled, and any hope the Manglers had of competing in the tournament with it.

Bundt glanced at the cheerleaders. Neither wore Manglers' colours, which was a mixed blessing. One was from the Galadrieth Gladiators, the other the Elfheim Eagles. Both teams had been knocked out of the Doom Bowl early, though the Manglers had played neither. He wondered how long it had taken them to notice that Marius was a stiff, and not the good kind. The elf-woman bent forward and made a peculiar gulping, heaving sound, before spilling the contents of her stomach on the floor. Her friend patted her back, his thin face twisted up in sympathy. Bundt frowned.

Decision made, he turned to Morgrim. 'What the sponsors don't know won't hurt us.' Bundt pointed to the door. 'Go find me a necromancer. A good one.'

'Good ones cost money.'

'Good point. Go find me an adequate one.'

'What about the *elgi*?' Morgrim said, hiking a thumb at the elves.

'What about them?'

'One – or both – of them probably did for Marius.'

Morgrim glowered at the cheerleaders suspiciously. The elves shrank back from the dwarf's gaze.

'There's only two of them,' Bundt said.

'They could've administered two poisons each!'

'I don't care who did for Marius. He was obstreperous, obtuse and off-putting, even if he did look good on the field. Someone, somewhere, at some point was bound to do for him.' Including Bundt himself, though he didn't say that. 'No, I care about *the game.*' Bundt raised his fists to the heavens. There were stains on the ceiling, and a pair of breeches hanging from the cross-guard of a knife. Probably belonging to Marius. 'We cannot lose this game. I *will* not lose. We have never lost! Manglers never lose! That's our mantra, our guiding philosophy.'

'What about our game against the Duffenbrau Decimators last month?'

'We have lost one game! Never again!'

'Or that time against the Catrazza Birdmen the month before that?'

'Two games – there will not be a third,' Bundt growled, still staring at the ceiling. His eye began to twitch. Loss was not in his dictionary. It was something that happened to other people. People who were not Tyros Bundt.

'Or–'

Bundt whirled, veins throbbing. 'Why are you still here? Go and get me a moderately priced, relatively capable necromancer. I'll meet you in the locker rooms. We've only got a few hours before game time, and I want this problem gone by kick-off.'

Morgrim gave a lazy salute. 'I'll do my best.' He reclaimed his axe from where he'd left it propped by the door and stumped out of the hotel room.

Bundt turned back to the cheerleaders. 'Now… how much to keep this under your pom-poms? Ten gold apiece, say?'

The elves glanced at one another, and then at Marius' purple corpse. The woman wiped her mouth and said, 'How much have you got on you?'

Bundt's hands twitched as he considered their fragile, elven necks. Then he sighed and reached for his coin-pouch. One corpse to deal with was enough.

After paying off the elves and the hotel staff, Bundt had managed to get the impressively limp body rolled up into the Arabayan carpet that had been on the floor. It wasn't his first time rolling up a body in a rug, and he knew to keep the loose bits folded in and all tied tight with curtain cords and belts. Wouldn't do to have feet or fingers flopping about, attracting unwanted attention. He had to break Marius' ankles to make it work, but he figured any necromancer worth the name could fix that.

Once he'd finished disguising the body, he awkwardly manhandled his burden outside, wincing every time his star player's bonce struck a step, and onto the streets of Drachenstadt. Drachenstadt perched precariously in the heights of the Grey Mountains, spreading outward like a stain from the collapsed ruins of the ancient castle which had given the border town its name. The castle had been abandoned since the ill-fated semi-finals of the Konigswald Classic, but the town was still a riotous cauldron of scum and villainy. The perfect place for a Blood Bowl tournament, in other words.

Drachenstadt was crowded this time of year. The streets were thick with accents from as far north as Praag and as far south as Tobaro. Orcs, men, mutants and worse things rubbed shoulders, traded punches and sang boozy team songs. Everyone was in team colours, and alcohol flowed freely. The sound of impromptu celebrations and the inevitable, accompanying carnage echoed out of taverns and public halls. The air smelled of smoke, and somewhere, something large was burning, flooding the crooked streets with a flickering light. The Doom Bowl brought money into the town, so the merchants' association was willing to overlook a bit of property damage – or impromptu urban renewal, depending on your perspective. Besides, it wasn't a proper tournament until something burned down.

Bundt had managed to find a willing pair of porters at the first tavern he stumbled across. Marius was heavy, and Bundt's knees weren't in the best shape. It cost him all the gold hidden in the hollow heel of his boot, but it was worth it. The sooner he got Marius to the stadium, the better. It was almost game time.

'I tell you, manling, it's a sure thing,' the one-eyed dwarf rumbled, as he shifted Marius' dead weight to his other shoulder. He was broader than any two men, with an orange crest of hair that added substantially to his height. He was doing most of the carrying, while his red-cloaked friend did most of the complaining.

'Yes, but that was all of our money. What happens if the Manglers lose?'

'The Manglers have never lost,' Bundt interjected. He'd only been half listening, most of his attention on navigating the crowded streets. He jerked to a stop as a drunken ogre lumbered past, trailing something that still whimpered from the sole of one hobnailed boot.

'What about when they played the Blue-Blood Bandits in the Frugelhofen last year?' the man asked, shifting his grip on the end of the rug. 'Zwemmer pounded their starting line into muck two minutes in.'

'Only after he infected them with Nurgle's rot,' Bundt

snapped. His eye was twitching again. He patted it, trying to get it to calm down.

'Hertz had mushrooms sprouting from his elbows,' the dwarf said. 'Kept playing though. That manling is almost as tough as a dwarf.'

Bundt glanced back at the rug. Marius wasn't so tough anymore. 'I'm just saying, you should have talked it over with me first,' the man continued. 'How am I supposed to write about your doom, if I meet mine first from starvation?'

'I'm not paying you to write or talk, I'm paying you to carry,' Bundt said. The man fell silent, a sour look on his lean, scarred face. The dwarf chuckled and thrust a finger beneath his eye-patch, scratching at the socket.

'Still haven't said where we're going,' the dwarf said.

'There,' Bundt said. He pointed. The dwarf grunted.

Drachenstadt Stadium was a bubo of rock and timber, rising outward from the side of the town, and somewhat over it. It was built on a shelf of stone, overlooking the slopes below. Rickety seating rose upwards away from the yellowing turf of the field at odd angles. The bleachers had been repaired more than once, and it wasn't unusual for one section or another to collapse mid-game, carrying hundreds of fans to their doom. Some fans even paid extra to sit in the most dangerous sections, just for the added thrill.

'What's in this rug?' the man asked, suddenly.

'I'm not paying you to ask questions either,' Bundt said.

'Only it's leaking.'

'What?' Bundt turned. The rug was leaking. Not blood – something less pleasant. Bundt had been in the game long enough to recognise when something inside a body had burst. The dwarf dropped his burden with a curse. The man hopped back, red cloak swishing. Bundt yelped and bent over the rug.

'What is that stench?' the dwarf demanded.

'Never buy cologne from a street vendor,' Bundt said. He grabbed the edges of the rug and began to back away. The dwarf set his foot on the other end, holding it firmly in place. He grinned, showing gap-teeth.

'Good advice.'

Bundt straightened. 'Your services are no longer required. I can get him the rest of the way.' The streets weren't so crowded, this close to the stadium. There were rumours that daemons of all sorts stalked these mean streets in the days before a game, summoned by the violent anticipation of unruly fans.

'Him?' the man said, quickly.

'It. The rug.' Bundt's hand fell to the dirk on his hip. His eye was throbbing. He couldn't allow them to find out. There was no telling who they'd spill it to.

The man pushed back his cloak, revealing a long sword. The dwarf groped for something, but came up empty handed. 'Where's my axe, manling?' he demanded.

'You left it buried in that tree-man back at the Poison Feast,' the man said, without taking his eyes off Bundt. The taverns in Drachenstadt all had colourful names – the Poison Feast, Oswald's Folly, Filthy Harald's Fine Ales and Spirits. Despite the names, they all served the same brand of knock-off, watered down Bloodweiser.

'What? Why didn't you tell me?'

'It's not like it's going anywhere. He set down roots.'

The dwarf turned. He thrust a meaty finger into Bundt's face. 'You. Stay here while I fetch my axe.' He turned and caught hold of his partner's cloak. 'You – come with me. I'm going to need to stand on your shoulders.'

'But–' the man began, as the dwarf dragged him away.

Bundt watched them go. When they'd vanished into the early morning crowd, he allowed himself a sigh of relief. His eye slowed its twitching. He looked around. No one was paying attention to him. It helped that he wasn't the only shifty looking fellow dragging a smelly, leaky bundle through the streets of Drachenstadt at dawn. He wasn't even the only one on this corner, he noted, as a hunched shape hurried past, a thrashing bundle under one arm. Drachenstadt was that sort of town. He reached down and grabbed the end of the rug.

Bundt was red-faced and puffing by the time he got to the side door, where players and staff entered the cavernous tunnels which served as the locker rooms. The tunnels stretched all the way from the ruins of the castle, and smelled worse than the sewers of Nuln. Bundt had seen worse in his time, but not by much.

Gritting his teeth against the smell, he shoved, kicked and heaved Marius' body down the corridor towards the locker rooms the Manglers had claimed as their own after a vicious three-day brawl in the opening hours of the tournament. There were only a few safe spaces in the tunnels. The annual free-for-all to claim one was used to determine the starting teams for the Doom Bowl. If you were tough enough to hold on to a locker room, you were tough enough to play. It wasn't unusual for whole teams to meet their doom before the Doom Bowl even properly began. And thanks to the Necromancers Broadcasting Circle, fans got to enjoy the pre-show bloodletting from the relative safety of the stands.

A silent line of spectral monks drifted past Bundt as he hauled Marius along the uneven corridor. They whispered the odds to him, placing bets on games that had been played centuries ago. The ghosts were as much a part of the tunnels as the screaming skull in the privies, and Bundt paid them no heed. It was the living that worried him at the moment.

Despite his protestations to Morgrim, Bundt couldn't help but wonder who'd poisoned Marius. The Manglers had made a lot of enemies this season, so there wasn't a lack of suspects. And Marius made enemies the way a spendthrift spread gold. He sighed as he dragged the rug and its contents into the locker room. 'If you weren't dead, I'd kill you myself,' he muttered.

Alive or dead, Marius was costly to keep around. The only reason he'd put up with the Blitzer for so long was Marius' almost supernatural skill with a ball. Some men were just built for Blood Bowl. Terrible at everything else, though. In Bundt's day, personal issues had been the leading cause of player death, besides the game itself. Nowadays, it was rare for a player to play injured, let alone go haring off to the far side of the world on a doomed quest for a missing sibling, and Nuffle be praised for that, at least. Annoying as Marius was, he'd needed the Blitzer. Bundt was willing to do anything – put up with anyone – to keep the Manglers in the game. Even if it meant selling his soul to a necromancer.

'We've never lost,' Bundt said, to himself. 'And we're not about to start now.' He dragged the rug along the row of lockers. He would hide the body until Morgrim showed up. He found Marius' locker easily enough – it was the only one stuffed to capacity with empty bottles, undergarments and fan mail. It was also the biggest.

The lockers were made from old, iron-banded coffins of varying sizes and degrees of craftsmanship. What hundreds of empty coffins had been doing down in the tunnels under the castle, Bundt didn't like to think about. Marius' was roughly ogre-sized.

The Blitzer always claimed the biggest locker for himself. Just like he got the best hotel rooms, the most fan mail… everything. Marius was the Manglers, in all the ways that counted. Even more so than the other players and even Bundt himself. He untied the rug and pried Marius' sticky corpse free. The smell hit him like a punch to the nose. Luckily, they were in a locker room.

As he opened the locker, it vomited its contents onto the floor – clothes, bottles and… gold? Bundt stared at the money. More than a few coins. In fact, there was a sack, hidden in Marius' spare helmet. He ran his hands through it, enjoying the feel of coins clinking through his fingers. Money was always in short supply. A competitive team, even a successful one, racked up expenses. He glanced at the body.

'Where did you get this?' he asked, frowning. Marius didn't answer. Bundt shook his head, as the barest shadow of suspicion took shape. Four poisons, and now money. What was going on? He forced the thought aside. None of that mattered. Only the game mattered. And he intended to win, dead star player or not.

Bundt unwrapped Marius. He needed to get him into his uniform before he hid him. That would make things easier. He unrolled the rug and leaned Marius against the locker. The poisons in his system had made him fairly floppy, and Bundt wondered if he had any ligaments left. It felt like trying to dress a bag of sand, but he got the flaccid limbs in the proper holes eventually.

As he was finishing up, a door slammed. Rough voices grumbled. Bundt, surprised, stumbled and fell back into Marius' open locker and inadvertently pulled the body towards him. The more he struggled, the deeper he sank into the coffin, drowning in unwashed, bloodstained clothes and perfumed fan mail. There was no way to get Marius in, or himself out, before the intruders arrived. He grabbed hold of Marius to keep him from toppling over, and leaned back. Hopefully it would just look as if the Blitzer were drunk and vomiting into his own locker. Purple, but drunk.

The voices got louder. Orcs, he thought. Lockers rattled as green fists pummelled them. Two sets of fists, two voices. 'Marius... come out to play,' an orc rumbled, as it stepped around the end of the row. 'Thought that were you, Hertz. They said you snuck out of the hotel in a rug. Dead clever, you are.'

'Knew we was on his trail, innit?' the other orc said, laughing nastily.

Bundt struggled not to make any noise. The orcs couldn't see him, wedged into the coffin-locker as he was, with Marius leaning against it. For the moment, at any rate. He didn't like to think about what would happen when they did.

'We need to talk, Hertz,' the first plug-ugly growled. The orc thumped a fist into his palm. Through the locker slats, Bundt could just make out a rat-skin jersey stretched tight over the greenskin's barrel chest. Screechers' fans. As if things weren't bad enough. 'Word is, you is planning on trying to win, tomorrow.'

'But you is supposed to lose,' the other orc growled. 'The boss paid you to lose. So you can't win, see?'

Boss? They could only mean the Screechers' coach, Red Warpbite. Red wasn't above a bit of strategic cheating when it suited him, on and off the field.

Bundt stifled a growl. That explained the money he'd found in the locker. He wasn't against a player making money on the side, but not during the finals. And certainly not without cutting the rest of the team in on the action. Especially his coach. He glared at Marius' slack, empurpled features. If the poison hadn't done for him, Bundt might've killed the Blitzer himself.

'We is supposed to hurt you a bit, Hertz. But we is thinking you might need a bit more than hurting.'

Bundt heard the sound of metal sliding over leather. He knew the sound of a knife being drawn when he heard it. The orc stopped, just on the other side of the locker door. 'Oi... why is you purple?'

Bundt jerked Marius to the side, driving his dead weight into the orc. The orc fell with a roar, and his companion lunged. Marius was wrenched from Bundt's hands, a knife jutting from the side of his skull. Bundt slammed into the locker door, causing it to smash the orc in the face. As one greenskin fell down, unconscious, the other scrambled back, piggy eyes wide in shock. 'What–?' he began. Then, 'Urk.' The orc toppled forward, a dwarf axe buried in the back of his head.

Morgrim clucked his tongue. 'What happened?' he asked, as he retrieved the axe from the orc's skull. A small, thin man, all in black robes, stood behind him, nervously cleaning a pair of tinted spectacles. He wore a cloak made from black feathers, and a tastefully distasteful necklace of finger bones.

'You killed him,' Bundt said, trying to free himself. It was no use; he was properly wedged into the locker. He had a momentary panic, as visions of being buried in a coffin full of stained breeches and perfumed letters welled up in his mind. Morgrim sighed and reached for him.

'I meant before that.'

'They killed Marius,' Bundt said, as Morgrim pried him out of the coffin-locker. 'Again.' Bundt crouched beside Marius' body and jerked the knife free. 'At least it was in the head. Nobody will notice the hole if we get a helmet on him.'

'He's leaking.'

'He was already leaking.' Bundt turned to the thin man. 'You're a necromancer?' Bundt asked, looking him up and down. He was certainly dressed like a necromancer – all in black, with that necklace and his teeth stained black. He wore scratched spectacles and had too many rings on his thin, pale fingers. As Bundt looked closer, he realised the feathered cloak wasn't made of crow or raven feathers, as he'd thought, but pigeon feathers, dyed black. His heart sank. What sort of necromancer couldn't even get proper crow feathers?

'I consider myself more a facilitator for the magic of death. Necromancer sounds so unpleasant.' The necromancer grinned, showing off his teeth. His accent was vague, from someplace full of sun and wine. 'I am Franco Fiducci. I can provide references.'

'I bet you can.'

'Living ones.'

Bundt blinked. 'Oh. Well, no time for that.' He kicked Marius. 'What can you do about this?'

'The colour, you mean?'

'No. All of it. His general state of – of…' Bundt shrugged helplessly.

'Death,' Morgrim said, helpfully.

'I can't bring him back to life, if that's what you're asking,' Fiducci said.

'I don't care if he's alive – I just want him to play,' Bundt said.

Fiducci smiled. 'That I can do.' He rubbed two fingers together. 'It'll be expensive.'

Bundt looked at Morgrim. 'I thought I said find a cheap one.'

'He is – comparatively,' Morgrim said. 'He only wants money, rather than your soul.'

'Preferably lots of money,' Fiducci interjected.

'Yes, it must cost quite a bit to dye all those pigeons.' Bundt sighed and reached into Marius' locker for the gold. 'Is this enough?' he asked, as he tossed the helmet to Fiducci. The necromancer weighed it in his hand and nodded jerkily, eyes wide.

'Practically a retainer.'

'Good. Consider yourself on the payroll.' He looked past the necromancer. Morgrim was questioning their prisoner.

'Why did you poison him?' Morgrim demanded, dragging the dazed orc up, until they were nose to nose. The orc's eyes crossed as he tried to focus.

'What?'

Morgrim punched the greenskin and let him flop back down. 'I don't think they poisoned him.'

'And I said I don't care *who* poisoned him. This is Blood Bowl, Doc. People die. Usually on the field, granted, but Marius was never all that considerate.' He looked at Fiducci. 'Well?'

'It will take much time to recall his ghost and–' Fiducci began.

'How much time to get him moving?'

'A few minutes. But he'll be a mindless husk, fit only for menial tasks.'

'In other words, the perfect Blood Bowl player.' Bundt rubbed his hands together in glee. 'Get him moving. The others will be arriving soon.'

It took Fiducci longer than a few minutes. 'It's the poison, you see,' he said, pushing his spectacles up the bridge of his nose. 'Poisons, I should say. It's rather like trying to animate an empty sack. Only the sack is full of rubbish.'

Zombie-Marius twitched and flopped on the floor like a suffocating fish. Fiducci gestured sharply, clawing at the air. Marius slid up, and sank down with a faint squishing noise. Bundt gnawed on a thumbnail. 'If he can't walk...' Morgrim began.

'As long as he can stumble to his starting position, I don't care. I'm not forfeiting this game. The Manglers have never forfeited a game!'

'What about the Wasteland Bowl?' Morgrim said.

'The dugout collapsed,' Bundt said. Eight players had died, his dreams (and their bones) crushed by cheap construction materials. A dark day for the team.

'We still forfeited,' Morgrim said.

'Not by choice!'

Morgrim shrugged. 'We call it now, we can get out of town before the fans realise what's happening. We might even make it back to Middenplatz without losing anyone else.'

Marius bobbed up again, feet slipping on the floor. His jaw hung slack, and something oily, and possibly acidic, drooled from his purple lips. His big hands twitched, groping blindly.

Fiducci waved a hand in front of the Blitzer's opaque eyes. The zombie lurched forward, reaching. Fiducci jerked back as Marius tried to bite him.

Morgrim caught the zombie's arms and Bundt crammed a helmet on the wobbling head. The visor of the helmet acted as a makeshift muzzle. Fiducci's fingers lit up with purple light and he tapped Marius on his chest. The zombie stiffened and slumped, dribbling quietly. 'That should do it,' the necromancer said.

'He can play?'

'More or less.' Fiducci cleaned his spectacles. 'Not as well as he did, obviously. But loss of skill is more than made up for by durability. The average zombie is good for... two, three games at least, if you take care of them.' He hefted his helmet full of gold. 'Now, I'll just be on my–'

'Oh no you don't,' Bundt said, grabbing the necromancer by his skull necklace. 'Retainer, remember?' Fiducci made to protest, but whatever he saw in Bundt's twitching eye silenced him. 'Welcome to the Manglers, Mister Fiducci. I only have one rule – the Manglers never, ever lose. No matter what.'

Fiducci frowned in puzzlement. 'Wait – didn't the Dwarf Giants pummel you in Dungeon Bowl last season?'

'That was a statistical anomaly,' Bundt said, from between clenched teeth. His eye was twitching so badly, it felt as if it were going to rip itself off his face.

'It looked more like a Deathroller.'

Bundt gently took Fiducci's neck in his hands. 'A. Statistical. Anomaly.' He stared deep into Fiducci's wide, terrified eyes. 'Are we clear?' He took Fiducci's squeak as a gesture of assent and loosened his grip.

Voices reached them, slithering through the corridors. The Manglers were arriving. 'Get him into Marius' locker,' Bundt hissed. Morgrim grabbed Fiducci and stuffed the protesting necromancer into the open coffin and slammed the lid. Bundt forced the blank-eyed zombie to sit, just as the first of the Manglers shuffled in. Most of them looked the worse for wear and, for a moment, Bundt wondered if Marius was the only dead man on his team.

Marius attracted a few second glances. Most of that was due to his new necrotic colouration, and possibly the copious drool. But some of those glances were more than curious. Bundt had been a coach long enough to tell when some of his players were feeling guilty. He traded looks with Morgrim. The dwarf nodded sourly and held up four fingers. Bundt sighed. 'Take a knee, lads – and lasses, sorry, Sora,' Bundt said, waving off a protest from Sora Oflrsdottir. The henna-haired, late-season trade from Vanheim Valkyries scowled and leaned her muscular frame against a locker.

Bundt studied the faces of his players. All of them were human, or close enough for book-keeping purposes. Nine men and one woman, as fine a team as one could get on short notice. 'Is Marius okay?' Sora asked.

'He's fine,' Bundt said.

'He's leaking. And not like normal.'

'He always does that. Ignore it.'

'Only it's eating through the floor...'

Bundt shook his head. 'Never mind. Now... what is it, Mueller?'

Horst Mueller shot a nervous glance at Marius. He was the team's thrower, with an arm like a trebuchet and a brain like one of those rocks that the trebuchet threw. 'There's a foot sticking out of that locker, Coach.'

Bundt leaned towards him. 'Do I pay you to look at lockers, Mueller?'

'No, Coach. Only it looks like there's someone trapped in there.'

'What about me, Mueller? I'm trapped in here – in a cage of despair.' Bundt slapped his chest. 'My heart is aching, Mueller. Why not think about me, for once?'

Mueller stared at him in horrified fascination. Bundt's eye felt as if it were doing a jig. He looked around, good eye narrowed in general reproach, of the players, the world, the fates themselves. 'Right. So which one of you poisoned Marius?'

Uncertain faces glanced nervously at one another. Bundt pinched the bridge of his nose. 'I'm not mad. Nuffle knows,

I considered it myself. But the night before a game? Especially *this* game? Which of you idiots is responsible for this?'

Five hands went up, including Sora's. Bundt wasn't the only one surprised. As the players looked at one another in shock, Morgrim chuckled. 'Guess I missed one.' He looked at Sora. 'Lahmian Rhapsody?'

'What? No. Lustrian Hisser. Makes the veins go kerplop.' She mimed an exploding vein. Then, defensively. 'He hogged the ball.'

Bundt shook his head. He looked at another player – Berkut. The Arabayan tapped his lips. 'Mine was the Rhapsody, Coach. I thought no one would notice if he keeled over during – ah… you know.' He gestured and shrugged. 'Served him right, after what he did to my sister… my brother… my cousins… our goat…' He trailed off. 'He was an honourless dog.'

The other three were much the same story – Marius had borrowed money from one, stolen a lucky charm from another, and had left the third with a bar tab the size of Altdorf. Old resentments, boiling over into murder. It was always the way. Normally, murder was confined to the field, but Marius had been a special case.

Bundt looked at Mueller. 'What about you? Anything to contribute?'

'No, I only stabbed him, Coach,' Mueller said. The others threw stray bits of armour at him, forcing him to cover his head with his hands. 'What? He kept snapping me with his towel – a man can only take so much!'

Bundt shot a look at Morgrim, who blinked. 'That explains the knife blade broken off in his stomach. I thought he'd swallowed it.' He shrugged. 'It didn't seem relevant to the poisoning, so I didn't think to mention it.'

'Why would he have swallowed a knife?' Bundt asked, his

voice deceptively calm. He wondered if hiring a dwarf doktor for a human team had been the smartest of moves.

'Who knows why you humans do anything? I'm a doktor,
not a philosopher.'

Bundt rubbed his face and patted Mueller on the shoulder. 'Thank you, Mueller. Your restraint is noted. As for the
rest of you... you're a bloody team! Why don't you act like
it?' He looked around. 'I know Marius was a living stain, but
five poisons? And a knife?' He wagged his finger. 'Next time,
gentlemen, consult with your teammates. Consult with me,
for Nuffle's sake! Set the play, follow it through. Trust each
other. What's a team without trust?'

Sora raised her hand. 'Are – are you sure he's fine?'

'Just a bit of an upset stomach,' Bundt said, with forced
cheerfulness. His twitch was growing worse, and it had
brought reinforcements. 'He'll be right as rain, soon enough.'

'Speaking of rain, he's leaking again,' Morgrim said.

'Stuff a sock in the hole to plug it up.' Bundt clasped his
hands behind his back. 'Let's go, Manglers. We've got a game
to win.'

Bundt had to admit that this year's Doom Bowl sponsors
had gone all out. A ghostly advertisement floated above the
field, surrounded by a flotilla of agitated spirits– 'DeathHex –
When they absolutely, positively have to die overnight!' –and
crackling with ominously cheerful, amethyst lightning.

Word was, with Tomolandry the Undying finally considering retirement for the fifth time in five hundred years,
DeathHex was looking for a new team to sponsor. Which
was convenient, given that the Manglers were about to lose
their current sponsors.

'This is an outrage,' the man from Errantry Magazine shouted.

'Errantry Magazine won't stand for this… this blatant violation of your ethics clause.' He was a big man, dressed in battered chainmail and a crisp, white tabard that was bright enough to blind the unwary.

'What violation?' Bundt asked, trying to keep one eye – the one that wasn't twitching – on the game. So far, the Manglers were holding their own – the Screechers had looked fairly put out at Marius' presence. Red Warpbite was probably gnawing his own tail in frustration. Bundt grinned. Served the scabby git right.

'Your blitzer – our spokesperson – is clearly an undead monstrosity.'

'You're only saying that because he's missing an arm,' Bundt said, wheeling on the other man. 'He gave a limb for you – what more do you want?'

'He's purple – bits are falling off,' the sponsor shouted, grabbing a handful of Bundt's shirt. 'There are knives in him. Multiple knives!'

'He's passionate… determined… tough…' The skaven had been trying to bring Marius down since the kick-off. But Fiducci's promise of durability had proven true – Marius had been tough in life. Now, in death, he was the next best thing to an avalanche.

'He's lost a leg now,' the sponsor shrieked, staring out at the field in horror.

Bundt slapped his hands away. 'We'll sew it back on. No one will notice – throw the gods-cursed ball, Mueller!' He shoved the sponsor aside and leaned out of the dugout, shouting at the hapless thrower. Mueller looked around desperately as a rat-ogre charged towards him, bellowing in fury.

Morgrim sidestepped the angry sponsor as the man stomped away, scowling. 'There goes another endorsement deal,'

Morgrim said. He winced as Marius lost his other arm to a chainsaw wielding skaven. 'And another arm.' Marius had the ball wedged in his helmet and was ploughing forward like a vaguely human-shaped battering ram. Skaven were stomped into squealing pancakes beneath his unfeeling feet.

'Who cares? Good riddance. When we win, sponsors will be lining up. DeathHex is looking for a new team.' Bundt stepped back as a stray bit of Marius bounced into the dug-out. 'Look at him go. He never ran that fast while he was alive!'

'He's only got one leg,' Morgrim said.

'He's streamlined. Shed all that offseason weight. Touch-down!' Bundt threw up his hands and howled in joy. Morgrim shook his head.

'While your pet zombie was stumbling downfield, we lost Mueller,' he said, as a pair of stretcher-bearers jogged out of the dugout, heading for the irate rat-ogre and what was left of Horst Mueller. The rat-ogre was repeatedly slamming the unfortunate Mueller into the turf. He was deader than Marius. 'And Sora just got mobbed by gutter runners,' Morgrim added. 'We're down four more players.'

'But we're up on points,' Bundt said.

'We barely have a team.'

'Easily rectified,' Fiducci said, fiddling with his spectacles. 'I can have them on their feet at half-time.' He slid his spectacles on and squinted owlishly. 'I am on retainer, after all.' He frowned. 'Indeed, we might even be able to make a few improvements...'

'Improvements?' Bundt asked.

Fiducci nodded. 'They're doing wonderful things with light-ning in Ingolstadt these days...'

'Lightning,' Bundt repeated. His eye ceased its twitching.

'What about Sora?' Morgrim demanded.

A mangled gutter runner bounced off the dugout and flopped to the turf. The former Valkyrie clambered to the top of a fuzzy heap, a handful of severed tails in her hand. She let out a long, ululating cry even as the half-time buzzer sounded.

'Sora's fine,' Bundt said. He looked at Fiducci. 'You mentioned lightning?'

Morgrim sighed. 'What am I supposed to do with a team full of dead men?'

Bundt looked at him. 'Is that what's bothering you?'

Morgrim glared at him. 'What's a team doktor supposed to do if his players are past caring about medical care?'

'Earn the easiest money of your misbegotten life?' Bundt said. Morgrim looked at him. He blinked. A slow grin spread across his battered features and he swatted Fiducci on the back, nearly bowling the little man over.

'Welcome to the team,' he said. 'Rule one: Manglers never lose.'

FIXED

ROBBIE MacNIVEN

The stadium was rocking. From the upper spires, where Grizmund and his gaggle of pale-fleshed vampire thralls had secured the best seats, to the pitch-side barricades, where half a dozen fights had already broken out between irate supporters, every man, elf and beast inside the Thunderdome Nordlander Arena was on up its feet, claws or paws. Cabal Vision were giving a pitch-side interview to a halfling pundit more preoccupied by dodging the remains of a Hackers Dunk Doughnuts advertising board being flung by the crowd, while the Nordlander cheerleading team were going through their flashiest routine, pompoms a yellow and blue blaze.

It was half time, and it was going well for the Nordland Rangers. Too well.

'Do you think the fixers have got to them?' Klimt asked. The rest of the Rangers shouted the lineman down, filling the dugout with their disapproval.

'Tell Kelled that,' Garr said over the outrage, nodding

towards the medical lean-to, where the team's apothecary, the butcher-turn-chirurgeon Mikal Frisk, was attempting to staunch the blood pouring from the catcher's mangled arm. A Kroxigor, the biggest creature on the pitch, had caught Kelled just before the halftime whistle. His screams were lost amidst the roaring of the crowd.

'There have been too many shock results since the split,' Klimt went on, ignoring the abuse he was getting from the rest of the huddle. 'Everyone knows someone's got to halve the coaches. They're making a fortune off these outcomes.'

'Who in Nuffle's name would the scalies do a deal with though?' Torvern, the stocky little catcher, demanded. 'They'd as soon rip legs off as take a bribe.'

'Depends on the bribe,' Klimt countered.

'That's enough,' snapped Coach Rife. The lanky, scarred ex-blitzer took off his feathered cap to mop his brow, glaring at Klimt. 'That sort of talk undermines everything we've done to make it this far. Everything *I've* done, Klimt. Do you want me to bin you?'

'No coach,' the lineman said, eyes on his boots.

Rife nodded, gaze sweeping the rest of the team.

'We're up eleven touchdowns to six, against a lizardmen team touted to finish a comfortable second in the playoffs. We're going to put this one to bed. Break these scalies and it's us versus the East End Boyz in the playoff final. I don't need to tell you all that's where we want to be.'

'Yes, coach,' the Rangers chorused.

'Same as we've done all season,' Rife went on. 'Garr, take us down the middle, box formation. Vulf, can you keep up?'

Kelled's substitute grinned and nodded.

'Damn scalies won't lay a claw on me, coach.'

'Good. Dumpf, just... do what you've been doing all game.'
The hulking ogre frowned, squinting down at Rife.

'Der...' he began to say, picking at his crooked nose.

'Tackle the Kroxigor, Dumpf. So Garr can get through.
Don't let that thing catch him the way it caught Kelled. Stop
the Krox, that's all you have to do.'

'The... croc see what?'

'The big lizard, Dumpf. The big, scaly bastard lizard. As
soon as he makes a move for Thunderbolt here, bring him
down.' Rife smacked Garr's battered helmet for emphasis.

'Sure thing, coach.' The ogre went back to picking his nose.

'Right. Okay then. Let's do this, Rangers!'

Garr dropped into his familiar central position, flexing his
back and shoulder muscles. The comfortable score line didn't
reflect the reality of playing against lizardmen – iron-hard
muscles and iron-hard scales meant a lot of hard knocks.

He glanced up at the main stand, and the rickety spire-
towers occupied by Grizmund and his bloodsuckers. In
over a decade of professional league Blood Bowl, Garr had
long ago learned to block out the crowd, at least until they
started throwing spiked projectiles or shrieking goblins onto
the pitch. Today, though, he couldn't shake the hypnotic,
black gaze of the ancient bloodsucker. He owed the dia-
bolical mobster money. Thanks to his gambling he owed
half the damn town money, but Grizmund was just about
the only one with the means to actually pursue a debt
from the most famous and successful blitzer in Nordland
history. The so-called Throat-Ripper, himself a long-retired
blocker from the Arterial Jets, had 'treated' Garr to lunch
at the Crow's Corpse only last week, an eatery that just so
happened to sit across the street from the dank, crumbling
stonework and rusting iron of the debtors' prison. For all

his on-pitch success this season, Garr knew he was running out of time.

'Let's end these coldbloods, Rangers!' he shouted, adrenaline spiking. 'I'll give two-to-one odds on the touchdown whistle blowing in under two minutes.'

The rest of the team growled their approval. Sadly, none of them actually took him up on the bet. More was the pity.

He slammed a fist against his chest plate and dug his boots into the ravaged turf near the line of scrimmage. To the Wastes with Grizmund and his corpse cronies. He looked away from the spire seats and took note of the skink runners making up the lizardman front row. The diminutive yellow-spotted creatures had been unusually sluggish so far, but Garr was still certain they'd try their hardest to slip through the Rangers' backline as soon as one of their bigger saurus team mates were able to wrestle the ball from the humans. Kriegveld and the other linemen had better be up to standard when it came to their blocks.

The goblin referee's whistle shrilled, the crowd's roaring redoubled, and the Rangers were going forward. Garr snatched the ball from where it thumped down after kick-off, its battered leather cradled in both spiked gauntlets. The scalies were defending a high line, racing to meet them. Garr felt a roar building in his throat, body driven on by the swelling howl of the crowd. He hit the line of scrimmage at full tilt. A skink simply disappeared beneath him, his outstretched fist slamming it down into the trampled dirt.

'On your left!' Gruber, the younger, rookie blitzer, shouted. Garr was vaguely aware of his offer of support, but he was still going, the chequered earth of the end zone beckoning him on. The catchers were almost in position. He barely knew what was happening either side of him – the thud and crunch of impacting bodies was all he heard. None of it really registered. It never did. Once he was committed, blitzing through the centre, nothing was going to distract him. That was why he was the best. That was why they were going to win.

'Watch for the block!' shouted Rell, one of the linesmen following the Nordlander attack. Garr had already spotted it. One last hurdle – a big saurus backliner. Garr had already taken the lizard down twice in the first half. It wasn't going to stop the Thunderbolt now.

He hit it with his shoulder, a classic barge, his spiked pauldron hammering the creature's scaly hide. The lizardman snatched for the ball even as it went down, claws raking off Garr's breastplate and gauntlets. The blitzer put his boot into the struggling coldblood for good measure, driving over him, launching himself at that final grassy expanse. Vulf the catcher was there – he'd made it through the scalies' backline too. He was screaming for the ball. The crowd was going wild. Garr pulled his arm back, ball in hand, winding up for a throw he'd made a thousand times before. It was all over. The playoff final was theirs.

'Garr, watch out!'

Gruber's shout came too late. Something hit him. He knew straight away that it wasn't a skink, or even a saurus. He was going down, the ball tumbling from his grasp, the air driven from his lungs. His left side crunched into the dirt, the force of the impact half spinning him onto his back and cracking his helmet off the ground. For a second he found himself staring through the grille of his visor up at a clear, blue sky.

Then the Kroxigor stepped over him. Clearly, Dumpf hadn't managed to stop the huge lizardman. The ogre was probably still too busy picking at a particularly intransigent wad of snot lodged in his nostril.

'Great Nuffle's hairy arse,' Garr panted, struggling for breath. The ball was embedded in the dirt next to him, spikes gleaming. He lunged for it.

And so did the lizardmen. With a shriek, a swarm of skinks mobbed him from every side, burying him in a mound of scrabbling, pale, leathery flesh. Garr tried to heave himself up, but found he was pinned. As the mound of bodies on top of him increased, the pressure became unbearable. He panicked, rendered helpless, unable to see for the creatures swarming over him. The last thing he felt before the darkness took him was the Kroxigor's grip on his leg, tightening.

Garr woke up reaching for the ball. It took a second for him to realise he was clutching at blocker Markus's thigh. He was on his back, and he was moving, though at first he wasn't sure how. Above was a cloudless sky, and faces. Girls. Garr realised that he was dead. He was dead, and in heaven.

As was, apparently, the entire cheerleading squad. Garr blinked. No, he wasn't dead after all. He was on a stretcher. Another face pushed its way in amongst the concerned expressions of the Nordlander cheerleaders. Torvern, streaked with sweat. The lineman was speaking, but Garr couldn't make out the words. His ears were ringing, the incessant buzz overlaying a distant roar that swelled like the crash of waves upon a far-off, jagged coastline. After a moment he recognised the sound – thirty thousand bloodthirsty spectators, howling equal parts approval and dismay.

He was being carried towards the tunnel and out of the rickety old timber stadium. His leg was in agony. He tried to sit, but even looking for purchase with his elbows set his head spinning. He slumped back, as the tidal roar rose up to swallow him. The last thing he heard were Torvern's words, repeated over and over, reaching him as though from far away.

We won.

The light filtering through the yellow canvas of the apothecary's tent stained everything the colour of stale urine. Garr gritted his teeth, as much to keep out the smell as to bite back against the pain infusing his leg.

'It looks bad,' said Frisk, looming over the table Garr had been laid on.

'Is that a professional medical opinion, sawbones?' Garr demanded, glaring up at the fat ex-butcher. Frisk grimaced, his heavy jowls streaked with sweat. The tent was infernally hot, and the apothecary's grubby blue overalls were stained dark with perspiration.

'As professional as it's going to get, I'm afraid,' he said, lifting the cloth away from Garr's thigh. The Thunderbolt focused his eyes on the canvas directly above – he didn't want to see it. He felt chubby fingers probe his limb.

'Does that hurt?'

'No,' Garr growled, knuckles white.

'How about now?'

Garr nodded through clenched teeth.

'I'm going to have to operate,' Frisk said, leaning over Garr so the Thunderbolt was looking up at him.

'You keep your damn rusty blades away from me,' Garr snapped. Before Frisk could respond the tent flap snatched back. Coach Rife ducked inside, pulling his feather cap from his balding head.

'Well?' he demanded, eyes darting from the apothecary to his star player. Frisk shrugged.

'Like I said, it's bad.'

'No one can see you like this,' Rife said, turning to Garr. 'The fans will go wild. There'll be a riot. We've got to get you fixed up.'

'Just keep this butcher away from me,' Garr said, forcing himself up onto one elbow. 'I'll not play in the final if he touches me, you can bet your last reikmark on it.'

'If I don't operate, you won't play again at all,' Frisk said. 'Then he won't be leading your lineout any more, Herr Rife.'

'Is that your professional medical opinion?' Rife asked.

Frisk sighed loudly, mopping at his chins with a stained handkerchief.

'This team pays me to treat it. The money comes out of your earnings as well. By all means, let your star player walk out of here right now – assuming he can even stand. But don't blame me when he finally comes to terms with the fact that he refused to have a career-threatening injury operated on.'

Rife looked at Frisk, then at Garr, then back to Frisk. He approached the operating table and peered at the Thunderbolt's exposed thigh. The stinking shadows couldn't hide his grimace.

'It's bad,' he said.

'I know, damn it,' Garr spat, still refusing to look at the injury. 'I'm not letting him give me the chop, Rife.'

'You'll still have two legs,' Frisk mumbled. 'I'll fix it. Just... don't worry!'

'What's that supposed to mean?' Garr snarled.

'You won't even notice the difference, trust me. In fact, you may even be able to play better!'

'Frisk is right,' Rife said, patting Garr's bruised shoulder. 'I pay him too damn much not to use his... abundant medical talents.'

Garr slumped back, eyes closed.

'Just not above the thigh, right doc?'

'Keep your knives away from his crotch,' Rife said to Frisk. The apothecary rolled his piggy eyes and picked up a tankard from a nearby bench.

'Bugman's XXXXXX,' he said, bending down to help Garr into a sitting position.

'For the pain?' Garr asked, reaching out shakily. He grimaced when, instead of passing it to him, Frisk gulped down the tankard's contents instead.

'For my hands,' the ex-butcher said, belching loudly. 'Helps keep them steady. Right, let's get started.'

They smuggled him from the stadium district in the back of an anonymous black hire carriage, the driver walking away with a few coins and promises that his family would suffer if a word of the Thunderbolt's state reached the papers. Garr lolled in the carriage's back seat, half covered by a team blanket, blessedly oblivious to every jarring rut. Rife had at least managed to convince Frisk to be liberal with the poppy tonic, or he had after Garr's screaming had run the risk of alerting people to his condition.

There were no opportunistic journos lurking around the Thunderbolt's luxury inner-town manse – the baleful presence of Nog made sure of that. The ever-faithful ogre ex-player was patrolling the perimeter, a big, lumbering shape in the fading light. Frisk and Rife managed to haul Garr from the carriage and put him into the ogre's arms.

'Take… him… bed,' Rife said, speaking slowly. 'Don't let anyone in until we return. Especially not any reporters, or Grizmund's debt collectors.'

Nog nodded.

'What did he just say?' Frisk asked.

'Put Thunderman bed,' the ogre said slowly, squinting. 'And… no let-ins.'

'Don't let him put any betting coupons on either,' Frisk said as they left.

Garr remained unconscious as Nog carried him through what had once been the most sought-after bachelor pad in the Lower Nordside. Now dark reikswood-panelled walls that had once been hung with signed sketches of the greatest Rangers were bare, their decorations auctioned off one after the other to pay for Garr's inveterate gambling. The floors were similarly unadorned, the thick Araby rugs long gone. Every surface was collecting dust, and cobwebs had started to conglomerate around the ceiling – he'd stopped paying the cleaner just over a month before. Of course she'd run to the press with reports about the state of Garr's finances, reports Rife had been quick to counter. A halfling cleaner would say anything for a free pie or two.

Nog placed Garr carefully on his cheap wooden bed and, with forefinger and thumb, tucked him beneath the blue and yellow covers. The ogre stood looking down at his master, a lazy smile tugging at his blunt features. After a while he seemed to snap back to the present. He tiptoed over to the window, the dusty floorboards squealing beneath his weight. Satisfied that it was closed, he glanced one more time at his master before lumbering from the room.

Two days passed. Frisk visited frequently with a variety of home-made potions and salves, keeping Garr under for what he described as 'bonding time'. Nog fed the blitzer during his rare moments of lucidity, Garr accepting messy spoonfuls only with glaring truculence. The papers would have a field day if they could see him – the highest capped, highest-earning, longest-serving blitzer in Nordland history – laid up and baby-fed by his big, clumsy house-ogre.

It all changed on the third night. Frisk had been and gone, demanding as usual that Garr keep his leg tightly bound, and refrain from putting too much weight on it. Nog had administered his evening repast – brutally hacked-up vegetables in a soupy mixture tarnished with far too much Stirland pepper. Garr was dozing off, the pain of his damaged limb a dull, distant ache.

A scratching sound disturbed him. He looked up at the ceiling's timber beams, but saw nothing. That was when something unusual struck him. He realised that he was cold.

There was a breeze. It was knocking, ever so gently, at the open shutters. Garr sat up, scowling. Nog had forgotten to lock the window. He drew a breath to bark the ogre's name, then thought better of it. He'd seen enough of the lumbering oaf over the past two days.

He threw back the covers, struck a spark to the candle stub and, after a second's hesitation, swung both limbs out over the edge of the bed. The injury had gone from painful to infernally itchy. He glared down at the inelegant wedge of bandages and plaster, willing the sensation to go away. Then, when it didn't, he stepped down onto the floor.

The itch turned to pain, and he flinched. Still, his other leg could take enough weight. He tottered over to the window, closed it, and banged the lock down. Then he slumped back into his bed.

The itching grew worse. It was unbearable. What in Nuffle's name had that damned butcher done to him?

He could stand it no longer. He snatched the covers back again and reached down to start tearing away the stiff bandages. They tore loudly in his fevered grip, cast across the room as he dug towards the source of the itch. Finally, his nails scraped something that wasn't just cloth and plaster of Parravon. Pain pulsed dully from beneath his fingertips. Only, he wasn't probing flesh. He frowned, wondering what sort of plaster Frisk had used for the lower cast.

More of the bandages fell away, and he saw something that made the itch vanish into insignificance. It wasn't plaster he could feel after all.

Before him was a thigh completely covered in thick, dark blue scales. They glistened in the flickering candlelight, hard to the touch. Slowly, mouth agape, he dragged away the bandages around his waist, exposing where Frisk had sewed and sutured the unnatural flesh to his own upper leg. The sight set his stomach churning. It only got worse when he moved the leg slightly, and the strange, leathery skin beneath the scales responded.

He'd seen this leg before. He knew exactly where it had come from. The coldbloods. One of the saurus blockers. Frisk had replaced his lower limb with a lizardman leg!

Maybe he'd have screamed, were it not for the scratching. The sound was back, digging away at the timber somewhere in the room. As he focused on it the heavy Guterdorf grandfather clock – the only one in the house not yet sold off or gambled away – counted sonorously past the witching hour. He started. The hideous limb twitched. Garr croaked a curse as the scraping sound continued. One of the worst things about going bankrupt was running out of money to pay the rat catcher. The old townhouse seemed permanently infested.

'Nog,' he said, his voice a dry croak. As he tried to marshal some spit he suddenly became aware of a presence beside his bed.

'Hippogriff's balls,' he grunted, twisting towards the figure. It stumbled back – curiously unstable – a tall, hunched man, wrapped up in an off-white cloak with a raised cowl. In one bandage-bound hand he gripped a crooked staff.

'I've got no time for apparitions,' Garr snapped, mastering his shock. 'And if you… by Nuffle's rusty knuckleduster, you stink! Where did you come from, the waste shaft? Is that how you got in?'

'Mister Greyg,' said the spectre in a curiously high-pitched voice. 'Allow me to introduce myself. I am Mister Squimper.'

'I'll allow you to get out of my damned house, you falsetto geriatric,' Garr said. 'Or I'll have my ogre snap your crooked back into shape.'

'I'll be gone soon enough, Mister Greyg, y-yes,' Squimper said, swaying unsteadily. 'But first, I h-have a proposition for you to consider.'

'What's wrong with your voice?'

The stranger paused for a moment, as if thinking. 'I… I'm Bretonnian,' he said.

'Now it makes sense. Is that brown stuff on your cloak what I think it is?'

'Your leg is badly damaged, Mister Greyg.'

'My leg is gone,' Garr snapped. 'I don't even know if this monstrosity *is* a leg.' He prodded the blue scales again.

'It will serve you well, if you have time to heal. But you do not. You will not play in the final, Mister Greyg. And without you, the Nordland Rangers will l-lose their last hope of promotion back to the Majors.'

'Listen, you stuttering snail-eater–'

The tall figure bent unsteadily over Garr's bed and placed one bandaged hand on his new leg, the long, bony fingers gripping him. An ugly green glow suffused the room, seemingly emanating from Squimper's crooked staff. The sewer-stink redoubled.

Garr cried out at the sudden grip on his scaled flesh, expecting a fresh flood of pain. Instead, all he felt was numbness. Cool, soothing oblivion. The green light faded, though the stench remained. In the distance what sounded like a town bell tolled, though it was long past the hour.

'What did you do?' Garr demanded, trying to wriggle away from the figure. It let go, yet the sweet numbness remained.

'I can heal this, and more,' Squimper said.

'You're some sort of stinking Bretonnian spell-weaver then? Well, magician or not, you still smell like sh–'

'These effects are not permanent,' Squimper interjected with his high squeak. 'They are dependent entirely on my goodwill.' The apparition clicked its fingers, and the pain in his lizard leg returned, worse than before. Garr moaned and slumped back against his pillows.

'I can make sure you compete in your playoff final, Mister Greyg,' said Squimper. 'And I have a further incentive, one that those you owe would surely thank me for, if ever they knew how you came by enough reikmarks to pay off your substantial debts.' A heavy bag materialised in the thing's hand. It clinked when he set it down on the bed next to Garr.

'This is half. You get the rest after the match.'

'What do you want from me, tricksssster?' Garr hissed, clutching his scaled limb. 'What's the catch?'

'What indeed, Mister Greyg,' said Squimper, leaning in closer, his stench overwhelming. 'I will make you s-stronger, faster, fitter, and wipe your debts. But you must d-do something for me too.'

* * *

The stadium hadn't been filled since the Nordlanders' relegation, three seasons earlier. Now it was packed to its old timber rafters, filled up with every conceivable creature. Halflings and elves, greenskins, humans and twitching, shade-wearing vampires, drawn like buzzwings to Bloodweiser by the alluring promise of violence both on and off the pitch. The Thunderdome was thundering, and the Thunderbolt was ready to strike.

Garr approached the centre point of the scrimmage line. He was vaguely aware of a vicious catfight breaking out on the sidelines between the Nordlander cheerleading team and the ridiculous, silk-ribbon-draped gobbos the East End Boyz counted as their own cheerleader squad. Garr ignored the shrill ruckus, eyes deliberately fixed not on the crowd, but on the towering greenskin coming to meet him.

He didn't remember Mister Squimper leaving after his nocturnal appearance, but he'd woken the next morning feeling more in shape than he had since the relegation, three years earlier. He'd spotted the strange white-clad figure again in the crowds during warm-up, deliberately seated near the dugout barricades. The sorcerer's gaze was making the hairs on the nape of his neck prickle.

The vampiric attention of Grizmund was just as discomfiting. Nog had taken delivery of a letter from the bloodsucker that morning informing him, in no uncertain terms, that unless his debts were paid within the next day there would be a knock on his door. Winning the promotion prize pot would go a good way to paying off the debts, but he'd still fall a little short. And Mister Squimper knew it.

Off-pitch worries took a back seat as a shadow fell across him. He'd reached the halfway line, and so had Krapnugg.

The huge, one-eyed captain of the East End Boyz leered down at the human blitzer, green-and-white scrap armour glinting, stinking of stale sweat, raw hides and fungus beer. Garr felt an upsurge of revulsion as he squared up to his team's most bitter rival. The elf refereeing the match kept his distance, clearly disgusted by both the human and the orc.

'Thundaboy, ya git,' Krapnugg growled. 'I heard you woz done for.'

'And I heard the Rangers are today's odds-on favourites with the betting scribess,' Garr croaked back.

'Dat's good you's fit for da game den. I gets to be da one who krumps ya good.'

'The only things getting krumped today are your team's promotion hopes, funguss-ball.'

Krapnugg hawked and spat a wad of green phlegm at Garr's boots. 'We do da talking on da pitch, Thundaboy. I'll see you in da scrum.'

'Gentlemen,' the elf said, investing the word with every ounce of scorn he could muster. 'Orcs or eagles?'

'Orcs,' Krapnugg bellowed, beating one great, green fist against his scarred breastplate. Garr nodded, not flinching away from the hate-filled gaze of the rival captain.

With a delicate flick, the elf sent a reikmark skyward. Garr glanced into the braying crowd, at where Mister Squimper was seated. He saw the cloaked figure make a brief chopping motion, unnoticed by the manic spectators surrounding him. The coin landed on the elf's outstretched palm and he slapped it down on his slender forearm.

'Orcs,' he announced. 'The greenskins have it.'

Krapnugg bared his tusks in what approximated a vicious grin. 'See you in 'ell, thunda-cripple,' he grunted. Garr said nothing. Unnoticed by the roaring crowds, a shiver ran up his spine.

It was game on.

Kickoff. There was nothing in the world Garr loved more. The roaring of the crowd had reached a frenzied crescendo, the noise setting the great stands of the rickety stadium quivering. Humans, ratmen, elves, greenskins and more, it was a sell-out. The only creatures who seemed absent in any numbers were the dwarfs – likely fans of Longbeard MineCorps were still licking their wounds after defeat to the East End Boyz in the previous playoff.

Out on the pitch both sides had taken up their starting positions. The Boyz had opted for their usual aggressive set-up, the leading edge of their offensive box formation commanded by the grey-scaled river troll that also passed as their hideous, leering mascot. The stink of rotting fish was reaching Garr, even from the far side of the pitch. It only made his stomach-churning discomfort worse.

This was not how he had seen the final playing out. He could take no pleasure from the hype of the crowd or the burning expectation of the rest of the team. Normally such things would have carried him to heady, adrenaline-fogged heights moments before the first blow of the whistle, but not today. Today was different. Today was a nightmare.

At least his body was ready for it. He put pressure on his scaled limb once more, feeling it take the weight easily. Rife had modified his strip so the freakish replacement was hidden, though the sensation of his scales grating against his clothes sent a shiver down his spine. He flexed, settled a shoulder-plate, gave his helmet a smack with a gauntlet. Instinctive revulsion aside, the leg was fine. He felt like he could blitz his way through every hoop-striped East End greenskin on the pitch, one after the other. Whatever Squimper was doing to him, it was working.

And that was just the problem.

It started to rain, fat, stinging droplets pinging from armour plates and turning the turf sodden. The sky had changed to a leaden grey. The crowd seemed to enjoy the worsening deluge, their demented shrieking reaching new heights. In fairness, it was probably the first wash most of them had enjoyed for months.

Distant thunder rumbled. Garr tried to decide if it was a good omen or not. The elf raised his hand, chiselled features riven with discomfort as the rain plastered his long, blond locks. He dropped his arm and blew the whistle.

Game on.

'Keep closse,' Garr hissed across to Gruber as he went forward. He didn't want the younger blitzer running away with all the glory. At least his leg responded perfectly. He felt young, he felt strong, but, for the first time in his life, seeing a green wall pounding towards him through the lashing rain, his heart quailed. It was a lie, and he knew it.

The East End Boyz were playing the Rangers at their own game – driving straight down the middle. Their troll was on a collision course with Dumpf, Krapnugg himself sprinting in the lumbering creature's path after having scooped the ball up under one trunk-like arm. The team's gobbo runners were attempting to slip either side down the wide zones. There was a reason the East End Boyz had vanquished their other great rivals, the dwarfs of the Longbeard MineCorps, to reach the playoffs – for a greenskin team, they were disciplined, and they knew their game plan.

Garr found his stride, and a surge of determination filled

him. Disciplined or not, they were still going down. There was no way the Rangers were going to lose their promotion bid this season. Win this game and they were going back up to the Majors. The team deserved it, and he needed it.

He hit the first orc full tilt. The greenskin was big, but Garr had learned how to take them out a long time ago. His right shoulder hit it in the stomach, his momentum deliberately driving him beneath its centre of gravity. It absorbed his charge with a grunt, its stinking, slab-like bulk forced back a step. Garr converted his forward drive into an upward thrust, pushing hard into the greenskin's chest as it attempted to wrap its trunk-like arms around him. The move sent it toppling, flailing for purchase as it slammed into the dirt. It tried to snatch at Garr's ankle, but he was still going forward, the front line defence pierced.

There was an audible crash as the rest of the two teams collided. Dumpf and the river troll hit with a crack that made the crowd gasp.

Garr looked left as he sprinted. Gruber had gone, taken down by a greenskin blocker.

'Vulf!' he bellowed, gesticulating at the end zone. Despite Gruber's holdup, the catcher had made it through and was making his run towards the Boyz backline.

'On it, boss!' Vulf shouted as he cut right across the pitch, into Garr's throwing arc. The blitzer wound up but, even as he prepared to throw, his eyes locked on the crowd, and the figure of Squimper. The sorcerer had risen, and had one crooked hand outstretched, a finger pointing directly at him from across the stands. Garr felt his blood run cold. A second later his right thigh twitched. He stumbled, sudden panic filling his thoughts. Squimper lowered his arm, and the pain went away.

'Garr!'

The shout, from Torvern, came too late. The split-second distraction had given a black orc blocker enough time to close with Garr. It hit him from the right, all snorting violence, scarred muscles and glaring, piggy red eyes. Garr knew better than to try and resist the brute's momentum – he let it take him down, hit the sodden turf, rolled with the impact. He was back on his feet again in a few seconds, fast and strong, body infused with an unnatural vitality.

He could do this. He knew exactly what he had to do – make sure the Nordland Rangers lost their playoff final to the East End Boyz.

Mister Squimper was the fixer, the mysterious charlatan who'd seemingly got to almost every single coach or star player in the Championship. He'd told Garr as much, as the blitzer lay with one hand on his new, unnatural, pain-infused limb. The exact nature of the scam wasn't clear, but the falsetto wizard had made one thing plain enough – if Garr botched his game plan and gave the East End Boyz the win, Squimper would provide just enough reikmarks to pay off his debts. If he played to the best of his abilities, the papers would discover the freakish surgery Frisk had performed. Even if the Nordlanders won, such a scandal would see their prize money taken and Garr's career ruined. And then Grizmund and his thralls would come for him in the dead of the night.

Such a reality left Garr feeling cold. But betraying the Nordlanders was easier said than done. Just seeing Krapnugg and his crew of green beasts on the pitch filled Garr with determination. It had overcome him earlier. Squimper was making clear what would happen if his instincts won out again. When the black orc took him down, he stayed down.

The greenskins won the first touchdown, punching their way to the end zone in season-record-breaking time. They won the second too, and the third. Garr found himself sprawled in the churning muck twice, once from the fist of a lumbering orc lineman, another time dragged down by a trio of bickering goblins. The move was a blatant foul, but the elf was far too busy lamenting his wet hair to care. Garr beat the goblins off with a snarl of pure frustration, but by the time he'd extricated himself the half-time whistle had sounded.

It wasn't going at all to plan for the Rangers, which meant it was going perfectly to plan for Garr. Or more accurately, for Mister Squimper.

If anything, it was a surprise the fixing had taken so long to reach the Nordlanders. The bag stuffed with reikmarks left lying on Garr's bed had amounted to exactly half the debts he owed Grizmund. The other half would see him in the clear. The damp stones and rusting grates of the debtors' prison seemed like a distant nightmare. The threat of tabloid scandals and emergency conferences seemed forgotten. Maybe his star playing career wouldn't crash and burn after all. Maybe, unlike so many before, he'd found a way to escape what had started to feel like inevitability. He just had to cheat. Worse, he just had to lose.

'What in the name of Nuffle's throwing arm is going on out there?' demanded Rife during half-time. 'Any explanations?'

Nobody answered. Everyone was drenched, bruised, and at least half the team were openly glaring at Garr. He kept his own gaze fixed on Rife, who in turn refused to meet his eye. It was obvious – the coach didn't have the guts to call out his star player on all the blatant mistakes he was making. The coach's plethora of feathers were drooping and sodden, and there was a look of panic in his eyes as he sought to blame anything and everything other than his pampered blitzer. The realisation made Garr feel even more sick.

'We're changing formation,' Rife said. 'Trying to match these green bastards head-on isn't working. Dumpf, you're going down the right-wing wide zone. Vulf, Muller, make use of any space he creates. On defence we need to watch the goblins more and that big damn fish-troll less. Also, Gustav and Wold, you're off. I'm bringing on Ulmann and Friedberger. Get our defence firmed up and we can work our way back into this.'

'What about Garr, coach?' Vulf ask, not bothering to hide the scorn in his voice. For the first time, Rife looked at Garr.

'Use your experience,' he said. 'And play roamer.'

In other words, just get out of the damned way.

The game changed. For all their ability at playing to a set plan, Krapnugg and his boys proved themselves woefully inflexible when it came to changing tactics. Dumpf punched through the wing defences time and time again, while the addition of two fresh, determined blockers, Ulmann and Friedberger, helped shore up the defence. After the three-quarter mark the Nordland Rangers had almost managed to drag themselves level. Even the rain had let up, giving way to weak, watery sunlight.

Throughout it all Garr had played in a dream-state, making minimal tackles and going down far too easily. He could feel the crowd's dismay resonating throughout the stadium. This wasn't him. It wasn't how he wanted to be remembered.

But he was afraid. Even as his heart soared at every successful Nordlander touchdown, so his mind quailed at Squimper's presence. He could imagine the mysterious sorcerer's dilemma – the Rangers were still competing, but it was through their own grit and determination, and not through their main blitzer's skills. Gruber was filling in well, winning two touchdowns on the trot. It stung Garr – he still felt strong; Squimper's charms were holding. But he knew that as soon as he made a point-winning move that could change.

The match ground on. Krapnugg was furious at the change of pace, driving himself from one flank to the other on a personal crusade to regain the initiative. At one point he went toe-to-toe with Dumpf, staving in the ogre's snot-choked nose before the huge player simply picked him up and flung him. The impact furrowed the double-skull crest painted into the centre line and threw up a great arc of glistening rainwater.

The Boyz brought on fresh black orc blockers, momentarily stymieing the Rangers' comeback. Rife responded by ordering deliberately brutal tackles on the goblin wingers the Boyz used as their catchers. By the time the whistle blew after a particularly vicious tackle by a black orc on Gruber, both teams were neck and neck on touchdowns. The last, decisive turn of the game started with the ball in the Rangers' possession.

'Make or break,' Rife said as the surviving members of the team huddled up. 'Dig deep one more time, Rangers. You know what you have to do.' He looked at Garr as he spoke, holding his gaze properly for the first time since the change of tactics. The blitzer found himself looking away, towards the crowd. Towards Squimper. The sorcerer was perfectly still, head turned towards him, seemingly oblivious to the brawling spectators surrounding him. Garr swallowed and looked back at Rife. The bestial chanting of the East End

Boyz, working themselves into one final game-frenzy, rose over the crowd's tumult.

'Let'ss play ball,' Garr said.

The whistle shrilled. The teams launched themselves forward, one last time. The second subbed-on blitzer, Welf, snatched up the ball from the kick-off and threw himself towards the right-side wide zone. The Boyz responded in force. Garr, holding a rear line behind Welf, felt his lizard thigh twinge again. This was it. Break point. He wasn't going to be allowed to interfere.

But in that moment, seeing his bruised and bloody teammates going forward around him, seeing Dumpf ploughing into a black orc and Torvern dragged down beneath two shrieking gobbos, Garr knew that interfering was exactly what he was going to do.

He was Garr Greyg, the greatest player in Nordlander history. He was going to win this one.

He ran. He ran harder and faster than he ever had before, his new limb powering him forward, spurred by a burst of raw energy that caused the crowd, already ecstatic, to start screaming manically. He was gaining ground on the front line as it continued to struggle with the greenskins, the damp air rent with screams, bellows and crunches. He saw Welf, ahead, try and weave round an orc lineboy, only to collide with something coming the other way – the wall of muscle and rusting green-and-white iron that was Krapnugg.

Welf crumpled. Krapnugg bellowed. The ball rose in the air, its spikes gleaming. Garr lunged. He felt pain sear through his body. But he was laughing, grinning. The ball was in his grip. And he was in Krapnugg's.

The greenskin snatched him by both shoulder guards as he plucked the tumbling ball from the air. Garr grunted as the pain in his leg returned. Krapnugg laughed, butcher's breath choking him.

'Puny lil' thundaboy. It's game over.'

Garr said nothing. Teeth gritted, he slammed the ball into Krapnugg's face. There was a wet thump as one of the spikes punched through the greenskin's sole eye.

The orc bellowed and let go. Garr found himself falling, the ball still in his hand, Krapnugg's eyeball impaled on one spike. The pain of his own injuries throbbed through every nerve ending. With the last of his strength, he tossed the ball over Krapnugg's head. Up, up and over, spinning, to where Vulf was making his run. The last turn, the last point.

The catcher snatched the ball from the air and leapt, green hands grasping impotently at him. With the Cabal Vision feeds flashing around him, he soared into the end zone.

Touchdown. Game over. Victory.

Garr was only vaguely aware of the carnage unfolding around him. He hit the ground hard, vision swimming. His ears were ringing. He managed to get himself up onto his elbows, where he could see the nearest stand. See where Mister Squimper had been. The cloaked figure was moving, stumbling for the exit, even as the rest of the crowd surged past him in the direction of the pitch. He didn't get far. A big shape rose up from the throng and snatched at the encumbered wizard – Nog the ogre, his blunt features contorted with fury. Garr had told him, in no uncertain terms, that if anything happened to him he was to grab the old man in the white cloak sitting a few rows down.

Except Squimper wasn't an old man at all. As Nog lunged the cloak came away, pulled apart by the frantic activity within. Two shapes burst out – hunched, scrabbling and grey-furred. They both squeaked shrilly as they were snatched by Nog. Garr suddenly remembered where he'd smelled the supposed old wizard's stench before. The Burrow Scrapers, before the season split. Ikkit's Backscratchers, from the lower leagues. The Warpfire Wanderers, from the Chaos Cup. They were skaven – vicious, dirty, cheating ratmen. He should have known from the start they'd be the ones behind the match fixing. They must have been hoarding a small fortune in their burrows.

For a moment Garr, still wracked with pain, wondered where said burrow could be, then realised they'd probably never find out where when Nog, agitated by the ratmen's wriggling and scratching, brought both their horned heads together with all his considerable strength. There was a gristly crack, audible even over the berserk crowd. Garr slumped back, drained and barely conscious.

That was when the dugouts exploded. The dwarfs of Longbeard MineCorps had been waiting almost two weeks to get revenge on the greenskins that had knocked them out of the playoffs. Nor had they been idly passing their time – for days the hardy stunties must have been mining a tunnel from the nearest brewery basement to the underbelly of the Thunderdome. Once they were underneath the opposition dugout, they'd packed their excavation with every barrel of gunpowder their illicit Bugman knockoffs could buy.

The few greenskin coaches, backroom staff and substitutes not atomised by the blast immediately launched themselves into Rife and the stunned Nordlander bench beside them. Rife was struck down almost immediately, his feathered cap trampled into the dirt. As the thunderclap echo of the explosion bounced back from the shuddering stadium's flanks, the spectators took it as the signal for a full-on pitch invasion. Barricades were smashed down, and within seconds the field was playing host to a riot. Above, almost unnoticed, the scoreboard proclaimed victory – and a return to the Majors – for the Rangers.

Gar was dimly aware of Krapnugg stumbling past. The huge greenskin was experiencing the nearest thing to fear his race could ever know – blinded, he was worse than helpless. He was useless. The orc's single eye was probably still impaled on the ball grasped in Vulf's hand as he was hoisted by the victorious Nordlanders through the crowd. Garr managed to find the strength to lift his scaled leg as Krapnugg staggered past. The orc tripped and, wailing, slammed face-first into the churned-up dirt that had once been the pitch. Garr, now delirious, realised he was giggling. The leg wasn't so bad after all. With a bit of training, and a few more stitches, odds were he could make it work.

The prize money combined with the crowns the ratmen had already given him would be enough to placate Grizmund. The fame from that last-gasp promotion win was bound to garner him plenty of marks in publicity tours and autobiography reissues. As he slipped once more into sweet, familiar unconsciousness with a smile on his mud-splattered face, Garr's last thought was a prayer to Nuffle that he wasn't about to be trampled to death. That sort of outcome really would have been a fix.

DA BANK JOB

ANDY HALL

The ball shot from the orc's arm as if fired from a cannon. It went spiralling high through the air in a perfect arc. By Nuffle's own definition, the throw was the epitome of a long bomb. The fans in the packed, ramshackle stadium – a noxious mix of dwarfs and greenskins – were silenced for the first time in what had been a brutal game thus far. The orc blitzer, wearing the captain's nose ring, looked on in momentary admiration as the ball went flying over the crowd, over the floodlights, over the stadium's high walls, and out of sight. He then looked at the thrower, stood next to him, and at the opponent's end zone… three yards away.

'You were meant to 'and it off, you stoopid, squig-sucking git.'

'Sorry, boss, it's just dat all season you've be on at me to throw a long 'un and I finally 'ad a chance.'

Before the captain could swear at his inept thrower again, the pair were set upon by the dwarf defence – piled into by eight bearded psychopaths, all eager to dig their elbows into the orcs' squashy bits. And then everything froze, as if a pause button had been pressed – most likely because it had.

'There you go, Bob,' snickered Jim Johnson to his fellow commentator, as the view switched from the frozen orc and dwarf scrum to an in-studio shot of a small, spectacle-wearing vampire with a rictus grin. 'As voted by CabalVision HD's viewers, that is last season's most hilarious play!' Large Cabal-Vision logos were revolving behind the studio sports desk at which the vampire presenter was sitting. Looming next to him was his fellow pundit, a brutal-looking ogre with scars that could only have been garnered off a Blood Bowl field.

'The irony is, Jim, it was a good pass… if the thrower had been standing two hundred yards downfield of 'is target, instead of next to 'im! But then dat's what we've come to expect from Brobrag's Big 'Uns!'

'True, Bob, they may have only formed at the start of the season, but they're quickly gaining a dire reputation. Err, where you going, Bob?'

'Dat's it, Jim. Season's done, I'm off on me jollies. See you in three months!'

'Right… Okay… well, as Bob leaves let's have another look at that humiliating clip of Brobrag's Big 'Uns. I bet their backer wasn't too pleased–'

The picture stopped suddenly as the ogre landlord smacked the large crystal ball positioned at the end of the bar, the vision within shaking for a second and then switching channel to the WOLF Network's post-season offerings. The nose-ringed orc breathed a sigh of relief and cautiously peered about as he supped his grog, wondering if the other 'patrons' in the heaving bar had recognised him from the footage. It was a big ask, as The Krafty Snotling was a hotspot for Blood Bowl players, their agents and autograph-hunting fans. The walls were adorned with trophies, MVPs, pennants, and many pictures of the ogre landlord – himself an ex-coach – posing with star players, past and present. The orc blitzer wasn't happy; this was the last place he wanted to be after the previous season, but those who wanted to meet him had insisted. So he sat in a corner booth, as far away from the bar as possible, with a picture above him of the smirking landlord giving a large thumbs up next to Varag Ghoul-Chewer. It was a nice shot, although the imprisoned daemon inside the CAMRA must have been running low on red pigment as the blood spatter on Ghoul-Chewer's loin-cloth looked a little too orange.

Luckily for the orc, no one seemed interested in him. The bar was propped up by some more orcs, and two large tables of humies glared at each other – one group wearing Reavers colours, the other clearly Marauders fans. A ruck was mere rounds away, the orc reckoned. Sat on his own, a few tables away, was a lone, robed humie; he had a frenzied air to him. His hand shook as he raised it to take a drink and occasionally he'd shout and grumble. In the far corner, a huddle of dwarfs were also looking about the place, and one of the stunty gits caught Brobrag's eye. They stared at each other across the bar, flinging eye-daggers. The orc had seen his like before – that one had grudge-fever, and if Brobrag didn't look out he'd be the target of the 'vengeance'.

'Mr Brobrag is it? Captain and owner of the Big 'Uns?'

The orc looked away from the dwarf – which, Brobrag knew, the bearded git would take as some minor victory – and saw two beings standing before his booth. One was a tall, pale humie in a scruffy, ill-fitting suit – the type Brobrag had seen moneyed agents and CabalVision executives wear.

The other was a goblin, wearing similar attire and looking even more dishevelled in his clobber.

'Dis is Mr Ger, and I'm Mr Bil,' said the goblin. 'Glad ya came. Got a drink I see, get yer another?'

Before Brobrag could even grunt in acknowledgement the pair had sat down. Now the orc's table was attracting more eyes than just the grudge-loving dwarf. He waved away the offer of another grog. The goblin caught the eye of a tavern wench dressed in a Darkside Cowboys cheerleader kit and ordered a drink for himself and his partner.

'So tell me,' began Mr Ger, 'how's your boss's pet squig?'

'Yoo know well enuff, humie,' growled Brobrag. 'It was in last week's *Spike!* magazine.'

'Remind me.'

'Leg-cruncha ate da critter. Da boss wasn't 'appy about dat. Bloody troll vomited da squig right back up. Poor fing was partly digested. 'ad to get Fingurs to put the blighter out of its misery.'

'It's been a tough first season, ain't it?' said the goblin with an evil glint in his eye. 'Yoo retire from raidin', start a Blood Bowl team with yer krew, get fundin' from yer warboss and promise 'im he'll get rich from all yer winnins. Instead, yer didn't win a single match, yer lost all the boss's teef and yer troll playa eats yer backer's fave squig.'

'It could've been worse,' ventured Brobrag.

'Well, you could be dead, I suppose,' answered Mr Ger.

'Yoo've dragged me 'ere just to gloat? Sod that, I'm off.' Brobrag began to rise.

'Let's not be hasty, we simply wondered how desperate you are. We have a proposal.'

Suddenly, the CabalVision ball sounded louder, as these things always did when the programming cut to a commercial break.

'Have you got the balls to challenge the Reikland Reavers? Blood Bowl balls that is!' This announcement was greeted with a cheer from the table of Reavers' fans. *'Can't wait for the start of next season? The Reikland Invitational is now accepting all-comers. Bring your team to the world-famous Altdorf Old-bowl stadium and play against other hopefuls – the winner then faces the Reikland Reavers! Beat them and take all the gate! Get noticed! Get more fans! C'mon, what else you going to do in the off-season? Raid and pillage? Boring! Play more Blood Bowl instead!'* The next advert was for Khorne-flakes – turns the milk all bloody! – and the volume seemed to calm down. The customers returned to their usual chatter.

'Fancy it?' asked Mr Bil.

'Wot?'

'The Invitational. Your boys win that thing, you'd be out of all that bother. Back on good terms with the warboss, the gate from a full stadium in your treasury and you'll have sponsors across the Old World all desperate to sign you up.'

'Dat's no tourney, dat's a stitch-up. Somefing the Reavers pull every off-season to keep da coffers flowin' and their 'ome stadium full. Every git on da circuit knows dat. I may be an orc, but I ain't dat thick.'

The inn's front door smashed open, sending an unfortunate halfling – who had been heading for the exit – flying across the tap room. A black orc filled the portal. A seven-foot slab of green muscle, with a ripped left ear. He scowled at the patrons, who all nervously looked back at him. On spotting Brobrag's group, the black orc made his way across, scattering the odd chair and smaller folk not quick enough to get out of his plodding way.

Mr Bil looked up at the towering orc as his shadow loomed over the booth.

'Fingurs, ain't it? Brobrag's second-in-command, and one of the only scorers in the team?'

Brobrag gestured for his black orc blocker to sit. Fingurs grabbed a small stool from the nearby empty table and plonked himself down.

'Wot I miss?'

'These two geezers reckon we should play in the Reikland Invitational,' said Brobrag. 'Fink we can win it, ha!'

'We could!' said Fingurs. 'Dey're only humies. Kill enuff of 'em, and den dere's no one ta stop yoo scorin'.'

'Erm... Let's not get ahead of ourselves...' interjected the only human at the table. 'The Reavers are one of the best teams in the world. Your captain is right, Brobrag's Big 'Uns don't stand much of a chance.'

While Brobrag didn't give a snotling's flea what the humie was saying – as it was annoyingly true – Fingurs growled from the back of his throat, the same growl he gave on the line of scrimmage. His ham-sized fist began to rise.

'However,' squeaked the goblin urgently, 'yoo lot playin' does present us with... an opportunity.'

Brobrag didn't like the sound of this, but he forced Fingurs to lower his fist all the same.

'Have you been introduced to your new team wizard yet?' asked Mr Ger.

'We ain't got no wizard!' said Fingurs.

'Oh, you have now.' As one, Ger and Bil turned to face the robed humie who sat two tables away. The man was still arguing with himself, and right then proceeded to smack the heavy wooden table with his head. Hard.

The orc captain frowned. He hated wizards and shamans; he hadn't got time for that magicky-nonsense.

'Wot kind of opportunity?' he asked.

'The best kind – one that makes you rich,' said Mr Ger with a wide smile.

It was match day. Brobrag looked at his team as they gathered in the visitors' locker room of the Oldbowl. They were all present – his mob of below-average line-orcs, the troll, Leg-cruncha, the gobbo twins known as the Chukka Brothers, Grappa, the thrower whose only ever decent pass was now CabalVision's favourite blooper, and finally, Fingurs the black orc. Standing slightly away from the team were the new 'coaching staff' supplied by Mr Ger and Mr Bil, and Chanzeemitt, the strangely paranoid and shouty wizard, also recommended by the so-called 'fixers'. Although, Brobrag wasn't sure he'd trust those two near anything broken enough it needed them to fix it. And yet, here he was! The locker room crowd looked on expectantly at the orc. He'd already explained the plan twice but knew what was coming when Fingurs opened his gob.

'So, why am I not playing in da game, boss?'

'I told ya, yer wiv dis krew,' said Brobrag gesturing to the orc coaching staff who had been 'recruited' just before the tournament. As orcs went, the four were as dodgy as they come. One had a broken tooth, one was missing an eye and the other two looked especially murderous, even when kitted out with cap, sponge and towel – the standard issue gear of any field-side assistant coach. 'Yer goin' into the vault wiv 'em, cos I don't trust dese orcs none – no offence. They're supplied by that pair of gits, so I need you to make sure we don't get stitched up! Dat's why yer in charge of 'em.'

'Okay, so it'z a bank job?' asked Fingurs, who still looked confused.

'Maybe I could explain, captain?' said the wizard, who then gave an involuntary yelp.

Brobrag gestured for the humie to go on.

'You, my fine green-skinned friend, will lead this group of err... experts... into the vault of the Imperial Treasury that's just across the road from this stadium. I will be providing the means of ingress. In the visitors' dugout is a stable portal – an escape route for the treasury staff and clients should they come under attack, I expect – I will open it with my magic and transport you directly inside the vault. HAAHAA!'

Brobrag flinched at the maniacal laugh the wizard used to punctuate his speech – stoopid loony humie, that's what you get for meddling with magic.

'Once inside, yoo grab all da loot yoo can and den leg it back out,' explained the captain. 'Me and da rest of the lads are gonna be playin' in da match. The longer we make the game last, the more time yoo 'ave in the vault to collect da shiny stuff. Right, let's get out dere!'

The team cheered, although most clearly didn't know why, and headed to the field.

Brobrag strode purposely through the player tunnel that led to the AstralTurf® pitch. One of the Chukka Brothers ran up beside him.

'Boss?'

'Wot,' growled Brobrag.

'I'm confused. Who we playin'? We're not fightin' da Reavers are we? Cos we don't stand a chance against them, boss.'

'I kno! We ain't playin' da Reavers. Dey don't play until da challenger is established. All da teams that come, fight amongst demselves, and the best one plays against da Reavers. It's da "official" challengers dat get all da coverage on CabalVision. Da match scheduler's been bribed, 'e's putting us against some halfling team... Even we should manage against dem. We need to string it out though, so da krew gets maximum time in da vault.'

Brobrag's team filed out into the massive stadium. The Old-bowl was a glorious temple to violence and sport. The orcs looked about, taken in by the atmosphere, the high stadium walls, the gloriously turfed pitch dotted with brown and crimson stains. And the packed crowds screaming and shouting from the stands. The Big 'Uns had never played at a venue like this before. Grappa and a few of the line-orcs started waving their arms as they strode onto the field, fully embracing the crowd's jeering racket.

'And here are Brobrag's Big 'Uns!' shouted the unmistakable voice of Jim Johnson over the stadium's 'state of the arcane' speaker network. Brobrag's gut shifted as it always did when he felt something bad was happening. The game was against the Merrywald Chums, a bunch of halfling farmhands. Such a match shouldn't be drawing a crowd like this, let alone the attention of CabalVision's presenters…

'Boss…' said the goblin who hadn't left his side since the tunnel. 'The fans – dey're all wearin' Reavers' colours.'

The reverb sped around the stadium, as Jim continued.

'The challengers are on the field, but here comes the team you've all come to see, eighteen-time Chaos Cup winners, voted best team of all time by *Spike!* magazine… the Reikland Reavers!'

The crowd broke into thunderous applause. In the stands just above the visitors' dugout, Brobrag spied Messrs Ger and Bil. The gobbo was wearing a sheepish grin; the humie met the orc captain's gaze and gave a 'wotcha gonna do' shrug of his shoulders.

'Zoggin 'ell!' murmured Brobrag.

* * *

The Reavers ran through the player tunnel and onto the field in a blaze of glory, and the fans went wild. While they basked in their welcome at the centre of the field, Brobrag corralled his team towards the visitors' dugout and sought out the nearest official. An elf in tailored zebra fur stood nonchalantly at the side of the pitch, twirling his whistle about on its twine.

'Wot in Nuffle's ball sack is goin' on?' demanded Brobrag.

'Problem?' snapped the elf.

'We're meant to be playin' halflings, not the Reikland zoggin' Reavers!'

'Yeah, about that, seemed the schedules got shifted,' the official said with a sly smile. 'The Merrywald Chums played a Chaos team called the Flesh Hounds this morning. I think they lasted all of two downs before they were slaughtered to a soul. The Flesh Hounds went on a killing spree afterwards, leaving you lot to face the Reavers – the final was brought forward and everything, someone paid a lot to make that happen. Didn't anyone tell you?' he sneered.

Brobrag had never liked elves, but this long-eared git had quickly risen to the top of his hate list. He headed back to his dugout. The players looked expectantly at the captain.

'Some gits want us to play da Reavers. So sod it, let's do it!'

Chanzeemitt cleared his throat. 'May I remind you the plan was that you fought against a weak team as a diversion and to maximise the vault-group's time in the treasury. If your team is all in the "dead and injured box" within ten minutes then we are… to use language your kind understands… screwed.'

'Can yoo still open da portal or not?'

'Well, yes.'

'Then get to it. Right ladz, it's our biggest game yet. We ain't just a diversion! We're Blood Bowl players, let'z bloody well play!' The team cheered and, led by Brobrag, ran onto the field.

Deep in the dugout, at the far end, away from the eyes of fans, the team wizard whispered in a language that made Fingurs shiver. The end wall shimmered and a black portal appeared where the cinder blocks had been moments before. Chanzeemitt let out a braying laugh but Fingurs was unsure if that was part of the spell or just one of the mage's strange tics.

'Go,' hissed Chanzeemitt. The black orc ran through the portal, closely followed by the four assistant coaches. Instead of sponges and buckets they now carried sacks and jemmies. As the last of the orcs from the vault-group disappeared, the elven ref's whistle was blown – the game had started.

The Reavers hit hard for humies. They slammed into the Big 'Uns' front line, which was sorely lacking their black orc blocker. Brobrag was in the middle of the defence, on the line of scrimmage, and found himself face to face with the Reavers' captain.

'And the two captains meet!' shouted an excited Jim Johnson over the stadium's arcane sound system. 'Griff Oberwald is a NAF hall of famer, one of the highest scorers in the sport. Brobrag... Well you can't really compare the two, can you?'

The orc and humie butted helmets in the middle of the scrum. Both were bent forwards with shoulders planted firmly into the opposing players.

'Don't worry, greeny, this'll be over for you soon enough,' said Griff through gritted teeth.

'Not likely, pigeon-'ead, we need to make dis last until full time!' Griff looked bemused at Brobrag's response. As if that wasn't the kind of trash talk he'd expected from the orc. Brobrag used the star player's momentary confusion to punch the smug git in his face. Oberwald spat out a tooth, and looked thunderous. He thrust downwards with his shoulders and stepped back, Brobrag's momentum carried him forwards and the blood-stained turf came rushing up to meet him. Without breaking stride, Oberwald stepped on the back of the orc's prone form and used it as a springboard to leap into the air. As if preordained by Nuffle himself, at the zenith of Griff's leap the ball flew into view, and he plucked it out of the sky. The Reavers captain landed far beyond the Big 'Uns' defensive line and then ran. The star player easily dodged the few half-hearted tackles by the remaining orc defence and jogged into the end zone. The crowd went wild. Brobrag got upright and looked back to see a triumphant Oberwald staring straight back at him. The first touchdown had been scored less than a minute after the starting whistle.

Fingurs was in the strangest vault he'd ever been in. Not that he'd been in any vaults before, but where was all the shiny stuff? They were underground, which he had expected, but they were in a long, square corridor of yellow stone covered in vines and other strange-looking plants. He wasn't the only one that looked confused. The rest of his 'away team' also seemed a bit lost as to where they were. Fingurs couldn't remember their names, or even if he'd asked for them in the first place, and so had decided to call them by their instantly recognisable feature.

'Oi, One-eye, where's dis treasure?!' Fingurs asked. The orc just gave him a shrug back. And then lost his head. A thin silver blade screamed out of a horizontal gap in the wall at head height and lopped off One-eye's bonce before the black orc could blink. The head rolled past Fingurs, who spun around to see Broken-toof looking guilty, his foot resting on a sunken flagstone.

'Soz,' he said, and carefully retracted the offending leg.

'By Gork's collected toe-jam, wot woz dat!?' shouted Fingurs to no one in particular.

'Booby trap,' said Angry-git. 'Bet dis place is full of 'em. Careful where ya tread.'

Fingurs wasn't happy. His place was on the Blood Bowl field, not here in this dark place, following a dungeon corridor to Nuffle knew where.

'This way…' Fingurs heard a whispery voice. It seemed to come from just behind his ear. 'Move it!' said the whispery, but now clearly impatient, voice. Fingurs gestured to Broken-toof, Angry-git and Nasty-git.

'Better go where da voice sez,' said the black orc, cautiously moving down the corridor. The others looked at each other and followed.

'Wot voice?' asked Broken-toof to Angry and Nasty.

The Big 'Uns were already down two-zero, but losing didn't bother Brobrag that much – after all, they'd lost every game in the previous season. No, what was troubling him more were the two casualties they'd already sustained. NAF rules were pretty flexible about how many players a team could field. There was a maximum of eleven per side – that was literally written in stone, as transcribed by the very first NAF commissioner, Roze-el, back in the day, and strictly enforced. As to fielding fewer than Nuffle's sacred number, well, it wasn't advisable but not technically against the rules. As long as you had players, you could play. However, as Brobrag knew all too well, you needed at least three players on the line of scrimmage at kick-off. If the team couldn't do that then they'd forfeit the game no matter how much time was left on the clock. While Brobrag's squad was large enough for now, if he kept losing players at this rate they'd be forfeiting before they even got to half time, leaving Fingurs and the loot stranded in the vault.

'The Big 'Uns are going to receive,' said a voice over the sound system. It wasn't Jim Johnson's, this announcer had a much deeper, metallic and troubling timbre. 'If they don't receive Nuffle's help, I know a few gods they can pray to for aid, hahaha!'

'Err, thank you, Lord Borak, I look forward to more of your comments throughout the game. Bob should go on vacation more often.'

The Big 'Uns had thirty seconds before the ref blew his whistle, so the captain called his players together for a huddle.

'We're gettin' butchered out dere,' moaned Grappa.

'Shut it!' growled Brobrag. 'We need to keep playin' and dose gits just want us off the field as fast as possible. We're green and mean, we should be da ones smashin' da humies ta bits, not da other way around. We gotta keep da ball out in our possession.' Grappa tried to speak, but Brobrag wasn't in the mood for more of his moaning and so carried on. 'Pick it up, don't pass it, we'll form a cage around the carrier and we'll march up the field real slow and steady...'

The ref whistled.

'Touchdown!' shouted Lord Borak, his voice reverberating around the stadium. Brobrag looked up from the huddle and saw a Reavers' catcher in their end zone.

'Wot the–'

'You were yabberin' too long, boss. Da Reavers kicked and then grabbed the ball while yoo were explainin' da plan. I did try and tell yoo.'

'Right, next play, we do dat plan.'

'Wot plan?' asked a line-orc.

Brobrag slapped him across the face.

Fingurs, Broken-toof and Angry-git stared down into the dark, fathomless hole that had swallowed Nasty-git two minutes ago.

'I fink 'e's ded,' said Broken-toof. Fingurs thought so too, and motioned them to move on. This left just the three of them to find the loot and get it back before the game ended. The black orc knew full well he wasn't the sharpest spike on the Blood Bowl ball, yet he sensed things were not going to plan.

'Dis voice you 'earin',' said Broken-toof. 'Sure it's not tryin' to lead us *away* from da shiny stuff?'

'Nah, it keeps gettin' mad if we stop an' talk or I go another way. It wants da gold as much as we do.'

Broken-toof was about to question the black orc's logic when they came to a door at the end of the corridor. It was made of stout-looking wood with metal hinges and handle. A dungeon door if ever you saw one, thought Fingurs, as he tried the handle. The door didn't budge. Broken-tooth pushed him out the way, and produced his jemmy. The orc worked at the hinge and then around the handle, and with a final push the door swung open and the three greenskins stumbled into a large, dimly lit chamber. It was a large square space, the roof made of different rectangular levels jutting inwards as they went up into the dark void, the only entrance – or exit – being the one the orcs had just walked through. Looking up, the would-be robbers could not even see the ceiling – they were at the base of a tower or some tall building. In the very middle of the room three chests sat upon plinths, each bathed in a cone of light.

'Shinies!' shouted Angry-git.

Before Fingurs could stop him, the orc ran forwards into the light and tried to open the chest in the middle. There was a flash, like lightning, and smoking bones clattered to the floor where the angry-looking orc had stood seconds before. The central chest was gone.

'Idiots!' screamed the disembodied voice, although only Fingurs could hear it.

'We ain't across the road in the treasury, are we?' said Fingurs.

'You think?' asked the voice, sarcasm dripping from both icy syllables.

'Well, da treasury building ain't got no tower,' said Broken-toof, actually making a good point, although Fingurs had been talking to the voice.

'I need what's in the left-hand chest, the others are just decoys. Get me the item in the chest and I'll guide you back out.'

As much as Fingurs hated the voice, he thought the best course of action was to follow its directions so he could get back to the ladz as quickly as possible. Now, if only he knew his left from his right...

The Big 'Uns were receiving. Not unexpected, as the team that concedes a touchdown always receives the ball at the following kick-off, and the orcs were down three-zero. The ball flew into the Big 'Uns half from the steel-shod boot of Jacob von Altdorf. Brobrag was relieved to see Grappa scoop up the free ball without too much fuss. As planned, four line-orcs surrounded the carrier, with Leg-cruncha herded to the rear. The formation slowly advanced to Brobrag's position where he took his place at the head of the formation.

There was now a cage of green flesh and spiked armour surrounding the ball. Even a team as good as the Reavers would struggle to break through.

'I can't think of anything more dull than a slow-moving cage play, Jim,' said Lord Borak across the speaker system, 'and I've dated daemonettes.'

'I'd have thought daemonettes are anything but boring. They strike me as quite… feisty?'

'Nope, they're all goffs. They just sit there and mope. Tedious. Talking of which, the Big 'Uns haven't advanced a yard since our witty banter started, Jim. They better get a move on!'

Brobrag didn't care one cold squig-fart what the commentators thought of his play. He was quite pleased, they had kept possession for well over a minute now, and the Reavers had backed off. All they had to do now was run down the clock, giving the vault-orcs time enough to collect the loot and get back. Brobrag managed a smile – maybe it would all work out after all. Then an axe embedded itself into his helmet. Swiftly followed by another that thudded into the ground between his legs, just as one of the line-orcs collapsed, an axe wrapped in a Reavers pennant lodged in his gut.

'It's da fans!' called Grappa. 'Dey ain't 'appy!'

The cage was getting pelted with more and more missiles, some less lethal than others, noted Brobrag, as a bottle of Bloodweiser went streaming past to clonk a line-orc between the eyes. Across the field, the orc captain saw the Reavers holding back, all sporting smug faces, happy to let the fans do the work.

'Da voice sez it'z dat one,' said Fingurs, and flashed Brokentoof a smile. Fingurs rarely smiled, so the effect was more unnerving than the black orc intended. Broken-toof looked suspicious.

'Which one?'

'Dat one!' pointed Fingurs at one of the remaining chests.

'Go on den,' said Broken-toof. 'Get da shinies.'

'Dat's yer job. I led us 'ere.'

'You fink I'm stoopid? I've seen Dungeonbowl, I kno what 'appens when you open a chest in a dungeon!'

'Fine, I'll grab da loot, but if you want a share you'll 'ave to take it from me.' Fingurs approached one of the chests to the side of the now empty central plinth.

'Oi!' Broken-toof rushed up to the black orc. 'You were pointing at the other chest before. Now yah gonna take da loot, yoo go ta dis one – da proper box! Nice try, but I told ya, I ain't stoopid.'

Broken-toof pushed Fingurs backwards, and lifted the lid of the right-hand chest. The orc's smoking bones fell to the floor. Fingurs looked at the remaining chest.

'So, dat's left.'

The cage formation had made it to the line of scrimmage, the Reavers' fans jeering and lobbing various detritus all the way. Brobrag had lost two of his line-orcs under the onslaught.

'Are there any halflings in that formation?' Lord Borak wondered aloud. 'They're taking so bloody long it's like they're on an endless quest.'

As the Big 'Uns staggered into the opposing half, the Reavers made their play. A fireball shot out from the sidelines, taking down a line-orc from the flank of the cage.

'The Reavers' team wizard is on excellent form,' said Jim.

'Unlike the Big 'Uns' new magic-user,' countered Lord Borak. 'Our field-side reporter say he's stuck in the dugout, waving his arms around and speaking in tongues like a skink who's had too much sun. Looks like another bad investment by the Big 'Uns' team captain.'

The spell had left the orcs in disarray, then the Reavers linemen tackled from the flank, while the Mighty Zug strode forwards and butted Brobrag right on the bridge of his nose. Orcs have thick skulls compared to humies, but Zug was a legend for a reason. The orc captain went down like a sack of squigs, creating the opening Griff needed. He wrestled the ball from Grappa and dodged past the troll before the beast could even register it. Within seconds the ball was back in the greenskins' end zone. Four-zero. The ref blew his annoying whistle again – it was the end of the half.

'Oh dear me. I think it's all over for the Big 'Uns. They'd need a miracle to come back from this,' said Jim.

'My gods give out miracles like candy, although this would be a big ask no matter how many souls you offered. To be blunt, they suck, Jim – even worse than you.'

Brobrag stumbled down the steps into the dugout. His teammates followed.

'We're screwed!' shouted a line-orc.

'No, we 'ave been screwed. Those fixers set us up,' said Grappa, his anger rousing the others. Brobrag smelt a mutiny. He heard a snigger from behind and looked around to see the wizard, eyes closed, arms waving around like an insane conductor towards the portal in the far wall.

'Wot you laughing at?'

'Oh, just how your teammates are obviously considering a change at the top. I love change, don't you?'

Brobrag growled. 'Where's Fingurs and da others?'

Chanzeemitt opened his eyes and gave an involuntary

screech that made one of the team gobbos jump. 'Sorry, comes with the territory.'

'Yer nutz!'

'No, not nuts, just unstable, there's a subtle difference.'

Before Brobrag could answer back, the wizard spoke again, this time in a different voice.

'The orc's right, you're crazier than Fungus the Loon! That's why I had to stop you, that's why I paid to have the Flesh Hounds play your halfling patsies!'

'What?' shouted Chanzeemitt in the first voice. 'You did this?'

'Of course I did, I hate you! Oh, look here comes another of your puppets now.' Fingurs shot through the portal, which fizzled out behind him. He was clutching something in his fist.

'Give me that!' demanded the wizard in his first, screeching voice.

'I wouldn't,' said Mr Ger, descending the dugout steps with Mr Bil closely in tow.

'You gits! Wot you doin' 'ere?' yelled Brobrag.

'Protecting our investment. We want to know why you aren't playing against the halflings as originally arranged.'

'So, you ain't got nuffin to do wiv dis?'

'No. We wanted da loot in the vault as much as yoo. We were gonna double-cross ya when you 'ad the dosh. So, not us, boss... Well, we may have put a bet–' Mr Bil was hastily nudged in the face by Mr Ger's elbow.

'You bumbling fools! You are puppets to be played with by greater minds than you are capable of comprehending,' said the wizard. He looked directly at Fingurs and gave an involuntary laugh. 'Now, give me it, or those scorched bones you saw in the Lost Temple will be nothing compared to my wrath!'

Just then, the elf official stuck his head over the dugout wall and treated the team to his most condescending smile.

'On the field!' he sneered.

Everybody in the dugout turned to look at Fingurs.

"Ave the bloody thing, ya nut job. Dis whole fing 'as been a waste of time.' Fingurs uncurled his fist to reveal a silver whistle.

'Yes-yes, hand it over!' said Chanzeemitt. Then the wizard howled like a direwolf, and the second voice sneaked out.

'No, keep it away! Don't give it to him-me!'

'Time!' shouted the elf ref from above and blew his own whistle.

'Yeah, time ta get our butts kicked!' moaned Grappa again.

Brobrag had reached his limit. He gave out a guttural roar that silenced everyone in the dugout and a good portion of the fans in the stadium above. Ever since he had given up raiding and started this Blood Bowl team he had been under the cosh, pushed, played and manipulated. But no more! He was an orc, and a bloody good one at that, it was time for him to do the pushing! He stepped between the wizard and Fingurs, grabbing the whistle out of the black orc's hand. Mr Bil had wheedled his way close to the action and looked at the whistle in awe, even as Brobrag waved it around in agitation.

'Wot's dis?' he growled, holding it up.

'It's nuffin boss, I blew it on the way back through dat vault. It didn't do diddly squat,' said Fingurs from behind.

'If you don't give me that whistle, I'll spend the rest of my days heaping humiliation upon humiliation on your pathetic team, orc. You think this performance is embarrassing? Well, wait till you see what an agent of Tzeentch can do when he has your full attention–'

Brobrag grabbed the yabbering humie by the throat and squeezed. There was an evil glint back in his eye that hadn't been there since before last season. The wizard choked and spluttered and ineffectively tried to prise the orc's hand from his fragile throat.

'I want to talk to da other one.' The wizard thrashed about. 'The second git you 'ave in that mangled brain of yours, send 'im up,' rumbled Brobrag. The mage seemed to calm momentarily and Brobrag relaxed his fingers slightly. 'Talk!'

We're both followers of the Great Conspirator. There was a rivalry, so our master thought it best to... merge us. Having two of us in here, it's made us a bit... unstable. The other one, my soul-rival, was trying to get that whistle. He couldn't enter the Lost Temple himself – another of our lord's caveats – so he engineered this situation.'

'Wot's so special about dis whistle? Every ref has one.'

The wizard jittered in the orc's hand and the first voice spoke.

'Fool! That is Nuffle's whistle. Once the correct rule from the Blood Bowl god's forgotten rulebook is spoken and the whistle blown, great power awaits.'

'I blew it, nuffin happened,' said Fingurs.

'Didn't you hear, you green ape? You need to speak the correct rule citation before using it. Ha! And I ain't telling you anythi–'

Brobrag squeezed again, and gave a vicious grin. From above, the elf popped his head over, met Brobrag's glare and quickly retreated.

'There's two of you sharing that 'ead. I reckon wotever you know, the other does too.' The orc grinned and let go of the wizard. 'I want to make a deal wiv da second git.'

* * *

The crowd was getting impatient; the Big 'Uns still hadn't surfaced, and the officials looked at each other, preparing to default the game. Then Brobrag emerged from the dugout and shouted:

'Rule 28B, sub-section 38G, paragraph 2 reads as follows: *Da whistle-blower will get his victory – as decreed by Nuffle.*' He then blew the whistle.

The piercing sound echoed around the stadium far longer than a normal whistle. The refs looked confused – players were not meant to blow whistles! And then the Big 'Uns stormed onto the field, with Fingurs leading the charge. The second half was on!

The Big 'Uns were receiving. Griff looked confident – the smug git. Before he could even lean into the Big 'Un's captain, the orc had side-stepped him and was up the field like a skaven rocket. Within seconds, the ball flew past and had been caught by Brobrag in the Reavers' end zone.

'That's four-one,' said Jim, sounding as stunned as everyone else felt. Griff Oberwald shook his head. The Reavers prepared for another kick-off, he got into his game-winning crouch – they'd be receiving this time. The ball was sent, but quickly intercepted. Before Griff could fathom what was going on, he saw a goblin fly overhead, ball in hand. The dumb-founded Reavers looked on, rooted to the spot, as the greenskin landed as if he were Jordell Freshbreeze and jogged into the end zone. In the next play, the Big 'Uns troll repeated the feat and soon the greenskins were four-three.

'It's a, erm… so… Bob Bifford is back off vacation next week,' stammered Lord Borak.

Then Fingurs came face to face with the Mighty Zug. The black orc nutted him in the face before Zug could bring his own noggin forwards as his usual devastating weapon. The infamous Reavers blocker fell to the ground and Fingurs gave him a substantial boot in the belly.

'Dat's for da boss,' he growled.

The Big 'Uns continued their wholesale destruction of the Reikland Reavers. Griff, Zug and the like ended the match in the dugout, nursing wounds. As the final whistle blew, Brobrag caught a long bomb thrown by Grappa. The orc charged through the solitary Reavers' lineman to score a touchdown as the whistle's shrill peep died away. The game ended four-seven.

For the first time ever, the Reikland Invitational had been won by a team other than the Reavers. The fans invaded the pitch in a rage. Like an angry tide they washed from their seats and onto the field. Under Brobrag's direction, the Big 'Uns formed a cage, and expected to be mobbed.

'Eat dis!' shouted Brobrag as he threw something into the troll's yearning mouth. The orc captain ordered his team to stay put and shot off at a blitzer's pace into the rabble. Yet the fans' ire was aimed firmly at Griff and his players. The Reavers quickly retreated down the player tunnel followed by an angry rabble. Some Reavers supporters thought they could have a pot-shot at the victorious greenskins, but Leg-cruncha and Fingurs quickly changed the minds of any who were stupid enough to try.

The orcs partied all night – Mr Bil, as a fellow gobbo, was in the midst of it; whooping with the Chukka Brothers, chanting with the line-orcs and shaking Brobrag's hand on more than one occasion. The gate alone was enough to keep the wrath of the warboss off the Big 'Uns – until next season, at least. With Nuffle's whistle in Brobrag's possession, the Majors were surely a given. And then the sponsorship,

promotions and inducement offers would follow. Annoyingly
for Brobrag, that meant he'd probably still need the services
of Mr Ger after all. Strangely, there was no sign of him; perhaps the humie was already making deals on the Big 'Uns'
behalf behind his back? The sneaky git.

As they wandered back to the locker rooms, Brobrag wasn't
surprised to see the wizard had done a runner. Maybe he
should have wrung the scrawny git's neck, but a deal was a
deal. If only his fixers-cum-agents had the same kind of integrity. Speaking of which, Mr Ger did turn up that night, but
he wasn't going to be making any deals on behalf of Brobrag's Big 'Uns. Fingurs found him in the dead and injured
box with a wicked blade shoved in his back. Mr Bil was suddenly missing… Brobrag urgently patted about his body and
kit. The whistle had gone…

Well, *one* whistle had gone. Nuffle's whistle was safe in
Leg-cruncha's gut, ready to be vomited out in time for the
next game. Brobrag gave his most orcish smile; he never had
liked that elven ref. The pitch invasion had made it easy to
hunt the git down and take his very normal whistle that had
hung around his very fragile neck.

THE HACK ATTACK

MATT FORBECK

'Welcome, Blood Bowl fans, to a special live edition of *Where Are They Now?*' the grinning vampire said on the crystal ball as it flickered to life. 'The top-ranked Cabalvision show that digs deep into the past of the Old World's favourite game to discover whatever happened to the Blood Bowl legends of yore! At least the ones that didn't die on the pitch!'

The vampire arched his pointed eyebrows over his circular sunglasses, the dark lenses of which resembled the empty ends of a double-barrelled shotgun. 'I'm Jim Johnson, and this drooling antique next to me is a legend in his own right, Bob Bifford!'

'That's right, Jim!' bellowed a massive, stitched-together sack of athletic flesh long since gone to seed. 'I am a legend – at least that's what your wife calls me!'

'How's she doing these days?' the vampire said to the ogre, a wicked glint in his eye. 'I haven't seen her since she went out for a nice, thick steak the other day and never came back!'

'I think she meant "stake," Jim! Maybe she's the victim of homicide by homonym!'

The vampire gave the ageing ogre a rueful chuckle. 'That's a lot of syllables for you to string together all at once, big guy! Don't hurt yourself! Hey, wait! I think those were the last words I told my wife!'

'Speaking of *Where Are They Now?*' the battle-scarred ogre said, turning back to the topic at hand. 'With some of the teams we focus on, we have to dig deeper than others. Those undead teams have a habit of digging their way back up from wherever anybody buries them!'

'But that's not the case with tonight's team. We're turning the spotlight on one of the greatest teams of the recent past, the Bad Bay Hackers!'

'That's right, Jim! The Hackers were more like a pack of losers up until a dozen years ago when Coach Captain "Peg-leg" Haken made the best investment of his life and hired rookie Dunk Hoffnung as his starting chucker.'

'The team rocketed out of obscurity after that, climbing up the rankings until they pulled off a nearly unheard-of feat – winning back-to-back Blood Bowl championships!'

'The wildest thing about those championship Hackers is that many of them survived! Can you guess how?' The vampire turned to the ogre, who hesitated as if he'd been asked to count past two while wearing mittens.

'Well, Bob, there are really only two ways out of a Blood Bowl team – death or retirement! Since I watched all those games back then, I'm going with retirement.'

'Right you are! There are different ways to retire from Blood Bowl though. The most common way involves eating most of your meals through a straw for the rest of your life!'

'I have a feeling a vampire like you would like that!'

'It depends where I get to put the straw!'

'But most of the Hackers didn't wind up being cared for by a full-time nursing staff. Well, except for Hackers linebacker Schlechtes Getrunken, but that was self-inflicted. After the Hackers won their second championship, he drowned in a vat of Killer Genuine Draft!'

'I hear his teammates pulled him out three times, but he kept jumping back in! They couldn't stop him until after he'd stopped breathing!'

'Well, let's check in with one of the surviving players who hasn't retired yet. None other than Dirk Heldmann himself!'

'Dirk started out as a blitzer for the Reikland Reavers, but when his older brother Dunk Hoffnung joined the Hackers, it seemed like it was only a matter of time before Dirk joined him over there. Now he's moved up to become team captain of the Hackers himself!'

'That's right, Bob,' Dirk said as the image on the crystal ball drew back to show him sitting at the announcers' desk with the vampire and ogre.

The man's blonde hair had thinned to almost nothing up top, but he compensated for that with a magnificent, bushy beard that looked like it had exploded from the lower half of his face. His bloodshot eyes had a haunted look, like the black paint he regularly spread below them while on the field had long since decided it would never leave him again.

'You've had one of the longest recorded careers in Blood Bowl – at least for someone who's not undead!' Jim said. 'How do you manage it?'

'It's a simple matter of killing my opponents before they kill me,' Dirk said. 'That and the fact I refuse to touch the football myself these days.'

'How's that work?' Bob asked. 'Don't you have to do that to score?'

'I'm happy to let the younger players worry about padding their stats. I've already set most of the Hackers' team records, and I don't mind sharing the spotlight. Especially if it means I don't have to die for it.'

'You don't worry that some people think that sort of play is the mark of a coward?'

Dirk gave Jim such a cold glare the vampire shivered. 'Those people are welcome to join me on the field to see who's scared of who.'

'Part of the reason you've decided to take such a hands-off stance is that you were recently promoted to coach as well, right?' Bob said.

Dirk broke off from staring at the vampire so he could answer the ogre's question. 'That's right, Bob. Captain Haken decided that he was done with day-to-day coaching and kicked himself upstairs.'

'He'd been handing over a lot of those responsibilities to legendary player Rhett Cavre over the past couple seasons anyhow, right?' said Jim.

Dirk nodded. 'Rhett and I are now co-coaches for the team.'

'Given how Coach Haken ruled over the team with a steel hook, that seems like an arrangement bristling with trouble.'

Dirk didn't respond. After a moment of dead air, Bob pitched in with a new question. 'Let's conjure up some images from the team's heyday. Who can forget what happened to your brother Dunk Hoffnung after he scored his first touchdown!'

The image on the screen morphed to show a dark-haired, hard-nosed athlete in a yellow-and-green Bad Bay Hackers uniform. He was standing in the middle of an astrogranite field at the height of a Blood Bowl match.

'The Hackers were playing against the Reikland Reavers. That was your team back then, right, Dirk?'

'That's right, Bob,' Dirk said. 'And to welcome my big brother to the big leagues, I trampled him flat.'

The image on the crystal ball cut to show a younger Dirk planting a spiked boot square in Dunk's chest as he knocked him to the ground. After Dirk charged past him, Dunk got up, and rather than going after his brother for some well-deserved revenge, he sprinted in the opposite direction.

Right towards the end zone.

'Of course, that was all part of Coach Haken's plan!' Jim said.

Dunk dashed past the Reavers' defenders and made it into the end zone just in time to see the football the Hackers' thrower had lobbed into the air there. He reached out and caught it, scoring his first touchdown.

'Not too many rookies manage to score their first touch-down in their first minute of play!' Bob said.

Dunk didn't even have time to celebrate, though, before one of the Reavers' players smashed into him from behind and knocked him into the stands.

'That hit still makes me cringe for him,' Dirk said, without an ounce of honest regret.

'And that was Spinne Schönheit who hit him, wasn't it?' said Bob.

'That's right!' said Jim. 'The same woman who later joined the Hackers along with Dirk here – and who is now mar-ried to Dunk!'

'I don't know if I could date someone who hit me like that,' Bob said. 'I mean, my wife knocks me around a *lot* harder!'

The image showed the fans in the end zone grabbing Dunk and body-passing him toward the top of the stadium. He struggled against them, but as strong as he was, there were far too many of them. The entire crowd began chanting at them, shouting, 'Over! Over! Over!'

Dunk tried to grab on to something – anything – but couldn't find a grip. As he reached the top of the stadium, he screamed in terror and then disappeared over the edge.

'The ref called a penalty on the play, of course,' Dirk said as the image cut back to him and the announcers. 'They flagged Dunk for "excessive celebration" for jumping out of the stadium like that!'

'How did Dunk survive that fall?' Bob asked. 'That's gotta be a five-story drop!'

'He hit a series of awnings all the way down,' Dirk said. 'That – along with the rat-on-a-stick cart he smashed into at the end – broke his fall. Of course, then the rat vendor beat him senseless for destroying his cart!'

'And he actually went on to marry Schönheit after that?' Jim asked.

'Let's just say it was a long engagement,' Dirk said with a chuckle. 'I think they'd both still be playing for the Hackers if Spinne hadn't gotten pregnant. And they have another on the way!'

'You heard it here first, folks!' Bob said.

'We hear they've holed up at an "undisclosed location",' Jim said to Dirk. 'Care to expose another family secret while you're at it?'

'Aren't *you* supposed to be the reporter here?' Dirk flashed a vicious smile. 'All I can tell you without fear of repercussions is that they're living in a wonderful grove tended by Edgar.'

'The treeman the Hackers picked up on a tour through Albion?' Bob said. 'He disappeared years ago! Something about a reproduction ritual that was supposed to take a full month?'

Dirk shrugged. 'Apparently the ritual took, and Edgar wound up with a little bundle of saplings all of his own. He's promised to return to the game once his wee ones are grown – but do you know how long it takes for treemen to mature?'

'How about M'Grash K'Thragsh?' Jim said. 'The ogre was a legendary player for the Hackers, but he left the team the year after Dunk and Spinne!'

'Once Dirkie came along–'

'Wait!' Jim said, shocked. 'Dirkie?'

Dirk flushed red. 'Dunk and Spinne named their little boy after me…' The menace in his voice dared anyone to interrupt him. No one did.

'Once Dirkie came along, M'Grash retired to become his full-time bodyguard.'

'The boy has an ogre for a bodyguard?' Bob chortled. 'Not even *my* kids get that!'

'He's more like a babysitter,' Dirk explained, 'but no one's had the guts to call him that.'

'Do you think there's any chance the boy will play Blood Bowl?' Jim asked. 'After all, he's got an amazing pedigree!'

Dirk gave the vampire a sad shake of his head. 'Dunk lost of a bit of his passion for the game after we won our first championship. He's told me he doesn't want his son to have to kill-or-be-killed for a living.'

'And how does Spinne feel about that?' asked Bob.

Dirk chuckled. 'When I gave the boy a plush ball with rubber spikes, she put it into his crib.'

'Dunk didn't throw it away?'

'M'Grash wouldn't let him.' Dirk grinned. 'He says the little guy uses those spikes as a teether!'

'I still get some shivers myself from that first Hackers' championship,' Bob said.

'Maybe little Dirkie can give you his stuffed football to keep you company at night!' Jim said.

'I don't blame you,' Dirk said to Bob. 'After all it's not every day the entire stadium you're playing in gets transported to the Realm of Chaos so you can play Blood Bowl for the fate of the entire empire!'

'Let's roll some footage of that!' Jim said.

The image on the crystal ball cut over to that championship game, pitting the Bad Bay Hackers against the Chaos All-Stars. The classic Hackers – Dunk, Dirk, Spinne, M'Grash, Edgar, Cavre, and so on – stood there on the astrogranite, facing off against a range of Chaos-twisted horrors. They included a motley assortment of beastmen, plus the tentacle-faced Kathula, the slime-covered troll Ichorbod, and their team captain, the triple-headed, dog-headed Serby "Dawgy-Dawg-Dawg" Triomphe.

'This game seemed to be a collection of everyone you and Dunk had pissed off throughout your careers!' Jim said.

'Mostly that fell to Dunk,' Dirk said. 'He's the one who got Skragger killed. And beheaded. And his head shrunken down to smaller than your fist. But, you know, it wasn't Dunk who turned that damn orc into a vampire somewhere along the way!'

'But did anyone see it coming that Skragger would wind up in cahoots with Zauberer, the All-Star's team wizard?'

'Well, it sure wasn't Triomphe!' Bob said as the image shifted to the three-headed dogman chasing Dunk down the field. An instant later, a bolt of lightning appeared from the sky and speared straight through the All-Star. 'How the Hackers lucked out with that strike, I'll never know!'

Jim slapped the ogre on the back of the head. 'It was all part of a plot to – never mind!' he growled. 'We were both there!'

'Right!' Bob said brightly. 'It was Zauberer who used the Chaos Cup to have us all sucked into the Realm of Chaos! What an arse!'

'He also had Skragger's tiny skull mounted on top of Ichorbod's decapitated corpse! That's some kind of heads-up magic for you!'

In the image, the sky grew dark, and the image of the Blood God Khorne towered over the field for a moment. The clouds roiling overhead crackled with crimson lightning. The sound of a million screams filled the air.

'Gotta like that game intro though!' Bob said. 'I mean, for a game produced by the forces of Chaos, they really had it together! I can't wait to see how it turned out!'

'How many head blows have you taken today?' Jim said. 'We all survived – well, most of us anyway – and the Hackers won!' The vampire gestured at Dirk as if his presence should provide plenty of proof.

'Praise Nuffle! But hey, spoiler alert!' Bob frowned at Jim. 'I haven't finished re-watching that game on my Debtflix account!'

Jim flashed the ogre a fang-filled grin. 'Be sure to let me know how it turns out!'

'We worked with Lästiges Weibchen on that game!' Bob said. 'She was the best sidelines reporter in all of Cabalvision! Whatever happened to her?'

'We got her fired last year!' Jim said. 'After all, we can't afford to have someone that good on the Cabalvision broadcast team! Think about our job security!'

'Ah, right!' said Bob. 'I still miss her though. Every time I throw anything at her! She's a nimble lady!'

'Actually, Dirk here used to date her, remember?'

Bob snorted. 'Remember? Wasn't that how we got her fired?

For dating a player? Some kind of "interest in conflict," or something like that.'

'I'm still amazed that worked!' Jim said. 'After all, I've been dating the cheerleaders for the Champions of the Dead for decades, and that's never gotten me fired!'

'You call that dating when they keep beating you up like that? That's more like all "conflict" and no "interest!"'

'It's pretty much impossible to get you two fired,' Dirk said with a grimace that would have looked foreboding on an undertaker. 'You have too much dirt on that scumbag Nuffle Commissioner Good-el.'

'That not fair!' Jim said. 'We worked hard to dig up all that dirt!'

'And, hey!' Bob said. 'Commissioner Good-el's been busy trying to cover up the long-term effects on Blood Bowl players sustaining countless concussions during the course of their careers. Do you know how hard it was for the wizards to figure that out in the first place? There aren't that many players that survive long enough to worry about it!'

'Bob! Are you insane? You can't just go flapping your gums about that kind of stuff in public!'

The ogre clapped a meaty hand over his own mouth for a moment. 'By Nuffle's hairy balls!' he said a moment later. 'You're right! Just imagine if I'd said that on the air!'

Jim gave the camra a deadpan stare. Then he turned back to Bob. 'Do you realise what a "special live edition" of this show means?'

'Sure!' Bob said with a toothy smile. 'It's special because we're still alive!'

Jim put his head in his hands and groaned.

'Hey, Dirk!' Bob said, unfazed. 'Let's get back to the subject. Whatever happened to Lästiges Weibchen?'

Dirk pointed off-camra. 'She's in the studio with us. Right over there. You threw a goblin at her just before we started this interview.'

'I know!' Bob said. 'I really do miss her. Every. Damn. Time!'

'So,' Jim said. 'Dirk! You've brought us up to date on most of the players on that double-championship Hackers team! But you've left one very important player out! What does the future hold for *you*?'

'I'm glad you asked, Jim,' Dirk said. 'As you know, not too many Blood Bowl players ever actually make it to retirement. It's not a forgiving sport.'

'So you're just going to keep playing until they either carry you out on a stretcher or sweep up your ashes into an urn?' asked Bob.

Dirk shook his head. 'I've made plenty of money. I've set enough records. Won enough games. I don't have anything left to prove.'

'Then what next?' asked Jim. 'We'd love for you to announce your plans here, live, on Cabalvision!'

'Well, there are really only two decent jobs for any self-respecting Blood Bowl player to take after their career winds down. You can be a coach – which I already am, co-coaching the Hackers right now.'

'But if you quit playing, will you keep coaching too?'

Dirk chewed on his lower lip. 'Much as I love the game, no. I'm going to give a shot at career choice number two.'

Bob gaped at Dirk in surprise. 'You're going to be an agent?'

Jim slapped the ogre on the back of the head. 'Weren't you listening? He said *self-respecting*!'

Dirk chuckled then stood up and gestured for someone off-camra to toss him something. A football spiralled toward him, and he caught it. 'Thanks, Lästiges!'

Dirk held the football up for the announcers to see.

'That's a funny-looking ball.' Bob stared at it, curious. 'It's all smooth. Where are the spikes?'

'This is a special ball,' Dirk said. He peeled apart the stitches on the ball and stuck his hand into the gap. 'It only has one sharp, pointy bit.'

As he said that, he squeezed something inside the ball, and a yard-long blade stabbed out from the ball's tip. Rather than having been forged from metal, though, it seemed to have been carved from a single piece of wood. 'But it's a killer.'

'So, ah, what job did you say you were going for?' Jim ran a nervous tongue across his fangs, never taking his eyes off the gleaming, polished tip of the blade.

'I'd like to be a Blood Bowl announcer.' Dirk brandished the football-blade in front of him. 'Actually, I think Lästiges and I would make a great team – and I hear there are about to be two openings!'

'Really?' Bob said. 'An opening? Where?'

Dirk lunged forward, and Bob jolted in surprise. Then he looked down at the new hole in his chest as if it had magically appeared there. 'Oh,' he said. 'There's one.'

'That's going to have to be it for now!' Jim said as he backed away from Dirk while still facing the camra. 'Tune in next week for the next edition of *Where Are They Now?* featuring a profile of the original Halfling Giants, who all disappeared ten years ago during a pre-game feast co-hosted by the Orcland Raiders! Of course, that's all assuming we survive our traditional post-show party today – which seems to have started a little early! Good night!'

MAZLOCKE'S CANTRIP OF SUPERIOR SUBSTITUTION

GRAEME LYON

'Excitement is at a fever pitch today here in the, er, where are we again, Jim?'

Jim Johnson sighed and shook his head at his co-commentator.

'We're at the Light's Hope Stadium in Talabheim, Bob,' he said, smiling at the viewers at home, 'here to witness what is likely to be a classic Blood Bowl match between two great teams, the Talabheim Titans and the Black Water Boyz.'

'Ah, yeah, that's right,' rumbled Bob. 'And we've been sent here to cover this seventh division match because of that incident with the goat during the–'

'The viewers at home don't want to hear about that, Bob,' said Jim firmly. 'All that matters is that the sport's top commentators are here to guide them through the athletic spectacle that's about to unfold. The match will be kicking off in about twenty minutes, folks, so stay tuned. We'll be back to talk about the teams after these messages.'

Jim watched warily, a broad – and entirely false – grin

on his face, until the warlock operating the image capture spell nodded, the light in his eyes blinking off, and then he slumped back in his seat.

'For Vlad's sake, Bob, remember where we are. Any more of that and you'll get us chased by a mob with burning torches. Again. I started playing Blood Bowl to get away from that sort of treatment.'

Bob sighed, his huge shoulders slumping. 'I know, Jim. It's just such a waste of time us being here. These little league games are so boring. We'll just be going through the motions. Nothing interesting is going to happen...'

'We've got this one in the bag.' Gerritt Vanderwald grinned as he looked at his team. The Talabheim Titans were in their locker room at the stadium they called home, and it was time for the pre-game pep talk. Fortunately, it was far from a difficult job. The team – thirteen humans and the lumbering ogre known as Ghurg – were relaxed and ready for the big match. In their crimson and white kit, they were hanging on his every word, eager to soak up his wisdom like the apothecary's sponge would soak up bloodied water later. So he gave them the benefit of his years in the game.

'The Boyz are on a losing streak a mile wide. You guys are the strongest you've ever been. Just keep it together and we're golden. And with the big city commentators here, and lots of media attention, some of you...'

He directed his attention towards Johann Walsh and Kurt Grafstein, the team's undoubted star players. Johann was a catcher of such skill that Vanderwald was sure he'd be poached by a team like the Reikland Reavers any day now, while Kurt was a competent blitzer, with the attitude of Griff Oberwald and about half the skill, but still better than the rest of them. Kurt's attitude was far better – he was sitting in rapt attention, leaning forward to catch every word, while Johann seemed to be barely present. No doubt lost in dreams of glory, or at least of the cheerleading squad. 'Some of you might just get a nice endorsement deal out of this. And that'll be good for us all,' Gerritt finished.

Times had been hard for the Titans lately. They'd had a nice winning streak, but in their position outside of the major leagues, that didn't equate to much money, and they were teetering on the edge of bankruptcy. This opportunity – a broadcast game, with the famous Jim and Bob commentating, here at the team's home ground – was a godsend.

'I don't need to tell you how much this can turn our fortunes around,' he said. 'Get out there, play well, and it's up, up, up for you all.'

'Up where?' asked Ghurg, peering quizzically at the ceiling, which given the size of him was mere inches from his head.

Vanderwald sighed inwardly and drew a deep breath.

'It means we'll be rich and famous, Ghurg,' said Walsh softly, looking up at the hulking ogre.

'Will Ghurg still get to hit greenies and pointies and beardies?' asked the ogre, his brows creasing with the effort of forming such a long sentence.

'Always, Ghurg. You and me are a team, buddy. You hit 'em and I'll score the touchdowns.' He raised one hand up to the towering ogre, palm out. 'Titans forever, chum.'

'Titans forever,' rumbled the ogre, a smile breaking across his scarred face as he slapped the catcher's hand surprisingly gently. It had taken a while, but Ghurg had learned eventually not to break fellow players' arms until he was on the pitch.

* * *

In another locker room on the other side of the stadium, eleven green-skinned orcs sat in silence on a filth-streaked floor while a pair of goblins chased a squealing squig round in circles. The diminutive creature had caused quite a lot of the aforesaid filth after eating everything in sight that couldn't fight back, including the benches and the metal door of one of the lockers.

It hadn't been a good few months for the Black Water Boyz. In fact, sitting in squig excrement could be considered a highlight. They'd lost every game they'd played this season – even, embarrassingly, against the halflings of the Tinkleheim Trotters – and were so hard up that they'd had to press-gang in the pair of older orcs who usually carried the team's gear just to field a full squad. Any casualties in the match ahead would be catastrophic.

Borgut, the Boyz' coach, stood in the doorway and watched his players. He'd never seen them so down before a match. Well, except Goblin, but he always looked like that. It was a goblin's lot in life to be down at heel, so that hardly counted. He wished he could tell them what he had planned, but since it was… not entirely within the rules, so to speak, he was better leaving them out of the loop. It would be worth it later, when the Titans were defeated and the Black Water Boyz were in the ascendancy once more.

'Boss?'

Borgut turned to see his assistant coach, Gazbag. 'Is he here?' he asked.

'Yeah. He's waiting for you.'

Borgut looked back at the players again, feeling a twinge of guilt at what he was about to do. It was for the team, he told himself. It was all for the team.

* * *

The Light's Hope Stadium was packed, with humans from across the Old World, orcs and dwarfs who had taken the long and dangerous trip down from the mountains for the big game. There were even a few elves, keeping to themselves in one corner of the stands, surrounded by haughty-looking guards and servants waving censers filled with sweet-smelling herbs to counter the stench of the rest of the crowd (especially the dwarfs). Gerhardt Mannheim looked around, enjoying the sight – particularly the sight of what looked like a group of Amazons down near the pitch's edge. He felt an elbow in his ribs, and turned to see his friend Tobias grinning broadly.

'Look at them, Gerhardt. Dunno about you, but I wouldn't mind seeing what's under them feathers.'

Gerhardt sighed with exasperation. 'What's under those feathers is more muscle and talent than you'll ever have in your life,' he said.

Tobias looked abashed for a moment, then grinned again. 'Yeah, but I'd still like to take a look. Besides, you're not exactly a star player yourself, mate.'

Gerhardt bristled. 'I have the talent and the knowledge,' he snapped. 'It's not my fault my mam overfed me.'

'Over*feeds* you, you mean. Them meals she makes when I come round are always massive. And tasty.'

'What are you talking about? I don't live with my mam.'

Gerhardt glanced around desperately and saw a trio of beautiful girls in replica Titans tops sitting behind them, giggling. 'I don't live with my mam. He's mad,' he said weakly. They giggled again, and he turned away. 'I don't know why I hang around with you,' he said. 'Anyway, I'd much rather get to know the cheerleaders…'

* * *

'Two, four, six, eight, Titans will annihilate!' Juliana belted out the cheer, jumping and waving her pom-poms in time to the rhythm. Around her, a dozen other cheerleaders did the same, performing a dance of intricate complexity that was completely wasted on the drooling Neanderthals in the stands.

'Three, five, seven, nine, beat them on the scrimmage line!' The words were painful to utter, so completely banal and pointless. Juliana hated what she did, but it was the only way, short of selling drinks in a kiosk in the stands, that she could be part of a game of Blood Bowl.

She loved the sport. She loved the strategy, the artistry, the adrenaline rush of a strong push into the opposing half of the field, the sheer exhilaration of a touchdown, the sound of an armoured elbow breaking bone, the noise of the crowd as they set upon a player stupid enough to loiter close enough to the edge of the pitch that a well-timed tackle could push them into the stands. She loved everything about it, or at least she was sure she would if she were ever allowed to experience it.

The cheerleaders finished their pre-match display and retired to the sidelines, to the audible dismay of certain segments of the crowd. They stepped back into the Titans dugout as the players filed past. Juliana braced herself, knowing what was about to happen. The same thing that happened before every match, however much she complained to Vanderwald.

'Hello, gorgeous,' drawled a voice from behind, laden with arrogance.

She steeled herself and turned to face Kurt Grafstein, the Titans' chief blitzer.

'Kurt,' she said through gritted teeth.

'How's my little good luck charm?' he said, grinning what

Juliana thought was supposed to be a winning smile, but just made her want to punch him even more.

'Don't you have a game to play, Kurt?' she asked pointedly.

He laughed a decidedly fake laugh, throwing back his shoulders and placing his hands on his hips ostentatiously. Then he looked at her lasciviously. 'Not until I get my pre-match kiss,' he said.

Juliana heard a sigh from behind her. Probably Emilia or Romana, or one of the others for whom getting attention from a player like Kurt would be a life highlight. 'I'm sure one of the others–' she began, before Kurt tried to grab her waist and pull her towards him. Juliana bit down the impulse to punch him and dodged out of his way, anger flooding her. As usual, he tried to move in again, but a hand on his shoulder stopped him.

'Get out there and play to your adoring fans, Kurt,' said Johann Walsh.

'But why do that when I have such an adoring – and adorable – one right here?'

'Because you're paid to make those ones happy,' Johann said firmly.

'And I adore you about as much as a dose of Nurgle's Rot,' muttered Juliana.

Kurt either didn't hear, or pretended not to. He leered at her again, then turned and ran onto the pitch, to rapturous response.

'Thanks, Johann,' Juliana said, leaning forward to give the catcher a peck on the cheek. 'You're one of the good ones.'

'Just looking out for a teammate,' Johann replied. He gave her a dazzling smile before turning and running onto the field to the adulation of the crowd.

* * *

'He don't look like much of a wizard,' said Gazbag in a whisper.

Borgut was forced to agree. The sorcerer was his last-ditch attempt to bring the Black Water Boyz back to glory. They were never going to beat a team like the Titans by legitimate means, and the limited magic that the Colleges allowed their licensed wizards to perform wasn't going to do the trick. Borgut had been directed to this Mazlocke character after making some discreet enquiries in the seedier hostelries of Talabheim. He hadn't met the wizard face to face, or even anyone who'd used his services, but he had seized the opportunity regardless. If Mazlocke could deliver what he promised, he'd be well worth his hefty fee, which had drained the last of the team's coffers.

The wizard was a small man (though all humans looked small to Borgut, to be fair), and wasn't as impressive as he'd expected. His robes were threadbare and patched, and his beard wasn't much better. He looked a lot younger than most wizards Borgut had met, though that wasn't many outside the College wizards who policed magic in Blood Bowl matches. This one could have been any age, Borgut supposed. You could never quite tell with those who dabbled in the dark arts.

'Are you, er, Gorbut?' the wizard asked, peering at a scrap of paper in his hand, his voice trembling.

The orc nodded. 'Close enough. Is the spell ready?'

'Yes!' The wizard sounded much more confident now. 'Mazlocke's Cantrip of Superior Substitution is just what you need. It'll send your players into the depths of space and time and replace them with some of the greatest Blood Bowl players ever, past and future.'

'And we'll get away with that, will we?' asked Gazbag.

Borgut sighed.

'How is the ref going to stop us?' he asked. 'By the time he sorts out who's supposed to be on the field or not, we'll have scored a load of touchdowns and knocked out most of the 'umies.'

'And then when the spell ends, the players will all go back where they came from,' chimed in the wizard.

'Yeah! So there'll be no evidence anything was ever different. It'll be fine.' Borgut turned back to Mazlocke and thrust a small bag into his hand. 'Alright. Here's yer first payment. You'll get the rest when we win. Now come on and cast the spell before the Titans score so many touchdowns we'll never catch up.'

The Black Water Boyz had trudged onto the field first, barely responding to the half-hearted cheers of the crowd. There were ten orcs, giant green-skinned brutes, each with more muscle in one arm than Gerhardt had in his entire body – not that he'd ever admit that out loud. Trailing at their heels was a goblin. The diminutive, wiry creature looked even more dejected and beaten than the rest of the team. Gerhardt opened his programme and rifled through it to find the team listings. He laughed when he saw the goblin listed as simply 'Goblin'. He pointed it out to Tobias.

'They prob'ly don't last long enough on the pitch to make a name worth bothering with,' he said, and his friend laughed.

Next came the Titans. Gerhardt sat up straighter. This was his team. He knew every player, and every stat. He could recite the touchdown and casualty records of each blitzer, reel off instantly how many interceptions the catchers had made (and against which teams, when and where) and put a number on the longest successful pass made by the throwers.

He knew exactly how many opposing players Ghurg the ogre had permanently crippled and killed.

And of all the team, Gerhardt was particularly knowledgeable about Kurt Grafstein. When asked, Gerhardt said this was because of Kurt's tremendous skill, his impressive scoring record and the fact that he had more confirmed casualties than any other human player in the seventh division. But in truth, it was because Kurt came from the same small village in rural Talabecland that Gerhardt did, and had achieved everything Gerhardt wished he could, but knew that he never, ever would.

In short, when it came to Kurt Grafstein, Gerhardt was as jealous as it was possible to be, and that jealousy had become what Tobias and Gerhardt's mother referred to as 'his little obsession'.

It had started with clipping out all articles mentioning Kurt from *Spike!* magazine and putting them in a scrapbook. Then there was the Titans merchandise featuring Kurt that covered every inch of Gerhardt's bedroom walls and ceiling.

Then he'd spent months watching Kurt's parents' house, hoping to catch a glimpse of him when he came to visit. He'd had to stop that when he was caught. He'd claimed that he was watching Kurt's younger sister, a comely girl about Gerhardt's own age. That had been awkward, especially when she'd been dragged out and publicly rejected him, but better than people thinking he was obsessed with Kurt.

Finally, he'd started writing to Kurt, long letters in his cramped, sloping handwriting telling Kurt how much he admired him, how much he wished he could meet him and talk to him about all the player's many triumphs and how good friends they would be. He had written dozens of them, and never received a single response. It really wasn't fair. But that didn't matter today. He'd support Kurt no matter what. He always would.

The coin flew into the air, glinting in the bright sunlight. Johann couldn't see it clearly from where he stood in the wide zone, but he knew that Kurt would have called heads. He always did. The referee – a stout dwarf with a bristling beard dyed into black and white stripes to match his jersey – caught the coin from the air and shouted 'Tails!' in a voice just audible over the roar of the crowd. Johann saw Kurt and his opposite number, a hulking orc in battered iron armour, shake hands.

Johann took a deep breath and enjoyed the moment. This was always his favourite time, just before the game began. He looked around, taking in the scope of the stadium – thousands of cheering fans, the great magical displays that showed the view of the various camra-wizards, the smells from the food vendors, the feel of the astrogranite beneath his boots. This was what he lived for.

The referee blew the whistle, and the Black Water Boyz kicked off. The ball flew into the air and Johann caught it and started to run. It was on.

Ten minutes passed as the two teams readied their plays. The ball passed back and forth, a few blocks led to some humans and orcs shedding blood onto the field, and a lucky tackle by one of the larger greenskins had a human lineman stretchered off the field with one leg at an angle that was entirely unnatural. It was business as usual.

'Well, Jim, I don't know what you think of this match so far, but I can't say I'm impressed,' rumbled Bob,

'Well, you can, Bob, you have that ability, but in this case I agree completely. Ten minutes in, and neither team has done anything daring. There's some talent out there on the field – Grafstein of the Titans is definitely one to watch – but they're not taking chances. Unless something exceptional happens, this is going to be a very dull match indeed.'

Bob nodded. 'That's right, Jim. And I think we both know what the chances of something exceptional happening are.'

Borgut watched Mazlocke work. The wizard stood at the centre of a circle painted on the floor of the cramped cupboard they'd cleared of cleaning products to perform the ritual. He was using a foul-smelling substance that Borgut decided he'd rather not know the provenance of. The wizard was chanting in a voice that sounded suspiciously high-pitched.

'I dunno what language he's speaking, but it def'nitely sounds arcane, dunnit?' whispered Gazbag, peering past Borgut to look into the cupboard. The two orcs stood out in the corridor, since there was only enough space for one inside.

'Yeah,' said Borgut doubtfully. He watched Mazlocke waving his arms in strange patterns, his utterances and movements growing faster and more urgent. The space inside the circle started to glow, as did the wizard's eyes. The intricate patterns he was tracing in the air were now visible. Borgut took a step backwards and pulled Gazbag in front of him, just in case. It never paid to entirely trust wizards.

The ritual came to its climax, Mazlocke now shouting arcane gibberish as a web of light shone around him. Then there was a strange pop, the world turned inside out for a moment and Borgut closed his eyes as the light became too bright to stand. When he opened them again, the circle was empty. Mazlocke was gone.

'Where'd he go?' squeaked Gazbag.

'I dunno, but he'll be back for…' Borgut trailed off as a horrible suspicion set in. 'The money.' He launched into a run, sprinting to the Boyz' stinking locker room. He pulled open the locker he'd stashed the much larger bag of gold in. It was empty.

Now that the game was getting exciting, the atmosphere in the crowd was nothing short of electric. Gerhardt had been frankly embarrassed by the poor showing from the Titans early on. They were capable of so much better. The early injury to Gellert Holstein had been a setback, and had given the Black Water Boyz a bit of hope and energy, which had raised the tempo of the match.

Gerhardt was on his feet, shouting himself hoarse as he watched the action on the pitch below. One of the orc throwers lobbed the ball in a perfect pass towards the diminutive goblin, who sped towards the end zone. All that stood between the Boyz and a touchdown was Johann Walsh. As Gerhardt watched, the ball seemed to slow down and stop, then the world spun around him, and he fell, but he was horizontal, and he felt his elbow impact on flesh and bone…

Johann leaped into the air, twisting to avoid a punch thrown by one of the burlier orcs, and reached for the ball as it flew past his face. Just as his fingertips touched it, he felt something hit him. The ball sped past out of reach and he was thrown forwards. He landed on the soft grass and rolled over, groaning in agony, oblivious to the unexpectedly high pitch of his voice…

Goblin ran, heedless of whoever might be around him. The end zone was ahead, but his eyes were fixed on the ball arcing through the air. A few yards more and he'd be in position to catch it and score. If he did, he might get fed tonight. He ran, arms and legs pumping, and then his vision blurred and he wasn't moving anymore. He couldn't see the ball and the ground suddenly seemed quite a lot more distant than it had been. Was he flying?

Kurt was showboating. The ball was on the other side of the field, so no one was paying him the attention he was due, and that was unacceptable. He kicked the leg out from beneath an orc thrower, then threw himself down on the greenskin elbow-first in an ostentatious display of skill and martial prowess. The blow didn't make contact. There was a bright light, and then the roaring of the crowd was much louder, and he fell back onto a hard wooden bench, crowds pressing in tight around him. He looked down, and uttered an unbelieving curse...

Juliana stood atop a pyramid of cheerleaders, held aloft by hands gripping her ankles. She cheered, waving her pom-poms towards the stands, and watched as Johann leapt and missed the ball. Then her head swam and she felt a force pushing her. She lost her balance and fell, the grips on her legs loosening, and then she was on the ground. She looked up and saw, much to her surprise, a rather large and heavily armoured orc about to land on her...

Ghurg was happily watching people running around. He enjoyed this. All he had to do was stand in the middle of the field, and when someone green came near, hit them until they fell down or ran away screaming. He was good at that, the hitting. A movement nearby caught his attention. A big orc (not as big as Ghurg, but bigger than most of the others) with very dark skin and spikes on his armour was running towards him, clearly wanting a fight. Ghurg raised one massive meaty fist to meet the oncomer. Then everything shook, and Ghurg was looking at the sky and running. He tripped and fell head over heels, and blinked up to see a ball hurtling down towards his face…

'And Raggut throws a beautiful pass towards the end zone, but it looks like Walsh is in position to intercept…' Jim Johnson's voice was high and fast as he related the events on the field to the watching audience.

'If he can avoid the fists of the blitzer Mugwort there, Jim,' interjected Bob.

'And it looks like he has, Bob, and he's reaching for the ball – oh, he's missed it!'

'Yeah, he has, and that could be bad for the Titans, Jim. On the other hand, it looks like Grafstein is bringing the hurt to poor Mugwort in retaliation,' said the ogre. 'This is turning out to be a pretty decent game, eh?'

'It is indeed, Bob, and–' Jim's voice choked off as several things happened at once. Down on the field, there was a flash of light, and several of the players seemed to convulse. As the flash reached the commentator's box, Jim felt his head swim. He shook it, and continued.

'Sorry about that, I felt dizzy for a…' He trailed off, paused for a moment and spoke again. 'Something seemed to hit the…' Again, he let his sentence end prematurely, as he wondered what was going on. He gave voice to his concern. 'Bob… Why do I suddenly sound like you?'

He looked to his right, but the ogre wasn't there. He looked left and saw, much to his surprise, himself, staring up at him in disbelief.

'I don't know, Jim,' his doppelganger said. 'But I have to say, you look a lot like me as well.'

Jim looked down, and there was a lot more 'down' than usual. Below him stretched the very large, quite fat, and undeniably ogreish body of Bob Bifford.

'Bob,' he said in the ogre's deep and grating voice, 'I think something exceptional has happened.'

Juliana rolled left moments before the orc's massive body landed. It missed her by inches, and the impact threw up mud that splattered her. She scrambled to her feet, but her body felt sluggish, as if it were somehow bigger and more densely muscled than before.

She thrust her confusion to one side and leapt backwards as the orc, back on his feet, threw a punch at her. She ducked beneath another blow strong enough to take off her head and put all her strength into a diving tackle. She hit the orc in the midriff with all her strength, and... it did nothing. She fell back, and the greenskin laughed and stamped a massive hob-nailed boot down towards her chest.

Juliana – or whoever she was right now – rolled, taking the blow to her left arm and feeling something break, then pushed herself to her feet, gasping at the pain. She evaded another of the orc's wild swings, then half-cheered as another Titans player, the lineman Phineas Crabbe, barrelled into the greenskin from behind.

'Ball's open, Johann,' Crabbe yelled as he and the orc went down in a tangle of limbs. 'Get it!'

Juliana looked around, trying to orient herself, before Crabbe's words really sunk in. He had called her Johann. She looked down and saw not her skimpy cheerleaders costume,

but the white cloth and red lacquered armour of the Titans...
on a man's body. Johann's body.

Looking over towards the field's edge, where she had been
atop the human pyramid, she could see the Titans cheerleaders clustering around a fallen figure. She watched in silent
horror as the girls helped the figure to its feet. No, to *her*
feet. Literally hers. The standing figure was Juliana. It was her.

'Juliana, what happened? Are you alright?'

Johann's head swam and he blinked as vision returned,
looking up into the face of Mariella, one of the Titans
cheerleaders.

'What... what are you doing on the field?' he asked, voice
slurring and, he realised, high. Not his own. 'What... what's
going on? Why do I sound like–'

'Juliana, I asked if you're alright,' said Mariella, impatience
tinging her tone. 'Come on, you've taken harder falls than
that.'

'Why d'you keep calling me Juliana,' Johann asked blearily. 'I'm–'

'You're going to be in trouble with Mr. Vanderwald if you
don't get up and start cheering again. You know he hates it
when the crowd gets restless.'

Hands grabbed at Johann and pulled him to his feet into a
mass of scantily-clad cheerleaders. In his bleary state, it half
occurred to him that he was in the midst of some sort of
fantasy, but that thought was quickly dispelled as pom-poms
were thrust into his hands and he was pushed towards the
stands, where fans were leaning forward, leering and clam-
ouring. Behind him, the cheerleaders started to chant.

'Why do you want me to cheer?' he asked, and finally the
haze lifted and he realised that his voice wasn't his own,

and neither was his body. He was a cheerleader. He was a woman. He was Juliana.

Goblin flinched as Krusha, the biggest and meanest black orc he'd ever been on a team with, barrelled towards him.

'What've I done, Krusha?' he squeaked in alarm, but his voice was much, much deeper than it should have been. Plus, Krusha looked… small. He was still massive, with arms and legs as thick as tree trunks and a fist raised that could have crushed Goblin into green paste with a single squeeze, but he looked strangely puny. Goblin lifted one arm in a vain attempt to try and fend off this confusing and unprovoked attack – he was sure he hadn't done anything wrong except miss the ball, and that wasn't unusual. His arm made contact with the black orc and lifted him from his feet, throwing him into the air and knocking him back. Goblin was stunned.

'Did I do that?' he asked. 'Sorry, Krusha. I dint mean to.'

The orc didn't respond. Goblin knelt down next to him, the movement slow and cumbersome, and prodded the orc in the face. His finger was huge. And it wasn't green. Goblin knew he wasn't the smartest creature in the world – though he could rightly claim to be a genius next to some of the orcs on the Black Water Boyz – but even he realised now that something about himself was different. He was big. He wasn't green anymore. He was…

'An ogre!' he shouted. 'I's become an ogre!'

Visions filled his mind of the things he could accomplish. A creature as powerful as an ogre with the cunning mind of a goblin – he could be famous. He could be rich and powerful, he could make his mark on the world. But, he realised, that could wait. There was one thing he wanted more than anything else. The one thing any goblin really, truly wanted and would always take given the opportunity. Revenge on the orcs who tormented him. He stood up, grinned, and stamped down on Krusha's stupid, drooling face, over and over again.

'Take that, Krusha. Take that, all orcs!' He raised his voice and shouted to the sky. 'I is Goblin, and I's gonna get you all!'

The ball landed just next to Ghurg. He ignored it, trying to work out why he was lying down on the grass. He remembered an orc running towards him and raising a fist. He couldn't have been knocked down. Ghurg was never knocked down. He was the one who knocked. He looked around, but didn't see the orc. And he wasn't where he had been standing, on the touchline. He was way down the pitch, close to an end zone. He'd never been this close to one before. He wasn't allowed to play with the ball, just to stand and hit anyone who came close.

He pulled himself to his feet, and was confused again. The ground seemed much closer than usual. And his arms and legs were skinny and green. His armour was gone too. This was very strange. Ghurg looked around to see if anyone else from the Titans had turned green and tiny. It didn't look like it, but he could see Johann. Johann was nice, was his friend. He didn't call him ugly or stupid like some of the other players did. He liked Johann. He decided to get up and go and ask Johann what to do.

As an afterthought, Ghurg turned to pick up the ball. It seemed big, but he scooped it up, carrying it in front of him in his two small, green hands, and started trotting towards Johann.

'What in Nuffle's name is going on?' shouted Kurt, as he looked down at the field in disbelief. 'Why am I sitting here among you stinking savages when I should be down there being magnificent?'

'Haha, nice one, Gerhardt,' drawled a voice to his right. He turned to see a spotty and unkempt boy in an oversized Titans replica uniform.

'Who are you?' he asked. 'And who's Gerhardt?'

'Duh, you are,' said the boy. 'Did you hit your head or something? And you know who I am. Stop being an idiot and watch the game. Your boyfriend just broke an orc's face.'

'My boyf... What are you talking about? I'm not Gerhardt, I'm Kurt Grafstein, and I... Wait, how did I get here?'

'You're Kurt Grafstein?' The boy looked incredulous. 'What are you talking about? You're Gerhardt Plumstader, and you've been sitting there for an hour, you moron.'

'Gerhardt Plumstader? Why is that name familiar?' Kurt wracked his brains. He knew the name, but from where? 'Plumstader... There are Plumstaders in Helheim, where I grew up.'

'Yeah, they're your parents. Seriously Gerhardt, what's going on? This isn't funny. I know you're obsessed with Kurt, but stop this pretending. It's creepy.'

Obsessed. Gerhardt Plumstader. It all clicked into place for Kurt. The letters, from a boy from Helheim. He hadn't read them – he didn't have time to read fan mail – but he'd been told about them by team security, who thought this Gerhardt Plumstader seemed a tad obsessed. *'Probably not dangerous, but if he contacts you in any other way, please let us know,'* the guard had said.

Cold fury overtook Kurt. He turned and grabbed the boy's chin, pulling his face level to Kurt's own.

'What did that little weirdo do to me?' he growled.

* * *

Gerhardt yelped as he felt bone crunch beneath his elbow and heard a grunt of pain.

'Oh, I'm so sorry, I don't know what happened. I was in the stands, and I was cheering, and–'

He was rudely interrupted by a very large and very powerful green fist smacking him very hard in the face. He was thrown back, feeling a sharp flare of pain and a surge of adrenalin.

'Ow, why did you do that?'

'You 'it me,' grunted the orc who was now towering over Gerhardt, cracking his knuckles menacingly. 'You might be some fancy-pants 'umie blitzer, but that don't mean you can 'it me.'

'Blitzer? I, no, there's been some mistake here. I'm just a fan, an ordinary person, I don't even know why you'd think I–'

Gerhardt stopped abruptly as the adrenaline wore off and his brain kicked back in. He looked up properly at the orc, as if seeing him for the first time, then down at himself, at the mud- and blood-flecked uniform he wore, in the white and red of the Titans.

'I'm on the pitch,' he said, mostly to himself. 'I'm a player. I'm a *Titan*!'

The orc laughed and threw himself at Gerhardt, who reacted with a punch to the orc's stomach. The orc's heavily armoured stomach. Gerhardt screamed as his fingers broke, then the orc barrelled into him and he screamed some more.

He kicked out, pushing the orc back, then threw himself to his feet and ran.

Borgut ran out of the locker room, Gazbag at his heels. He sprinted up out of the dugout to the field and sto~ belief as he saw the state of the pitch. Th~

of skilled players weren't anywhere to be seen. And neither were the Black Water Boyz, at least not in any effective, organised way. They were getting hammered.

'That cheating little scumbag!' he roared.

Gazbag peered around, squinting at the orcs who littered the field, most of them on their backs moaning where the Titans' ogre had left them as it rampaged across the pitch. 'Boss, where's the special players?' he asked eventually.

'There are none,' hissed Borgut from between gritted fangs. 'I don't know if that little weasel Mazlocke conned us, or if he was just rubbish, but nothing's happened.'

'Maybe it's just gonna take some time, boss. Maybe the spell caught the players sleeping or something, and they're getting their kit on.'

Borgut goggled at his assistant. 'Sleeping? *Sleeping?* The only players sleeping seem to be the Boyz! Look at them – I've seen fewer casualties on a battlefield!'

Gazbag shuffled from foot to foot awkwardly. 'What's gonna happen to the Boyz then?' he asked.

Borgut glared up at him. 'What do you think? We were already about done, and this disaster is it. The end. It's over. All our gold is gone, the team are getting hammered out there, and when the Colleges of Magic find out what I did, I'll be deader than our chances of winning this game.' Misery overtook him and he slumped to the ground. 'This is the end of the Black Water Boyz.'

'In that case, I'm gonna leave now and get the first caravan back to the mountains,' said Gazbag cheerfully. 'I hear the Gunbad Giants are looking for a new coach. I fink the spiders ate the old one. See ya, boss.' He turned and wandered towards the stadium's exit.

Borgut watched him go, then started shouting incoherent

curses at the universe in general and unlicensed wizards in particular.

This was Juliana's chance. She was on the field, the ball was nearby and she could finally prove what she could do. Okay, it wasn't exactly *her*, but that was a small thing. She scanned her surroundings for the ball as Crabbe, now aided by Pearce, put the boot into the orc who had tried to tackle her, and the dwarf referee moved in to break them up.

A short distance away, she saw a goblin struggling to balance the ball in both hands while running forward, tripping, falling, picking itself back up and grabbing the ball again. Oddly, it was running *away* from the end zone and towards her. She shrugged and sprinted towards it.

Goblin was having so much fun. He'd beaten up more orcs than he could count (more than one). None of them could stand up to his massive strength. He saw two of them moving towards him at once, one from each side. Laughing maniacally, he jumped and dropkicked one while swinging his massive ogre fists at the other. They both went down, and he landed bodily on top of them, relishing the crack of bones breaking and the gurgles of pain.

Goblin pulled himself back to his feet, stopped to wipe blood from his hands and then he saw… himself. Halfway across the pitch, the body he knew and hated was running unsteadily, ball in hand, towards a human, who was sprinting towards the goblin.

'No!' Goblin shouted at the top of his, now considerable, voice. 'You no hurt Goblin!' and charged towards them.

* * *

Kurt was pushing his way through the stands, moving down towards the field. He needed to find Vanderwald. 'Get out of my way,' he shouted at a group of dwarfs who seemed to be having a drinking competition, judging by the empty ale barrels around them. 'Don't you know who I am?' he screamed as he tried to push one of them aside.

'No!' the dwarf said, standing up to his full height, such as it was, and cracking his knuckles menacingly. 'But I do like to know a fella's name before I beat him to death with his own leg, so who are ye, laddie?'

'I don't have time for this,' Kurt muttered. He took a few steps back and sprinted, then leapt over the dwarf. At least, he tried to. Had he been in his own body, he'd have succeeded. In the clumsy, unfit body of an obsessed fan, he instead tripped over a trailing shoelace and fell head-first into the dwarf, who reeled back, blood welling from his newly-broken nose.

'What in Nuffle's name do ye think yer doing, ye human bampot?' the dwarf yelled, his beard rapidly turning red. 'Think ye can treat me like that just 'cos I'm a dwarf, do ye? Well I'll show ye what we do to folks with that attitude up in the mountains, laddie.'

The dwarf made a fist and lashed out at Kurt, who reeled backwards to avoid it. He overbalanced and tumbled over the seats on the next level down, colliding with a group of smelly Bretonnian peasants, who tumbled away. The dwarf followed, vaulting over the seats on the third attempt. Hob-nailed boots landed inches from Kurt's borrowed head.

'I don't have time for this,' he growled, grabbing the dwarf's legs and yanking hard. The bearded, bleeding dwarf fell on his back. Kurt pulled himself up, stomped on the dwarf's face, enjoying the sound of bone cracking, and sprinted away as fast as he could in his new body.

As he ran on, Kurt heard the dwarf saying, awe in his voice, 'I dinnae ken who that is, but he's a violent wee lad. He should be a player.'

He saw Vanderwald on the touchline, yelling abuse at the referee, who seemed to be trying to drag two of the Titans off an orc. Further along, he saw the Black Water Boyz' coach on his knees, having some sort of fit. Pushing his way to ground level, he went to leap over the barriers separating the crowd and the players, but his borrowed body wouldn't make it over. Sighing in exasperation, he raised his voice and shouted to the head coach.

'Vanderwald! VANDERWALD!'

The coach's head turned, and Kurt waved. 'Over here! I need to talk to you!' Vanderwald snorted and turned away, and Kurt shouted again. 'NOW! Get over here.'

The coach hesitated, then trotted over to the barriers.

'Look, son, I'm busy just now, but if you want an auto-graph, hang around after the game.'

'Oh, shut up, coach. No one wants your autograph, they want mine,' snapped Kurt.

'Why would anyone–'

'It's me, you stupid old man. Kurt. Kurt Grafstein.'

'Are you mental, boy? Kurt's out there.' Vanderwald ges-tured to the field, then looked at where he was pointing.

Kurt focused on the same point, and saw himself running away from an orc, screaming. 'What the hell is he doing?' Vanderwald asked.

'He is not me,' Kurt yelled. 'I mean, he, the me out there, is this person, who I am right now. I mean, I am Kurt, in this body, and this body's owner is, presumably, out there run-ning away from a very large orc.' Kurt looked back out at the field, and felt a surge of fear. 'Running very slowly, actually.

Oh god, he's going to–' He winced as, out on the field, the orc caught up with 'Kurt' and, almost casually, knocked him to the ground.

Gerhardt felt something hit him from behind and he fell face-first to the ground. He tasted blood and mud, and then he was in the air. He looked frantically around to see himself being lifted by the orc he'd punched.

'Oh, I'm so sorry, I really am, I didn't mean– oh nooooooo!' he squealed as the orc started turning around slowly, gripping Gerhardt's leg in both hands and spinning him like a goblin fanatic with his ball and chain. The orc sped up and Gerhardt tried to scream, but couldn't as the motion made him queasy, then violently ill. He heard the orc laughing madly, then it spoke.

'I thought you were supposed to be some kinda star,' it sneered. 'Let's see how the crowd likes you, eh?'

Then Gerhardt was flying through the air, still spinning, and below him he could see the press of the crowd and hear baying voices and then he was landing and hands were tearing at him and then everything went mercifully dark.

Johann felt utterly exposed. He'd never told anyone, but he had a recurring nightmare that he turned up to team practice naked. It was the worst thing he had ever imagined. What was happening now was worse.

It wasn't the skimpy uniform he was wearing. He didn't mind that too much, actually. The skirt was pretty comfortable, and feeling the breeze on his skin was quite nice.

It wasn't the dancing either. As a catcher, he was used to being athletic, and he'd spent enough time watching the cheerleaders to have some idea of their moves. He was quite sure he wasn't doing as well as Juliana usually did, but he wasn't entirely embarrassing himself. Well, her.

No, the part that was making him feel horrendous was the shouts coming from the crowd. On a drunken night out with the team, he'd once ended up in an 'exotic dancing' bar in Bretonnia, and even there, the customers had been more polite to the dancers than what he was hearing now.

Then the world went wobbly again. He blinked, hoping that he would suddenly be back in his own body. Instead, there was a blinding flash and someone fell on him. It was a short man with a stubbly beard, terrible skin and what looked like a homemade attempt to replicate the kind of robes worn by College wizards. It seemed to have been patched together from stained old blankets and what looked like feedbags used by Bretonnian warhorses. Crude mystical-looking symbols had been stitched onto it in haphazard fashion.

'Oh, I'm so sorry,' the man muttered. 'I should have appeared where there wasn't anyone. My, aren't you lovely, in your, ah, is that a cheerleader's costume, my dear?' The man looked worried. 'In white and red. Oh dear, those are Titans' colours, aren't they? Oh no. Oh, nonononononono. I'm still here. I should be miles away. That stupid spellbook!'

The man looked around frantically, then jumped to his feet. 'I'm sorry, but I really have to–'

His words were cut off as Johann leapt to his – her, whatever – feet and punched him in the stomach with a pom-pom-wielding fist.

'That's for calling me "my dear",' he growled in Juliana's voice. 'Now, who in Nuffle's name are you?'

The man opened his mouth to answer, but before he could speak, a large bag popped into existence in the air. It hung there for a moment, with everyone around gaping at it. Then gravity seemed to catch up with whatever magic had created the bag, and it fell, landing on him with a loud thud and knocking him out cold.

'Well, that was unexpected,' Johann said, gaping at the unconscious wizard.

Wizard! That was it. This wizard must have had something to do with what happened. Johann threw down his pom-poms and opened the bag as the wizard moaned gently. It was full of gold marked with orcish symbols. Johann looked down at the wizard, then to where a burly orc was weeping on the sidelines.

'Ah,' he said. 'I think I have an idea what's going on here. Where's Vanderwald?'

Juliana sprinted towards the goblin, utterly focused on it and the ball it half-carried, half-dragged. She was so focused that she almost missed the ogre barrelling towards her at high speed, shouting something about goblins in his guttural voice.

She skidded to a halt at the last moment and threw herself backwards as the ogre thudded past, towards the goblin.

'What are you doing, Ghurk?' she shouted to him, but the ogre ignored her. He reached the goblin and, to Juliana's utter astonishment, scooped it up and sat it on his shoulder. The goblin was clearly equally astounded at this turn of events, as it dropped the ball and waved frantically at her instead, squealing, if she heard it correctly, 'Johann! Johann, it's me! Johann!'

The ogre turned towards her, looked at her for a moment, then looked over at where the referee was still trying to disentangle Crabbe, Pearce and an orc. A grin split the ogre's face, and it shouted 'Goblin will help!' then thundered towards the scrum.

Juliana blinked, then caught herself. The ball was just feet away. She scooped it up, and turned. She was close to the orc end zone. She needed to be at the other end of the field to score, but there were bound to be loads of opponents between here and...

'Ah,' she said to herself as her gaze took in the tableau of the match. There were barely any orcs standing. It looked like a dwarf deathroller had cut a swathe of destruction through them. Small clumps of Titans players were taking the opportunity to pick on the few orcs still upright while the referee was busy. Near the stands, one greenskin was spinning a human player around his head. He let go and the human sailed up and towards the crowd, screaming. It looked like Kurt.

Juliana knew she should feel sympathetic, given what he would face when those animals in the stands got hold of him, but in truth she didn't care, especially given the way he pawed at her given any opportunity.

The orc turned and saw her, and spotted the ball in her hands. It roared and started towards her. Grinning fiercely, Juliana ran.

'What did you do?' screamed Vanderwald into the shabby wizard's face.

'N-nothing,' the wizard said, weeping. 'Honestly, I–'

'I think it was the orcs, coach,' Jul–Johann said. 'He had this bag of orc-stamped coins.'

'They're not mine. They're hers. She's blaming me,' the wizard muttered.

'Shut up, you,' Vanderwald said. 'What do you suggest, Julia– I mean Johann. I think.'

The coach was still trying to wrap his head around what

was going on, but the cheerleader and the strange stalker-boy were adamant that they were actually Johann and Kurt, and it made as much sense as anything else that was happening today.

'I think it might be a good idea to see why the orc coach is crying,' the cheerleader said, pointing to a crumpled and broken-looking greenskin a few yards away.

Vanderwald prodded the orc coach with his foot. Hard.

'Oi, Borgut!' he yelled. 'Have you been trying to cheat again?'

The orc looked up through bleary eyes, saw Mazlocke and blinked once, then again. Then he launched himself at the wizard.

'Where's my gold, you no-good, thieving, useless excuse for a shaman?' he shouted.

Kurt and Johann stepped forward and pulled the orc back.

'What exactly did you do, Borgut?' Vanderwald asked through gritted teeth.

The orc sighed. 'I hired this charlatan to cast a spell that would substitute my players for... better ones.'

'Mazlocke's Cantrip of Superior Substitution,' the wizard piped up. 'Guaranteed to... Eh, never mind,' he said as four pairs of eyes glared at him. 'I'll shut up now.'

'What went wrong?' Johann asked.

'Well, I got the spell from an old book, and it was in an obscure language, and I might have mistranslated it a bit. I'm not exactly College-trained. The same thing happened with the teleport spell,' he said, looking abashed. 'Otherwise I'd be miles away by now.'

'Can it be reversed?' Vanderwald asked.

'Um... I really don't know,' Mazlocke admitted, red-faced. 'I have the book here.' He reached into his dingy robes and pulled out an ancient tome with arcane runes on the cover.

Vanderwald sighed and turned to Johann.

'We need a real wizard. Go and find one of the ones running the camras. It's time to reverse this idiot's spell and put you all back where you belong.'

Juliana was yards from the end zone. A touchdown was in sight. Unfortunately, so was the orc. It bore down on her, grunting belligerently. She wasn't going to make it. This called for a risky play. She stopped on the spot, threw the ball straight upwards and then, with a deep breath, leapt after it. The orc charged and grabbed her by the legs, pulling her to the field. She tasted mud and rolled from the greenskin's grip onto her back. She looked up as a shadow passed over the sun.

It was Ghurg.

The ogre slammed into the orc, bellowing incoherently. On its shoulder, the goblin still held on for dear life. The ogre kept moving, taking the orc with it, and the ball landed just feet in front of Juliana. She silently thanked Nuffle – and Ghurg – grabbed the ball and threw herself over the touchline.

The crowd went wild, and the world went weird. Again.

The College-approved wizard finished chanting and Vanderwald looked at him.

'Is that it? Have you reversed it?'

The crimson-robed figure shrugged. 'I don't know. It's never easy with–,' he turned his gaze on Mazlocke, who was shifting uncomfortably in the grip of two surprisingly burly security mages, and his voice hardened, '–*unlicensed wizards*.'

Vanderwald was struck by the contrast between the two. The College wizard was resplendent in embroidered robes, and power crackled from his eyes. Mazlocke, by contrast, was simply shabby.

'How did that idiotic orc think this fool was a real wizard?' he asked.

The College wizard raised his staff and uttered more arcane syllables. He turned back to the coach. 'Actually, this sort of thing happens surprisingly often. Enthusiastic amateurs who think a College education is optional, not realising that the only thing standing between turning a player into a frog and sucking the stadium into the Realm of Chaos can be the knowledge we provide.'

Vanderwald paled. 'That could have happened?'

'Oh, yes,' said the wizard cheerfully, making shapes in the air with his staff that glowed with power. 'Remember that incident with the Schonburg Sentinels? The entire town's just a crater now. That was one like him.' He gestured back to Mazlocke. 'Right, that should be it now.'

Vanderwald glanced at the bodies of the fan and the cheerleader, whoever they contained right now. 'Do you two feel any different?'

They just gazed blankly at him. He thought there might be a bit of drool around their mouths.

'Well,' he said. 'I suppose something's happening.'

Juliana blinked. Her vision cleared and she was standing by the side of the pitch, with Coach Vanderwald waving his hand in her face.

'Coach?' she said. 'Did you see? Did you see what I did? I scored.'

'I don't think it matters, really,' Vanderwald said dismissively. 'We'll have to replay the match after what this idiot did.' He slapped the orc coach on the head with the back of his hand.

'But… I scored. I won us the match. I was a player.'

'Oh, don't be stupid, girl. You're, well, a girl. You can't play Blood Bowl.'

'Is that so?' said a voice from behind him. He turned and gaped up at a very tall, very well muscled and very angry looking woman wearing what looked like a dress made of brightly coloured feathers.

'And just who are you, madam?' he asked in the moments before she punched him in the face.

'Patronising patriarchal prat.' She turned to face Juliana. 'You were in the body of the player out there? The one who scored?'

Juliana nodded.

'You were very good. I could use a player like you.' She produced a small card from somewhere in her feathers. 'I'm the head coach of the New World Warriors, a team from the Lustrian League. How do you fancy becoming an Amazon?'

Juliana smiled.

Johann was sitting by the touchline, the ball in his hand. He pulled himself to his feet, readjusting to his own body and wondered if there was any place in the world for a male cheerleader.

One minute Ghurk was sitting on top of his own shoulders enjoying the ride, the next he was back in control of his own heavily muscled body, jumping up and down on the mangled remains of an orc. He stopped and looked around. He felt something on his shoulder and reached up, grabbing it. He hung the goblin in front of his face for a second, then casually tossed it away with the force of a crossbow firing a quarrel.

* * *

Goblin flew. He was happier than he'd ever been. He'd been an ogre, taking out all his years of frustrations on the orcs who'd been mean to him. And now he was flying. It was the best day ever. He put his head down and spread his arms, and shouted, 'Wheeeeeeeeee!'

Gerhardt's vision turned multi-coloured, then went back to normal, just in time to see a goblin in a battered metal helmet flying towards his stomach at immense speed. Not for the first time that day, he screamed.

Kurt woke up lying on his back. He blinked and tried to look around, but couldn't move his head. Above him was a high wooden ceiling, arched and criss-crossed with ornate beams carved with doves. The last thing he remembered was spinning in the air and flying towards the crowd, then… pain. *Pain.* It came flooding back, and he screamed. A face swam into view above him. It was Juliana. He tried to speak, but she shushed him.

'It's okay, Kurt. You're in the Temple of Shallya,' she said. 'You – well, your body – got hurt really badly. The sisters think it'll take months for you to heal.' She grimaced. 'And you might never play again. I just wanted to say, before I headed off to play in the Lustria League, that if you recover enough, there'll be a place for you as a cheerleader for my new team. Maybe. I'm sure Johann will put in a good word for you anyway. He's nice like that.'

And then she was gone. Kurt lay in silence – not that he had much choice – until another voice broke his reverie. A very familiar voice, one he'd last heard speaking in his own voice.

'Hello, roomie!' it said. 'This is amazing. I can't believe

I get to share a room with my favourite Blood Bowl player ever. And since most of my ribs were broken, I might be here for months. This is going to be great!'

Jim Johnson looked up at his ogre companion, glad to be comfortably back in his own undead body.

'Well, that did turn out to be quite a match, didn't it, Bob?' he asked brightly, grinning into the camra-warlock's glowing eyes.

'I dunno, Jim. It's not like we were really paying attention,' Bob shrugged. 'We were a bit busy getting to know each other better.'

'Please don't phrase it like that, Bob. It's very distasteful,' Jim said through his grimace.

'Well, one good thing came from all this, Jim.'

'Oh, and what's that?'

'Well, you know that saying that if you want to understand someone, you should walk a mile in their shoes?'

'Yes, Bob.'

'Well, now that I've been you, I know why you're such an uptight, humourless git, Jim.'

'Oh, and why is that?'

'Your shoes are far too tight. I don't think I even could walk a mile in them.'

Jim sighed.

'Thanks, Bob. And thanks to you viewers at home for sticking with us through the drama in this match between… some team and some other team. We'll see you again soon.

'From the Light's Hope Stadium in Talabheim, good night.'

PRIDE AND PENITENCE

ALEC WORLEY

Dolph Gutmann, coach of the Bright Crusaders, gazed at the gnawed and splintered bones piled in the wheelbarrow before him. His eager young assistant, Tomas, beamed as though he were presenting his employer with a wheelbarrow full of birthday cake and not the mortal remains of lynch-pin player Ulrich the Virtuous.

'The skaven said we should get the head back before the end of the game,' said the boy, eyes wide with enthusiasm. 'Rat-ogres have a terribly efficient digestive system, apparently.'

Dolph gave a brittle smile. 'Can this wait? I'm in the middle of a pep talk...'

Tomas gazed round at the surviving members of the Bright Crusaders, all eight of them. They were seated in a semi-circle, mesmerised by the contents of the wheelbarrow, their faces contorting as if in competition to see who could strike the most horrified expression.

Dolph ushered his assistant from the locker room, kicked a

chewed femur out of sight and clapped his hands, as if about to introduce a fun new activity to a class full of schoolchildren. He winced as Tomas hissed at him from the doorway.

'Sorry, coach. Shall I put this lot with the others?'

Anger was something of a foreign language to Dolph. His first season as coach of the Bright Crusaders had given him plenty of opportunity to become fluent, but the only expression of rage he could seem to master was a steady throb in his temple and a growing collection of stomach ulcers.

'If you could, that would be lovely,' said Dolph, his voice trembling with restraint. Tomas disappeared with a whistle so cheerful that it made Dolph's eyelids twitch.

It was this eerie patience that had not only earned Dolph his nickname – 'the Saint' – but also served him well during his own time as a star thrower for the team. Despite serving for eight long, silverware-free years, Dolph remained proud to serve the Bright Crusaders, a team famous for its devotion to the virtues of sportsmanship, which included a problematic contempt for cheating of any kind.

He regarded what was left of his beloved team, most of them now blinking up at him like a basket full of pigeons curious to know whether the cook was going to serve them roasted on a stick or baked in a pie. Had he pushed them too hard during training? Were they overawed by the importance of the event? This was the Purity Cup Final, after all, the Crusaders' first shot at a major trophy in years, a chance to stop everyone from sniggering at the mention of the team's name, a chance to prove that good guys could finish first for once.

Dolph returned his players' attention to the tactics chalked on the board beside him, rebuilding his expression into something resembling an encouraging smile as he outlined the plays for the second half against the Doomtown Rats. He praised the valour of his blitzers in breaking the skaven line and enabling the Crusaders' first two touchdowns, applauded the fortitude of his linemen for holding back the skaven's persistent offence, and commended the thrower for not sobbing too loudly at the sight of Skrut Manpeeler, the skaven's marauding rat-ogre, disembowelling his third Crusader player in a row. That last casualty had allowed one of the skaven gutter runners to scurry into the Crusaders' end zone to score a touchdown for the Rats seconds before the half-time whistle blew.

Facing a tenuous two-one lead, Dolph marvelled at the lunacy of his own optimism as he tried to reassure his team that all would not be lost in the second half so long as they maintained a strong defence. His assertions inspired nothing but a surge of protests.

'They have a twelve-foot monstrosity that eats every player who tries to mark it,' said Klaus the Forthright.

'Those gutter runners are going to have a field day now there's only eight of us,' said Hans the Doubtful.

'At least they haven't bribed the referee,' said Dieter the Naive.

Dolph nudged the team's bard, who quickly struck a heartening chord on his lute, silencing the quarrelling players long enough for Dolph to cut in, his voice firm with conviction.

'Our passing game has been the best in this competition,' he said. 'Have you forgotten what we did to the elves? Every one of you is skilled enough to be worth two skaven players. If you ask me, it's us who outnumber them.'

The bard's fingers galloped over his lute-strings, his soaring melody evoking all the romance of valour in the face of uncertain odds.

'They're weak,' Dolph continued. 'They're worse at dodging than you think and their co-ordination is pitiful. They don't work as a team. Whereas we stand united, armed with faith and decency. We face the impossible as we have always done. Do we not strive to honour the sacred code of fair conduct in a sport lost to madness? Is this not victory enough? Is this not who we are?'

Dolph's heart soared at the sight of his players nodding in agreement, joining hands in a gesture of unity, the bard's heroic air rousing them to righteous war.

A bell clanged in the corridor outside, summoning both teams to the players' tunnel for the second half.

'Who are we?' demanded Dolph.

The players would have roared back, 'We are the Bright Crusaders!', only the hulking blitzer responsible for their first touchdown had sprung to his feet.

Gerhardt the Penitent.

The vein in Dolph's temple began throbbing, his eyelids fluttering like they were trying to escape from his face.

'I understand, Coach Gutmann,' said Gerhardt, his face enraptured as though receiving private instruction from Sigmar Himself. 'You're saying we have an unfair advantage!'

Before Dolph could correct him, Gerhardt dropped his trousers.

The coach and the other players gazed in horrified awe as Gerhardt struggled to untie his bootlaces, hopping around the locker room like a half-naked ogre on a pogo-stick.

It wasn't the strangest thing Gerhardt the Penitent had done since joining the Bright Crusaders last season. He had set fire to himself during that qualifier against the Athelorn Avengers. Then there was the time he insisted on playing while lying on a bed of nails. Or the time he had apologised for an expert tackle on a kroxigor by spending the rest of the game trying to kick himself into the nearest end zone.

'I shall play without armour,' he bellowed, shrugging off

his spiked shoulder-pads and tearing off his vestment. 'I shall bear no unjust advantage, for a victory won unfairly is no victory at all!'

During an interview with *Spike!* magazine, Dolph had been sincere when he described Gerhardt's arrival as a 'blessing'. He had scored four touchdowns in his debut match against the Khazad Steelers and was probably the only rookie Dolph had ever seen who could listen to the threats of a rabid Trollslayer without soiling himself. The man had all the makings of a legendary blitzer, as strong as an ogre, as quick as an elf and regarded pain as an interesting theory he might be lucky enough to one day understand. But it soon transpired that Gerhardt's physical gifts were tempered by a moral outlook that was severe even by the impeccable standards of the Bright Crusaders.

It turned out Gerhardt was an ex-monk from St Apologia of the Immaculate Piety, a cult of flagellants who believed that only through constant hardship and penitence could one achieve true enlightenment. The monks wore nothing but fleas, lived on a diet of their own tears, and slept on beds of gravel, but only if they'd run out of hedgehogs.

Gerhardt the Penitent now bared himself before his teammates, surrounded by torn clothes and discarded armour, announcing his readiness to return to the pitch by snapping the waistband of whatever meagre rag it was he was trying to pass off as a loincloth.

The bell outside rang again, more urgently this time.

'Gerhardt,' said Dolph, urging the other players to remain seated. 'We agreed that you would no longer carry out acts of penitence on the pitch. The fact that you've managed to abstain from doing so all season is the reason we've been able to get this far in the competition, yes?'

A pair of familiar shadows materialised behind Gerhardt.

Dolph had regretted allowing the blitzer to hire a pair of dark elf 'trainers' (their business card had read 'Freelance Sadists'), but Gerhardt had insisted that he would need help in maintaining an acceptable level of personal contrition if he was no longer allowed to debase himself in public. Last week they had helped Gerhardt bury himself during training and it had taken the groundskeeper hours to find him again.

'Yes,' said Gerhardt, inspired as the dark elves whispered in his ear. 'I have abstained from penance for too long. I must atone for the arrogance of our previous triumphs.'

One of the linemen was now sobbing.

The bell rang a third time and Dolph took a deep breath, struggling to dispel the image of his own hands garrotting Gerhardt with a loincloth.

'What about Sister Bertilda and the orphans?' he said, snatching a sheaf of letters pinned to the team's portable shrine. Gerhardt looked bewildered. He'd become even more forgetful since he'd ordered those dark elves to break things over his head during morning prayer.

Dolph rifled through the letters, pausing now and then to read aloud.

'"Dear Gerhardt",' he read. '"We are eternally grateful for your assistance."'

Another letter: '"The children see you as an inspiration. Without your help we would be forced to sell them all for wizarding experiments."'

Yet another: '"Sir, we beseech you, in Shallya's name, do all you can to help your team achieve victory on the day of the final."'

Gerhardt examined a child's sketch, charcoal scribbled on parchment, of a robed stick-figure and her tiny charges celebrating as a hulking figure covered in spikes trampled through a scrawl of dismembered limbs. The blitzer turned to his teammates, hoping they might offer him a further clue.

'We pledged to buy her orphanage with our winnings,' said Felix the Chaste. 'If we win we'll be saving her and a hundred orphans from eviction. They're the reason you promised to stop sabotaging every game!'

Gerhardt's face suddenly brightened with recognition, then darkened with what Dolph desperately hoped was sensible thought.

'Those orphans need you, Gerhardt,' he said. '*We* need you. Your strength, not your devotions. Just for one game more.'

The other players had already gathered up Gerhardt's discarded armour. They offered it to him in unison, nervously, like devotees hoping to placate a volcano god who was just looking for an excuse to smite something. Gerhardt returned their gaze with a troubled look.

'It is no small thing you ask of me, brothers,' he said, wrinkling his nose at their offering. 'Our victories have afforded us some of the finest armour money can buy. We wore no such finery when we were losing games with blessed humility. I fear it is a symbol of our vanity.'

Dolph saw the other players glance at each other, perhaps wondering if there was anything in the Crusaders' code of ethics that might excuse the murder of a teammate.

'If I wear this armour,' said Gerhardt, 'if we win this game, then you must agree, all of you, to join me in an act of penitence, only this can assure the virtue of the Bright Crusaders as we claim that trophy.'

Dolph and the other players almost mobbed him with relief.

'Anything, for the love of Nuffle. Anything! Just get us that win!' cried the coach. The other players nodded in agreement.

Gerhardt's smile became a roar. 'Who are we?'

Dolph and the other players would have roared back, 'We are the Bright Crusaders!' only there came an urgent knock at the door. It was Tomas.

'The bad news is the referee is threatening to penalise us if we don't hurry up,' he said, then produced a sack that reeked worse than the stadium outhouse. 'The good news is I managed to get Ulrich's head back.'

'I wish I could have been a fly on the wall of the Crusaders' dressing room, Jim.'

'I know a wizard who could arrange that, Bob.'

'What I want to know is how the Crusaders plan to stop a full team of some of the best runners in the game from getting through their lines when they've only got seven and a half men.'

'Seven and a half, Bob? I count eight. Is someone missing a limb?'

'I'm talking about Gerhardt the Penitent, Jim. He's certainly not the most reliable player. Do you remember how he apologised for that touchdown against the Iron Tusks by trying to saw off his own leg?'

'That was a while ago, Bob. In this tournament, he's been downright boring. No stopping in the middle of the game to pray to the ball, no covering himself in leeches, no chaining himself to a rock.'

'But will he be able to stay focused enough to help the Crusaders secure their lead? I mean, this could be the game that saves these goody-goodies from being a permanent laughing stock.'

'Well, we're about to find out, Bob. The players are back on the pitch, and there's Gerhardt. He looks focused enough, but who's that he's waving to in the crowd?'

Gerhardt could just make out Sister Bertilda waving at him from among the seething wall of fans to his left. She was cocooned inside the humble grey habit of a priestess of

Shallya, her face a perfect oval as she waved her handkerchief. He fancied that she resembled a courtly lady granting favour to her champion, although he knew she was just as likely trying to wave away the stench of ale and vomit that permeated both the stands and the majority of the other fans. The group of orphans under her charge jumped up and down behind the advertising boards in a frenzy of excitement, swathed in tattered scarves with adorably oversized caps askew on their heads as they waved their crutches or rapped spoons upon their gruel bowls.

But the sight of those he had promised to save did little to ease Gerhardt's nagging conscience. He had struggled all season to control his addiction to repentance, to stop himself from whispering the Crusaders' tactics to the opposition players and applauding their bootwork when they fouled him. Gerhardt's conscience haunted him like a ghost that had nothing better to do, urging to him to repent, always to repent. If only Coach Gutmann knew how close Gerhardt had come to firing himself out of that confetti cannon at half-time.

He wiped away another rivulet of drool oozing from the brow of his helmet and looked up into a pair of glowing green eyes. They glared down at him like emerald fires above a snout wrinkled with fury. Skrut Manpeeler was a festering tower of muscle, claws and whiskers, a rat-ogre stitched together by some demented skaven alchemist for reasons beyond the grasp of human sanity. Like the rest of its rancid species, the monster stank like it was really putting in the effort, its chest heaving with rapid rasping breaths that fanned Gerhardt's face with an aroma somewhere between 'cesspit' and 'something that had smelled pretty bad even before it was found dead in the gutters behind a harbour tavern on a hot day'.

The other skaven players had assumed a strong offensive

formation beside this monstrosity. The ratmen were hunched, as if barely evolved from scurrying through sewers on all fours. Their clawed hands pawed restlessly at the ground, snouts twitching, bodies encased in armour or draped in rags, both the colour of luminous mould. Those standing beside Skrut snickered to themselves, relishing not only the power of their monstrous teammate, but also the vulnerability of the diminished opposition. It took all of Gerhardt's internal resolve to stop himself from wishing them all good luck.

The whistle caught Gerhardt by surprise, the crowd surging with a tidal roar as the ball sailed overhead into the skaven half. Then it happened. It always did. While all eyes were focused on the trajectory of the ball, one or several members of the crowd would take it upon themselves to start a fight, assassinate the referee, or attempt to burn down the stadium.

This time a skaven fan had taken the opportunity to launch something at one of the Crusaders' players. Blood Bowl fans were extraordinarily inventive when it came to selecting things to hurl at the players. Gerhardt had seen everything from rotten fruit and startled livestock to halfling snack vendors and all manner of homemade contraptions that ticked or sizzled for a few seconds before exploding. He was almost disappointed to see that today's missile was merely a rock.

It descended almost lazily, like a perfectly placed pass, towards the head of Felix the Chaste. The catcher was busy studying the skaven lines, no doubt calculating how best not to die during the second half of the game. Gerhardt couldn't recall telling his legs to start moving. All he knew was that he felt overwhelmed by a familiar sense of need. He was sprinting towards Felix, his eyes fixed on the hurtling rock. He'd been so good all season. He'd agreed to wear his armour. Wasn't that enough? Surely Coach Gutmann would allow him just one bit of penance, just a smidge. It was only a little rock after all. He heard Felix cry out in alarm seconds before Gerhardt shoved him aside, sprang into the air and caught the rock square between the eyes.

Gerhardt picked himself up, helped a shaken Felix to his feet, then gave everyone else a thumbs-up before promptly keeling over. Coach Gutmann suddenly appeared at his side trying to explain something to him while the apothecary asked Gerhardt to count how many fingers he was holding up, which – in all fairness – would have been a tough one for the blitzer even without the concussion. Gerhardt pushed them all aside and jogged back into position, burbling something about a rainbow stealing his unicorn.

The whistle blew, activating some kind of switch in the rat-ogre's fevered brain, one that sent it from 'unnerving stillness' to 'berserk rage' in a millisecond. The monster fell upon Gerhardt, eyes blazing green, huge claws raking the air with terrifying speed, ripping at the turf as the blitzer staggered backwards, still trying to shake away the buzzing in his skull.

Gerhardt glimpsed downfield as the skaven thrower scooped up the ball in its claws, its teammates bounding towards the Crusaders like an armoured tide. The creatures seemed to multiply as they ran, fanning out across Gerhardt's blurred vision in twos or threes until the pitch appeared overrun.

The rat-ogre attacked with the persistence of a machine, gurgling with exertion, its jaws awash with foam, claws flashing as it sought to pin its prey, like a cat trying to trap a mouse that didn't have the sense to run away. Gerhardt caught something in his peripheral vision. He turned instinctively as he brought his spiked kneepad up into the face of a skaven lineman diving at his legs. The blow collapsed the creature's snout with a sound like a warhammer hitting a basket of eggs. The skaven crumpled to the ground with a congested squeak. The rat-ogre's gauntlet came down, slashing a line down Gerhardt's arm, forcing him further back.

As he retreated, Gerhardt could see the stormvermin blitzers clashing with a pair of stout Crusader linemen as two more skaven players scurried past them, streaming like foetid water across the grass into the Crusaders' half.

Gerhardt took the searing pain in his arm under advisement as the rat-ogre's claws streaked down yet again, plunging deep into the turf. He drove his studded boot down onto the back of the monster's hand, pinning its rooted fingers. Sensing the monster's snout had been lowered to punching level, Gerhardt swung his gauntleted fist into its lower jaw, slamming it aside like a door through which someone had just made a dramatic entrance. But the rat-ogre was too consumed by its frenzy to care and went to plunge its sickly yellow incisors into Gerhardt's throat.

The blitzer seized the chisel-like teeth near the gum, gripping them in his armoured hand as he struggled to hold the monster's thrashing head at bay, still pinning its fingers beneath his boot. Gerhardt felt the other set of claws grasping his body. He grabbed two long fingers before they could close around him, twisting them aside with a crack as he drove his weight forward, pressing his face into Manpeeler's greasy, reeking fur. He shouldered spikes deep into its belly, forcing it off-balance, almost toppling the rat-ogre onto its back. As he grappled with the squirming giant, blood streaming from the gash in his arm, every muscle in his body straining to subdue the murderous fury before him, Gerhardt could hear his conscience tutting, disappointed that he couldn't have done more to give the poor beast a sporting chance.

A Gutter Runner streaked past him. Gerhardt sensed it moving into the space behind him and knew it would wait there to receive the ball. The skaven thrower was still down-field, sniffing its way left and right, the ball clutched tight in the crook of its scrawny arm as it sought the safest passage through the Crusaders' line. Gerhardt's teammates seemed to be drowning in a sea of verminous bodies either side of him, fending off claws and teeth as the frantic skaven strug-gled to drag the men to the ground.

Gerhardt felt the rat-ogre rip its claws out from beneath his boot as it twisted itself free of his grip. He braced himself to receive its next attack, but the monster only snarled at him, pounding the turf like an angry gorilla demanding to know who ate the last banana. It hissed at the surrounding fans, surrendering momentarily to its feral nature, finally giving up its feeble attempt at restraint as a thoroughly bad job.

The Crusaders' fans cheered with renewed vigour as the justly named blitzer Jurgen the Upright crashed through a wall of skaven and charged at their exposed ball-carrier like a maddened bull. The thrower froze as Jurgen dived at him, but somehow managed to slip from between his hands like a revoltingly hairy bar of soap. It scampered away, leaving the blitzer to perform the even more impressive feat of using his face to plough through several yards of turf.

Manpeeler seemed to have forgotten Gerhardt was there. The blitzer sensed another accurate strike at its broken jaw could see the creature stretchered off the field, but that thrower was streaking towards a gap where several Crusaders lay sprawled.

Gerhardt left the rat-ogre to snarl at the crowd, leaping over its tail as it wriggled after him like a questing tentacle. As he ran, he focused on the ball cradled in the arms of the skaven thrower, visualising himself stripping it from Manpeeler's grasp and tossing it into the hands of Felix the Chaste, who now sprinted alongside him towards the skaven end zone.

The skaven thrower had seen them. It was flinching in a zig-zag, trying to distract Gerhardt as he bore down on it like a meteorite. The skaven's wriggling course made Gerhardt feel suddenly seasick. His skull buzzed and his vision blurred once again. The skaven shimmered into triplets. Gerhardt squinted as he picked one, then snatched the ball.

He seized the blurred oblong and tore it from the skaven's grip, tossing it without thinking into the waiting mitts of the catcher beside him. Felix gave a strangled yelp, letting the thing bounce between in his hands as if it were red-hot, before finally dropping it on the grass. Gerhardt peered down at the ball, his head spinning, dimly wondering why the referee hadn't blown the whistle for a fumble and why the ball appeared to possess whiskers and a startled expression.

He turned and saw the headless body of the skaven thrower stumble several more paces before collapsing, releasing the ball into the paws of the waiting gutter runner. Gerhardt could have sworn the foul creature winked at him before scuttling past a lonely Crusaders lineman and into the end zone to score.

The referee blew the whistle and the skaven fans erupted into a squall of delighted squeaks, a sound that made Gerhardt's battered brain feel like it was being nibbled. The screen of the Cabaltron mounted above the players' tunnel filled with the image of the gutter runner gyrating in a manner that was as enthusiastic as it was horrifying.

Gerhardt clutched his head, trying to stop the stadium from whirling around him as he scanned the stands for Sister Bertilda. His vision cleared, but his heart clouded at the sight of the priestess sobbing into her habit.

'And there's the equaliser, Jim.'
'And there's Gerhardt looking very unhappy for failing to pick

up that ball. He's not going to make that concussion any better
by beating his head on the ground like that.'

'I've never seen the Crusaders so demoralised. They're not even
applauding the other team's touchdown.'

'I doubt the odds of their winning this final will do much to
raise their spirits either, Bob. The Crusaders may have the skill,
but I'm afraid the Rats have the numbers.'

'That reminds me, Jim. Did you know a ratman can squeeze
through a hole the size of a gold piece?'

'Is that so?'

'Yep. Kweequik the Kontorted of the Skavenblight Scramblers
once proved it by squeezing his entire body inside a football. He
would live to see his name in the record books too, if the team's
rat-ogre hadn't used the ball for kicking practice. Hur! Hur! Hur!'

Those smelling salts had certainly cleared Gerhardt's head,
although the apothecary had been rather short with him
for drinking the entire bottle. At least the number of opponents he could see now corresponded with the number of
opponents actually on the pitch. Not that it made much difference; the skaven still dominated the field with their speed
and superior numbers.

The scoreline remained two-two and as the Crusaders con-
cluded what was shaping up to be the final drive of the game,
Gerhardt was flailing on the line of scrimmage like a man
on fire. Three skaven clawed at his armour, thrashing him
with their tails, the urinary stench of their bodies cloying as
he fought to shake them off. One of them struggled with
his legs, trying to buckle his knees and probably wondering
why Gerhardt wasn't falling over the way most humans did
when you gnawed at their hamstrings.

The pain in Gerhardt's legs was nothing compared to the

guilt he felt in his heart. His gluttony for punishment had lost his team the lead, causing him to betray his pledge to help win the game and save Sister Bertilda's orphanage. Until the priestess had written to him, explaining her desperate plight, Gerhardt had never believed that victory could be more important than humility. He had never before given a thought to how his acts of penitence might serve as anything other than a glorious inspiration to the rest of the team. The other players certainly never did anything to stop him, although Coach Gutmann had once suggested they were just being polite.

The coach himself seemed to take the skaven's equaliser rather well, although he had done that thing where his eyelids twitched like they were playing ping-pong. As he directed his players back into position, he had given Gerhardt strict instruction to hold the centreline and tie up as many skaven players as possible. But it turned out the skaven were just as intent on tying up Gerhardt, smothering him like a fur coat that had seen better days.

The other Crusaders remained mired in a persistent scrum. White-armoured bodies clashing and knitting shoulder-to-shoulder with the sickly green of the skaven, both sides smearing the bloody grass to mud beneath their feet as they heaved and growled, spiked fists and iron-capped boots striking here and there, attempting to break the deadlock. The Crusaders had formed a cage around the ball-carrier, Felix the Chaste, and were trying to grind their way upfield, but more and more skaven were charging into the fray, inching the Crusaders back.

Gerhardt felt another surge of guilt to know that he was the cause of his team's plight. He had abstained from penance for so long, his hunger for it had grown so acute, that he had forgotten what Bertilda had taught him: that his actions had consequences for the rest of the team. Now his best chance of rectifying his mistake was to trust Coach Gutmann, who had forbidden him from moving out of position, and made sure that Gerhardt understood this didn't mean gluing or nailing himself in place.

A filthy pink tail lashed around Gerhardt's face. He bit down on it without thinking, which was probably just as well. One of the skaven screeched in pain as it leaped from his body as though electrified. Gerhardt grabbed it by the scruff of its neck and hurled the creature to the ground, freeing his hand to tear away the second skaven and fling it on top of the third still clawing at his legs. The creatures squirmed to their feet as Gerhardt staggered back, panting, wondering for the first time in his career whether he might be bleeding too much.

The timer on the Cabaltron was ticking down the final five minutes of the second half, beyond which play would continue into sudden-death overtime. With fresh substitutes and an offensive drive, the nimble ratmen would secure the win for sure.

The three skaven leaped at him with a collective squeal. He crouched as they crashed into him, feeling their spikes clash like swords upon his armoured shoulders. But the dexterous creatures had ducked lower than he anticipated, all three clawing at his legs. As he fought for a stable footing, his boot slithered along a patch of mud and he fell face-first into the muck. His squeaking attackers threw themselves on top of him, pinning his shoulder-pads, making it difficult for him to rise even if one of them wasn't jumping up and down on the back of his head. Mud oozed like worms up Gerhardt's nostrils, while his ears filled with squeals of skaven laughter.

The crowd roared and the beating ceased. Gerhardt managed to pull his head up out the mud with a slurp, blinking away the filth to see Jurgen the Upright trample one of the stormvermin underfoot as he raced forward. Felix the Chaste ran after him, head down, clinging to the ball.

The Crusaders' cage had broken the skaven line, but Skrut Manpeeler had been positioned downfield, ready to welcome any such intruders. Gerhardt could see the feral monster already bounding towards the Crusaders players, its broken jaw wagging, arms flailing excitedly, as if it couldn't decide which of these two fleshy gifts it wanted to unwrap first.

The goblin referee stood nearby, pretending to examine the hourglass around his neck as the cheating skaven forced Gerhardt to return his attention to the dirt. Gerhardt knew that Jurgen and Felix stood little chance against the ravenous rat-ogre. Guilt weighed upon him as heavily as his own armour, that and the three skaven players currently employing it as a trampoline. If he were to help both his team and Sister Bertilda, and absolve himself of his own sins against them, he would need to go against Coach Gutmann's instructions and think for himself. Like a spark struck from a tinderbox, three pairs of skaven feet struck an idea from the flint of Gerhardt's brain.

Still pinned inside his armour, Gerhardt tensed the slabs of muscle across his back, tightening the straps of his shoulder-pads. He felt the buckles snap as the skaven stamped on him again. The creatures were so focused on their efforts to pound Gerhardt's head into the earth like a tent peg that they failed to notice the blitzer wriggle free of his helmet and shoulder-pads. By the time they realised he had vacated his armour, a shirtless Gerhardt had smashed into their startled midst.

One of them managed to claw at his legs as it was dragged across the grass, pulling what was left of Gerhardt's britches down to his ankles. A lesser player would have tripped, stumbling over his own drawers, felled like the world's most undignified tree. But Gerhardt the Penitent instead bounded into the air, kicking off his boots and slipping free of his trousers with the grace of an exotic dancer shedding her final veil.

'Whoah! It looks like we got a streaker, Jim! I can see the referee calling for his tranquiliser crossbow.'
'That's no streaker, Bob! It's Gerhardt! And he's snorting mud out of his nostrils as he makes a blistering run down the wide zone towards his teammates!'

Gerhardt saw Jurgen attempt to swerve a flanking tackle from one of the skaven, but the creature caught him around the waist, ramming him towards the fans. A mob of orc hooligans surged forwards to receive him, but threw up their hands in disappointment as Jurgen crashed into the advertising boards. According to a tradition most Blood Bowl officials were too afraid to oppose, any player shoved off the pitch and into the stands was subject to whatever penalty the supporters could think to administer at the time. Luckily for the players, most fans were too dim-witted to think of delivering anything more than a severe beating, although Chaos fans were justly feared for their terrifying creativity.

Undaunted by the loss of his wingman, Felix kept running for the skaven end zone, racing perilously close to the crowds on his left as the rat-ogre charged towards him from the right.

Gerhardt sprinted faster than he thought possible, his bare feet a wondrous blur, gobbling up the distance between himself and the frenzied rat-ogre as it finally pounced upon Felix. The catcher managed to dart backwards and the monster drove a pulverising fist into the turf where he had been standing, forcing Felix back along the advertising boards. The orcs surged forwards in anticipation while Felix stood seemingly transfixed by the sight of the rat-ogre's gaping jaws.

Gerhardt bore down on Manpeeler, feeling invigorated by the whistling of both the fans and the refreshing breeze rushing through his loincloth. He was thrilled by the thought of meeting his foe on gloriously equal terms, every advantage surrendered, prepared to pit naked skill against raw fury, two forces matched as perfectly as light and dark.

Gerhardt leaped, distracting the rat-ogre as it went to swing its claws at the helpless ball-carrier. The giant's shining green eyes registered something like confusion seconds before its vision was blotted out by an expanse of forehead that descended into its snout with a symphony of splintering cracks. A number of dwarfs and norsemen in the crowd completely forgot themselves, swooning like schoolgirls in admiration of such a magnificently delivered headbutt, a perfectly placed 'Khazad kiss' that shattered the monster's muzzle, slamming its head backwards, momentum launching its enormous body over the advertising board and dropping it in a dazed heap surrounded by several pairs of orcish boots.

Skrut Manpeeler disappeared beneath a mob of greenskins as Gerhardt regained his senses, making a mental note to ask the apothecary whether he should be concerned that his head now rattled like a moneybox when he shook it. Felix was streaking towards the skaven end zone with two skaven scurrying far behind him as the timer on the Cabaltron winked towards its final zero.

Felix planted the ball over the line a split-second before the whistle blew and the stadium exploded like a volcano full of confetti. Cannons blasted shimmering streamers overhead as Gerhardt watched the scoreboard flip three-two in favour of his team. The Bright Crusaders and their fans went berserk, which for them meant respectfully applauding the losing team.

As the ogre security guards dragged away the skaven players, who continued squeaking threats at the referee as they were escorted off the pitch, Gerhardt searched the stands for Sister Bertilda. She was desperately trying to restrain her orphan charges. The youngsters had apparently become so overwhelmed with excitement they had joined in the orcs' assault upon the fallen rat-ogre, hammering at the unconscious monster with their crutches. Their caps and scarves had fallen away to reveal faces bright with glee. Gerhardt took a moment to assure himself that orphans could indeed be green. It probably meant they were unwell or something. He stared, intrigued. Apparently, their condition had caused them to sprout long pointed ears and teeth that gleamed like rows of needles as they cackled. Gerhardt laughed to himself. It was as if someone had paid a bunch of goblins to dress up as orphans. He paused, the thought lingering in his head like an unwelcome smell.

Sister Bertilda was now hoofing up the stairs towards the exit, hitching up her robes to reveal a pair of impressively hairy legs. Maybe she was desperate to use the toilet. Maybe she had forgotten the orphans' medication. Gerhardt vaulted over the advertising boards and dashed up the stairs after her, keen to offer assistance. The applauding fans tried to avert their eyes at the sight of the near-naked blitzer streaking up the steps beside them. Sister Bertilda tripped and something tumbled out of the front of her habit. Gerhardt saw a buxom pair of turnips bounce past him. He tried to tell himself that maybe she had brought a packed lunch, but his usually indomitable ignorance was already facing a rare defeat by the forces of reason.

Gerhardt caught the fleeing priestess with a diving tackle, bringing her down before she could reach the top of the stairs. Sister Bertilda barked an astonishing variety of swear words as the pair of them bounced back down the steps. Gerhardt eventually landed on top of her, pulling open her habit to reveal the dazed face of the Tomas, Coach Gutmann's assistant.

'I'm sorry,' said Dolph, clambering over the advertising board to join Gerhardt at the foot of the stairs. 'Let me explain.'

He forced himself to look into the blitzer's face, his expression that of a kitten wondering what it had done to deserve being fed to a minotaur. The fans paused in taking another bite of their cat burgers, hundreds of hands hovering over boxes of deep-fried cockroach nuggets as the tension rose unbearably.

'Sister Bertilda, the orphanage...' said Dolph, his head bowed under the weight of his confession. 'It was all a–'

Gerhardt interrupted. 'You... lied?'

'We all did.'

Dolph turned to see Felix the Chaste joining the rest of the shamefaced team as they gathered behind their coach. Tomas sidled away, straightening his habit and replacing the turnips down his front for reasons no one thought to question.

'It was the only way we could stop you from... well, from being you,' said Felix, his voice suddenly echoing from the Cabaltron nearby, as a Cabalvision camera-goblin eagerly broadcast the team's confession to the entire stadium.

Gerhardt sat down on the steps in shock.

'You're a star player, Gerhardt, the noblest of us all,' said Dolph, approaching him, almost in tears. 'You are the brightest of the Bright Crusaders, but we were losing every game because of you. Sometimes victory must come before piety, surely, otherwise what's the point of playing?'

Gerhardt stared at Dolph as though he were gibbering in a foreign tongue. The betrayed look upon the blitzer's face ignited within the coach a monumental sense of shame. Dolph had prided himself upon his impeccable record. For eight years as a player he had faced every defeat with bewildering gallantry, his patience unbreakable, the inspirational legend of Dolph 'the Saint' Gutmann unquestionable. But now his legacy had been sullied by a single lie.

The irritated voice of the goblin referee broke the hush that had descended upon the stadium.

'You haven't actually broken any rules, you know,' he said as he shoved his way through the players' legs. 'So do you want this bleedin' trophy or not?'

Dolph felt countless eyes upon him. The Crusaders fans glared at him, many of them so wild with rage they looked as though they might lose control at any minute and write him a very, very stern letter. The other players stared at their boots as if in mourning. Gerhardt gazed up at Dolph with a childlike look of hope.

Dolph gave a long, melancholy sigh before turning and addressing the stadium.

'A victory won unfairly is no victory at all,' he said before turning to his players. 'Who are we?'

They answered with what little enthusiasm they could muster.

'The Bright Crusaders,' they said.

Dolph nodded, feeling a pang of bitter satisfaction. 'Maybe next year,' he said.

His attempt to lead his team in a dignified exit from the pitch was marred somewhat by Gerhardt elbowing him into the stands as he roared to his feet, his voice amplified to an earthquake by the speakers of the Cabaltron.

'Good people,' he boomed, his words vibrating through the stands. 'The code of the Bright Crusaders has not been compromised!'

'We lied to you, Gerhardt,' said Dolph, clambering out from between the legs of several fans. 'It's not how we win games.'

Gerhardt ignored him, leaning over the advertising boards and yelling at the camra-goblin. The image of his face filled the Cabaltron, raining the inside of the screen with spit.

'My team swore an oath to me at half-time,' he said. 'They swore to join me in an act of penance that would assure the virtue of the Bright Crusaders as we claimed victory.'

He turned to his teammates. 'Is this not so? Did you not all swear?'

The other players nodded, exchanging fearful looks as they realised that exactly what they had sworn to had never been made entirely clear.

Gerhardt continued. 'Then I can assure you all that our victory has been achieved fairly, that our piety has not been compromised, that the strictures of virtue and honour have been obeyed! So swear I, Gerhardt the Penitent, the bright- est of the Bright Crusaders!'

The fans erupted into forgiving applause and Gerhardt threw his arms around Dolph, who suddenly found him- self trying to extract his face from the player's cleavage. The applause intensified as the goblin referee shrugged and stomped off to inform the officials.

'So...' said Dolph, his features pinched between two slabs of pectoral muscle as he peered up at Gerhardt. 'This act of penance you mentioned...'

Gerhardt beamed at Dolph as a pale arm snaked around

the coach's neck and pressed a foul-smelling rag to his nose. Blackness rushed over Dolph like a shroud.

'Dolph,' said Astrid Smallbeer, the halfling interviewer from CabalVision News. 'The stadium's empty, you've bared your soul before thousands of fans, and you've won the Bright Crusaders their first trophy in years. Now the excitement's over, you appear to be in a contemplative mood.'

'Well, it's been a tough season,' said Dolph. 'We've all had to make sacrifices, but really I'm relieved more than anything that we could achieve victory without compromising our principles.'

Astrid nodded sagely and took another bite of an immense meat pie. 'Principles have always been important to the Bright Crusaders,' she said, spraying Dolph with pastry crumbs. 'But even die-hard fans are questioning your decision – and, indeed, your sanity – in allowing Gerhardt the Penitent to bury the entire team!'

'To be fair, he only had us buried up to our necks,' said Dolph, puffing aside the blades of grass that kept tickling his nose as he looked up at Astrid, now shaking crumbs out of her plaits. 'Knowing Gerhardt as I do, I think that shows tremendous restraint on his part. But really all we're doing is what the Bright Crusaders have always done, and that's demonstrate humility in the face of victory. We hope this gesture serves as an inspiration to the entire Blood Bowl community.'

Astrid fought to keep a straight face.

'You're clearly a firm believer in achieving the impossible,' she said. 'But some have suggested a month could try even the patience of Dolph "The Saint" Gutmann.'

'I'm sorry, a month of what?'

'Of being buried up to your necks.'

'A month?' yelled another head from somewhere further down the line of scrimmage. 'I didn't agree to that!'

'I'm terribly sorry, Astrid,' said Dolph, trying to maintain his composure as he felt yet another subterranean invertebrate seek refuge in his trousers. 'But is Gerhardt around?'

'He's buried right behind you,' she said. 'He's upside down, but he can still hear you. Look, he's waving his feet.'

'Ah, so he is,' said Dolph through teeth gritted so hard he could hear them cracking.

Someone cried out. 'I've had it! I quit! I don't care! Just dig me out of here right now!'

Astrid hesitated. 'Gerhardt's trainers told us they were under strict instruction to leave you here until the stadium reopened. They had crossbows. Big scary ones.'

Dolph watched in horror as one of the dark elves slithered into view and whispered in Astrid's ear.

She nodded. 'They said not to worry. Your assistant has promised to feed and water you. Oh, and the groundskeeper's said he'll try to mow around you as best he can.'

'The groundskeeper?' said Dolph, struggling to make himself heard above the others wailing in his ears. 'You mean Wulfe the Drunkard?'

'The one with two eyepatches, that's him,' said Astrid. 'Erm, Coach Gutmann are you alright? It's just that your eyelids keep twitching. Coach Gutmann? Hello? Sorry, viewers. Dolph 'the Saint' Gutmann seems to have drifted off there, no doubt meditating on the glories that await the Bright Crusaders next season. This is Astrid Smallbeer, CabalVision News. Back to you in the studio, Jim.'

THE SKELETON
KEY

DAVID ANNANDALE

The temple was buried far below a cemetery that had been abandoned for centuries. It was the forgotten beneath the forgotten. Its gods were dead, its idols without meaning. It was a ruin sinking deeper into the abyss of time. Or it would be, if it had been left to the dignity of its slow oblivion. But it had been reclaimed, and a new purpose imposed upon its corridors and vaults. It was a temple of sport now. And in a dugout that might once have been a prison, or a meditation cell, the most ancient of players brooded over the fallen, ruined nature of the age, and pronounced his judgement.

'Idiots,' Ramtut the Third muttered. The voice of the star player of the Champions of Death was a harsh whisper, scraping with the sands of history.

'And we're back! Jim Johnson and Bob Bifford with you once again after the Dungeonbowl opening ceremonies. Bob, weren't they splendid?'

'Rubbish,' said Ramtut. He sat in the rectangular chamber that passed for a dugout, watching the CabalVision inanity unspool in the crystal ball. He clenched a bandage-wrapped fist. Dust crumbled from the wrappings. 'Idiots,' he said again. It bore repeating.

'*That they were, Jim. And a big shout-out to the Bloodweiser Orchestra for a knock-out performance.*'

'*You know, Bob, that's the first performance of Morrheim's Egregious Fanfare in its original arrangement for strings and scalded cats here at the Dungeonbowl, and I can't think of a better introduction to the match we have for our viewers today.*'

'*It's a doozy, all right. Folks, this is it – the Bright Crusaders against the Champions of Death. Doesn't get more tense than that.*'

'*Indeed not, Bob, and it's fair to say the crowd is lapping up that tension. It's a battle of the extremes. The Bright Crusaders are the league's most honourable players. There isn't a single penalty for cheating in their history, and that's not even getting into the spectators whose lives they've saved, even when that meant losing the game.*'

'*They're all about the honour of the game before the glory of victory. Which is just as well, given their win-loss record.*'

'*And facing them is a team that has racked up an impressive series of triumphs* and *body counts.*'

'*They managed to take out an entire stadium of spectators five years ago, didn't they, Jim?*'

'*They sure did, and swelling the ranks of their post-life fans. So there you have it, viewers: the incorruptible heroes fighting the undead horrors.*'

'*Uh, but aren't you…?*'

'*Undead* horrors, *Bob. Horrors.*'

'*They are a bit crumbly, that's for sure.*'

The skeletons clattered back into the dugout, accompanied by the Champions' necromancer coach, Tomolandry.

They had watched the opening ceremonies from just below the bleachers. The skeletons crowded Ramtut on the bench as they clicked and shook, teeth chattering with excitement.

'They enjoyed the show,' Tomolandry said. He leaned against the dugout entrance. His features were obscured by the hood of his robe. Only the tip of his protuberant nose was visible. It shone in the torchlight.

Ramtut grunted. He turned a jaundiced eye on his team-mates. They had glyphs on their skulls to identify one from the other, but they were faded or smeared with dirt. Even Ramtut could barely distinguish them. He could pick out some by their physical variations. Spurs had bone growths spiking out of his shoulders. Dropjaw kept losing bits of himself. Straightline had trouble with the concepts of stopping and turning. Cup was missing the top of his skull.

'Best show ever, was it?' Ramtut growled. By which he meant the worst. In his day, there had been real opening ceremonies, with proper ritual sacrifices. None of the diluted, undignified spectacle of the present day.

More excited clatters. The skeletons had never been good at detecting sarcasm. Spurs began to clack his fingers against his jaw, beating out his answer in code. *It was amazing!*

'It was twaddle,' Ramtut said. 'Pap vomited onto the unthinking hordes on the bleachers. The best that can be said of it was that it and its audience were well-matched.'

Spurs lowered his hand, seeming abashed.

'They enjoyed the fireworks,' Tomolandry said. 'Very bright, close and hot underground.'

'Vulgar,' Ramtut snorted. 'Once, there was real grandeur to these events. None of this sad pandering.' He turned back to the crystal ball.

'It's worth repeating, Bob, that the College of Wizards is really

playing up the theme of this year's championship, and who can blame them?'

'The people who don't want themes in their Blood Bowl matches, Jim.'

'And what a lost opportunity that would be. What we have here is nothing less than a classic confrontation in a classic setting. Noble heroes venturing into the dark dungeon to seek out and destroy the monsters therein. That's the story of this Dungeon-bowl, Bob. And the crowd is eating it up. What a welcome the Bright Crusaders are going to receive!'

'That could be a real advantage for them, Jim, though I see a few unhappy faces in there.'

'Well-spotted and well said, Bob. If my eyes are not mistaken, those are supporters of Da Deff Skwad.'

'In a crowd of humans, orcs and goblins stick out like green thumbs, Jim.'

'Uh... yes. Quite. I must say I'm surprised they're here at all, given their team's surprise defeat at the hands of the Bright Crusaders.'

'I'd say any victory through honesty is a surprise victory, but I agree.'

'I think there is a lesson here for us, Bob. Whether Da Deff Skwad fans are here to boo the Crusaders or cheer the Champions, they're here. And isn't that what really counts in–'

'Please shut up,' Ramtut growled. He smacked the crystal ball from its mount. The images winked out and it rolled to the far corner of the dugout. He stood up. What stung was that the commentators were right. This match had a narrative. If the opposing team were anyone other than the Bright Crusaders, he would have guessed the fix was in. 'Let's go,' he said. There was still half an hour before kick-off, but he was tired of waiting in the dugout.

The skeletons filed out ahead of him. The exit from the

dugout opened onto the dank, dripping, nitre-encrusted walls of the vestibule. The masonry was massive, but decaying. Ramtut glanced at the crumbling blocks and sniffed. The dungeon had all the structural integrity of rotten bone. No one knew how to build anything to last anymore.

Beyond the iron door on the other side of the chamber was the Champions' end zone.

'We'll be going on first,' Tomolandry said when Ramtut reached the doorway. 'The crowd is filled with Crusaders supporters, so they get the build-up.'

Ramtut pulled his shrivelled lips back over his teeth. 'Monsters before heroes, is that it?'

Tomolandry shrugged.

'And that, I suppose, is your stirring pre-game speech?'

'The skeletons don't need one, and you would walk out before I was finished.'

Point taken. Ramtut could remember some speeches of old, though, that had value. That fired the spirit. That he had memorized the first time he heard them. Like everything else, oratory was a fallen art in this sad age.

'About the skeletons,' said Ramtut. 'Are you sure we don't need at least one ghoul? Or even a zombie? It feels like we're conceding before we start.'

Tomolandry tapped the side of his nose. 'They're vital to the strategy,' he said. 'You know that.'

'I still say it's a bad idea.'

Tomolandry clapped his cloth-wrapped shoulder. 'Trust me. I know what I'm doing.'

Ramtut didn't trust him and didn't believe him.

The betting chambers were nestled beneath an overhang of the bleachers. There were a score of the low booths. Beyond them, at the foot of the stone bleachers, vendors plied the crowd with slabs of indeterminate meat on sticks and tankards of ale. The people milled, shouting and laughing, the din growing louder as the start of the match drew closer.

Lots of noise. No one could hear what Greezing was saying to the dwarf bookie, especially with the other goblins crowding around to keep the conversation private.

'Are you betting on the Champions of Death or the Bright Crusaders?' the dwarf asked again. His quill was poised over the accounts ledger resting on the booking chamber's centre.

'Neither,' Greezing said. 'We're not betting on a win.'

The dwarf raised eyebrows almost as voluminous as his beard.

'We want to bet the Bright Crusaders will be caught cheating.'

The dwarf stared at Greezing for a long moment before he burst into laughter. Greezing waited the fit out. Eventually, the dwarf wiped the tears from his eyes and said, 'Very good, very good. Seriously, though, how do you want to bet?'

'I was serious.'

The dwarf blinked at him, grinning happily. 'You want to throw your gold away, I won't stop you.'

He laughed all the way through the transaction.

When the goblins were done, they turned their attention to the halfling who had been leaning against the wall between betting windows, one hairy-toed foot against the brickwork.

'All done?' the halfling asked. His name was Pillip. His clothes were dirt-smudged and dark, though his ruddy cheeks undermined the dangerous look he was trying to achieve.

'Done,' said Greezing. 'You placed yours too?'

'I did.' Pillip straightened up. 'Time to see my uncle, then.'

* * *

Pillip's uncle, Hallic, was a referee. He was also a halfling who believed in doing business, and doing it smartly. Greezing had found him to be very receptive in the days leading up to the match, and now he was delivering what he had promised. It didn't hurt that his nephew had placed gold for him on the same bet.

'The way I see it,' said Hallic, 'Dungeonbowl is already an unorthodox approach to Blood Bowl.' He spoke quietly but didn't whisper, rolling his words lovingly, as if appreciating their taste. He was standing beside one of the dungeon's portcullis gates, his hands on a wheel, waiting to turn it. The portcullis was out of sight beneath the foundations of the bleachers, which only had a direct view of the centre of the dungeon. With half an hour to go, CabalVision had not opened its all-seeing eye on the playing field yet. Greezing and his fellow goblins would have all the time they needed to make their preparations. Once the game began, they would have to hug the shadows more carefully, but Greezing felt sure they could avoid detection and do what needed doing.

'Unorthodox,' Hallic said again, pleased with himself. 'Yep. So what we're looking at, I say to myself, and I don't disagree, is *enhancement* of the unorthodox. And since the unorthodox is a selling point, then this is *enhancement* of the entertainment. That's the opposite of cheating the customer.'

'You said it, uncle,' said Pillip.

Hallic glanced at an hourglass. He said to Greezing, 'You boys know your way around in there?'

Greezing chuckled. The laugh spread to the other goblins behind him. Veelber and Gilspat almost dropped the heavy load they were carrying between them. 'We know,' Greezing said.

'Good.' Hallic looked at the hourglass again. The timing

had to be precise. The last inspection of the dungeon by the representatives of the Colleges of Magic had just finished. Between the departure of the College officials and the arrival of the teams, there was a window for *enhancement*.

This was it.

Hallic turned the wheel. The well-oiled portcullis rose in surprising, but satisfying, silence. 'Off you go, then,' he said.

The goblins ran into the tunnels beyond.

'Well, we're moments away from the teams taking to the field, and the excitement is at a fever pitch. Everything is pointing to this being a memorable match, if I do say so, Bob. Even the start is something different.'

'Too right, Jim. For the teams AND for us.'

'Exactly. As you know, Bob, one of the features of Dungeonbowl that makes it unique is the fact that the teams don't know where each other's end zone is. So there are three stages to the match. There are six chests scattered around the dungeon, and the first challenge is to find them. Then players have to get the ball, which is in one of those chests, while the other five are traps. Finally, the teams have to find where they're supposed to take the ball. And on top of that, they can only start with six players on the field.'

'There's a good reason why a single touchdown is all you need to win.'

'You said it, Bob. But today we're looking at a historic first for the game. There has never been a Dungeonbowl championship where the spectators don't know where the end zones are, either.'

'It's a brave move by the Colleges of Magic, Jim. The teams are being teleported straight from their end zones to the centre of the dungeon, and that's where we'll see them first. I don't know if this idea will catch on, but points for trying something new.'

'I doubt you'll get Ramtut to agree with you there, Bob!'

'Oh, touché, Jim!'

[forced hearty laughter]

'Hold on, Bob, I think this is it… Yes… yes… HERE THEY COME!'

The teams were sent on one at a time, and a deafening storm of boos arose when the Champions of Death appeared. On his front-row seat in the bleachers, Pillip looked back and forth between the centre of the dungeon where the Champions of Death were arriving, and the giant CabalVision crystal screen that floated above centre field. It would show the other regions of the dungeon as gameplay advanced, but for now it displayed close-ups of the team. Most of the images were of Ramtut's shrivelled features, which snarled through his wrappings. The skeletons were too difficult to tell apart.

A human sitting next to Pillip clapped him on the shoulders almost hard enough to knock him off the bleacher. 'Some home crowd advantage, eh?' she shouted happily, her words almost lost in the din of the hate aimed at the Champions.

Ramtut greeted the crowd with an unambiguous gesture. People rose in their seats, promising him a slow, painful death.

Pillip kept a straight face as he contemplated the stupidity of the threat.

The Champions moved off into a hallway heading north, and the Bright Crusaders entered centre field. The crowd's frenzy reached new paroxysms, but the storm was a joyous one now. Pillip winced at the piercing cheers.

'What's the matter with you?' the woman asked. She gave Pillip's shoulder another clout before she sat down.

Her companion glared at Pillip. 'What's wrong? Got something against heroes?'

Squeaky clean drips, Pillip thought, but kept the sentiment to himself. Both humans looked strong enough to punch him through a wall.

'Just worried,' he lied. 'I have money riding on them.' Which was half-true.

'They're finally winning a championship,' the woman said. 'I know they are.'

'It's Sternright and Gallant!' the man shouted. 'Sternright and Gallant!' He was on his feet again, and the woman joined him.

'Arik! Dirk!' the woman yelled at the Crusaders' Star Player and his right-hand man.

Flowers rained down from the crowd on Sternright. To Pillip's disgust, the man blushed. He rubbed his square chin bashfully. His face, framed by blond locks, turned a bright crimson. Dirk Gallant gathered up the flowers and set them aside carefully.

'I was there in '88 when Dirk ran out of bounds to save a kitten,' the woman confided.

'I'm jealous,' Pillip said dryly.

'Arik really is sensitive, isn't he?'

'Just what you want for a Dungeonbowl player.' Pillip hoped the Bright Champions wouldn't lose before the goblins had the chance to trick them into cheating.

The whistle shrieked through the damp corridors of the dungeon. Ramtut led the Champions of Death at a run up the north passage. They had barely started when the two of the Bright Crusaders appeared from central chamber. Ekerd Honourschine and Conrad Knightstandt raced up behind the skeletons. Ramtut had expected the move. The humans were splitting up to cover as much of the dungeon as fast as possible in the hunt for the ball. Ramtut couldn't trust the skeletons on their own, so he had to keep his team in one group and use force to counter speed.

Honourschine and Knightstandt were fast. They were closing with the Champions.

A vaulted entrance was coming up Ramtut's left. He slowed as he reached it. The chamber was shaped like a bowl, the ribs of the walls sloping in towards the centre of the floor where a chest waited in plain sight. The chest looked oddly rounded, even soft. It was also present too soon. Ramtut couldn't believe the ball would be in the first room he passed, but there was no choice. The chest had to be opened. He spun on his heel. He pointed at Cup.

'Open the chest,' he said, and charged back down at the Crusaders.

The other skeletons collided with each other in their effort to turn around, but Straightline managed to pivot and ran ahead of Ramtut and the pack. He barrelled directly into Knightstandt as if expecting to run straight through the Crusader. The impact blew Straightline apart. Bones rattled against the corridor walls. Knightstandt staggered, winded. Ramtut hit Honourschine at an angle, knocking him off his path and into his teammate. Knightstandt slammed into the wall and slumped down.

'Unclean fiend!' Honourschine yelled at Ramtut and tackled him around the chest. He tried to throw Ramtut to the ground. The skeletons pulled him off. Ramtut yanked the Crusader's helmet from his head, reversed it, and hammered Honourschine into unconsciousness.

There was a loud boom. Ramtut turned to see dust and bone fragments puff out from the chamber. Cup's skull hit the wall and fell, spinning, to the corridor floor.

'Down two,' Ramtut muttered. The Crusaders had lost two players also, but they were still covering more ground, and faster. Tomolandry had said this was to be expected. That this was when the strategy would begin to kick in. Ramtut hoped it would soon.

Ramtut led the team north again. The corridor branched, and he turned left. There were two more chambers opening off this tunnel. Ramtut checked the first, and there was another chest there, as crudely built as the first. He frowned. 'Wait here,' he told the skeletons, and ran ten yards down to the next chamber.

There was a chest there too.

'This can't be right,' Ramtut muttered.

Greezing knelt and pulled another assembly of painted pig's bladders from his sack. He blew into a tube at one end, inflating the sewn-together bladders into a decoy chest. He tied the tube off, then removed a clay glyph from the sack and placed it on the chest. He rubbed away the charcoal counter-glyph from the tablet's surface, and the trap was activated. The pig's bladders would explode when they were next touched. The decoy barely resembled the official Dungeon-bowl chests scattered around the rest of the temple, but for players in a frenzied rush, a chest was a chest.

Greezing nodded to himself. He ducked out of the chamber and ran down the tunnel towards the next open doorway. He had three more decoys in his sack, then he would be done. With a bit of luck, the rest of his team would also be wrapping up this stage of the operation. This plethora of false exploding chests should slow the Bright Crusaders down nicely. The plan was to get them so hurt and desperate that they wouldn't notice the real trap being laid for them.

They had to hurry, though. The goblins were in a rush to stay ahead of the Bright Crusaders, and those detestable prigs were nothing if not fast. The eyes of CabalVision would be on the players, so as long as Greezing and his gang stayed out of sight of the Crusaders and the Champions, he counted on their activities remaining secret.

He was in the next chamber and placing his trap when he heard the muffled *whump* of a chest going off at some distance. He frowned, but didn't think more of it until, only a minute later as he was catching up with Gilspat down the tunnel, he heard another blast. It too sounded far away, he didn't like that, and he didn't like that it came so soon after the previous one. And both of them right at the start of the match. He had been placing his chests some distance away from centre field. They needed to look genuine. The traps couldn't be too obvious or they would backfire.

The explosions he was hearing also seemed to be going off in the north sector of the dungeon, in the direction the Champions of Death had gone to start the match. None of this was right.

'Why am I hearing chests going off?' he asked Gilspat.

'Probably Yugwitz and Veelber's traps.'

'Why do they sound like they're coming from the north?'

'Because I sent them there.'

'*What?*'

'You said we should have them spread out as much as possib–'

Greezing grabbed him by the throat. 'Everywhere *except* the north, you idiot! We don't want to nobble the Champions!' With a sinking heart, he could picture what was happening. The lazy fools had planted their chests in the first chambers they'd found, and now they were blowing up one skeleton after another. The Champions of Death were being ground down before the Crusaders even knew there was a contest.

Greezing pushed Gilspat away and sighed. There was still a way to salvage this.

'You have the ball, right?' Finding out where *that* was had been the single greatest expense so far. Da Deff Skwad's operating budget for the next season had taken a serious hit to acquire that piece of information. Greezing couldn't guess how Hallic happened to know which chest had held the ball, and he didn't care. He was grateful that corruption went as high as he needed.

'Yes,' Gilspat said. 'I have it.' He lifted his sack.

'And the fake one?'

'In the western side. Right in Sternguard's path.'

'Good.' There was still a good chance the Bright Crusaders wouldn't notice they had a fake until it was too late. 'Put the real one in a chest near the Champions.'

That would put more pressure on the Crusaders. Greezing wasn't sure it would be enough to make them crack before the temptation he would place before them, but he was running out of moves. Things were getting messy.

'How do I put it in a trapped chest?' Gilspat asked.

'I don't care!' Greezing shouted. 'Use one of ours! Put it on top! Just *go*!'

Boom. Boom! Two more trapped chests, and fairly close together. Ramtut distrusted good luck, but this much bad luck was suspicious too. Spurs and Dropjaw were the only skeletons still with him. Tomolandry could get more skeletons into the field quickly, but only to teleport pad locations. Ramtut had seen one since the centre field, and he, Spurs and Dropjaw had left it behind several branches back. The team was getting scattered and there still wasn't a ball in play. At least the Crusaders didn't have it yet. The horn signalling possession had not sounded.

The corridors branched three more times. The next chest was in a much larger chamber than the others, which was ferociously hot. The chamber was divided into two by a canal of molten lava running down the centre, emerging from one wall and then plunging down under the other. Huge, snarling idols stood on opposite sides of the lava, reaching out to each other with massive pincers. The pincers held a platform over the canal. The chest was on the platform, veiled in the shimmering heat rising from the lava. It was weirdly rounded, like the others. A ball rested on its lid.

'What?' said Ramtut.

'Jim, we're looking at a highly irregular incident here.'

'We are, Bob. Someone has completely fallen down on the job, or else the irregularity is even more serious. The league is still recovering from the Scrygate scandal. Let's hope this is just a case of extreme carelessness.'

As Ramtut stared at the ball, Honourschine and Knightstandt barrelled into him from behind. The three players rolled in a struggling tangle over the floor. Ramtut cursed himself. He had been too focused on the rushing from one chest to another, he hadn't realised the Crusaders had recovered and were on his team's trail.

'Get the ball!' Ramtut yelled at the skeletons. Dropjaw ran for the nearest idol.

With Ramtut down, Honourschine tried to disengage. Ramtut wrapped his mouldering fingers around the Bright Crusader's facemask and hauled him back into the scrum.

'Your unholy hands shall not touch the ball!' Knightstandt shouted, wrapping an arm around Ramtut's throat.

'And you're a sad excuse for an opponent,' Ramtut said. 'Back in my day... Oh, never mind.' He jerked his head forward. He broke Knightstandt's hold, but now Honourschine's mass kept him trapped. The three players fought and clawed, and rolled further across the floor.

Until there was no floor.

Ramtut saw Honourschine's eyes widen as he realized, too late, he and Knightstandt had made a mistake. The scrum tilted off the temple floor and into the lava.

The Crusaders lost their grip on Ramtut as they sank, howling, into the molten rock. Ramtut heaved himself back out of the flow with a grunt and smacked the flames off his wrappings. He looked up in time to see Dropjaw touch the ball.

A great horn sounded. The ball was in play.

Ramtut saw his luck finally change for the better.

Then the chest exploded. The singed, deflating ball whistled through the air, rising and falling in erratic flight before it came down with slap on the lava. The pig's bladder caught fire, and sank beneath the surface just as the horn sounded to announce the ball was in play.

A rain of bones clattered to the ground.

Ramtut eyed the spot where the ruined ball had vanished.

Do we dive in? Spurs rapped out against his cheekbone.

'No, it's gone.'

What do we do now?

Ramtut sighed. Ancient dust puffed out from between his withered lips. He suddenly felt very tired.

In a crevice of the ceiling hidden above the platform between the idols, Greezing stared in disbelief. Gilspat had forgotten not to set the booby-trap on the chest. Greezing mentally tallied what was left of the plan. He had to hope Gilspat hadn't bungled the placement of the counterfeit ball as well.

The plan could still work. Victory for the Champions was unimportant. What mattered was that the Crusaders be caught cheating.

In the dugout, the sound of the horn was Tomolandry's cue. The ball was found. Now the hunt for the end zone would begin. Time to put his strategy into action. Almost all the skeleton players had been taken out of action. That was more than he had expected so soon, but no matter. The key now was coverage. Get as many players into the field as possible to find the end zone.

Tomolandry chanted the spell of raising. One by one, skeletons rose from the floor of the dugout and headed for the end zone teleport pad that would project them, at random, to another pad in the dungeon. One after another, rattling as they ran. He sent three off in short order.

Tomolandry kept going.

West of centre field, in a vault filled with shattered, empty sarcophagi, Dirk Gallant said, 'I've been hearing a lot of explosions.'

'Me too,' said Arik Sternguard. 'The fates are with us today. Victory through virtue, brother!'

'Victory through virtue!' Gallant replied. He clutched the ball tightly to his chest. It was an honour to have it in his possession. Sternguard was the star player, and had every right to launch into the quest for the end zone with the ball in his arms, but Gallant had been the one to open the correct chest. The Crusaders had split up to search more quickly, and the ball had been in the first chest Gallant had tried. He had crossed paths with Sternguard just after his discovery, and Sternguard insisted he keep the ball.

'Sigmar has blessed you and us,' Sternguard told him. 'Our piety is its own reward, but it brings wondrous gifts too.'

They gave thanks as they ran.

They reached another intersection. 'Which way, brother?' Gallant asked.

'The paths both go north, and as our end zone was in the south, either could be the correct route. I'll take the left.'

'And I the right. We'll meet again in triumph!'

Sternguard raised a fist in solidarity, and took off at a sprint.

'So that was a bit confusing, Jim.'

'It was Bob, but if we look at the replays, I think you'll see that Champions lose the ball in the lava just before Guy Gallant of the Crusaders finds the replacement.'

'Unusual for the replacement ball to go back in a chest.'

'That's right, Bob. Just as it is unprecedented for the correct chest to explode. I think there have been some technical difficulties on the field today.'

'Looks even more like there will be some hard questions asked after this match, Jim.'

'There will be, Bob. There certainly will be.'

Tomolandry raised three more skeletons and sent them into the temple.

Then three more.

The rules specified six players to *start*. No upper limit was mentioned. A useful oversight, Tomolandry thought.

* * *

Yugwitz crouched in a fissure that was tall but so narrow he had some doubts about being able to get out again. He could barely move, but at least he was hidden from CabalVision's gaze. And there was just enough room for his equipment. He saw the Bright Crusader charge forward with the ball. The player was tall, fair-haired, his face miraculously unblemished by scars. Yugwitz remembered that pretty face from Da Deff Skwad's defeat. Time to rearrange it a little. As Gallant drew near, Yugwitz pulled a potion out of his sack and downed it.

Then he grabbed the stilts.

'Help!'

Gallant screeched to a halt beside the chamber entrance. The woman's voice called again.

'I'm coming!' he called and ran inside. Game or no game, he could not ignore a cry for aid.

In the centre of the chamber was a deep pit, crossed by a thin, rickety wooden bridge. The span was so narrow, it barely seemed possible to cross it at all. On the other side of the bridge, the most beautiful woman Gallant had ever seen was gazing across at him. 'My saviour!' she cried, as if she'd always known it would be him. She clasped her hands. She wobbled a bit on her heels. She batted her thick eyelashes. Gallant's pulse trembled in rhythm with their fluttering. 'You've come at last!' the woman breathed.

'I have!' Of course he had. 'How can I be of–'

'The pit,' the woman said, her voice like honey and the caress of roses. 'It frightens me so. And I've hurt my ankle. Won't you help me cross?'

Gallant moved to the edge. The darkness below seethed with hissing, whirring and grinding. As his eyes adjusted, and he saw the bottom of the pit was deep with writhing serpents. They were huge, the smallest several yards long. They raised their heads to look at Gallant, spreading their hoods and baring fangs. They coiled around a forest of spikes fifteen feet high. Reaching higher than the spikes, but still a long drop below the chamber's surface, was a score of poles with scythe blades spinning around the top of them.

Gallant took a step back, his mouth suddenly dry. *At least there isn't any lava*, he thought. He cleared his throat. 'Of course I'll help you,' he said. 'It will be my honour!'

'Oh, thank you,' she said. She took unsteady steps back, until she was close to a crack splitting the far wall. Her dress swayed, its slit revealing a long and shapely leg.

'Be careful!' Gallant called. 'Don't back up any further!' He started across the bridge.

The woman smiled. She extended her arms in welcome.

Gallant was at the peak of the bridge's arc when the woman seemed to collapse in on herself. Her back hunched. Her glowing hair dissolved into mist, revealing a green scalp. Her clothes fell in a heap. Her legs were stilts. The goblin grinned, crooked a rude farewell at Gallant, leapt from the stilts and vanished into the crack in the wall.

Gallant blinked.

Something changed in the surface he was standing on. He looked down.

The woman had never been there. Neither had the bridge, or the spikes, or the snakes. He was standing in mid-air.

He dropped with a cry of horror into the lava.

Concealed once more, Yugwitz giggled at the Bright Crusader's fate. That was a fine success. He couldn't wait to tell Greezing.

He was in mid-caper when a thought struck him.

Wait. He had the ball. Was I supposed to do that if he had the ball?

Then he remembered the fake, and was much less eager to share the news with Greezing.

'That's two balls lost to lava, Jim.'

'And one Bright Crusader.'

'Did I see a spectator in the field?'

'I'm not sure. She definitely wasn't from either team. But there's the whistle, and I see the ball is back in play, bouncing out of the centre field teleport pad. This is still anyone's game, Bob.'

At the sound of the whistle, Ramtut put on a burst of speed, heading back south. No more nonsense with chests now. No more nonsense at all. He had run out of patience for that thousands of years ago. Right now, he was going to turn this game around. He pounded through the dungeon tunnels, wrapped feet thumping dully against stone, Spurs at his heels. Other skeletons joined them from connecting tunnels. Still more ran off in other directions. He didn't know where they were going, and he was quickly losing track of how many there were. He didn't care. He cared only about restoring some measure of his dignity and ending this farce.

There was a flash as he ran past the last teleport pad before centre field. Another skeleton appeared. A moment later, the pad flashed again. The replacements were showing up, but he didn't recognise any of them. They all looked the same.

No matter. He had better numbers now. Ramtut led the run out of the last tunnel and into the vast centre field chamber. In the bleachers that surrounded the space, the crowd was on its feet, howling with excitement. There was the ball, and on the other side of the field was Sternright. Two other Crusaders, Harald Goodstar and Jorn Puresoul reached the chamber and pounded across the stone floor to join their Star Player.

Ramtut roared, exhaling a cloud of dust, and charged the foe.

'The Champions of Death are all over the pitch, aren't they, Jim?'

'That they are, Bob. I'm guessing that Tomolandry's strategy is to have part of the team search for the Crusaders' end zone while the rest take the ball, but I don't mind admitting I'm having trouble keeping track of who is going where.'

'Another one just teleported in, Jim. I'm losing count.'

'Yes. We're looking at multiple feeds here, and it... uh...'

'Another!'

'This seems...'

'And again!'

'That's definitely more than six players...'

Better stop, Tomolandry thought. He'd just realized he had lost track of how many skeletons he had sent into the game. He might have overplayed his hand. Time to bring closure to the spell.

'Niffle fumr ari-bal-car,' he intoned, then froze. That was wrong. Should he have said *ari-bal-den...*?

The broken ground of the dugout should have ceased to churn. It did not. Eldritch light still circled around it, and skeletons continued to force their way into the light. Tomolandry moved to block the exit from the dugout. 'Stop!' he said. 'That's enough!'

The skeletons didn't listen. They shoved against him in the effort to reach the door to the dungeon. He pushed back. More and more and more came out of the ground. Soon the dugout was full. The pressure of the mob grew too great, and Tomolandry flew out of the entrance like a popped cork. The skeletons charged into the dungeon.

Sternright scooped the ball up just as Ramtut was reaching for it. They had both run far ahead of their teammates. *No*, Ramtut thought. *No no no.* He would not be outrun and out-played by this priggish whelp. Ramtut growled and lunged for Sternright. He closed his fingers around the Crusader's shoulder pads. Before he could tighten his grip, Sternright jinked right. The spikes of the pad tore through Ramtut's wrappings, and Sternright was free.

Ramtut sprinted after him. They ploughed through the crowd of skeletons, scattering bones. Ramtut wondered why the Bright Crusader was heading north. The Champions' end zone was through one of the main entrances heading south. Why was Sternright going this way, running like he was bound and determined to score an own goal?

Answers later. Catch him now.

Goodstar and Puresoul followed close behind, running interference. Ramtut charged between them, and threw his weight left and right. He checked them hard enough to send them careening into the narrow tunnel's walls. They banged back into each other, stunned, and Ramtut put on a burst of speed. He was only a few paces behind Stern-right now.

There was a teleport pad just ahead. The Crusader was making for it with blinding speed.

No you don't, Ramtut thought, and made a desperate leap to tackle.

The teleport pad seemed to explode.

* * *

The conclave invoked by the College of Magic would eventually pronounce that the overload was inevitable. The skeletons poured into the dungeon too quickly for the teleport pads to accommodate them all. The critical point was reached when there was a skeleton arriving on every pad. The chain reaction began. Every pad attempted to transmit, but no location was receiving. The feedback loop of energy lit the entire dungeon with shrieking blue lightning.

Ramtut caught Sternright around the legs. They tumbled onto the pad together, into blazing, convulsed magic and a shifting kaleidoscope of confused skeletons. The dungeon disappeared in a searing flash. Ramtut tumbled through an eruption of non-light and howling colours. Space lost all meaning. Something *tore*.

And then…

Ramtut and Sternright dropped onto the peak of a huge structure. Ramtut looked around, trying to make sense of what he was seeing, and failing. They were in an inconceivably vast city, whose structures were impossibly tall. The city was at war. Bursts of unimaginable power shattered buildings. Huge engines of war, larger than any dragon, flew through the air, unleashing cataclysm. Swarms of towering, all-devouring monsters attacked walking metal mountains. And…

And…

Were those *pyramids*? Pyramids larger than any Ramtut had seen with living eyes.

Flying pyramids?

In the midst of incomprehensibly vast conflict, of war and war and war raging to the horizon and filling the skies, Ramtut found himself thinking, *Now this is more like it.*

Sternright was standing still, mindless with shock. His jaw was wide open, and slack. A string of drool fell from his chin to his chest. His arms were hanging limply at his side and he had dropped the ball.

Ramtut heard a sound like a tide snarling. He looked down and saw a swarm of creatures climbing the façade of the building towards them. They were about the size of a man, but had four hideously clawed arms. Bony structures like spinal columns rose from their carapaces. Their elongated, violet-hued heads gaped ravenously, serpentine tongues tasting the air.

'What what what what…' Sternright was saying.

The centre of the rooftop began to crackle with light again. The sorcerous vortex spun. Ramtut knew better than to second-guess the possible exit. There were glories in this place, but he could not remain here. He picked up the ball and turned to go.

Sternright did not move. The terrors of this world had broken him.

Ramtut sighed. He grabbed the Crusader by the scruff of the neck and hauled him towards the light. As he did, the first of the monsters reached the roof. It lunged at them. Ramtut leapt back and pushed Sternright away. The beast's jump carried it between them. One of the elongated claws of its forelimbs sank into the ball and yanked it out of Ramtut's hand. The monster tumbled into the vortex and vanished.

The storm of magic convulsed, sending sorcerous fireballs in all directions. It was about to disintegrate.

A horde of monsters clambered over the parapets.

'Come *on!*' Ramtut yelled at Sternright, grabbing him again and running into the maelstrom.

* * *

'And we're back. CabalVision and the College of Magic wish to apologise to viewers for the technical difficulties, but it looks like we have eyes on the game again, Bob, and… and…. uh…'

'Jim, what is that?'

'I… I'm at a bit of a loss, Bob. I can tell you that there are no records for any player matching that description.'

'Well it has the ball and look at it go! It's tearing through the opposition like nobody's business! It's pounding through the skeletons like they're not even there! The clean-up teams are going to have a lot of smashed bones to pick up when this is done. Gotta say, though, Jim, it sure doesn't look like your typical Bright Crusaders player.'

'It doesn't, Bob, and… Ah. Well, it looks like it isn't one of the Champions of Death either.'

'Nope.'

'It will be of small comfort to Harald Goodstar, but his was the most efficient decapitation I've seen in a score of championships.'

'What a move, Jim! I'm telling you, if we'd had that player as a ringer back in my day…'

'I can well believe it, Bob. Meanwhile, there's still no sign of the star players for both teams and this mysterious new player is on a rampage.'

'That's no metaphor, Jim.'

'No, and the ball has seen better days, too.'

'It's just a flapping pig's bladder now.'

'Please, Bob, a deflation scandal is the last thing we need to think about right now. The ball is, still, technically in play, even if we don't know for whom. And now the player is barrelling south, and…'

'I don't believe it, Jim.'

'Neither do I, Bob, but that's an end zone!'

'Whose?'

'We still don't know, and I guess we won't until both have been revealed.'

'Is it going to cross the line?'

'It is, Bob! It is! AND IT HAS! TOUCHDOWN! I think! And–'

'Ouch. Wow, that was bright.'

'I'm a little dazzled, but the player seems to be gone.'

'I don't think those tremors are supposed to be happening, Jim.'

Greezing was making his way towards Hallic's portcullis through a warren of crevasses in the temple ceiling. He was just north of the central chamber when there was second furious blast of light throughout the dungeon. The teleport pads exploded, and the tunnels began to shake. Greezing fell from his place of concealment in the ceiling. He tried to get to his feet, but fell as the floor cracked and heaved. This was all going wrong. The Bright Crusaders had been savaged by whatever that thing was that had come through, but everyone was so confused that Greezing's strategy was a shambles.

He stumbled down the tunnel, surrounded by a mob of panicked skeletons. Femurs knocked him back and forth and he squinted against the explosive magical discharges. There was no point hiding now. He headed in the direction of centre field, hoping against hope he would not be noticed in the sea of clacking bone and could make one last attempt against the Bright Crusaders.

He was almost there when Sternright and Ramtut dropped out of the air in front of him. There was crack of thunder, and the blasts of magic stopped.

The tremors did not, though.

On Greezing's right, the cracks in the walls widened.

A blizzard of dust fell from the ceiling. The rotten bricks crumbled, and the walls began to fall.

'Bob, I've just been informed that the creature's touchdown has been ruled invalid because it was not clear whose team it would count for. There's also some odd language here about it not being clear whose end zone that was.'

'You'd think the referees should know that, Jim.'

'Be that as it may, Bob, the game is still on, and a new ball is in play!'

'With a playing field undergoing total collapse! Exciting times, Jim!'

'I couldn't agree more, Bob.'

The walls fell into the lava. The canal was growing wider, becoming a violent river swallowing more and more of the dungeon. Chunks of stone fell from the ceiling, splashing into the molten rock and sending burning waves on all sides. The maze was disappearing, turning the dungeon into a single vast tunnel. A large portion of the centre field chamber was still intact. Ramtut was running for the ball. So was Puresoul. Sternright was curled up on the floor, gibbering. Wherever he had been, Greezing thought, it had not agreed with him.

Greezing reached into his pouch. His careful plans were in ruins, but he wasn't going to flee this disintegrating ruin without making one last attempt. He opened his pouch, took out the scroll he'd been keeping there, and ran, weaving against the shaking of the floor, to Sternright. The Bright Crusader blinked down at him. Greezing pushed the scroll into his hands.

Sternright held it limply.

Greezing took the scroll back, unrolled it and shoved it in Sternright's face. *Look!* he thought. *Look at what this is! It's a map, you fool! Do something with the knowledge while it still matters!*

Sternright sat down and began to whistle tunelessly.

Greezing covered his face and wept.

There was only the great flow of lava now. The last stone memories of the temple were tumbling into the blazing canal. Hundreds of skeletons bobbed and sank. The centre field chamber had collapsed, and the bleachers were perched precariously over bubbling rock. To the north, there was only the raging source of the lava. To the south, visible at the far end of the canal, was Ramtut's end zone.

The mummy dredged up his most ancient, foul curses. He had the ball, and he had nowhere to take it. He was standing on a narrow ledge above the lava. South of his position, Puresoul was shaking Sternright, and the Bright Crusader star player was finally beginning to respond. Puresoul kept facing north, looking past Ramtut with a puzzled, frustrated expression.

Odd, Ramtut thought. He would have thought the Crusaders would be relieved their end zone was now utterly inaccessible.

But why had they always been struggling to take the ball north?

The answer came at the same moment that Puresoul's face cleared.

One end zone, Ramtut thought. Everything made ridiculous sense now. That was why the Bright Crusaders had seemed to be struggling to go the wrong way. They had come from the same spot as the Champions of Death.

This, he thought, *is the most degraded excuse for a game I have ever seen.*

'One end zone!' Puresoul shouted at Sternright. 'There's only one end zone!'

The shock of the absurd revived Sternright. He stood, and the two Bright Crusaders rushed along the ledge for Ramtut. He leapt with the ball into the flowing lava.

'He's in the lava, Jim! Ramtut is in the lava!'

'Being indestructible, he's the only player who could attempt such a bold move, Bob. And he's managing to hold the ball above the flow!'

'The crowd is going nuts! And refusing the evacuation orders!'

'Indeed so, Bob. I think we should pause to reflect on the reversal we see here. The lone Champion of Death is now the underdog. Outnumbered, he is literally walking through fire to snatch victory for his team in the midst of unspeakable calamity. How far we have come from the proposed theme for this match, Bob. Where is the traditional good versus evil, heroes versus monsters narrative now? There's a lot to learn from this, Bob, and maybe the crowd will look back on this moment in times to come. This is the transformative beauty of the sport, Bob, and—'

'HE'S HEADING FOR A TOUCHDOWN, JIM!'

The Bright Crusaders ran along the crumbling, heaving bank of the river, a sobbing goblin just ahead of them. The lava sucked at Ramtut's limbs. It tried to pull him under. It could not kill him, but he felt the consuming fire. The edges of his being eroded, the closest he could know to real pain. He walked through a haze of shredding, uncertain self. Bitter determination held him together. He would not leave the lava. If he set foot out of it before the end zone, all the

Crusaders would have to do was take the ball and victory would be theirs. There were no skeletons to help him. He saw a couple on the other side of the river, but the falling ceiling crushed them to dust almost immediately.

Through the writhing heat of the lava, Ramtut saw the doorways and walls tumble away, and the end zone appeared. The lava flowed underneath the goal post. He walked with it to the bitter end. The wrappings on his face caught fire in the last moments, and he could no longer see. It was only when the horn sounded that he knew he had scored the goal.

Ramtut moved to the right until his hand found the bank. He hauled himself up onto the uncertain floor. He batted out the flames on his face. The Bright Crusaders faced him on other side of the goal, honest to the last and defeated, but standing firm as the dungeon broke apart around them.

Ramtut hurled the ball into the lava with all the force of his contempt. Then he brushed off the bits of molten rock and stood firm and silent in his victory. The match was a joke. The game was even more degraded than he had believed. But he still had his dignity. That, in the end, was his real triumph.

He caught the slight nod Sternright gave him. Ramtut nodded back. The Crusader understood.

Dignity. It was all about dignity.

'Some late-breaking news, Jim. We're getting some reports of Referee Hallic and an unidentified halfling spectator being taken away in chains by officials from the College of Magic.'

'Thanks for that, Bob. We'll be following that story as it develops. In the meantime, let's get back to our post-game panel discussion, and a consideration of what the surprise announcement of Da Deff Skwad's financial straits will mean for the next season…'

SCRAPE TO VICTORY

GAV THORPE

'Kikkit!'

The sound of Oversneer Skreet bellowing his name made him flinch, expecting an accompanying blow or lash. Early life in the slave pits had given him certain instincts that no amount of time in the higher tunnels could overcome. It had also taught him swift reflexes, honed a sharp mind and developed an incorrigible sense of self-preservation, character traits that had served him well as he had clawed his way – often literally – to his current place within the hierarchy of Crookback Mountain.

As one of the clanrats working in the verminhive, his life was tedious, painful and fraught with the politicking of his ambitious companions. All of which was preferable to constant whippings and beatings, the peril of being fed to the rat ogres when supplies fell low, or suffering random and potentially lethal mutation while mining the warpstone deposits.

Yes, all in all, his lot had improved much.

Shoulders hunched, ears flat to his head, Kikkit looked around from the bench where he had been working – filing cog teeth along with thirty other workers for shipments to the factory-workshops of Clan Skryre in Skavenblight.

'Yes-yes, oversneer?'

The burly skaven responsible for second shift bared yellowing teeth in a broad grin. It looked awfully similar to the oversneer's grimace of anger, so Kikkit kept his posture and expression neutral. The clanrats to either side of him surreptitiously moved a little further away, leaving him in a void of his own uncertainty.

'It's official, Kikkit,' said Skreet, waving a rag of parchment covered in the ink scratchings of the skaven. 'The commission of the Southern Cabal of Associated Blood Bowl have released the latest figures. You, Kikkit, my mangy little rat, have forty-two confirmed injuries to a downed opponent.'

A ragged cheer went up at this announcement and Kikkit allowed himself a pant of happiness.

'I knew-knew that goblin would count,' he crowed, jabbing a finger toward Snarlitt. 'Forty-two! One more and I'll have the league record!'

'That's right, you scrawny backstabber. Nobody in the history of SCABB has kicked more people when they're down.'

'And the Crookback Cretins is through to the final,' squeaked Chuchuk, waving his rusty spanner. 'Win that and it's a place in the Blood Bowl tournament itself!'

This roused another desultory cheer, and a few sour glances. The Grey Seers had, to a certain degree, lavished praise and attention on Kikkit and the others that had made the grade to be linesmen in the Cretins. Kikkit had more warpstone and gold than he had ever known, which wasn't saying much seeing as he had known so little in the past. But it had bred resentment too, in those that had to cover his shift while he was playing, particularly on the long journeys across the mountains or the Dark Lands.

Kikkit didn't care though. The elbows in his ribs at the trenchers, the tacks left by his bedding, the urine in his daily ration of teatwater. Even the risk of death and injury at the hands of some orc or ogre player were worth the risk because he had, rolled up and hidden in his most secret place behind the bilge pumps, an invitation for a try-out at the Skavenblight Scramblers.

It was conditional on getting the 'Most Injuries of a Downed Opponent' record at the end of the season.

Never mind the Cretins reaching the Blood Bowl, they would get annihilated in their first match, most likely literally. But the Scramblers... They were his tunnel out of Crookback to the life of a full-time professional Blood Bowl player.

'Kikkit!'

The growl of the oversneer snapped him from his reverie.

'Back to work, you maggot-ridden furbag, the final's not until tomorrow. Shift doesn't end 'til sundown.'

'Yes-yes, oversneer,' replied Kikkit, bending back to his task. As he rasped his file between the points of a large gear, his thoughts drifted away again, picturing piles of gold coins, warpstone tokens, and platters upon platters of food with hardly any mould on it.

The Big League beckoned.

The howl of the ratwolves signalled dusk and the end of second shift. Kikkit left in the scrum with the others, casually biting and scratching his neighbours as they pressed through the narrow workshop entrance, battling against the flow of the other shift trying to get in.

He loitered for a moment outside the feeding hall, content to let the others push in front. It was a big match tomorrow and his gut felt shrivelled, his appetite absent.

Watching his fellow clanrats punching and wrestling each other to get at the sagging trenchers reminded him of the day he had caught the eye of the Grey Seers. It had been just such a dinnertime, he had been ravenous after a long day of toil, and in the eating melee he had spied one of his companions on his back, dazed by a blow. Kikkit had leapt, ducked and climbed through the sprawl to snatch a rancid chicken from the downed skaven.

It was, on reflection, pretty much the same as trying to get the ball from under a pile of players, and it was his natural timing and ruthlessness that had earned his place among the Crook-back Cretins and now saw him so close to achieving his dreams.

It was with a bit of a swagger that he turned away from the food hall and headed through the twisting gnaw-tunnels to the chambers of Nyak Longtooth. As he turned into the corridor where the cave of his representative lived – his 'agent', Nyak insisted, though he was nothing more than a loan-ratshark – Kikkit slowed, suddenly aware that something was amiss. Usually, the curtained door to the warlock's laboratory was guarded by Nulk, Nyak's huge rat ogre. There was no sign of Nulk but the flicker of warpstone light betrayed movement inside the chamber.

'Nyak?' He tugged aside the ragged curtain and poked his twitching nose into the room.

His eye was first drawn to the broken crucibles and scattered pieces of magical equipment on the floor. Next he noticed the shattered glass vials and alembics on the warlock's experimenting bench. His gaze flicked back to the stone floor. Was that fresh blood?

He took all of this in at the same time that he registered the three figures standing just inside the doorway. Two were skaven a little larger than Kikkit, dressed in the thick hide aprons, gloves and kilts of Clan Moulder packmasters. They had coiled whips at their belts. One had a long ragged scar down the side of his face, his front teeth prominent even for a ratman. The other wore thick goggles of scratched green glass, his right hand replaced with a crude angled hook of iron.

The third figure was Nulk, looming over Kikkit with ropes of drool hanging from his bared fangs.

'Sorry! Wrong-wrong turn,' shrieked Kikkit, spinning around to leave.

'Not so quick-quick. Grab him, Nulk!'

Kikkit knew better than to run and instead went limp, becoming an unresisting furry sack of bones as a massive clawed fist snatched up the loose skin at the scruff of his neck. The rat ogre lifted, presenting him to the two packmasters.

'Got 'im,' rumbled Nulk.

'What has we got here, Packmaster Kratch?' said goggles.

'One of Nyak's "assets", I think, Packmaster Snurk,' said Kratch.

'No-no, no-no, not-not asset, not-not me. Just worker, mangy rat, yes-yes, mangy furry maggot. No-nobody.'

'Star player, I hear,' said Kratch.

'Most injuries of a downed opponent, that's the talk,' said Snurk.

Kikkit said nothing, dangling sullenly from Nulk's fist. Snurk stepped closer, the smell of warpstone on his breath as he whispered in Kikkit's ear.

'Nyak got a little greedy, he did.'

'Greedy,' echoed Kratch.

'Nulk here wasn't cheap, was he?'

'No, Snurk, he was not.'

'And the wolfrats. And the warstoats. And the diremice. It all adds up, it does.'

'More than a few gold crowns and warpstone tokens, let me tell you,' chuckled Kratch.

'That little contract of yours? The one you had with Nyak? It's ours now.'

'Right-right.' Kikkit nodded ferociously and started to swing in Nulk's grip. 'Fair to me.'

'And you owed Nyak thirty thousand gold crowns.'

'Thirty…' Kikkit swallowed hard.

'The loans for your kit, the warpstone poultices to heal you afterwards, representation with the Grey Seers, and forty per cent of your winnings. We'll take fifty thousand and call it even, yes-yes?'

'Fifty thousand… Where-where am I supposed to get-get that much?'

Kratch grinned and it was not a pleasant sight. He poked a broken claw into Kikkit's malnourished pot belly and then squeezed the clanrat's scrawny arm muscles.

'I think we could do a thing or two with a body like this. More than just fodder for the beasts.'

Kikkit shuddered, knowing well what happened to skaven that ended up on the operating tables of the Moulder packmasters.

'Right-right, fifty thousand. No problems. Big match tomorrow. Final. Win-win, big prize.'

'Yes, win-win, big prize indeed,' said Snurk with a curled lip. He pulled a bonesaw from the pocket of his apron. Rust flaked from the old blade. 'Or else it's the chop for you, *star player*.'

* * *

Along with the rest of the team, Kikkit crammed into the dingy caves that served as the changing rooms for Crookback's algae-carpeted Blood Bowl pitch. The sunlight coming through the slits overhead made him squint, but it was league rules that all finals were to be played above ground. He moved into the more comfortable shadow of Nulk, who doubled as their linebreaker, and strapped on fur-stuffed leather kneepads.

The three Grey Seers, the true power of Crookback, stood on one of the benches glaring at the Cretins. Clad in thick robes, warpstone charms and looted bracelets hanging about them, staffs in hand, they stood imperiously over their minions. Their leader, Quittit, banged his rod against the mildew-slicked wood of the bench to get their attention.

'Final time, worthless ratbags,' he declared. 'Big-big match. Win this, many, many prizes for all of us.'

A few of the skaven gave a half-hearted cheer and pumped their fists. The others were less than enthusiastic, knowing that there was a 'but' to come.

'But,' continued Quittit, to a chorus of inhalations and suppressed groans, 'lose-lose and it will be bad. Very bad-bad.'

'Bad-bad,' chorused the other two Grey Seers.

'With all gifts and boons we have given you, failure means only one thing. Means you have displeased the Great Horned Rat. Means we will displease the Great Horned Rat if we tolerate your failure. So, lose-lose this match and you will all be sacrificed to the glory of the Horned One!'

They knew better than to make any protest – even Skrankor the captain-vermin bowed his head in acceptance, darting a silencing look at his team-rats.

The Grey Seers scuttled out, leaving a last spray of musk to remind the team who was in charge.

'We history,' groaned Thork, the first-pick thrower. 'We never beat Morglum's Marauders! They not conceded touchdown all season!'

'They can't defend if they can't stand,' snapped Kulvik, one of the gutter runners. 'Break their legs in the first half, score in the second.'

'We can do this,' growled Skrankor, lifting up his helmet like a trophy. 'We play terrible, hate each other, fight amongst ourselves all season, and still get to final. If we play together just once, we can win.'

Kikkit was less confident but said nothing. He had his own plan, and it didn't rely on beating the best team in SCABB.

They limbered up in the dugout carved into the mountainside next to the pitch, observed by Quittit and the other coaches. They were decked in their almost uniform purple gear, the triskele daggers of the Crookback rune daubed onto their kit. Nulk was busy punching slaves into paste in one corner, while the throwers tossed a much-patched ball back and forth. On the nearby stretch of pitch the gutter runners sprinted to and fro, testing each other's reactions with glinting throwing daggers and stars – banned during the match, of course, but good practice all the same (and 'it's only illegal if you get caught' was the unofficial motto of the team).

Skrankor and the other Stormvermin practised their gouging and biting on straw-stuffed mannequins while the clanrats loitered together performing their individual routines – desultory stretches, claw sharpening, checking their flimsy armour pads.

Kikkit whispered the mantra that had got him to the place he was.

'Kick them when they're down. Kick them where it hurts. Kick them 'til they stop.'

He noticed the others had stopped their warm-ups and were staring down the winding track that led into the mountains. He joined them at the edge of the dugout and saw a line of carriages making their way up the road – the visiting team.

But he didn't recognise the colours. Morglum's Marauders played in black, checked with black, with a black flame motif and numbers in black. It was a singular style statement but also very confusing and… black.

Contrary to this, the three covered wagons that swayed up the hill were decked in garlands of red and green, the grey ponies that pulled them – not snorting boars – had ribbons of the same plaited into their manes. A smell preceded the small convoy on the mountain wind, not of offal and dung that accompanied orc teams, but of roast meat and jam. The second was a bit of a guess for Kikkit as he had only ever heard of jam, never tasted it, but the sweet fruitiness that assailed his nostrils was exactly what he imagined jam would smell like.

Kriskit, offensive coordinator, sent Chikkirt, one of his gutter runners, to investigate. The black-clad skaven hared down the track, tail twitching, and they waited in silence while he leapt from a rock up to the driving board of the lead wagon, terrifying the diminutive figure sat on it. What appeared to be a brief conversation followed and then the gutter runner raced back.

'War,' Chikkirt told them. 'Morglum and the Marauders have joined an invasion into the Northern Wastes and have forfeited their place in the final.'

'So who we playing?' asked Skrankor.

'The team they beat in the semi-finals. The Tinklebrook Trotters!'

The team were wracked by rubbing of hands and cruel laughter at this announcement.

Halflings! The match was as good as won.

While the others congratulated themselves on the victory to come, Kikkit had other plans. The ability to exploit an easy win had set him on the road to success and he wasn't about to pass up another.

He slipped out of the dugout and back to the tunnels, ready to plead pre-game nerves for a quick break, but nobody challenged his departure. Once back in the caves of Crook-back Mountain he accelerated, darting down the gnawholes to the bilge caverns beneath the warpstone mines. Here he located his hiding spot behind the creaking, wheezing pumps, dodging between the spinning gears driven by the slave wheels in the levels above.

He found the hidey hole, removed the rotten plank that covered it and drew out his two most prized possessions. In fact his two *only* possessions if one didn't consider the rags on his back and the Blood Bowl kit for which he was now in hock to the Moulder packmasters.

First, he drew out the message from the Skavenblight Scramblers inviting him to their pre-season try-outs. He stroked the worn vellum – real ratskin! – and sniffed the blood it had been written in. Then he pulled out a pouch containing his entire savings – a few warpstone tokens and nearly three thousand gold crowns worth of coins. It was, in Crookback terms, quite a lot of money, but nowhere near the fifty thousand he would need to buy out of his contract.

His win bonus would not be enough, not by a long way, and even though all he needed was one more injury to a downed opponent and a one-way ticket to Skavenblight, the arrival of the halflings gave Kikkit an opening to pursue his career free from the Moulder shadow that had fallen over him. They had contacts everywhere and it would only be a matter of time before they caught up with Kikkit, possibly with interest but more likely than not determined to take their debt in flesh and blood.

So he stuffed the savings and letter under his team shirt and headed back through the skavenhold.

Ensuring he was not followed, he scuttled to the tunnels that led into no-rat's-land further towards the other mountains. It was easy enough to elude the patrols of the stormvermin – nothing compared to dodging a three-line blitz coming downfield – and he headed out in the wildercaves.

It was not long before he found the tell-tale gleam of luminous fungi that led him to the current whereabouts of Bogsnik, an itinerant night-goblin bookmaker that plied his unofficial business near the outskirts of Crookback. Guarded by a pair of ferocious squighounds, the greenskin gangster had set up his business in the undercroft beneath a waterfall of a subterranean river.

Kikkit ducked past the water into the cave beyond, keeping flat to the wall as the squighounds snarled and drooled. A few vague shadows disappeared into the depths of the cave, doubtless other customers not wishing to be identified.

"Ello, my furry friend,' said Bogsnik, standing behind an upturned crate covered with the remnants of a looted dwarf banner. He was hard to hear over the gushing water that echoed in the cave. "Avin' a little flutta today, are we?'

Kikkit dragged out his savings and plonked them on the makeshift table.

'All of that on the Cretins to win.'

Now, Bogsnik no doubt prided himself on his ability to

keep abreast of events and trends, but Kikkit was betting his life that news of the change of opponent had not yet reached the bookmaker.

The night-goblin eyed the pouch and then peered suspiciously at Kikkit, making note of his kit.

'Dat's ten-to-wun, Cretins to beat da Marauders. Was finkin' of 'avin' a look when I'm done. Yoo know sumfin I don't?'

'Need a lucky day, owe people big-big,' confessed Kikkit. He gave the night goblin a conspiratorial wink. 'Ten-to-one for me, maybe not for the next one that comes in, eh? Three thousand here.'

'I see...' The greenskin rubbed his hands together with a sly look. He slid a wooden marker over the table and plucked the pouch from Kikkit's twitching fingers. 'Right yoo iz. Ten-to-wun.'

Kikkit nodded, took his marker and fled as quick as he could, skirting past the snarling squighounds on his way out.

Even lighter of step, he raced directly back to the pitch, coming overground to the dugout. The stands were starting to fill up with a few diehards, and he found his team-mates sitting on the benches. As he approached, he felt their mood was sober compared to when he had left. Downright glum in fact.

Nerves on edge, he joined the other linesmen.

'What's happened?' he asked, sitting down at the end of the bench.

His companions said nothing but one of them pointed down the road. Coming over the last hill, ponderous but implacable, were two huge figures – gangling giants with leafy limbs and creased bark for skin. Each long stride seemed to take an eternity, moving the figures with the slow inevitability of a root cracking stone.

Treemen. Two of them. Wearing the colours of the Tinkle-brook Trotters.

'Oh,' said Kikkit.

A flailing limb – a branch to be more precise – missed Kikkit by the smallest of margins as he ducked past the treeman, intent on breaking through the Trotters' front line. A plucky halfling with a round, jam-stained faced tried to intervene, grabbing at the skaven with pudgy fingers. Skrankor hit the distracted halfling like a bolt of warp lightning, bowling the player into the dirt in a frenzy of gnashing teeth and punches. The stormvermin blitzer ran straight over the unfortunate Trotter, claws tearing cloth and skin and rucking up the dirt.

Kikkit bunched his muscles, ready to pounce on the halfling, but the small linesman was rolling around in a puddle of his own blood. There was no way the commission wouldn't rule that as already injured. Kikkit glanced to the sidelines to see the league officials standing at the halfway line – two dwarfs and a human with clipboards and styluses.

That had been the tale of the match so far. The halflings were so puny that if they went down, they were likely already hurt. Kikkit had roamed the line looking for unsuspecting targets, but most had already been unconscious, or bleeding, or cradling broken arms or legs.

There seemed to be little shortage of substitutes and a steady stream of cheery-faced Trotters swamped the skaven offence, helped in a large part by the two immovable tree-men anchoring the centre of the line. Even Nulk was smart enough to steer clear of the scything swings and entangling roots of the forest giants.

The halflings had somehow scrambled and bundled their way over the line to score first, but a quick response from the Cretins had levelled the game and then gone one score up by the time the whistle blew for half-time. Feeling less cheery about his prospects of getting the season record, which meant winning was neither here nor there as far as he was concerned, Kikkit retired to the dugout with the rest of the team.

They munched on their mouldy rations while the Grey Seers lambasted them for poor tackles, failed passes and missed fouls. Kikkit let his gaze slide over to the visitors, where the halflings were almost lost from view behind baskets filled with iced buns, doughnuts, lollipops, currant buns, cream cakes, candy canes, frosted fruits and malted loaf. In fact, buns, confectionary and cakes featured exclusively in their half-time 'snack'.

By the time the referee blew his whistle to get the teams back on the pitch, the Tinklebrook Trotters all had a sugar-rush-wild look in their eyes. Twitching and blinking, the halflings lined up, each of them vibrating with unreleased energy. The treemen had barely moved, their roots dug deep into the soil of the pitch, branches stretching far to either side to protect the halflings around them.

The whistle blew and the Cretins received the kick-off, but no sooner had Thork picked up the ball than he was set upon by a shrieking mob of sugar-frenzied halflings. The skaven did their best to protect the thrower, but no matter how hard they punched, kicked and bit, the diminutive Blood Bowlers seemed impervious to pain.

Kikkit suspected there had been something more than sugar in the half-time food – the smug look on the halfling coach's big red face spoke volumes – but any evidence had been devoured right under the noses of the officials.

He joined the general scrum around the ball, picking his

moments to land punches in the backs of unwitting opponents' heads, chop-blocking the backs of their knees, aiming
kicks at their kidneys, but all to no avail.

A few halflings hit the dirt in the general ruck of bodies,
but they bounded back to their feet before he could reach
them. Frustrated, he lost his cool and waded into the fighting, forgetting his personal mantra of only kicking when the
target was down.

No sooner had he made the error than he felt twiggy fingers
grasping his arm. He was hoisted out of the melee and tossed
bodily across the pitch to land head-first in the crowd. Their
snarls and jeers around him, the Cretins' fans tossed him back
onto the pitch, where he sat groggily watching the vague silhou-
ettes of the players dashing around him through a stunned fog.

He heard the whistle blow again and staggered to his feet,
thinking the game was over. Despondency turned to relief
when he realised the ref was only signalling a score – the halflings had run the ball over the line for a second touchdown.

'Get over here!' snarled Quittit, signalling that he was
going to replace Kikkit. 'You're out on your feet, you useless scat-head.'

'Don't take me off, coach,' pleaded Kikkit. He started
bouncing from foot to foot, twitching his tail and trying to
look as alert as possible. 'I can do this! I can do this!'

There was nothing the Grey Seers could do as Kikkit took
his place on the line ready for the restart. He lined up next
to Nulk, knowing the rat ogre was bound to put down an
opponent or two at some point.

Play began again, but Kikkit had no mind for the ball. He
shadowed Nulk's every step, waiting for his moment. The
halflings knew better than to stay anywhere near the rat ogre
and they scattered from his path.

'Nobody fight me,' moaned Nulk. 'All run away.'

'There-there!' squealed Kikkit, spying a halfling limping toward the sidelines in response to a signal from his coach. Just a sprain, in Kikkit's experienced estimation, not enough to officially count as injured. Yet. 'Hit-hit!'

The halfling must have heard the lumbering rat ogre. He looked over his shoulder, terror in his eyes, pain screwing up his mouth as he tried to get away on his damaged ankle.

Nulk reached out a long arm and slapped the player across the back of the head, pitching him face-first into the dirt.

'Yes-yes!' Kikkit launched himself at the fallen halfling, stamping again and again and again.

But the Trotter seemed to be made out of rubber. Whatever Kikkit did bounced off his armour, or his bulbous gut, or his fleshy thighs, as though stomping on a particularly tough piece of jelly.

He slipped off his spiked elbow pad and gripped it like a knuckleduster ready to stove in the halfling's face. He lifted back his arm, ready to strike.

The whistle blew for full-time.

With a wordless yell, Kikkit fell to the mossy ground, kicking and flailing in an uncontrolled tantrum.

'So-so close!' he screamed.

He lay there for some time, until he felt a shadow fall over him.

'Get up,' Skrankor snapped at him. 'Extra time.'

Extra time?

Kikkit looked at the scoreboard. It was 3-3. A tied game. Extra time.

Sudden death extra time.

Next score won.

He had another chance, but he wouldn't have long.

He dashed to the sidelines, splashed water on his face and got himself ready for the next play.

Alert to everything now, looking for the narrowest opening in which to strike, Kikkit prowled the periphery of the scrimmage line like a waiting wolfrat.

The treemen reeled from a combined offensive of Nulk and the stormvermin, threatening a breakthrough in the centre. Retreating, the halflings formed a second line not far from the end zone. Thork had the ball in hand, the gutter runners were heading for the end zone...

At this rate, the Cretins were going to score. Kikkit needed to act.

He tripped Thork with his tail, 'accidentally' falling on top of the thrower a moment later. Rolling away, he searched the pitch, desperate, heart hammering.

And then he saw his opening.

Just behind the halfling line, next to the end zone, one of the Trotters was on all fours, forehead to the pitch. Perfect.

A gap opened up in the halfling line, between the two treemen.

'Block-block!' roared Skrankor, pointing to the breach, no doubt wanting Kikkit to hurl himself into the fray to let one of the stormvermin dash through for the touchdown.

He looked at the endzone, and then at the halfling. That was his choice – go for the season record, or go for the win...?

Kikkit broke into a run, arms and legs pumping. He heard the shouts of the crowd intensifying, become insanely loud but just background noise behind the thunder of his heart and the rush of blood in his ears.

He saw only the gap and the halfling beyond.

To the Horned Rat with victory, he had a try-out to win!

He gathered speed, leaping over a halfling who threw himself in the way, ducking beneath the swiping bough of a treeman, leaves scratching over his helm.

He kinked left and then right, faked a jump and spun past another tackle. Every moment on the training field, every practice run through the food hall, every match up to now had been preparation for this instant.

Time slowed. The halfling by the end zone turned his head, eyes widening in shock, mouth opening to shout. A wall of hairy faces beyond the end zone was going mad, baying with glinting eyes and sharp fangs and raised fists.

Kikkit hadn't known his record-breaking season had meant so much to anyone else. He recognised some of his fellow workers amongst the throng. He thought he even saw Oversneer Skreet among them, urging him on.

He felt elated and vindicated. So what if the team were all sacrificed to the Horned Rat? Crookback would revel in his fame. They would read the newsrags about the Skavenblight Scramblers, see his name on the team sheets, and they'd nudge each other and say, 'He was one of ours, you know?'

He planted his lead foot for ready for the punt, picking a point right on the halfling's chin to aim for.

Kikkit relaxed into the kick, letting momentum and physics do their work.

His rag-bound foot connected solidly, snapping back the halfling's head with an audible crack. Teeth and blood showered from the Trotter's jaw as he spun away from the impact.

Such was Kikkit's impetus he could not stop himself tumbling over the halfling. He became entangled in the strapping of the halfling's shoulder pad and twisted, falling backwards into an ungainly somersault to land on his backside in the end zone.

His first look was at the halfling. The Trotter was out for the count on the score line, blood trickling from mouth and nose, jaw obviously broken.

His second look went to the league officials. One of the dwarfs met his gaze and gave him the slightest of nods.

Grinning, Kikkit turned back to the pitch to see his whole team converging on him, whooping and shouting.

Nulk swept him up with one hand, raising him onto the shoulders of the waiting linesmen. The Grey Seers and everyone from the coaching staff were running onto the pitch.

Everything was spinning, the roar of the crowd intoxicating.

'You did it!' bellowed Skrankor.

The stormvermin gave him a toothy grin, slapped him on the helmet and pointed at Kikkit's right shoulder.

There, impaled upon the spike, slightly deflated, was the ball.

Kikkit realised he must have accidentally spiked it when he had thrown himself onto Thork.

Not only had he broken the record, he had scored a winning touchdown.

'I-I did-did it-it,' he mumbled, echoing Skrankor, not quite believing it had happened.

He had broken the 'Most Injuries of a Downed Opponent' record for a single season. The Scramblers were going to give him a try-out. The enforcers of Clan Moulder would be history. No more back-breaking, knuckle-aching work at the cog factory. Gold and warpstone beyond counting.

Next stop, Skavenblight and the Big Leagues.

His voice rose to a shout as he punched the air.

'I did it!'

DOC MORGRIM'S VOW

VOW

JOSH REYNOLDS

'This is a mistake,' Doc Morgrim growled. The thickset dwarf stood braced against the rail of the gondola, staring out of the window, listening to the omnipresent cacophony of creaks and groans. The Makaisson and Sons airship echoed constantly with the stress of travel through northern skies, and its crew were ever in motion, repairing this, tightening that, and muttering prayers to Grungni, Valaya, and whoever else might be listening.

Morgrim flinched with every squeak and squeal. He was of the opinion that if the venerable ancestors had wanted dwarfs to fly, they'd have given them golden wings and instruction manuals. Others didn't agree, as the airship proved. Makaisson and Sons ran three flights a week from Praag to Sjoktraken, and once a month to the Dragon's Hold. Airships were the latest thing and said to be safer than sea travel. Fewer dragons, at any rate.

'No, this is an opportunity,' replied Morgrim's companion.

Tyros Bundt was big for a human, mostly width-wise. The coach of the number-four-ranked Middenplatz Manglers was a former blitzer, one of the best Nuffle had ever seen fit to bless, and starting to run to fat, as the old muscles went flat from lack of use. Even so, he was still more than capable of prying an opponent's skull open like a bottle of Bloodweiser.

'It can be both,' Morgrim said. In contrast to Bundt, Morgrim was as hard as slate. Beneath the greasy smock he habitually wore in his capacity as team sawbones, his broad form was covered in tattoos and scars. His hair and beard had been stiffened with bear fat and dyed in Manglers' colours, giving him the look of someone who'd lost a fight with a feral rainbow. Despite his appearance, he was one of the best physicians in the league.

'Stop ruining this. I'm happy. Why won't you let me be happy?'

'I'm a dwarf. We are not at home to happy.' Morgrim thumped a fist against the side of the cupola and stared down at the white wasteland visible below. Norsca. Why did it have to be Norsca? The high, snow-capped crags below reached up towards the underside of the airship like the claws of some vast beast. Somehow, it looked worse from the air.

Morgrim had always hated Norsca. It wasn't the cold, so much as everything that went with it. Also, the cold. He'd sworn never to set foot in these wild lands again, but Bundt had insisted. And Morgrim had taken an oath, on the field of battle, to always stand by his teammate. To stand by the manling who'd saved his unworthy life. 'Never should have played in that game,' he muttered.

'What?'

'This is a mistake.'

'You already said that.'

'And I intend to keep saying it until you listen.' Morgrim turned from the window. 'The Tournament of a Hundred Woes is a meat grinder. It's chewed up and spat out more teams than I can name.'

'Then it's due an upset.'

'I don't know how I let you talk me into this.' Somehow, the Manglers had been invited to the tournament. It might have been their win in the Doom Bowl, or maybe Bundt had put out feelers. Regardless, there weren't many teams interested in travelling that far north, and the ones who were often went for one of the better known tournaments – the Manticore Bowl, the Troll Country Classic – rather than trekking into the mountains to take part in a tournament known only to a few dedicated enthusiasts. The Dragon's Hold Drakeslayers were probably desperate for opponents. Which only made them more dangerous. And there were other perils than those to be found on the playing field.

Despite his misgivings, Morgrim had agreed to go. He still wasn't entirely sure why. Perhaps some part of him missed his home town. Also, without his skills, he had no doubt the Manglers would return in more pieces than they'd left in. And there was no denying that it'd be a coup to pull off. Like the Chaos Cup or Mork's Thumb, the Angry Dragon Cup was a legendary artefact in Blood Bowl circles. The sort of trophy spoken of in whispers.

'I didn't have to talk you into anything. Deny it all you like, but you've been wanting to come back to Norsca for ages. And how better to do it, but as a champion?' Bundt flung out a hand. 'Feel that, Doc? Winds of change!'

'Yes. That's why the hull is studded with protective runes.' Morgrim frowned. 'The Dragon's Hold is dangerous. They play for keeps up here. There's a reason the Angry Dragon

Cup has never gone south.' The dwarfs of the Dragon's Hold were staunch traditionalists. It would be a cold day in Grungni's forge before they surrendered any of their treasures, especially that cup.

'Like I said, it's due a change, then,' Bundt said, stubbornly. 'Besides, we've got a secret weapon. Isn't that right, Fiducci?'

The black-clad shape froze in its attempt to creep past them, towards the galley. Franco Fiducci was a Tilean by birth, a necromancer by inclination and a horse, if you judged by appetite. This would make the fifth time he'd gone to the galley since they'd left Sjoktraken, and it showed. Wrapped in black robes, black furs and black feathers, with black-stained teeth and black spectacles, he was his own best advertisement. The robes were looking a bit tighter than they had before.

Morgrim hadn't yet warmed to the little man, but he'd come in handy the last game, after the Manglers' star player, Marius Hertz, had succumbed to a bout of pre-game hijinks. At the moment, a large portion of the team was only in one piece thanks to Fiducci's abominable rites. Thankfully, they had him on retainer.

Fiducci straightened and whipped off his spectacles. He began to clean the lenses on the edge of his sleeve. 'Ah… yes?' he said, hesitantly.

Bundt's eye twitched. 'The team are all intact, aren't they?'

'Well, yes…'

'Don't say "but",' Bundt said.

Fiducci swallowed. 'But–'

Morgrim interposed an arm, halting Bundt's murderous lunge. Normally, the coach's temper was fairly slow burning. But the Manglers' recent victory in the DeathHex Doom Bowl had added some fuel to that simmering fire. The team had climbed a ranking, deposing their long-time rivals, the Haakenstadt Screechers, and were now being sponsored by DeathHex – 'DeathHex – When they absolutely, positively have to die overnight!' – which meant more money, more fame... and more trouble.

The stress of success had shortened Bundt's fuse drastically. He'd headbutted a reporter from *Errantry* magazine before they'd left Drachenstadt, and fed a photogit from *Fungus Digest* to his own squig in Wolfenburg. At this point, Morgrim was just praying that Bundt wouldn't snap and run amok through the airship, tossing crewmen left and right. If that happened, they might not survive long enough to die horribly later.

'What's wrong?' Morgrim demanded, glaring at the necromancer.

'It's the cold,' Fiducci said. 'It's making the zombies stiff. Stiffer than normal, I mean.' After the Doom Bowl, half of the Manglers' current starting line-up were ambulatory corpses of one description or another. Zombies made for excellent linesmen. They could take a punch or six, and didn't mind being set on fire. Always a plus, when it came to Blood Bowl players.

'Can you fix it?'

Fiducci shrugged. 'I know a few rituals that might help.' He smiled thinly. 'If you're willing to pay extra, that is.'

Bundt growled. 'You're already on retainer.'

'I have expenses.'

'Expensive tastes, you mean.' Morgrim poked him in the belly.

'Winter weight,' Fiducci said, looking offended.

Morgrim snorted. 'Don't think I didn't notice that powdered warpstone you've been putting on your puddings.' At

Fiducci's incredulous look, he added, 'Doktor, remember? I know the signs of warpstone bloat when I see it. Besides, your teeth glow in the dark.'

'I can quit any time I want!'

'I don't care. But if you so much as sprout an extra finger, you're done.'

'You can't fire me,' Fiducci spluttered.

'Who said anything about firing you?' Morgrim patted the axe in his belt meaningfully. Fiducci goggled at him, eyes wide behind his spectacles.

'Stop it, the pair of you,' Bundt snapped. He pointed at Fiducci. 'You want a raise? Fine. But you're going to earn it. Clear?'

Fiducci glowered, but nodded. 'Clear.'

Bundt looked at Morgrim. 'See? No problems. We're fine. Everything's fine. Manglers never lose.'

'We did two years ago,' Morgrim said, annoyed.

Bundt blanched. 'You promised you'd never mention that.'

'The Grimfane Grundle Bowl. You remember?'

'A statistical anomaly,' Bundt sputtered. His eye was twitching again.

'We lost the game and half our players.'

'A technicality!'

Morgrim shook his head. 'This is a mistake.'

'Stop saying that,' Bundt said. He looked at Fiducci. 'How's Marius? Moving smoothly?' Marius Hertz had been the Manglers' star player, before he'd overdosed on poison. Now he was a dripping, violet corpse that occasionally tried to bite the other players. All in all, not much had changed.

'He's stopped leaking.'

'Wonderful,' Bundt exclaimed.

'By which I mean, it's all frozen,' Fiducci said.

Bundt's face fell.

'Can he play?' Morgrim asked. He hoped the answer was 'no'. Without Marius, he might be able to convince Bundt to return south.

'As well as can be expected,' Fiducci said. 'Corpses are delicate things – too much heat and they rot, too little and they go brittle. It's all about balance…'

'Balance? Balance – this is Blood Bowl,' Bundt hissed, grabbing a double handful of Fiducci's robes. 'I don't care if they're losing bits and pieces… Get them in fighting shape or, so help me, I'll find a necromancer who will.'

Before Fiducci could reply, a horn sounded somewhere in the depths of the airship. The melancholy sound reverberated upwards and outwards through the gondola. Bundt looked around. 'What was that?'

'We're either being attacked by a manticore, or… ah.' Morgrim gestured to the window. 'Behold, Karaz Ankor. Known to my folk as Krakadrak or the Dragon's Hold.' Even now, the sight of that great city took his breath away. Even now, it was magnificent. A jutting edifice of carefully hewn rock, every peak and cliff shaped to perfection by generation upon generation of dwarfen artisans. To the untrained eye, it was merely one mountain among many. But to one who knew, it was the very essence of a mountain – a mountain among mountains, crafted by a folk who knew what a mountain ought to be.

'That's it?' Bundt asked.

Morgrim looked at him. 'What do you mean?'

'Only, it looks like a mountain.'

'It *is* a mountain,' Morgrim said. 'A fine mountain. The greatest mountain in this range. Look at those crags. You think snow-capped peaks like that come natural, my friend? No, that is all hand crafted and organically produced.'

'It's snow,' Fiducci said.

'Dwarf-made snow,' Morgrim said, sharply. 'Better than the other kind.'

'It's snow,' the necromancer repeated.

'Artisanal,' Morgrim snapped.

'You sound like you've been here before,' Bundt said, peering at him. 'You've never mentioned that.'

'No,' Morgrim said. 'I haven't.'

Bundt, for once, took the hint.

The landing was rough. They always were, this side of the Sea of Claws.

The crater on the southern slopes of the mountain hold had been specially carved and flattened for airship arrivals. Protected from the deadly winds by a rising barrier of stone, it was the only place in the mountains safe enough to attempt a landing. Even with the crags acting as a windbreak, it was still precariously gusty. Even so, the crew were old hands and had mooring ropes secured and anchor weights deposited within moments of arrival.

As the Manglers disembarked down an iron gangplank lined with safety ropes, Morgrim heard a scream from above and peered upwards. 'What was it?' one of the players asked from behind him. He glanced back at Sora Oflrsdottir. The crimson-haired, late-season trade from Vannheim Valkyries was an experienced blocker and another expatriate from the grim north.

'Doom diver. Someone heard we were coming.' *Waaagh! Monthly* employed photogits strapped into aerial harnesses, and launched from catapults, to get the best pictures. Or so they insisted. Mostly what they got was a slew of blurred images, followed by a splattered photogit. 'Must've launched him from nearby. Looks like he caught an updraft.' He watched the tiny figure spiral up and away.

A series of flashes startled him. He heard Fiducci curse and turned. The necromancer stood poised halfway up the gangplank, glaring up at the side of the gondola. 'Paparazzi,' he snarled, summoning a handful of amethyst energy. He hurled the crackling purple ball at a half-frozen skaven dangling from a strut on the airship, snapping away with a flash. The skaven gave a despairing squeak as the energy enveloped it, and reduced both it and its image-capture device to dust and bits of bone. 'I hate paparazzi,' Fiducci spat.

'Still, you have to admire their dedication,' another player said, as he pushed past the trembling necromancer and made his way down the gangplank. Horst Mueller was the team's thrower, with an arm like a catapult and a brain like something a catapult might throw. His face, never the prettiest to begin with, was a mass of angry red scars – a parting gift from the Haakenstadt Screechers. 'Little fella must have hung on all the way from Sjoktraken, just to get the perfect shot.'

'The perfect shot of the back of our heads,' Berkut Balcan, the Manglers' catcher, said. The Arabayan was wrapped in three layers of furs, and still shivering. 'Why is it so bloody cold here?'

A pale hand laced with dark veins stroked his furs, causing him to jump. 'Is it? I find it quite balmy.' The woman's voice was a thing of unnatural resonance, echoing through the marrow of Morgrim's bones. Then, that wasn't surprising, given her unnatural nature. Mimi Scream, the Manglers' newest blocker, had joined the team in Drachenstadt. The banshee was beautiful, at a distance. It was only when you got close that you realised you could see her bones through her flesh. By then, it was too late.

Berkut flinched away from her skull-like visage and hurried down the gangplank. Mimi laughed and took Fiducci's arm. The necromancer patted her hand in paternal fashion. He'd introduced Mimi to Bundt, not long after they'd secured the DeathHex sponsorship. Between the banshee and the zombies, the Manglers had more dead team members than living. Not that that was exactly a disadvantage.

Bundt was last down the gangplank, dragging the remainder of the team behind him by their chains. The zombies were a stumbling, moaning lot, wrapped in armour and studded with spikes. There was no point in removing their uniforms, and it was dangerous to make the attempt besides. What was left of Marius Hertz was easily distinguishable from the others – his flesh had turned a vibrant shade of violet, and he lurched with purpose. There was an evil glint in the former blitzer's eye – a bloodlust that was far from human. He wore an iron muzzle over the front of his helmet, to prevent any unfortunate biting incidents. Off the field, at least.

Morgrim wasn't sure how much of Marius was still in there. The blitzer had been unpleasant while alive. Being dead hadn't changed his disposition much. Marius groaned and threw up his hands, clawing at the air, as if to strangle it. 'He's testy,' Morgrim said, as Bundt guided the zombies down the gangplank.

'I think the trip riled them up,' Bundt said. They'd left the zombies penned in the hold with their gear. It was the only way the airship crew had been willing to transport them. 'You know how excitable they are. Especially Marius.'

'Nice to know some things never change,' Morgrim said. He ran his hands through the stiff bristles of his hair. 'This is a mistake, by the way.'

'Still harping on that,' Bundt said, sourly. He took a deep

breath and looked around. Besides the crew scurrying about their appointed tasks, there was no one else around. 'Where is everyone? Where are the journalists? The fans?'

'What fans? What journalists? The Dragon's Hold has neither.'

'No fans?' Bundt looked shaken at the thought. 'Then who are we playing for?'

'No one. The Tournament of a Hundred Woes is played only for a select group of nobles and notables, who watch from the comfort of their clan halls.' Morgrim shook his head. 'I warned you. There's a reason few teams bother with it, besides the obvious.'

Bundt's features hardened. 'Well, we'll see about that.'

Morgrim shrugged. 'Don't say I didn't warn you.'

'It's not like you'd ever let me forget it,' Bundt said, acidly. 'This is our shot, Doc. A win here puts us in soup bones and sponsorships. It'll add lustre to our gold.' He swept out a hand, eyes vague with imagined triumphs. 'Think of it – the Middenplatz Manglers, undefeated holders of the Angry Dragon Cup. From strength to strength.'

'The Wolfenburg Harpies beat us last year,' Sora said. 'And quite badly.'

'A momentary setback on the road to greatness,' Bundt said, fixing her with a glare. His eye was starting to twitch again. 'Manglers never lose. Now come on… I want to get these lads out of the cold before their fingers start snapping off.'

'Not that they need fingers,' Morgrim said.

'Don't worry, I can replace them,' Fiducci said. 'As long as we don't lose them. Everyone keep an eye out. Nothing more frustrating than a missing digit.' He peered at the ground for emphasis.

A set of massive double doors occupied an immense archway

in the far wall of the crater. The archway had been carved
to resemble the brooding countenance of the creature which
gave the hold its name. As Morgrim and the others made their
way towards it, the great doors ground open with a thunderous whine of ancient hinges. Morgrim stopped, and Bundt
ran into him.

The doors swung outwards ponderously, releasing a gust
of relatively warm air from within the mountain. The faint
sounds of industry reverberated up from within. A dwarf
city sounded like any other, just a bit louder due to the
echoing effects of the mountain's interior. A group of dwarfs
trooped out. They carried handguns and wore mail beneath
their vibrantly dyed furs. At their head marched a heavily
armoured dwarf, his face hidden behind a helmet, and a
massive hammer braced on his shoulder.

The newcomers came to a stolid halt before the astonished
Manglers, and lowered their handguns from their shoulders.
While the gesture wasn't entirely hostile, it wasn't friendly
either. 'What's going on?' Bundt hissed. 'I thought they knew
we were coming.'

'They did.'

'Is this a welcoming party?'

'Of sorts,' Morgrim said, tersely. He eyed the Thunderers with suspicion. He'd been afraid of this. He'd hoped to
avoid it until after the tournament, but some people had
no patience.

'Morgrim,' the armoured dwarf said. The Ironbreaker was
shorter than Morgrim, but twice as broad, with shoulders
thick enough to support a cannon barrel. His heavy armour
was adorned with gold and silver, and his war mask was
chased with bronze and sapphires.

'Gazak,' Morgrim said, fists clenching. He had an axe stuffed through his belt, but the Thunderers arrayed behind the Iron-breaker would fire if he so much as twitched towards it. Gazak Thunorsson nodded, as if reading Morgrim's mind.

'You won't make it.'

'I know,' Morgrim said. 'And I wouldn't give you the satisfaction anyway.'

'You always were disagreeable.'

'How's your sister?'

'Better, now that you're here.' Gazak's eyes glittered icily behind his war mask. 'She insisted we provide you a proper honour guard upon your arrival. Our father agreed.'

'Of course he did,' Morgrim said, sourly. An image wavered across the surface of his mind – the face of the woman he'd loved and then left behind when he fled Norsca, never to look back. Or so he'd thought. The old guilt came back, bringing with it its boon companions, shame and anger.

Bundt leaned over. 'Something you want to tell me?'

'Yes. This is a mistake.'

'You're *married*?' Bundt said, staring at him. His voice carried strangely. As a group, they had been herded into an antechamber just inside the doors. The antechamber was open on three sides, looking out over the hollowed-out interior of the mountain, and the civilisation that had taken root in its depths. Reinforced flues over their heads allowed for the open flow of air and free-standing steps descended from the antechamber plateau into the depths of the hold. Wide, tall pillars, marked with runes and intricate carvings, rose along the edges of the antechamber, marking its borders.

'Yes,' Morgrim said. Gazak had departed to summon whoever had asked him to take the Manglers into custody. But the Thunderers were still there, stationed in ones and twos throughout the antechamber. Bundt and the others remained clumped together, looking variously worried, calm, annoyed or, in the case of the zombies, vacant. Blood Bowl players, as a rule, took a lot of scaring. A few dwarf handguns pointed in their general direction wasn't going to do much more than make them wonder what was going on.

'You?' Bundt said.

'Yes.'

'Married.'

Morgrim sighed and tugged on his beard. Behind him, he heard the tromp of feet on the ancient slab steps. 'Engaged, actually. I swore no oath of marriage.' He'd made sure to leave well before that.

'Merely an oath to swear an oath, which you broke.'

Morgrim turned. 'Hrulda,' he said, hoarsely. Hrulda Thunorsdottir was as lovely as he remembered, with shoulders you could crack stones on, and a round face that put him in mind of a perfectly formed dumpling. But there was something different about her. He blinked. 'Are you doing something different with your hair?'

The yellow plaits he remembered had been replaced by a stiffened coif, dyed a vibrant orange and arranged in artful spikes. His heart sank. 'You took the Slayer oath,' he said. 'Are you mad, woman? Why would you do something so foolish?'

'Why, he asks,' Hrulda said. 'Why do you think, husband?' She looked around fiercely. Nearby Thunderers edged back, grips tightening surreptitiously on their weapons. The roster of the Dragon's Hold Drakeslayers was made up exclusively of the mad, the bad and the dangerous to know. Every player had to take the Slayer oath at the shrine of Grimnir before being allowed to don the blue and gold.

'Technically, we were never married.'

'Technically, we weren't not married either,' she growled. For the first time, he noticed that she wore not robes or even ceremonial armour, but instead the war-plate of a Blood Bowl player. It had seen much use. Too much. 'In the eyes of the gods, it's all the same. You deserted me. Dishonoured me. And now... you're back.'

Morgrim hesitated. Then, weakly, 'Surprise?'

A second later, he was staring up at the ceiling, wondering how he'd gone from vertical to horizontal. The pain caught up with him soon enough. 'Ouch.'

Bundt looked down at him. 'In fairness, you deserved that.'

'Shut up and help me.' Bundt, Fiducci and Horst helped him to his feet. He saw Hrulda eyeing him balefully from the other side of a Manglers wall, composed of Sora and Mimi. He rubbed his mouth. His fingers came away bloody. 'You always could throw a punch, Hrulda.'

'I'll do worse than that,' she began. She took a step, and Mimi hummed a trill of warning. Morgrim winced. The sound made his molars ache. Hrulda shook her head and stepped back. 'Why did you come back, Morgrim?'

He glared at Bundt. 'It wasn't my idea.'

'If you'd said something,' Bundt began.

'Would it have mattered?'

Bundt opened his mouth. Closed it. He shrugged. Morgrim snorted. 'That's what I thought.' He looked at Hrulda. 'You're wearing Blood Bowl colours.'

'So are you.'

'I don't play anymore, Hrulda. These days, I just put players back together.'

Hrulda laughed. 'Safer on the sidelines, is it? Why am I not surprised?'

Morgrim shrugged. 'I didn't expect you to be. Just like I

didn't expect your father and your brother to let you join the Drakeslayers.'

'We didn't *let* her do anything,' Gazak said, as he entered the antechamber, followed by a second, older dwarf. Gazak clutched his helmet under one arm, revealing a stern visage, partially obscured by a thick flare of black beard. 'I tried to stop her and she broke my arm in three places.'

'Takes after her mother,' the older dwarf said, as he pushed past Gazak and stumped towards the Manglers. 'I told you not to come here, girl. Not until I had spoken with the oathbreaker.'

'It was my dishonour, father. I have a right...' Hrulda began. The old dwarf waved her to silence and fixed a steady glare on Morgrim.

Morgrim eyed him right back.

'You look well, Thane Thunorsson,' he said.

Thunor Thunorsson, second of his name and Delvemaster of the Deep Tunnels, was as imposing as Morgrim remembered. He was as broad as two boulders, with the muscles to match. His battered features peered out of a well-groomed hedge of ice-white hair and beard. He wore Drakeslayers colours like his daughter, which was only fitting, given his position as coach. He looked Morgrim up and down, his gaze lingering on Morgrim's hair. 'And you look as foolish as ever, Ironbane.'

'Who's Ironbane?' Bundt said, looking back and forth between them.

'Me,' Morgrim said.

'Your name is Ironbane? Why didn't I know that?'

'You never asked.' Morgrim inclined his head towards Thunor. 'And you are as perceptive as always, Thunor Thunorsson.' He straightened. 'Tyros Bundt, coach of the Middenplatz

Manglers, might I introduce Thunor Thunorsson, coach of the Dragon's Hold Drakeslayers.'

'Always a pleasure to meet a peer.' Bundt offered his hand. Thunor looked at it as if it were spillage from a pump. Morgrim pushed Bundt's hand down, even as the coach's eye began to twitch. As bad as things were, they would only get worse if Bundt punted Thunor out of the antechamber.

'If you wanted to join a team, Ironbane, I would have welcomed you into the ranks of the Drakeslayers. You didn't have to foreswear yourself and flee south.' Thunor eyed Morgrim's smock with distaste.

'Oh, I think I did,' Morgrim said. 'Why did you detain us?'

'You have much to answer for,' Thunor said.

'But we just got here,' Bundt said.

Morgrim waved him to silence and said, 'I demand to see the king.'

'It is my clan you have shamed. And my right to clear the grudge. The king agrees.' Thunor spoke confidently, but Morgrim knew that wasn't the whole of it. It never was, with thanes like Thunor.

'Does he?'

'When I ask him, I'm sure he will,' Thunor replied, grudgingly. As coach of the Drakeslayers, and the thane of one of the hold's largest and most influential clans, he could get away with that sort of thing. Thunor had done plenty worse in his time. 'Until then, this affair will be kept private.' He looked at Bundt and the others. 'You lot are free to go. I have no quarrel with you.'

Bundt hesitated. Then, with a sigh, he dropped his hand onto Morgrim's shoulder. 'You have a problem with one Mangler, you have a problem with the whole team.' He smiled. 'Besides, we're here to play a game.'

'Game?'

Morgrim peered at the thane. 'The Tournament of a Hundred Woes. Someone invited us.' He'd assumed it had been the king, or the council of thanes. But if Thunor didn't know… He realised the truth, just as Thunor did. They both turned towards Hrulda. 'Hrulda…?'

'What did you do, girl?' Thunor demanded.

Hrulda frowned. 'We needed an opponent. It's getting harder to find decent challengers. They're all afraid of us.' She glanced at Morgrim. 'I caught the Manglers' last game on the Necromancers Broadcasting Circle. Living men might fear us, but dead ones…'

'So you went behind my back?'

'If it helps, my people go behind my back all the time,' Bundt interjected.

Thunor glared at him and Bundt stepped back, hands raised. 'Guess not.'

'That wasn't the only reason, was it?' Morgrim said. Hrulda looked away.

'It doesn't matter. What's done is done.' Thunor slashed the air with his hands. 'There will be no game. You will be wed, and that will be that. Honour will be satisfied.'

'Wed? That's why you detained us?' Morgrim laughed. 'I doubt either of us would be happy with a forced marriage.'

'Your happiness is immaterial,' Thunor growled. 'You will be wed. And the grudge will be satisfied.'

'What grudge?' Morgrim snarled. Always the oaths and grudges. They were part of the reason he'd fled. Thanes like Thunor were another reason. Blood Bowl was more honest, even if Morgrim didn't play anymore. The rules were clear and simple. 'I made no oath.' He looked at Hrulda. 'Tell him!'

'I have,' she said, sourly. Morgrim blinked. She didn't

sound like a woman interested in marriage. He looked at Thunor. The thane glowered at him. Like many dwarfs, he'd set his mind on the world working a certain way and he'd be damned if he wasn't going to make it do what he wanted.

Morgrim met Thunor's glare. 'I won't be bullied into marriage.'

Gazak tapped the floor with his hammer. 'Then you'll be buried, oathbreaker.'

Morgrim felt, rather than saw, the other Manglers stiffen. Sora stepped forward, thumping her fist into her palm. Marius stirred in his chains, as if excited by the scent of impending violence. Morgrim's hand dropped to his axe.

Bundt, red faced, eye twitching, said softly, 'I told you – mess with one of us, mess with all of us.'

Gazak stepped back, an order on his lips. Incipient violence hummed on the air.

'Wait,' Hrulda said. All eyes turned towards her.

'Girl, I told you…' Thunor began.

'I'm team captain, father, whether you like it or not. And I have as much say in how and when we play as you do. And I say we play the Manglers.' She met her father's gaze and held it. Thunor looked away.

'Enough of this foolishness. Gazak, take them…'

This time, Morgrim interrupted. 'We came in good faith, Thunor Thunorsson. Would you now break one oath, in order to avenge another?'

Thunor whirled, face darkening, fist raised. 'You talk to me of oaths?'

'I talk to you of honour. Yours and ours. I know a way to keep both intact,' Morgrim said, talking fast. Thunor grunted, eyes narrowed.

'Speak.'

'If the Drakeslayers win, I will wed Hrulda. If they lose, I am free of all oaths, real or imagined.' He spread his hands. 'Either way, the dishonour is expunged.'

Hrulda stared at him, in what he thought might be consternation. She glanced at Gazak, who shook his head. Then at her father, who gave no sign of what he felt either way. Then Thunor smiled without humour and nodded. 'So be it. The Tournament of a Hundred Woes will commence at daybreak.'

Dawn found Morgrim standing in a makeshift dugout on the mountain's northern slope. A strange wind was blowing in off the Sea of Claws, and the air tasted of warpstone. At any other time, he might have thought that it was the perfect weather for a match.

'You look sour, Morgrim.'

He turned. 'Shouldn't you be over there, Hrulda?' He gestured to the mountain's summit, where the Drakeslayers' dugout sat on a high crag, overlooking the ruins.

'I will go there directly. But until then, I am here.' Hrulda was dressed for war, or the closest facsimile thereof. She had even daubed her round features in ash, as was the tradition. She carried her helmet in one hand, letting it bounce against her leg. 'Will you really stay?'

'Despite what you might think, I am a dwarf of my word.'

She laughed. He couldn't help but smile. It was a lovely sound, like hammers ringing on an anvil of silver and gold. 'Perhaps I don't want you to.'

'No?'

She didn't answer. Morgrim sighed. 'Why did you invite the Manglers here?'

'I told you,' she said. 'We're running short of decent opponents. And sponsors.' She grimaced. There was more going on beneath the surface, Morgrim thought, than was immediately obvious. When he'd left, the Drakeslayers had been in a relatively stable position. But if interest were flagging, it was no wonder Hrulda had gone looking for a different calibre of opponent. Blood Bowl teams, especially small, isolated ones, lived or died by their sponsorships. 'And… perhaps, yes, I wanted to see you once more.' She tugged at a spike of hair. 'When I saw you in the dugout during the Doom Bowl broadcast, I knew I had to bring you here. To ask you…' She trailed off.

'Ask me what?'

'It doesn't matter now.'

Morgrim was silent for a moment. Then, 'Thunor looked as if he wanted to kill me. Gazak too. They might have, if you hadn't interfered.'

She frowned. 'That interference saved your life. We take oaths seriously, here. When you broke yours–'

'I broke nothing,' Morgrim said, firmly. 'I wasn't ready to be married. I wanted more than to sit in this hold forever, petrifying.'

'Even if it was with me?'

He looked at her. 'You weren't any readier than I was. Thunor only started up with the whole scheme because you decided you wanted to play Blood Bowl, and he was against it. Not proper, for a *rinn*.'

She sighed and looked at her helmet. It had a hole cut lengthwise along the top, so that her crest of hair could stand upright. 'Father has always been a traditionalist. Especially when it comes to Blood Bowl.'

'And you've never met a tradition you didn't want to pulverise.'

Morgrim looked away, out over the snow and rock. Ruins

climbed towards the mountain's summit, following the curve of the peak. There were hundreds of semi-collapsed buildings, broken bridges and shattered statues littering the slope. He looked back at her. 'Admit it… My leaving was the only way for both of us to achieve our dreams. I saw the world. And you get to pummel all the players you like.'

She laughed, not unkindly. 'Maybe so, Morgrim Ironbane. But it looks as if our dreams have come to an end.' She put on her helmet. 'The Drakeslayers have never lost a tournament, and I don't intend to start now.'

'If it must be done, let it be done well,' Morgrim said, softly.

She smiled, briefly. 'That is the only way to do anything.' She turned towards the steps. 'I will see you when this is done… husband.'

Morgrim didn't reply. He watched her trudge across the field and sighed. Some days, he wondered what it might have been like, if he'd just accepted his fate. And on other days, he knew. From behind him came a polite cough.

'Everything all right?' Bundt said.

'Is it ever?' Morgrim glanced at Fiducci, as the necromancer sat cross-legged on the hard stone floor. 'Things will be starting soon.' The rest of the team soon joined them. They were in their away-game gear, which was, if anything, more brutal than their normal uniforms. Spike-studded pauldrons and helmets, heavy gauntlets and boots, all reinforced to the barest edge of what was considered legal. The Manglers had a reputation for casual violence to uphold. Besides, it wasn't really Blood Bowl unless you had someone's brains on the bottom of your cleats.

'Good.' Bundt rubbed his hands together. 'I think we have a shot here. Where's the field?' He leaned over the stone rail and peered out. 'Is it underground?'

'You're looking at it.'

'Behind the ruins?'

'It *is* the ruins.'

'That's not a proper field,' Bundt said as he gazed up at the heat-blackened ruins, which sprawled across the mountain's northern slopes. 'What sort of field *goes vertical*?'

'This field. Also, I told you so.' Morgrim shook his head. 'It used to be an *elgi* trading city. Good riddance.'

'What happened to it?' Fiducci asked, adjusting his spectacles.

'A dragon, what else? The very beast that the hold is named for. When it was slain, my people moved into its lair and created a hold worthy of legend. This is all that remains to mark the beast's passing.' Morgrim looked at Sora and the other players. 'We've all played Dungeon Bowl, so you know how this goes – find the ball, get it to the end zone. Dragon Bowl is a little different in some aspects, however...'

'How different?' Berkut asked. The Arabayan had traded his furs for a uniform bedecked in spikes. He flexed his fingers, causing the joints of his gauntlet to creak.

'Instead of explosive chests, it's monsters.'

The players looked at one another. 'Monsters,' Berkut repeated.

'Lots of them,' Morgrim said. He studied the ruins. 'Also traps... fire pits, deadfalls, collapsing walls, self-launching ballistae, war machines... I could go on.'

'I'm starting to see why they called it the Tournament of a Hundred Woes,' Bundt said. 'No wonder no one comes to this thing.'

'I told you so,' Morgrim said. 'We have one advantage.'

'Most of us are already dead?' Mimi said. She bumped knuckles with Marius, who then stared at his fist, perplexed.

Morgrim nodded. 'Two advantages. The second is that the Drakeslayers are – well – Slayers, and that means they're mostly more concerned about the monsters than the game. In fact, they've never actually won, save by default.' Slayers, as a general rule, tended to get distracted by the opportunity to die gloriously in battle.

Fiducci started. 'You mean they've never found the ball?'

Morgrim chuckled. 'I doubt they ever actually looked for it. That's not really the point, from their perspective.' He looked around. 'They expect the ruins to kill you, the same way they've killed every other team that tried its luck.' He gestured to Marius and the other zombies. 'But we're the Manglers.'

'And Manglers never lose,' Bundt said, clapping him on the shoulder. 'All right team, you heard him. Now get out there, and win one for the *grint*.'

Morgrim frowned. 'Did you just refer to me as a piece of waste rock?'

'We're all waste rock, in our hearts,' Bundt said, piously. He rubbed his hands in glee. 'Now, get out there and play some Blood Bowl!'

'No announcers, no crowds – are we sure this is even Blood Bowl?' Bundt said. He leaned over the dugout rail, his breath pluming in the frosty air. The team had dispersed quickly at the distant clangour of a gong, after briefly squaring off in the middle of the field. There'd been no coin flip. That required a referee, and the Drakeslayers had lost theirs in the ruins and never bothered to replace him.

The tournament was like some weird hybrid of Dungeon Bowl and Blood Bowl. The teams had to find the ball and then race to their end zone, while battling monsters, angry dwarfs and booby traps, if they wanted to win. The Manglers' end zone was just below them, on the edge of what was left of a market square. The Drakeslayers' was nearby, on the other side of the square. The field wasn't large, but it being ridiculously dangerous made up for that.

'There are announcers, we just can't hear them out here. And there are crowds.' Morgrim pointed at the ground. 'Sitting quietly. Down there. Proper dwarf crowds.'

'I've seen dwarf crowds. Sitting quietly isn't what they're known for.'

'Southern dwarfs. These are proper dwarfs. Real dwarfs.' Morgrim tugged on his beard. 'Or so they like to think of themselves.'

Bundt shook his head. 'I'm starting to see why you left.'

'And why I didn't want to come back.'

'I said I was sorry. I – never mind. It's starting.' Bundt looked up at one of the crystal balls set into the wall of the dugout. The enchantments laid on the ruin captured images of what was going on from every angle, and sent them back to the crystal balls. Morgrim watched as the two teams searched the ruins, dodging the opening fusillade of traps. Or in the dwarfs' case, looking for monsters to kill.

He winced as the ground gave way beneath one of the zombies, dropping the corpse into a hole filled with ravenous snow-wyrms. One of the Drakeslayers' linesmen was caught coming and going, first by an unbalanced section of street, and then hurled into the path of a ballista bolt. It wasn't an honourable death, but at least it was messy.

The Manglers split up, moving quickly. Most of them had played Dungeon Bowl before – find the ball, win the game. He saw Sora slam a spiked fist into the skull of an ice-troll, knocking the lumbering brute senseless, even as Berkut hunted for the ball. Across the ruins, two of the Drakeslayers rushed Horst, even as he leapt out of the path of a snarling arctic sabre tusk. The Manglers' thrower stumbled back, cursing, as the two Slayers charged at him. One ignored him entirely, bypassing him for a chance at the sabre tusk. Horst ducked the other, and scrabbled for safety.

Morgrim flinched as Mimi's scream echoed over the ruins. One of the crystal balls fuzzed and squawked as the banshee's cry interfered with the enchantment. 'Where's Marius?' Bundt asked, peering up at the crystal balls. He sounded anxious, as well he might. In life, Marius had been tough. In death, he was nigh unstoppable, and the most valuable member of the team. The other zombies were little more than mobile obstacles for the Manglers' opponents, but Marius was still the best blitzer in the league, as a pair of Drakeslayers soon discovered to their chagrin.

'There he is,' Morgrim said, as he watched the purple-faced dead man bull through the two dwarfs, bowling one over and tossing the other through a free-standing wall. Marius was on the hunt, and there was little that could stop him from getting his hands on the ball. Even dead, he hogged it at every opportunity.

Bundt nodded in relief. He glanced at Fiducci, who was concentrating on his charms and runes. The carved stones and bones were scattered on the ground before him, and he waved his hands over them as he muttered incantations beneath his breath. 'How are the others?' Bundt asked.

'Still moving,' Fiducci said, without looking up. The strain of controlling the zombies under such conditions showed on his face and in his voice. 'Now stop bothering me.'

Bundt twitched, but said nothing. Short tempered as he was, he knew they needed Fiducci in one piece. He looked at Morgrim. 'Nervous?'

'About what?' Morgrim said, not looking away from the crystal balls.

'The prospect of your potential nuptials.'

'Manglers never lose.'

'Then you'd better hope that this isn't one of those times we don't not lose.'

Morgrim made to reply when he caught sight of a familiar figure on one of the crystal balls. Hrulda was moving fast, for a dwarf, skimming in and out of the ruins, a look of determination on her face. She had something in her arms. The ball.

He heard Bundt's intake of breath, and hunched forward, heart thudding. Then he saw why Hrulda was moving so determinedly. The dragon wasn't large, as far as such creatures went. Its scales were the colour of frost, and it had a long, almost serpentine body. Stubby wings flapped as muscular limbs propelled it along with ever-increasing speed. A mountain-drake. 'Looks like you might not have to worry about getting married after all,' Bundt said, as Hrulda ricocheted off of a chunk of rock and launched herself at the monster.

The dragon burst through an archway, scattering frost-covered stones. One clipped Hrulda on the shoulder and interrupted her attack. The blow sent her tumbling through the snow. The ball bounced from her grip as she rolled. A gout of fire spewed from the dragon's mouth, nearly catching her. She threw herself into the snow to extinguish the flames that clung to her armour.

Bundt was still talking, but Morgrim couldn't hear anything save the thud of his heart. Hrulda had taken the Slayer oath. All she'd ever wanted was to play Blood Bowl, and this was a Blood Bowl player's death. He wondered if this was what she wanted. Then he realised that it didn't matter.

Morgrim snatched his axe from his belt and vaulted over

the rail, dropping to the snows below. Bundt was shouting, but Morgrim ignored the coach and started to run towards the smoke from the dragon's fire. He'd wanted to be free of this place, of his responsibilities, but not like this. He heard shouts and screams as he stumped along – the game was still going on and, from the sound of things, the Manglers were giving as good as they got. Small comfort.

He burst through a hole in a crumbling wall and skidded to a stop as he got a face full of dragon scale. The dragon was small, as most northern dragons were. But it was still more than large enough to swallow a man or dwarf whole. It padded towards Hrulda, head swaying, jaws open. Heat rolled from its mouth, melting the snow, as she scrambled to her feet. 'Hrulda,' Morgrim roared. He swung his axe, chopping into the beast's flank.

The dragon whipped around, jaws snapping shut just shy of his beard. Morgrim stumbled back, and the dragon followed. It snapped at him again and again, coming perilously close each time. With a convulsive lunge, it caught hold of his smock and slung him aside. His axe clattered from his hand as he fell into a pile of rubble. The dragon approached, tail lashing, steam rising from its nostrils. Past it, he caught sight of Hrulda, scrambling for the ball. Even if she got it, he wouldn't be able to fulfil his vow. But she'd be alive. He saw his axe, lying on the ground. One jump would place it within reach. The dragon reared up over him, jaws sagging open, its scales gleaming as the heat built up in the blast furnace of its stomach. Snow boiled to steam as it took a step towards him.

'Oi – turn around, you overgrown newt,' Hrulda shouted as she hurled the ball at the dragon. The dragon whirled and plucked the ball out of the air. It vanished down the creature's snaky gullet with barely a ripple. Even so, she'd bought him time. Morgrim lunged for his axe. He felt the heat of the dragon's breath as it clambered after him, shrugging aside pillars and broken statues in its haste. Morgrim didn't turn around. No sense in wasting his last moments counting a dragon's teeth.

He snatched up his axe, and came face-to-shin with a familiar pair of spiked greaves. He looked up, into slack, purple features. Marius stared down at him, as if wondering where he'd come from.

'The ball, Marius – get the ball,' Morgrim shouted.

Marius lunged towards the dragon, hands outstretched. The dragon jerked back in surprise and belched fire. The zombie blitzer vanished. For a moment, Morgrim thought he'd been consumed. Then, blackened bone fingers burst through the flames. Whatever spells Fiducci had cast on the blitzer's corpse were still holding strong. Marius was still in the game. Fleshless hands caught hold of the dragon's upper and lower jaw and wrenched them apart. The dragon yelped then gave a strangled squawk, as Marius stamped on its bottom jaw and thrust a smoking arm down its throat.

The zombie retrieved the ball and released the dragon. The creature wriggled away, whining in pain. Marius clutched the partially melted remains of the ball to what was left of his chest and started to stumble swiftly towards the Drake-slayers' end zone. He was still on fire, but it didn't seem to bother him overmuch.

'Are you alive, Morgrim?' Hrulda asked, approaching him.

'Singed, but breathing.' He gestured. 'You lost the ball.'

'How about that,' she said, pulling off her helmet with one hand. Her other arm hung at a wrong angle. 'I'm injured.'

Morgrim touched her gingerly. 'Dislocated.' He took hold of her wrist and shoulder. 'This will hurt.'

'It always does.' She winced as he popped things back into place. She rotated her arm and then drove her fist into his nose, knocking him onto his rear. 'That's for interfering with a play in progress. Illegal participation is a penalty. You're lucky our referee got eaten by cave-squig last year and we never bothered to replace him.' She flexed her fingers.

'You're welcome,' Morgrim said, feeling his nose. 'I think you broke my nose.'

'Good. Consider our grudge settled.' She helped him to his feet. A gong sounded, echoing through the ruins. 'Game's over. I guess your friend made it to the end zone.' She frowned. 'We should increase the size of the field.'

'Probably.' Morgrim tugged on his beard. 'Thunor will be livid.'

Hrulda laughed. 'Yes. Grimnir save us, we might actually have to leave Dragon's Hold to get our cup back. He'll hate that. But at least the team will survive.' She looked around. 'It'll be nice to play somewhere else for a change.'

Morgrim nodded. 'What now?'

Hrulda smiled. 'What else? Rematch.' She gave his beard a tug. 'It was nice seeing you again, Morgrim.' She turned and trotted away. Morgrim watched her go, suddenly feeling a lot lighter. As if some heretofore unnoticed weight had been lifted from his shoulders. He turned at the sound of running feet. He saw Bundt hurrying towards him, followed by Fiducci.

'We won,' Bundt shouted.

'I suppose we did.' Morgrim smiled. 'Maybe this wasn't such a mistake after all.'

A LAST SNIFF OF GLORY

DAVID GUYMER

He stared, unblinking, at the silhouette on the other side of the candle flame. The air curdled with tension, marrow spilt too long ago from the bone. The candle flickered. He wondered what it was for: it stung his eyes, tickled his nose, and they could all see perfectly well in the dark without. Fur and rags rustled edgily on the bench beside him. Someone in the gloomy undercroft coughed.

'Would you like me to repeat the question?'

Shadows licked at his clawed muzzle as Rurrk glared into the untidy flame.

His trainer, Kato, squeaked in alarm.

The rat was padded throat to ankles in a cracked leather suit, arms and legs stiffened to either side, a piebald scruff of head and a twitch of tail sticking out from either end. He scrunched his eyes tight as Rurrk's broad shoulder took him through his belly padding. Air fled clenched fangs in a foetid mewl, and his footpaws squirmed at the end of their pipe-like leg padding as they were snatched from the ground. By the time Rurrk had grunted off him and stuck a cleated kneepad into his throat Kato was squealing with fright.

'Done-done!' Kato squeaked, trying to clap a paw on the dirt and managing instead a maggot wriggle of his tackle suit. 'Good-good. Very good. Time out. Enough practice for now, I think.'

Groggily, Rurrk released his grip on his knuckles. The cloying scents of dirt and droppings and fur moult panted in and out of his mouth. His lungs were still paying out on the debts they owed, and for a moment he'd been confused about who it was beneath him. Kato's supine muzzle swam in and out of focus and he lowered his fist, his knee issuing a protesting 'pop' as he released the pressure on Kato's throat and stood.

Kato struggled to get up too, but could not.

The temptation to kick a rat when it was down was difficult to resist, but Clan Moulder trainers didn't exactly grow out of the ground. By some miracle of better judgement he withheld even a correctional shot across the kidneys, and bent to haul Kato up by the collar.

While the clanrat squirmed out of his armour, Rurrk leant against the claw-cut wall of the practice field cavern system to wheeze, pretending to watch the other vermin train.

They were whelps mostly, practising scrimmage line-ups and tossing around under-inflated balls that had been filched (judging by the faded logos) from the training fields of Karak Izor and Miragliano. A black-furred Clan Rictus bully with a lumpen cudgel and a vest of rusty chainmail stood guard at the tunnel mouth. A plank of mouldering wood had been hammered into the wall behind him and scratched with the words:

Skavenblight Scramblers training field – no ball games.
Trespassers will be eaten.

Some rats thought just anyone could be a Blood Bowl player.

Rubbing the old lump at the back of his skull, Rurrk recalled how it was that he had first come to the attention of the Scramblers' then head coach. The plague priest had given him a nasty crack, but he remembered taking three of his novices down first. He'd learned sometime afterwards that the team's apothecary had needed to cut the fourth in half to get him out from under Rurrk's arm before they could fix his head. The lump of bone sticking through the fur of his head was just another memento. Nothing that a pasting of skalm hadn't fixed at the time, but it ached like bathwater whenever he had to play above ground.

An intrusion by the present made him grimace, and he twisted some of the stiffness from his wrist, elbow and shoulder.

He could have sworn it had hurt less back then.

'You in good-good shape,' Kato chittered, despite the evidence, hyperactive claws making a meal of unfastening the strapping of his vambrace. 'You improve, yes-yes. Muscles good for their age-years. My regimen good, I think, yes. Yes, I think it is.'

Rurrk grunted.

'You keep to my exercises?' Kato asked, then brushed the vambrace off his arm and skipped around the strewn pads as though he had won and they had lost.

'Every day.'

'And the diet?'

He reached for his gut with a wince.

'Good-good. Need every edge can get-steal, I think. Yes?

Not so young as used to be. No. Stop playing with arm. Joint pains are side-effect, give-give.'

Kato's expert claws kneaded the ache from Rurrk's bicep before moving on to the joints. Rurrk's eyelids flickered in pleasure. 'Litter-brother of mine has slave who once had master who mucks out spawn cages for Hell Pit Harridans. He squeak-slips to slave that Princedom of Pain razed three Kislevite villages during off-season. Then had fun-way with dead-things after.'

Rurrk snarled. 'Kislev village-places get razed all time. They not even trying any more.'

Kato frowned at him, claws working. 'Ear to the ground, master. Squeak-talk of Underway is that the Inviolate Prince stronger than ever. Not too late to back out-down.'

'Seven years too late.'

'You squeak-talk yet to Razzel?'

Rurrk sniffed. 'Course I have,' he lied.

His eyes adapted to the wavering light. It became a slow sting around the eyes, a rim of golden-red that lanced the corners of the undercroft. His attention wandered. The smell of human fear permeated the stonework. Sweat and blood. Rust from ancient chains. From some distantly connected corridor there was a clink, as of iron on stone, and a whimper.

'You are held as one of the modern legends of skaven Blood Bowl. How hard has it been to make way for younger blood this season?' The word 'modern' was uttered with some spite, 'blood' as if it needed the tongue wrapped fully round it in order to encapsulate it.

Rurrk drew his attention back from the architecture.

The eyes that stared back were red as his own, but cold, set like ice, while his flickered like a fly over frozen meat. The patrician figure was draped in a long black coat, the brassy glint of a Cabal-Vision pin on his high collar.

'You must have been surprised to find your name on the roster for this match.'

Grey Seer Razzel sat in the high, cushioned chair of his palanquin, borne on the backs of eight wiry skavenslaves to wheresoever whimsy dictated that the Horned Rat would, at any given moment, bestow his tactical acumen upon this willing servant. At this moment, that position was halfway up one of the decrepit spires of Skavenblight's Blood Bowl Quarter.

The Grey Seer peered near-sightedly through a crumbled window that overlooked a courtyard. The squeaks of drilling players and the sounds of balls being tossed and caught echoed up the mossy stonework. Razzel had been appointed to his current position off the back of some debacle or other, the installation of a new head coach to skavendom's most famous (and varyingly successful) Blood Bowl team being generally considered cheaper than assassination.

'You never care about playing before now. What changes, hmmm?'

For half a skaven heartbeat, Rurrk managed to meet Razzel's gaze. The Grey Seer's black eyes shimmered like magic mirrors in the weak second-hand sorceries of the Clan Skyre foundries. The breeze caused the charms that bedecked his horns to tinkle. Rurrk quickly looked away, his eyes feeling as though they had been removed, turned over a warpstone brazier and then carefully returned. With great relief, he found a safe place for them in the window behind the Grey Seer's back.

Age had gnawed it down so completely that, perversely,

fissures of the original white stone had become visible where time's teeth had eaten through the grime. The decorative friezes that surrounded it had in most part already fallen away. Rurrk gave the carpet of rubble a distracted stir with his footpaw, black and grey hair drizzling from his thigh as he did so. Some of the frame's carvings were still visible, effective-looking teams of man and dwarf wearing kits that looked like archaic versions of modern Tilean squads. This had been a place of Blood Bowl, even in the distant when-ever when the credulous would have it that the ancestors of men and dwarfs had had the run of Skavenblight's warrens. For some reason that was comforting. He could almost feel the spirits of past glories snarling supportively from over his shoulder.

From the window came the shrill note of a coach's whistle, the skitter of rearranging footpaws.

Could Razzel really not know why this mattered?

'I can still play. I fit-ready.'

'I let you play season opener, did I not, hmmm? Against Mootland Raiders? Did the Horned Rat not show great faith in mighty Rurrk?'

Rurrk glowered. Always he had to dig that up. 'You want-need big rat like me against the Inviolate.'

'I want-need the young Red Claw Rurrk. This one can't run. His knees like maggoty cheeses. He out of breath just from come-climb up here.'

Rurrk self-consciously puffed out his chest as Razzel bur-rowed under a cushion. The next thing he knew, something that felt like a nut had plinked off his forehead. He snarled at the air in surprise.

'And his eyes!' Razzel threw up his paws in despair, and addressed his next words to the horned idol atop his staff.

'Who want-need Blood Bowl player than cannot run-scurry and cannot catch, hmmm?'

Rurrk's tail lashed as if from its own irritation. His fists clenched in imaginary gauntlets behind his back, the feel of metal on fur on skin so familiar that he felt it even when his paws were bare or the morning numbness made them tingle.

'Red Claw never run. He never catch. Put me on scrimmage line and you not want me move. I train hard. I...'

He patted his chest with one clenched fist, tongue fumbling with words his heart did not know how to convey. Like this tower, age had caught up with him. He had felt for a while that he had been on the way out, but the Raiders game had been the moment when everyone else had realised he was no longer the player he had used to be. He should have retired then, when he still had the chance.

But then he'd seen the teams entered into this season's Eight Point Star Cup

And he'd come to a different decision.

In a part of his mind it would always be Erengrad: it was wintry, his muscles shivered with fitness and youth, the scent of wet astrogranite excited his nose with his first sniff of glory. And on the other side of the painted line... He closed his eyes as if to clothe himself in the fur of his younger self... Prince Amaranth the Inviolate, star player of the Princedom of Pain, never in his three-hundred-year career on the losing side of a Blood Bowl match.

Until that day.

'I... feel it. I still Red Claw Rurrk.'

'Pah!'

A chorus of panicked squeals sprang up from the courtyard. It appeared that there was still a kink or two in the new 'poisoned wind' ball for the team's warlock engineers to work through.

'Semi-final of Eight Point Star is biggest-big match of my glorious leadership.' And an unexpected opportunity to grab one more year's breath, Rurrk thought. 'And you expect great Razzel to tinker with the Horned One's winning formula because Rurrk say he *think* he no longer rubbish-meat? No-no!' The Grey Seer shook his head, setting off a discord of clanging charms.

Rurrk looked through the window as scattering claws cleared the yard below.

Smog clotted the breaks between towers and rat-runs, crumbling stonework held together by bits of wood and the prayers of rats like a teetering mountain of cards. He stared dimly through the sporadic flash of warp lightning, his mind an unobtrusive blank, while the Grey Seer prattled on about providence and favour.

'… paid right bribes in right paws to speak-squeak to Head-splitter's handler-rats about two-match contract. Expensive. But worth it when I win.' He snickered, gazing into the idolatrous carving on his staff as though he looked admiringly on his own reflection. 'Let rat-ogre take-handle Prince Amaranth. I see it already. The stadium chant-sings my name. It will be feted in every corner of skavendom. Razzel and the Great Horned Rat! Yes-yes, the Great One loves this plan of mine.' He turned back to Rurrk as if just then remembering he was not alone. 'Whole pawful of stormvermin before need call Old-Meat Red Claw.'

He covered his mouth with the paw that he already had held up to demonstrate the many rats in his mighty paw, and tittered at his cleverness. 'He of the all-smelling nose loves this plan too much to let something befall them *all* in two weeks.'

* * *

'I covered your debut game in Erengrad for CabalVision and I was impressed. But that was nearly seven years ago, a lifetime for...' The smile was predatory. *'For your kind. With the success you have seen in your career, I wonder if you've given any thought to retirement? There is still an hour or two...'*

The Reeks was a squalid mire of permanently flooded warrens and a tangle of mouldering pontoons that hazarded into the forest of cattails and sawgrass that sucked on the borders of the Blighted Marshes. The local economy consisted of petty piracy directed against the punt-craft that took the marsh channels from the Tilean Sea to Skavenlight's scrap-pushers, and stealing one another's slaves. Even the agents of Clan Eshin moved in packs. The clanless rats that dwelt there were better than slaves only in name. Slaves, at least, got fed. Or in less denigrated parts of Skavenblight, they sometimes did. Here they were the food. It was a cesspool without bottom into which any rat without eyes or wits about him might slip, and from which attempts at escape only put more slime on increasingly despairing claws.

It had been a choice that had put Rurrk here.

The entrance to his burrow was high enough above the swamp to be dry at least some of the time, rain kept out by a curtain of marshweed for which he had traded an old shoulder pad scratch-marked by Hakflem Skuttlespike. The four malnourished heavies he had paid to guard his things put away their fangs when they saw it was him. He dropped a quarter-token into each rat's paw, then brushed aside the waxy sheet and ducked into his burrow.

It was musky and dank, and he scuttled into the darkness by scent and familiarity alone. His back hunched, tension seeping out of his muscles as he left the game of being a bigger, stronger rat than he was at the curtain.

A manskin bag had been left on the three-legged table he kept in the middle of the burrow. It was sealed with a string tie. Rurrk hurried to it, a spring in his scurry that made his ankle click.

He undid the tie and a green light smeared the underside of his muzzle and printed the walls of his burrow with shadows without the prior courtesy of light. Saliva dripped from his jaws and onto the tabletop. A gut-ache of craving formed a knot there. He massaged it away and with a long out-breath he re-did the tie.

The unlight went out.

Kato's supplier had good warpstone, but it wasn't cheap. Pushing his way back to the top had cost him everything. But it would be worth it. What else was there?

He clutched the bag to his breast and checked over his shoulder.

Satisfied that none of his guards had snuck in or listened too closely at the curtain, he scurried over to the naked fire-pit in the loamy muck by the burrow's back wall. Getting stiffly onto all fours, he clawed through ash, pausing once in a while to suck the cooking fat off a bone scrap, to dig up a metal vial with a screw lid.

With much less enthusiasm, he unscrewed the vial and sniffed inside.

Empty. Expected, but dispiriting all the same.

You could say this for skaven – they're optimists.

Stuffing the vial into the same paw with which he held the bag, he scurried towards another apparently random spot and began to dig. After a few minutes his claws struck wood. He cleared it, digging round the edges, until he looked down on a worm-eaten wood chest of the sort that might have been lifted from the wreck of a Sartosan galley. Taking a deep breath he dug his claws around the short sides and, bracing thighs and shoulders, hauled the thing out of the hole.

Brackish water gushed from its seals and from a hundred tiny wormholes as he brought it above the water table and squelched it onto the floor. Lowering himself onto crossed legs, he flipped the catch and creaked back the lid.

He paused for a moment, paw on the lid, staring down, as if caught by the sort of petrifying enchantment that would have saved him a warptoken a day on guards if he had been able to afford it.

The chest was filled with memories.

Trophies, medals, other mementos he had not yet traded or sold, all packed in with reverence and care. A tooth from the infamous squig thrower, Grubba Greenback, the red paint from Rurrk's gauntlet still on it. The deflated matchball from the famous 10-10 draw with the Har Ganeth Executioners. A scratching of astrogranite from that day in Erengrad.

Nostalgia wrapped around his heart like a clinging mother.

Putting it to one side, he reached instead for another bag. It was depressingly flat, and gave a light clink as he lifted it out. He sniffed at it, and took another quick look over his shoulder.

The guards stamped their footpaws and complained about the damp in subdued squeaks. At least he wouldn't have to fork out on sentries for much longer.

He counted out twenty full warptokens. Almost everything he had left. Then he put the twenty into the vial, screwed the cap, and re-buried it in the firepit where he'd found it. He swept the ash back over it, stamped it in, and then scuffed

it back up to look acceptably unintentional before scurrying back to the chest.

He was about to shut it again and drop it back in its hole
when the nostalgic ache in his chest tightened, leading him
instead to remove his paws from the lid and rummage inside.
Reaching through the keepsakes, he drew out something large
and heavy, but jointed in the middle so as to fit inside, and
coarsely wrapped in burlap.

He held it in both paws as if weighing it up before decid-
ing whether to open it.

Reverently, he unwrapped it.

There in his paws, bundled up like the meanest offspring
of the union between rat and machine, was a wearable steel
claw. It was three times the size of his own. The foreclaw in
particular was long and terminated in a flared muzzle with
a swollen knuckle of copper wires and rusted valves. Eldritch
glyphs and technosorcerous symbols decorated the gauntlet,
chief amongst them the emblem of Clan Skyre on the cuff
and on the muzzle of the big talon.

He had been given the gauntlet when the name 'Red Claw'
had been big enough to earn the sponsorship of one of the
Greater Clans.

Not the Skavenblight Scramblers.

Him.

Above the gauntlet was a rickety scaffold of pulleys and rods
custom-built for his arm. He slid the arm in with a soft squeak
of pleasure, then wormed his claws into the control glove. He
flexed his fingers, and made a fist. The old gauntlet emitted a
plaintive squeal as mechanisms left to drown and choke on
their own rust struggled to ape it. He chittered satisfaction
nonetheless and looked to the bag of warpstone still held
clutched to his breast, provoking a spasm of unnatural hunger.

Just one nibble now wouldn't hurt. There would still be more left for later.

He wiggled his fingers and the mechanical steam-claw cried for mercy.

He could almost hear the crowds scream 'Red Claw' again.

'Let's turn our attention to the match at hand.'

Rurrk licked his lips and grunted assent.

'The Eight Point Star is so beloved because it features only the eight most evil teams in Blood Bowl, as voted for by the fans. I confess to a little bias, but with the tournament finals right here in Drakenhof this year, the Drakenhof Templars are everyone's favourite to lift the trophy. Are you nervous about the prospect of facing them, or are you hoping that the Evil Gitz will do you a favour in tonight's other match?'

Rurrk stared blankly.

The interviewer shook his head, amused.

'Moving on then. Again. The talk outside the ground right now is all about your first head-to-head with Prince Amaranth since that famous night in Erengrad. Your careers have taken very different trajectories since then. Can the fans really look forward to a re-match? Will you meet him head on as you did seven years ago?'

Razzel leaned forwards, blinking rapidly as the candle's flickering glow was turned towards him.

'Our plan-scheme for Prince Amaranth is between the Great Horned Rat and me.'

Clanking in his armour, Rurrk huffed up the tunnel from the away team dugout. The silence that cheered him from the solitary wooden stand as he emerged into the night was as thin as the moonlight that draped it in Mannslieb's home colours. Astrogranite crunched under his footpaws as he neared the sideline and took a sniff of the open space. The lump in his head ached.

With a week to go, Grey Seer Razzel had grudgingly paid out for a training session in what some local official had disingenuously described as a similar arena.

Rurrk suspected that the stadium of the Waldenhof Pipers had never been anything but the runt of the Drakenhof litter, but even what there was had smelled better days. The seating in the wooden skeleton of a stand was long gone. The field was cracked and furry with flowering weeds. And Kato had gleefully reported something large living in the away arming chamber before venturing in with a grabber and a net.

Puffing out his cheeks, Rurrk slugged the final few yards to the field.

He'd never been the quickest. There was even a joke about it.

'Who quicker, Red Claw Rurrk or treeman? Depends, is treeman still sleeping?'

Now though, it was obscene. He was immense, put-on muscle squeezed into his old armour as though a warlock had stuck him with a needle and inflated him. Every step shot pain up his shins. It felt as if his legs would have given by now if not for the triple-winding of strapping holding in his knees.

A couple of stormvermin were warming up on the sideline with some light relays and they laughed, jogging on the spot, as he clunked towards them.

'Thirteen!' squeaked one, a three-season veteran called Bisk, and tittered in mock amazement. 'It move-moves!'

'Quiet. Do not be rude-bad.' His relay partner, Grist. 'Do you not see-smell? Great Red Claw is back.'

'You mean Rust Claw,' said Bisk and exploded with chittering laughter. Rurrk made no reply as he clumped past, but did pause long enough to punch Bisk in the chest.

The stormvermin folded around his steam-claw with a pathetic mewling noise, then collapsed on the ground, whimpering with pain. Rurrk would have trodden on him too if he could have lifted his knee so high, but could not, and so settled for crushing the other skaven's tail. You couldn't have everything.

Grist, meanwhile, wisely shut his muzzle and scampered for the safety of his teammates with his tail between his legs.

'Starting places! Not have all night!' Razzel waved his staff, tinkling like a wind chime. His white fur and puritan robes lit the Grey Seer like a brazier in the moonlight. He had been in a bad mood ever since Likkish and Skat had failed to turn up for the team's sedan convoy from Skavenblight.

Rurrk patted his gurgling belly.

Add to Kato's many talents, he was a splendid cook.

Kato pointed excitedly to Bisk's splayed figure from the decrepit little stand, a pocket of furry bodies comprising the team's treasurers, cooks, engineers and assorted hangers-on. He mimed a 'sleeping' gesture, and then squeaked something encouraging that Rurrk couldn't wholly make out.

The players positioned themselves over the field to the squeaked instructions of the coaches. Both teams had been drawn from the Scramblers' roster, with the team expected to line up against the Princedom of Pain in a week's time facing off against the rest.

Rurrk's number was with 'the rest', which for today suited him perfectly.

Wheezing like a bellows with a hole in it, Rurrk shoved a stormvermin with a sleek coat of black fur and shiny red-brown armour off his favoured spot right in the middle of the scrimmage line. He bared fangs then brandished his claw, and the whelp quickly found himself another place on the line. Ignoring the shrill appeals of his side's coach, he turned round and passed his gaze along the opposing line-up.

They were all familiar faces. Household names even. Big stormvermin in spiked guards. Line-rats grizzled by white eyes and torn ears and more scars apiece than years between them. Their hunches were loose, confident.

At the end of the opposition flank was a brooding rat-ogre part-armoured in green plate bearing its owners' emblems. Its rough hide was tattooed with further advertisements and covered with scorched cankers and sores. It glared stupidly at its handler as the skaven chittered at it, pointed at the terrified line-rats in front of it and occasionally emphasised a salient point with a slap across the snout.

A braver rat than Rurrk.

It wasn't Headsplitter.

That was one more reason for Razzel's current searing temper. The legendary rat-ogre had, despite the near-magical disappearance of a fortune in bribes and agents' fees, been otherwise employed on the other side of the world in Lustria for some months. All of which meant that the Grey Seer could now add a difficult-to-explain hole in the team treasuries to his end-of-season summons before the Council of Thirteen. The last-minute find of a halfway like-for-like replacement in Manwrecker (what its sponsors had in mind touring the provincial Sylvanian leagues Rurrk didn't know and Razzel had been in no position to ask) had calmed the head coach down enough to squeal coherent instructions, but no more.

An assistant coach in black and white checked rags standing

in as referee scurried back from the scrimmage line and blew his whistle.

Like a slave conditioned to his master's call, Rurrk's mind switched on.

The blinkers came down. The excited squeaks of the understaffers became a muted backdrop, the dull creak of a tunnel. The moon disappeared from view, a source of light, nothing else, as the world shrunk to a hundred and twenty tail-lengths by fifty-four and with him at its middle. He felt the kicker run up to the ball as he would an itch up his tail. The line-rat smacked his footpaw through it, the meat-slap clarion rang along Rurrk's whiskers, bypassed his brain, and scurried down his spine to his arm.

The stormvermin on the other side of the painted line was still watching for the kick-off when Rurrk's rusted claw smashed through his snout. With a squeal, the big rat went down, and with a dozen more shrill cries just like it the two scrimmage lines crashed together.

Skaven hissed and squealed. Claws scratched on metal. Tails clobbered heads and poked for eyes. Moonlight glinted on a previously concealed blade.

Even in 'friendlies', skaven weren't renowned for fair play.

From somewhere, the ecstatic squeak of the thrower. 'Long-long! Run-quick!'

A stormvermin with something to prove went down under the challenge of a heavier model with better armour, and short-sightedness be damned, Rurrk got a good look as the black-furred behemoth followed through and came at him.

The blitzing player cannoned off Rurrk's shoulder and rolled muzzle-over-tail back across the scrimmage line. With both a gape and a giggle making their own shapes of his muzzle, he watched the stormvermin's head disappear in a tuft of weeds. His iron claw whistled out greenish steam as his bulging bicep prematurely activated against the mechanism.

He could have hugged Kato!

The rat he had laid out during kick-off issued a groan and scratched meekly at Rurrk's greaves. He stamped on the stormvermin's helmet, crushing it like a stage prop. Blood and brain juices splattered through the flattened opening in the front, a spray pattern darkening the silvered ground.

With a squeaked roar, Rurrk struggled to free his footpaw from the ruined helmet.

His heart ran like a bull centaur on fire. His gut roared, hungry as a warpstone furnace, but strength pumped through his old muscles with the willing fizz of power.

With a shrieking tear of metal, he got his footpaw out.

He should have done this years ago.

He could hear Kato's squeaks of excitement from the stands, the roar of the crowd in his mind, the thump of their drums and the blare of their horns pushing blood through his ears.

He swung his claw in a hiss of gadgetry and near-beheaded a line-rat that tried to jink past him. The rat's footpaws skidded under him and he crashed onto his back and performed a boneless reverse somersault.

Rurrk looked down on him, and so caught the flight of the ball late as it sailed over his head. He made a half-hearted flap at it with his unaugmented arm, but was too outrageously top-heavy to make a proper jump and the ball zipped past.

He hardly needed to make his thick neck turn to see the ball sink soundlessly into the arms of the gutter-runner, Silkpaw. The black-shrouded runner smoothed the ball into the folds of his sleeve as though it were a bawling man-thing infant held for ransom, then spun on a warptoken and broke through the cage of squealing line-rats that had thought him marked.

And then he decided to start running.

Tinny cheers broke out from the minuscule crowd as Silk-paw took a lap of the end zone while his pursuers caught up. Then he tossed the ball nonchalantly over his shoulders and wove back to his own half as the line-rats folded over knackered legs and gasped like fish caught out of water and made to play Blood Bowl. His circuitous victory lap took him by Rurrk and he winked as he scampered by.

Rurrk gave a wave of his bloody gauntlet.

The fans loved Silkpaw. Everyone else wanted his legs broken. Another place where Rurrk's opinions took tangents. He appreciated a good player, and they didn't come better. That and their utterly contrasting playing styles left a jealousy-shaped absence in which a friendship of mutual ambivalence could prosper.

'This not game-play!' Razzel shrieked. His eyes were beginning to turn fully black and his palanquin bearers were beginning to squirt fear musk. Dark magic flowed through the Grey Seer's voluminous robes and licked about his horns. 'You get ball, you score fast-quick. And remember.' Those throbbing disks fixed on Rurrk as if they might, on another day, have willed him to ignite. 'This practice-play!'

Warlock apothecaries lugged pots of skalm onto the field. One of them, red-cloaked against the night cold and with a green-lensed monocle, squatted by the flattened line-rat. He wafted a jar of warpstone snuff under his snout, then cocked an ear before pronouncing the rat dead. A pair of kitchen hirelings came along with shovels to scrape the first stormvermin off the astrogranite. It did not take an apothecary to tell anyone he was dead. Elsewhere, Manwrecker's gore-slicked snout was coaxed out of the entrails of a line-rat whose eviscerated remains the clear-up crew were keeping way back from. The rat-ogre's handler waved some kind of lure attached to a long stick and then, once he had the mutant beast's attention, walked the goad back up the field to its position in the line-up.

Rurrk watched, lips pursed, and came to a decision. He clanked slowly down the scrimmage line. Razzel watched his approach towards Manwrecker with an explosive expression.

If rats could sweat...

The referee took a quick tail-count to make sure no one had snuck on an extra player during the restart, then brought his whistle to his muzzle. He took a deep breath. His cheeks inflated.

And Razzel cracked.

'Fine! Fine! You play next week.' The Grey Seer pointed a trembling finger at Rurrk. 'But no more practice for you!'

The interviewer nodded in feigned understanding, and Razzel fidgeted back down, chittering under his breath. He returned his attention to Rurrk and the candle flame shifted with it.

'I was fortunate enough to be at the Skavenblight Scramblers' season opener and saw you knocked out by the previously unheralded Stovel Jamsalad. May he rest in peace. I can't help but notice the improvement in your physique since then: a grey hair here and there, but you almost look like the Red Claw of old.' He gestured to the rusted iron harness about his right arm and smiled, something practised and yet very far from perfect. 'I'm sure every mortal of a certain age wants to hear your secret. Perhaps

you can tell us something about your training?' He leaned in, his smile conspiratorial.

'Anything... special?'

Kato rubbed down Rurrk's fur. The wires of his brush were already thick with his fur, and the menial's tongue lolled from the side of his mouth as he tried to clear them out. They had both given up on trying to get Rurrk out of his armour. Kato had undone the buckles at the back of his greave only for the muscles of his lower leg to hold the plate exactly in place. 'Have to keep them on for the week,' Kato had shrugged. It suited Rurrk.

He never wanted to take them off again.

'They squeak-say that Amaranth possessed by daemon, that why he so strong.'

The voice had come from behind him, and Rurrk twisted round with a snarl. Silkpaw was there, sitting on the crumbling ruin of a wash basin. Its stone fascia was gone or had never been fitted, and there were cobwebs where there should have been water.

'How you get in here?' said Rurrk. He'd been facing the tunnel.

The gutter-runner idly kicked the air with his footpaws. 'I need no practice-play. Like you.' He tilted his muzzle and looked at Rurrk piercingly. 'I no old-meat, but I around long enough to know signs of warpstone poison. Fur loss. Hunger pain–'

Rurrk bared his teeth.

'–Temper.'

'Sneak-rat should mind his own business. He still has glory ahead. Mine already far behind. Maybe... maybe just one more day.' His eyes turned gauzy and he unclenched his fist.

His gauntlet let off the steam it had built up with an acrid wheeze. 'You not there that day in Erengrad-place.'

Silkpaw lowered his snout and bared his throat. Just for a moment, but all the same. He gestured with his nose to the arming chamber's dirt ceiling. 'I was there. In crowd. I saw you play that day.' He sat back then, flicked out his tail. 'Not care about warpstone. All stormvermin need-take. Most line-rats too. But this? This too much.' He shrugged, sorrowful. 'You going to die, Red Claw, before whistle blows if you not careful.'

'I don't know about the people watching, but I'm excited.' He smiled coldly, teeth sharpened by candlelight. 'CabalVision and our official tournament betting partner, Other Side, have now stopped taking wagers on your dying today after a flurry of betting in the run-up to the match. What do you have to say to those people who've already voted with their money pouches?'

Rurrk sprung from the bench with a high-pitched growl.

Aggression filling his muscles, he lashed out his tail and snapped the damned candlestick in half. It was still sputtering out on the floor when he pounced onto the stone-lidded sarcophagus it had been fixed upon and raised his claw to strike at the man sitting behind it.

He squealed wordless fury as a pair of ghoulish heavies took him under each arm and lifted him back off the slab. He snapped for them, green-flecked and faintly luminescent froth spraying their dead faces, and thrashed his tail in a useless rage. He squealed an insanity of sounds which even in his head hadn't begun as words.

Throughout the episode, the interviewer did not bat an eye.

He glanced over his shoulder to the cowled mummer who was magically transmitting the interview live, mimed a 'cut' across his throat and then turned back to Rurrk. He winked.

'I like the temper. The fans will love it.' For a moment, the measured facade slipped and the vampire bared fangs. 'If you should die then try to do it neatly. Arrangements are already in place for your remains.'

The crowd roared as the hunched figures of the Skavenblight Scramblers and the broken knights of the Princedom of Pain marched onto the Drakenhof's famous field, and everything that had come before was forgotten. Rurrk's too-short life became a broken tableau of loosely connected moments: the crash of a tackle; metal on leather; teeth flying; a ball in his hand; banners rippling, in the stands, held across scores of febrile paws and emblazoned in glittering claw-scratch with the name *Red Claw*. The only shared feature was him, growing progressively then noticeably and then unmistakably older as they passed.

The crowd roared.

He closed his eyes and let the tide of adulation carry him from past to present, onto the pitch and his place in the lineout. He had no idea how he had got here. The moment. He was a dead-thing, called from unlife only to play, with only the dimmest recollection of what passed in the times between. And nor did he care.

He was alive now. He opened his eyes.

And despite everything, he had always known exactly what he would see.

Prince Amaranth the Inviolate was near enough to reach out and shove, and it was a triumph of match discipline that he did not do so.

The champion of Chaos was half again his height, and must have been three times his weight or more. He was clad in plate steel, reddish purple, cast as if moulded to the contours of his gargantuan physique so that he appeared to bulge with muscle like a beast of shining hellmetal. A fluted helm enclosed his face behind a mask of perfect con-descension, but Rurrk saw through the slits of his eyes. They were jaded.

'You have aged,' said the prince. The voice that rang from the sealed helm was so similar to the euphoria of the crowd that he could scarcely tell them apart. 'There will be precious little sport in this, but the people want what they want.'

Rurrk snarled for an answer.

The whistle blew and he barely heard it. A teammate he could not name hoofed the ball downfield and he did not care. He swung for Amaranth's head.

At last.

The Chaos champion arched back, a moment of sublime grace that belied his monstrosity, and Rurrk's steam-powered claw chuntered across his muscled plate. Purring with aggres-sion, the Amaranthine Prince came in high over Rurrk's swing, his heavy gauntlet cracking Rurrk's lighter shoulder armour like a warhammer.

Rurrk gasped in sudden searing pain, then snarled, shoul-dered Amaranth back a pace and shoved him off. He turned with the momentum of his bull-like forward charge, not exactly quick, not for a skaven, but he had grown into his new bulk and was still a sight quicker than Prince Amaranth. Like his muscles, his tail too had been hardened and taut-ened and it lashed across Amaranth's ridged neck guards like a severed cable.

Amaranth reeled, his arms whirling, but his boots were weighted like anvils. It would take a cannonball to knock him down.

The crowd brayed and in Rurrk's head it was all for him.

He was nevertheless half aware when a beastman with fur painted bright purple and with pennons of the same fluttering from his goat-like horns picked up the ball and began to run. In what was clearly a training ground routine, heavily armoured Chaos warriors beat back the opposing formation of line-rats and stormvermin to clear their runner a path. The rat-ogre, Manwrecker, blundered into the flank of the drive like a cave-in with claws. A bellow caused teeth to rattle against fangshields, and a blow from the monster's fist smashed a Chaos warrior into the stands. Crude fireworks popped the sky, and the rat-ogre sniffed at the unexpectedly vacant patch of astrogranite in confusion as the beastman clattered past with the ball.

And Prince Amaranth came back for more.

'I am immortal,' he roared, to the melodic belligerence of a horde of chanting fans. Hate had burned the listlessness from his eyes and now he glowered like a thing possessed.

Their arms tangled, attacking one another with knees and tail. Metal scraped against metal as they fought. Amaranth smashed his sneering mask through Rurrk's half-armoured snout and brought it away bloody. Rurrk slid from the brawlers' embrace, head filled with singing, and shook his head. He clapped his paw to his head, but the singing only got stronger.

Amaranth spat out a final verse that brought sparks from the tip of his tongue, and as though his armour were doused in daemonic oils, he erupted in screaming flame. He laughed, and his next punch lifted Rurrk from his footpaws and threw him a dozen tail-lengths back into his own half.

The Inviolate was far too couth for anything so boorish as spitting on the ground, but condescension dripped from his armour like libations to insatiate gods.

'You think you have recovered your strength of old, but it will not be enough. I have refined my skills since last we met.' The unnatural flames spat balefully and receded back into his armour. 'This is no longer diverting.'

Rurrk squealed in fury as Amaranth turned to run after the ball-carrier. He levelled his claw, steam escaping through whatever thing it was had come loose when he had hit the ground as the chambers built to pressure. It shook his arm, ready as a volcano, and then in a great, whistling geyser, emptied its reservoirs over the Amaranthine Prince. The Champion's armour took on a glow, crimson, like the backs of eyelids held too long on the surface world. He roared in scalded ecstasy and Rurrk chittered gleefully.

'Ball-thing!' Razzel shrieked at him from the sidelines.

Rurrk saw the beastman clattering towards him on cloven feet, panic in its ungulate stare at the sight of him in its path, but then shrugged his shoulder to it and bouldered instead into the reeling Prince Amaranth.

Razzel clawed at his horn chimes in a rage.

The Grey Seer had arguably the perfect temperament for a Blood Bowl coach, an incendiary cocktail of thwarted ambitions, sudden, pious furies and a sorcerous temper.

Admirable traits in the dugout.

The air throbbed with rising power, as if one half of a canal lock to the Realm of Chaos had just been opened. The Grey Seer's eyes turned black as sordid gemstones and with an implosive clap that rippled out from his idolatrous staff a spear of purple-green lightning struck from the sideline to envelop the ball-carrier in a flash of unlight. For a moment, Rurrk could see the beastman's deformed bones, white against its furry body's black, and then the whole disintegrated into ash.

Miraculously unscathed, the ball sailed free. It squirmed

through the grasping paws of the Chaos warriors and line-rats that dived to claim it, and then bobbled between Rurrk and Amaranth. Both ignored it, except occasionally to knock it one way or the other as they fought, but never far enough to get it out from between their legs.

The crowd roared their appreciation for the absurd, the stricken body language of the other players causing them to hoot and holler. The game stuttered to an incongruous pause as players weighed their odds of retrieving the ball from the scrum against that of the brawl burning itself out some time before the half-time whistle and coming down in favour of the latter. The two sets of coaches remonstrated with each other and with their players' cowardice, but no one shifted except to yell back, and the crowd's ironic cheers grew louder.

Relishing the noise, Rurrk smashed his steam-claw into Amaranth's breastplate, right over the heart, and knocked the prince onto his heels. The Slaaneshi fended him off, open palm pushed under Rurrk's snapping jaws, and bunched his other fist tight.

With a beatific shriek he called again on the daemonic patron for whom he was host.

The astrogranite began to shake, cracks opening up and spreading out from beneath Amaranth's boots. Again flames licked his armour, but this time they were multi-hued and urgent, orgiastic coils that squeezed around the princeling's clenched fist and boiled.

Rurrk backed away, claw raised to ward against the intense light.

The metal and skin of Amaranth's hand began to run together, and though the Inviolate was clearly in agony he seemed to be enjoying it. Through twitching whiskers and raised, iron claws, Rurrk saw Amaranth's gauntlet lengthen until it was a blade of flesh-coloured hellsteel. It stiffened as it cooled. Daemon fire simmered gaily along its dripping edge, and Amaranth the Inviolate laughed with a thousand voices.

Rurrk feinted with his tail and backed quickly away, or meant to.

He felt a gentle push against his back, without strength, but enough and at exactly the right time with his heels off the ground to send him stumbling forwards when he had wanted to be scuttling back.

He gasped.

A sudden, moist pain spread through his chest and arrived at his back. Blood appeared in his mouth. It spilled over his fur as he looked down to find Amaranth's throbbing spike in his chest. He chittered up a gurgle of fresh blood as he finally noticed Silkpaw, near invisible even up close, scavenge up the loose ball and sprint for the end zone. The gutter-runner flitted through the still-unresponsive Princedom players to score what would have to go down as one of the most effort-less touchdowns of a celebrated career.

Rurrk could hear Razzel's squeals of delight, riding on the roar of blood like a raft.

But the crowd did not join in. They had not noticed, trans-fixed by the endgame being played out on the scrimmage line

He slid back off the fist spike and fell.

It seemed to last an eternity, until he realised he was already on the ground and just had not felt it. A chitter of laughter burbled up from his throat as the first shouts of 'Red Claw!' rose around the stands. The first of many. He felt warm, as if he had found a burrow in which he might close his eyes and sleep in safety. And so he did.

And dreamt one last dream of glory.

* * *

'So how does it feel to have signed for the Drakenhof Templars, and before such a massive occasion as the Eight Point Star final?'

Rurrk issued a foetid gasp, a moan that rattled up from the depths of his throat. With glassy eyes he stared, unblinking, at the silhouette on the other side of the candle flame. His whiskers were brittle, his fur already beginning to come away in patches. His muzzle opened slackly. A smile.

The CabalVision mage caught it.

'He very-very excited,' said Kato, preening in the flickering light. 'Is what he would have wanted. Legend like Red Claw should not-never end with defeat and he looks forward to lots-many more games.'

Rurrk's lips gristled in silent agreement.

'Well it sounds as if the crowds are entering the stadium and I'm sure Prince Amaranth is looking forward to an early rematch.' The interviewer smiled keenly. 'Let's play some Blood Bowl.'

FOUL PLAY

ANDY HALL

There was a knock at the door. The thief stopped rooting through the owner's breeks drawer and waited, hoping the visitor would go away. Why had they come to the house anyway? Didn't everyone know that Gerald Frost-thumbs would be at work? The CabalVision weatherman was a ratings hit with his mid-day weather forecasts. Of course, it helped being a weather-mage, if you could not only predict the weather but ensure it happened that way too, but the viewers didn't seem to mind.

The knock came again, louder than the first one. The thief tip-toed down the stairs of the empty house in time to see the door rock in its frame. It visibly lurched once more as a third burst of knocks came even louder; someone was losing patience. The thief approached the door – he now knew who was knocking. The bosses had come to visit. His hand hovered over the latch.

'Are you in dere, Sulk?' spoke a deep, cruel voice from the other side of the door.

'Yes,' replied the thief.

'Den open up.'

He hesitated and thought about running... Turning around, sprinting into the back room and out of the window he'd jimmied open to gain ingress in the first place. He thought about it, but didn't.

'Open up,' said the voice from beyond, threat creeping into its tone. Sulk lifted the latch and opened the door to see two ogres in ill-fitting suits and shades. One, the closest, had his arm half-risen.

'Took yoo long enough,' the ogre said. 'I wuz about to remove the zoggin' thing off itz hinges. Right, let'z go see yer handywork.' The ogres barged through, forcing Sulk against the wall. He closed the door and followed after a couple of recuperating breaths. He wasn't looking forward to the next few minutes. The Kobassi Brothers were not just any old gangsters: they were *the* gangsters, running the toughest firm in Altdorf. This job – the one they'd seemingly come to personally inspect – was low-level. He was in the midst of stealing some incriminating evidence the gangsters could then use against Mr Frost-Thumbs for leverage.

'Found anyfing yet?' asked one of the Kobassis.

'Not yet, I was in the middle of looking when you knocked–'

'Checked the undies drawer? They always keep the real kooky stuff hidden in their smalls.'

'I have, nothing's come up yet...' answered Sulk. He was wary. Coming here, now, during the robbery, was close to the ogres getting their hands dirty. And these days, the Kobassis only got their hands dirty when dealing with 'grasserz'. They despised gobby gits, tattlers, informers and stoolies more than anything else. Sulk knew this all too well. He'd not worked for the Kobassis that long since leaving the Marauders, but had already witnessed what the brothers did to anyone who talked to the Watch. It had involved a barrel and troll vomit; lots and lots of troll vomit...

Sulk couldn't help thinking that someone must have set him up. Another enforcer perhaps, jealous of how quickly he had come to the attention of the brothers since leaving the leagues? Bald Shrew had it in for him, he knew that.

'Alright,' said a Kobassi nonchalantly. The ogre picked up the jimmy bar Sulk had carelessly left on the dining room table after gaining entry. Sulk prepared to plead his innocence, even though he knew it would do him no good. If the brothers were here it was because they'd already made up their minds he was guilty.

'Wrap this up. We got another job for ya. One more pressin' dan dis.'

Confused, Sulk continued to stare, waiting for the other boot to drop, waiting for the iron bar to be used on him.

'Let'z talk about Blood Bowl,' said the other Kobassi.

The thief was confused by the sudden change of subject. 'What about it?' he asked.

'Well, you used to play da game, didn't ya? Or was we not correctly informed?' A low growl came into the ogre's voice, the barest whisper of threat.

'No, you're right, I did. I was with the Marauders, a lineman – before injury forced me out and I had to look for other... er... career opportunities.'

'The Marauders, didn't they have trouble wiv dere mascot recently? Lost a goat, or was it swiped? Wot was itz name?'

'Janet,' said Sulk. 'Janet the goat. They were going to kill it, because someone on FaceTome started a rumour that it was a beastman in disguise. Well, not even in disguise, just a gor on all fours.'

One of the Kobassis broke into a rare smile.

'Anyway, yoo left the humie team, and here you are,' said the Kobassi. 'Yoo'll do.'

'I'm not sure what this is about... still.'

'Then yoo better keep up, 'cos the only thing I dislike more than grasserz iz repeating meself. Dere's a match on in two days' time at the Oldbowl. The Gouged Eye are playin' the Dwarf Giants. The Eye are out of form. Expectation iz da stunties'll win it easy–'

Sulk tried to stifle out a laugh that broke the ogre's flow. He gave Sulk a deathly stare.

'Sorry,' said Sulk. 'It's just the Giants are all short, bearded psychos, more interested in testing out their latest weaponry on the field than actually playing Blood Bowl. And they despise greenskins. They'll win alright and then some. I feel bad for the sorry git stuck ref'ing that game.'

'Da only fing I dislike more than grasserz and repeating meself is being interrupted...' growled the Kobassi. Sulk gestured respectfully that the ogre should continue. 'Everyone expects the dwarfs are goin' to win. So we've gone and put a massive bet on the Gouged Eye beatin' 'em.'

Both ogres smiled at each other, clearly pleased with a cunning plan that didn't actually seem that cunning. Sulk suddenly felt he should have run instead of answering the door. He saw himself as a mouse by a trap, knowing he shouldn't eat the cheese, but strangely compelled to do it all the same.

'But what happens if the Giants win? Like everybody thinks they will.'

'Then we'd lose a ton of money, and a lot of status, and

our enemies would swoop in. They've already started betting against us. But if our flutter pays off, well, we're gonna be stronger than ever. Dat's why *yoo're* gonna ensure the stunties don't win.'

'Me?'

'You.'

'How?'

'We got loads of minions and enforcers on our staff... but only one that used to play Blood Bowl. Dat's yoo. We gonna put you in zebra togs and yoo'll be da ref for da match. We got contacts in da NAF. Dey'll have yoo sworn in and match-ready in no time.'

'But-but I was a player, not a ref.'

'It'z close enough. I gotta say, you're sounding awfully *reluctant* about dis opportunity. Fink about it as a promotion,' said one Kobassi.

'Fink about what happens if you say no,' said the other Kobassi.

'Well, I've always wanted to blow one of them whistles,' said Sulk with mock enthusiasm.

'Dat's better. Right, we got places to be. Seems news of our wager is spreadin' already. Dere's a few chancers betting the other way. Bless 'em. We're off to see some bookies, make sure da odds stay in our favour. And I'm starvin'. Hungry game dis business!' The Kobassi gently but firmly gave Sulk a 'friendly' slap on the cheeks with a mighty ham-sized hand and headed out of the weather-mage's house.

'We'll be in touch,' said his brother as he bent to get back through the front door. Then he turned to face Sulk. 'Just throw some stuff on the floor and smash a few plates. Make it look like a botched robbery, The Watch have promised us they won't come investigating for another hour or two.'

Sulk was left on his own in the big empty house. He tapped his pocket to check that the small book of suggestive images he had found in the sock drawer was still there. If the Kobassis didn't want to blackmail Gerald Frost-thumbs, it was something he could do freelance, once all this Blood Bowl malarkey was over.

'At least they didn't punish me for being a grass,' mused Sulk aloud, which was mildly fortunate, because he was. In fact, he was the worse type of grass going.

Sulk lived on the top floor of a particularly wretched tenement deep in Altdorf's notorious slums, known as the Stinkend, due to their proximity to the Reiksport. He entered his squalid two-room garret the worse for wear, numb from the day's events. The first thing he did was to peek in the smaller room, where he was greeted by Janet's welcoming bleat. He gave the stolen mascot a reassuring stroke. Let folk like Bald Shrew think he was in it for the greed, that was easier for them to understand and made sure they didn't come snooping about. If they knew he was harbouring an innocent creature... well, that was dangerous, that was leverage.

Sulk stumbled into the room that served as his sleeping quarters and kitchen. He wasn't normally a big drinker, but had stored away a bottle of Bloodweiser Champion's Brew in the tallest cupboard. He searched for a tankard amongst the debris of pots and pans that scattered the small kitchen area. He found one, opened the bottle, poured the beer in and drank it down in one long drag. It was warm, but surprisingly good, and went straight to his head. He didn't intend on getting drunk but he thought he was well within his rights to get a little tipsy considering his current predicament. If

Sulk knew how much worse it was about to get, he'd have stayed far more sober.

As he blundered towards his sleeping pallet, a shadowy figure wearing a black cloak emerged from the far corner. Sulk staggered back, grabbing a rusty skillet from the worktop, and held it aloft in a quasi-threatening manner, all while feeling slightly dizzy.

The figure approached the skillet-armed Sulk, clearly not in any way intimidated.

'Had a busy day?' asked the intruder, and removed his hood to reveal a plain looking man of middle age, wearing a smug grin.

'Nuffle's balls! Zog off, Hinter!' sniped Sulk as he dropped the skillet and headed towards his pallet. Hinter put out his arm, blocking the way.

'I notice you haven't made a report recently,' stated Hinter.

'There's nothing to say.'

'How can we be the Eyes of Altdorf if we can't see what our enemies are up to? You are one of our little eyes, Mr Sulk, but you seem to be closed. If you cannot keep us informed about what the Kobassis are doing, then what good are you?'

'Can't you go and stalk Griff Oberwald? I've had a really bad day, let's talk about it tomorrow.'

'I'm afraid that won't do. You are requested.'

'Requested? By who? Look, when I agreed to do this, under considerable pressure I might add–'

'When trying to justify it, don't forget your compensation. Let's not pretend it's all stick and no carrot.'

'I don't care, I didn't sign up for late-night visits.'

'Well, seems your employers – the ones you publically work for at any rate – are up to something. So, you're on call.' With that, Sulk felt a cloth bag being slipped over his head – some git must have sneaked up behind him. He felt drawstrings tighten around his neck; they met his skin but didn't bite too deeply. A strange, sweet smell filled his head.

'Hinter, you utter s–' he managed to say before collapsing.

Sulk awoke. His head felt like he'd been in a particularly vicious blocking play on the line of scrimmage… against a troll, although he wasn't sure if this was a natural hangover or the aftermath of whatever substance they had used to knock him out. He looked around. It was dark. A lone, guttering candle spluttered some yellow light about, revealing a dank but grand chamber with a large sarcophagus lying in the centre. Other standing tombs were dimly visible in the darkness, but this one was the grandest.

'Gulden von Sulkenhof,' said a voice. Sulk started and scanned the darkness, looking for the voice's owner. A tall figure emerged from around the head of the stone coffin and came to stand just within the perimeter of light offered by the candle. 'There you are, Gulden. How like you to be skulking in the darkness. Tell me, why should I *not* have you killed right now?'

'Sorry?'

'It's a simple question. Are you a good man? An average Blood Bowl player cast aside by the Marauders as soon as you were injured. You could have leveraged your limited celebrity, like many ex-players do. But instead you end up as a thug working for the Kobassi Brothers, and you're not even loyal to them. I've met skaven with more integrity. So… why should I root for you, why should anyone?'

'Erm… I don't care if anyone roots for me. I'm in it for myself,' lied Sulk.

'Indeed, how wretched. But then wretched men are easy to control.'

The figure stepped further into the light. Sulk recognised the face but didn't know from where. The man was older than the usual lot he dealt with. His long face and grey hair gave him a shrewd if noble appearance. But there was an intelligent malevolence around the eyes. He wore fine clothing, over which was a heavy cloak emblazoned with a crest above the left breast. He saw Sulk studying it. 'That's the crest of the Lord Chamberlain, for I am he, and you are my agent, willing or not,' he said. Sulk gulped. 'The Eyes of Altdorf is my network, and its glare is currently fixed on you. Do you not know where you are?'

Sulk shook his head, although he had an uneasy suspicion.

'The Imperial crypt. I thought it an apt place to talk. A reminder that all will meet their end – from the poor to the mighty; both the meek and the powerful,' he said, tenderly tapping the sarcophagus. 'The time of those ogre gangsters is also at its end.'

'Good luck with that,' said Sulk with mock confidence.

'Now, Gulden, don't be so hasty in ruling yourself out. You have a part to play.'

'I'm just an enforcer, a low-level thug, as you said.'

'At the moment you are, but in two days' time you'll be an NAF-sanctioned referee,' said the chamberlain with a devious smile. 'Come now, you don't think it timely – the day the Kobassi Brothers tell you about their massive bet, I bring you here?'

'Maybe it was because I haven't sent in a report?' said Sulk.

The chamberlain gave a short laugh. 'I'm not sure you understand the, shall we say, *prominence* of my role? I have my more trusted agents to deal with matters of compliance. No, we're meeting in person because the Dwarf Giants are playing the Gouged Eye.' The candlelight highlighted a gleam in the chamberlain's eyes.

'Sports fan?' asked Sulk with a meek innocence.

'Blood Bowl? No, I can't stand it. I think you've got me confused with more murderous chamberlains.'

'I've heard it said it's a good outlet for those who like to plan and plot? The demographics for Tzeentchian cultists were off the charts when I was in the game,' ventured Sulk in an attempt to keep the chamberlain distracted while he tried to figure out an escape plan.

'My nefarious plots are rather straightforward, I'm afraid. I don't have time for anything quite so labyrinthine. Let's take your situation as an example. The Kobassi Brothers want you to ensure the Gouged Eye win. I insist that the Gouged Eye lose. It's as simple as that.'

'No offence,' said Sulk, whose niggardly streak had started to resurface as the hangover receded, 'but the brothers are ogres and big terrifying ones at that. If it's down to threats, they win.'

'Well, let me persuade you instead. We want the Kobassis broken. Losing this wager will leave them more than vulnerable, the Burgomeisters will be grateful.' Sulk wasn't moved by the chamberlain's words. The old man could see it, and so his demeanour hardened. 'Hinter mentioned something of interest to me on your delivery.' The chamberlain began to prowl around the sarcophagus, wandering into and out of the candlelight with his hands behind his back in a relaxed gesture. 'Why do you sleep in the corner of your kitchen when you live in a hovel with two rooms? I wonder...' Sulk felt an icy stab in his heart. 'Could it be because you keep something else in the other room? Something stolen. Well, you are a thief.' The chamberlain came back round the head of the long-dead emperor. 'Is it true love?'

'No!' retorted Sulk. 'Nothing like that. I just care about animals, I hate to see them threatened or maltreated.'

'You're not quite the selfish thug you make out to be are you, Mr Sulkenhof? That's why we should root for you,' the chamberlain said in a self-satisfied way. 'Don't worry, it's our little secret. Of course, if you wish to shun our gratitude and don't ensure the Dwarf Giants win, I could always tell your ogre bosses about it… and that you have been informing on them. From what I hear, they hate "grasserz"'.

'No,' said Sulk.

The chamberlain gave him an ungracious smile. 'Why don't you sleep on it?'

Before Sulk could answer, a hood was slipped over his face. A familiar, sweet smell filled his nostrils. 'Send him back, Hinter.'

'You utter–' was all Sulk managed as he lost consciousness, flickering out long before the guttering candle did.

Sulk spent the next two days agonising on his impossible choice. The Lord Chamberlain demanded the Dwarf Giants win the game, and had the resources of an entire city to make Sulk's life miserable. On the other hand, the Kobassi Brothers expected him to swing the game for the Gouged Eye, and they did not suffer failure either. A sharp knock at his door told him the time for worrying was over, the game was imminent. He gave Janet another handful of hay and made his way to the ground floor.

He stepped out of his building to see the Kobassis' personal stretched carriage was waiting for him. He had no doubt they were inside, waiting to give him one last 'pep talk' on the way to the stadium. He was ushered into the carriage by Bald Shrew, who gave Sulk an evil wink while closing the door. The ogres were sat on leather seats. Even though the carriage was large by any human standards, the ogres were clearly cramped. Sulk was directed to sit between them. It was all far, far too cosy, and very sweaty. The pong of ogre sweat was far stronger than a player's underoos, even after a match, he thought.

'Sulk!' said one of the Kobassis. 'Yoo've been quiet since we last spoke. Haven't left yer squat, we heard.'

Sulk was relieved that the ogres didn't seem to know about his midnight excursion to the crypt. That could have been a difficult one to explain.

'I've been studying,' he lied. 'I wanted to get on top of the rules and regs. Even in the time since I stopped playing there's been some rules changes.'

The ogres looked at each other in an approving manner. 'Glad to see we made da right choice. But just remember, we don't give a ratman's arse about da rules, just as long as da orcs win.'

'Yeah, they really are out of form...' ventured Sulk.

The Kobassis both gave him a stare that would have curdled milk. 'Dat's the point,' growled one. 'Dat's why dere odds are high and why we've bet on 'em. We gonna win big, cos yoo're gonna make sure dey win big.'

'How about a draw?' asked Sulk. 'I know a win would be best, but a draw would mean you get your money back...'

'A draw is da same as a loss,' rumbled a Kobassi. 'Get us a win, Sulk. And let'z have no more talk about ifz an' butz.'

The rest of the trip passed in silence, and soon Sulk was delivered to the staff entrance at the Oldbowl. As he got out, the nearest Kobassi leaned forwards. His face mere inches from Sulk's, his breath stank like the River Reik combined with a year-old corpse.

'Don't let us down, Sulk. My brother isn't as forgiving as me.' Sulk managed a sheepish grin before Bald Shrew shut the carriage door. The ex-player, ex-thug and now ref wandered to the stadium entrance muttering a prayer to Nuffle without the slightest idea what to do.

Sulk stood on the astrogranite, dressed in black and white with a whistle dangling on twine around his neck. The coin had been tossed, the receiving team decided. It was the Dwarfs. Both teams seemed quite mad about that. He was in the middle of twenty-two adrenaline-fuelled and bloodthirsty warriors in spiked armour. On his left, they were short and bearded. To his right were hulking green-skinned beasts. Surrounding them were the raised stands of the ancient Oldbowl, packed to capacity with cheering fans. The supporters of the Dwarf Giants were in the south end of the stadium – easily spotted not just because of their diminutive height, but also for the sea of blue and gold as they proudly wore their team's colours. The Gouged Eye's rabid fans were in the opposite end. They were less concerned with wearing the Gouged Eye colours of red and white, because being green was probably enough to identify with their team. There were a fair few inflated Gouged Eye balloons bobbing around those stands to further reinforce the crowd's support.

Separating the rival fans in the middle part of the oval on both sides of the Oldbowl were neutral parties. This was the area where the sponsors, corporate blaggers and parties with more financial – rather than tribal – interests spectated. The Kobassi Brothers stood out like sore and irritable thumbs in their seats despite the crowd numbering in their tens of thousands. Sulk saw the ogres and they stared back at him. Time seemed to slow, but it hadn't really – at all – and both the players and fans were getting impatient.

'By Roze-el's bearded chuff, blow the whistle, you

bumbling umgi git!' shouted Grimwald Grimbreath, the Dwarf Giants' captain. Startled by the rebuke, Sulk blew into the whistle and the shrill noise carried across the stadium. A great cheer went out from the crowd and the players on the line of scrimmage crashed against each other like a tidal surge against rock-hewn sea defences. Sulk was standing in the centre of this mass and his old player instincts quickly told him to duck as ancient enemies – black orcs and bearded blitzers – crashed into each other at full velocity. Sulk managed to crawl out of the scrum relatively intact. He kept crawling until he reached the side of the field. In theory, he was meant to be keeping an eye on the game for infractions, rule-breakers and fouls, but he'd spent the first half minute glaring down at the blood-caked astrogranite surface as he moved to the side of the field on his hands and knees.

An arm reached down, offering to pull him up. Sulk took the proffered hand, noticing the zebra-coloured sleeve. So, this was his assistant referee – they had not met before the game, due to Sulk's dawdling, but there was no time like the present. Sulk let the assistant's arm drag him up and he looked into the face of its owner for the first time. He was met with a smug grin. It was Hinter's face.

'What are you doing here?' hissed Sulk.

'Same thing as the Kobassis, reminding you to make the correct decision.' Before Sulk could answer back, he heard a shout from over his shoulder.

'REF!'

Sulk turned to see two orcs kicking the absolute snot out of a prone dwarf. The remaining Giants were running towards the incident as fast as their stumpy legs could carry them and screaming at Sulk in the eternal way all players appealed to officials – with jaws wide and arms splayed in 'Can-you-not-see-this-injustice!?' fashion.

'No foul, play on!' he shouted. The Giants' fans voiced their objections – fully half the stadium exploded in boos and khazalid death threats aimed at Sulk. The Gouged Eye fans cheered in delight. One of the orcs in mid-foul celebrated with a flying elbow into his victim. Sulk turned his head to give Hinter his own smug grin. But his assistant was no longer smiling, now there was anger.

The game continued, and Sulk was not making himself popular with the Giants' fans. While not as infamous for it as rival dwarf team, the Warhammerers, the Giants were prone to bringing their experimental and illegal weapons onto the field of play. Some refs deliberately turned a blind eye to this outright cheating; they either feared being skewered on the very weapons they were banning, or had received a hefty purse of dawi gold before the game. Sulk was in neither category. He had already stopped a chainsaw-wielding dwarf from coming on to the field. The fans were not amused. Grimwald Grimbreath pushed past Sulk and nearly knocked him flying.

'You're in my personal book of grudges, laddie,' spat Grimbreath as he strolled back into his own half.

In a way, the dwarfs' willingness to cheat made Sulk's job easier, as he didn't have to manufacture any reasons to penalise them. Of course, he still had to consider letting the dwarfs win to please the Lord Chamberlain, but at the moment he wanted to agitate Hinter more. Before the end of the game, he still had to figure out how he could please the ogres *and* the Eyes, although, deep down, he knew someone was going to lose – and that was probably him.

There was a roar from the Giants' end zone. It wasn't the outraged roar of the crowd; more mechanical – like a lawn mower that had drank a potion of strength. Sulk looked up to see a deathroller churning up the turf around the stands and heading for the astrogranite. Dwarf deathrollers were the ultimate 'secret' weapon, the irony being they were not subtle at all due to their enormous size. Initially developed by the Warhammerers from antiquated sports field rollers, it was a steam-driven contraption with a large, spiked roller at the front which was about four foot in height and seven foot wide. The roller span at a fearsome rate, even when stationary. The machine was ridden by a player-pilot whose job was to mow down enemy players, until only dwarfs were left on the pitch unopposed. It was a fan favourite with good reason. Sulk knew if the machine got on the field then there wouldn't be any orcs left to win the match.

He sprinted across to the Giants' end zone and stood before the deathroller, red card in hand. The Giants' fans were shouting and screaming at him at the top of their lungs, cursing his ancestors and swearing countless grudges against him. The deathroller continued to slowly advance, its spinning drum whipping up the air currents around the referee. The deathroller inched forward, until the roller came within a beard's length of him. Sulk held his ground, even as he struggled to hold his bowels in place.

'Hold it!' shouted Grimwald. The Dwarf captain came to stand by Sulk. 'You've got balls, lad. Big, spiky ones, I'll give ye that.' He turned to the player in the deathroller pilot seat. 'Spin her around, Thorek, we'll try again later.'

Sulk let out a sigh of relief but quickly regained his composure as Hinter came to join him.

'If you'd let that machine on, it would have been game

over, fool,' he said. Sulk moved into Hinter's personal space, their heads almost touched.

'Don't push me, Hinter!'

'Or what?'

'I might push back!' Sulk walked away before Hinter could respond.

The clock was rushing towards half time. Sulk didn't know if that was a good or bad thing. The sooner the ordeal was over the better, but then what fate would befall him once he blew the final whistle?

'Illegal procedure!' a shout called out from the sidelines. Without turning his head, Sulk knew where the shout had come from. As the ranking match official, technically, Sulk was the only ref allowed on the field during play. Assistant refs were confined to the sidelines but could call out fouls and other rules breakages. Most never did, rightly letting the head ref take the heat from resentful players and fans for halting play. But Hinter had his own agenda. Sulk looked askance from the field, and the CabalVision camras followed his gaze.

'Gouged Eye player four doesn't have his boot laces tied up. That's a clear breach of NAF code 122, paragraph C. According to the laws of the game, play must reset with Dwarf Giants in possession.' Hinter's face didn't look as confident as the words he spoke. Even he knew that he was not just poking a hornets' nest but drop kicking it down the ravine. And yet, his interpretation of the rules was foolproof. Unlike the head referee, he must have been swotting up on his NAF regs before the game. Sulk had no choice but to concur. Grimbreath sidled up to Sulk.

'Well now, lad, isn't he a despicable, sanctimonious oik?

Glad he's a Giants' supporter!' He gave a gruff laugh and patted Sulk on the back before ordering his players into formation.

The Gouged Eye fans were not happy. Some of the mascot balloons were thrown onto the pitch, where one burst over a goblin, covering him in gloop. Sulk dared a glance at the Kobassis. Their faces were stone – not just hard to read, but impossible. However, their eyes – yes, their eyes – gave away their true feelings, and it was pure, unadulterated anger.

The game restarted with half-time only moments away. Despite all that had gone on, neither side had managed a touchdown yet. While the Gouged Eye were genuinely out of form, the Giants' were simply being self-destructive, too hung up on getting their illegal weapons on the pitch. If they had just played the ball, thought Sulk, they'd probably be two up by now. It was a thought he certainly wasn't going to voice to the dwarfs. Although, he worried that Hinter might say something. And as if on cue...

'Foul play!' shouted Hinter from the sidelines. 'The troll is picking his nose, a clear breach of NAF player protocol–'

'Shut yer zoggin mouth!' shouted the Gouged Eye captain. The orc came storming up to Sulk. He was big and angry, with a row of broken fangs jutting from his bottom lip. Sulk was thankful it wasn't Varag Ghoul-Chewer. Part of the reason the Eye were not on form was their absent captain, who was still recovering from injury from when a witch elf had kicked him in the groin last season.

'Yoo betta get dat assistant git to shut it wiv his weird rulez, or I'm holdin' *yoo*' – with that, the orc poked Sulk hard in the chest with a knotted, clawed finger – 'responsible.'

Sulk was now sure that every player and member of the crowd was out to get him... Play resumed, the dwarfs were mere yards from the end zone, Sulk had the whistle in his mouth ready to blow as soon as the half was up. He would call it early if he could, but due to Hinter's constant interference, scrutiny of the match officials was now off the charts. Then Grimbreath was handed the ball.

'Out the way!' he roared as he charged past. Sulk blew the whistle, trying to stop the game before the dwarf captain crossed into the orcs' end zone. But it was too late – an undeniable touchdown was scored.

'Half-time!' shouted Hinter from the sidelines. His smug grin had returned.

The teams retreated to their dugouts to be shouted at by their coaches. Sulk was in no doubt that both he and Hinter would be the topic of much of that discourse. He dared a look into the crowd and saw the Kobassis glaring back. Their anger had given way to malice and hatred. If the score line remained the same, he was a dead man.

His assistant ref approached him from behind and looked at the Kobassis. They returned his glare with the same hatred they had shown Sulk.

'It would be best for everyone if the score stays the same from now on, or even if the Giants can increase their lead.' He gave the ogres a friendly wave as he spoke. It wasn't returned. He then faced Sulk. 'Do you know what I've got here?' He tapped his breast pocket. A small, black book was sat in it. The books were normally carried by match officials used for recording cautioned player numbers... and bribes. Sulk was non-plussed. 'It's evidence. All the information we have that you are my informant. Think the ogres are mad at you now? Wait till I show them this,' he tapped his pocket again, 'unless of course, you stop being so stubborn and *let the Giants win.*'

Sulk walked away, partly because it was already time to get the second half started, and partly to stop himself from throttling Hinter there and then.

Let the Giants win, mused Sulk. Maybe, just maybe there was a way out of this...

It was kick-off time once again and the Gouged Eye were receiving. The dwarf kicker hoofed the ball high into the air and into the greenskins' half. A goblin snatched it before it bounced and orc linemen quickly surrounded him. The greenskin cage started to march upfield. The dwarfs, always better at defending castles than taking them, struggled to grab the goblin as the Gouged Eye moved ever closer to the opposing end zone. Hinter moved along the sidelines, following the ball. Twice he called foul play, but this time the orcs refused to listen. No doubt a direct order from their manager at the half-time talk. Hinter, looking slightly panicked, beseeched Sulk to intervene, but the chief ref pointedly ignored him too. The dwarfs attacked deep in their half. The two team captains were trading heavy blows when a gobbo broke from the cage and made a run for it. He scored, and the Gouged Eye fans erupted in jubilation.

'I've had enough of this!' ranted Grimbreath, as the dwarfs gathered for kick-off once more. 'Thorek, you're back on!' The roar of the deathroller reverberated around the stadium. The dwarf captain looked to Sulk, daring him to stop it. In the crowd, the Kobassis glared at him, and on the sidelines Hinter looked on with a scowl, expecting Sulk to send it off. However, Sulk didn't, he looked past it, as if the rumbling, smoke-belching machine wasn't there.

'Play on!' shouted Sulk in his most ref-like voice. The Gouged Eye fans turned their howls from triumph to outrage.

The ogres, who had been stony faced throughout, roared their disapproval. Hinter's scowl disappeared, and a familiar, irritating smile spread across his face. At last he had got through to Sulk.

The deathroller trundled up the field, but the greenskins had no answer. As it advanced the Kobassis gestured at Sulk, desperate to attract his attention. Hinter moved down the sidelines, looking self-satisfied. The deathroller made it to the line of scrimmage – the line that bisected the field at the centre – when Sulk called a foul play.

'This dwarf's beard is too long,' Sulk shouted, pointing to a runner, whose cheeks burned red with embarrassment as he quickly tucked his beard into the top of his breeches. The game halted, and all players stopped what they were doing. Sulk stood at the centre of the field, with the deathroller stationary but its drum spinning menacingly before him.

'No!' shouted Hinter. 'You can't stop the game now, that's not even an infraction!' He strode onto the field in a clear breach of official etiquette. Hinter stormed up to Sulk, ignoring the dwarf and orc players about him, and the rumbling deathroller.

'What are you up to, Sulk? The game is a draw, full-time is close. You need to let these bearded fools win!'

'No,' said Sulk, looking calm.

'Then you'll pay. I have all the evidence, I'll show it to your bosses and watch them pull you apart.'

'That's all the evidence? There in your pocket, no copies?'

'It's all here,' gloated Hinter. 'Ready to give to the Kobassis. And once they're done with you–'

Sulk gave Hinter a push. It wasn't hard, but was just enough to tip the assistant off balance. Hinter fell sideways and into the deathroller. There was short scream followed by an unpleasant crunch. The drum of the deathroller turned red.

'Told you I'd push back.' Sulk noticed the shredded pages of Hinter's notebook blow in the wind and get trampled into the astrogranite in the ensuing panic. No more evidence to worry about.

Players from both teams looked surprised at what had just happened. If they had seen the push, none cared to mention it. Sulk quickly took charge of the situation.

'Penalty on the Dwarf Giants, an illegal construction has caused the death of a match official. Send it off. The Gouged Eye take possession!'

Even the dwarfs struggled to argue against that decision. None picked up on the irony that they were being punished for a murder Sulk had committed. The Gouged Eye were emboldened and surged deep into the Dwarfs' half with the ball. It was full-time, but with the score still a draw Sulk let the game play on. The Giants' fans jeered, calling for the final whistle, but Sulk ignored them.

Then the orcs fed the ball to their speedy gobbo, and he dodged a slayer's tackle and sped into the end zone, scoring a second touchdown. Sulk blew the final whistle – the Gouged Eye had won! The orcs on the field let out a celebratory 'Waaagh!', which was echoed by the fans in their half of the stadium. Gouged Eye balloons bounced around and goblin fans were thrown onto the field. The loons joyously laughed, even as they landed with a splat.

The ogres would be happy and Altdorf's Eyes had no hold on him. Sulk hoped he was in the clear, although he would need to avoid dwarfs for a while.

* * *

Sulk entered the refs' locker room. He was desperate to get out of the bloody kit, although at least it wasn't his blood for the most part. He walked to his locker.

'Pleased with yourself?' said the chamberlain. He emerged from the shadows just as he had done in the crypt, his long face stern, but the flaring of his nostrils revealed rage. 'I had high hopes for you, Gulden.' The chamberlain closed the locker door. 'I should have you killed right now, have my Eyes swoop in and slice your throat. But no, a more efficient message needs to be sent. I can't have my other informants betraying me, can I?'

'Do your worst!' said Sulk, managing to sound far braver than he actually felt.

'You don't want my worst, Gulden. Believe me, my worst is reserved for enemies with far more potency than a petty thug and thief! No, I'll let the Kobassi Brothers deal with you.'

'You have no evidence – it got chewed up with Hinter.'

'I admired your little deception back there on the field, but you are so, so naive. How hard do you think it would be for me to manufacture more evidence? Or, maybe I shall just take Janet. The Marauders are still looking for their mascot.'

'You'll stay away from her,' whispered Sulk. 'If you want my services.'

'Why do I need a low-level thug?'

'I'm no longer low-level. I'm now the Kobassi Brothers' most trusted man,' stated Sulk. 'Their wager is won, and they're now more powerful than ever because of me! I'll be even closer than before.'

The chamberlain thought about this, and did not disagree.

'And if you want my cooperation, if you want to know what I know, then you'll leave me and my charges alone.'

'Or I could have my agents steal the goat and make you work for me anyway?' said the chamberlain.

'As you said, wretched men are easy to control. I am not wretched – not anymore, at any rate. If you want the intelligence, I think it's best you throw away the stick and keep an eye on my carrots to make sure nobody else ever eats them!' Sulk gave a threatening look. The chamberlain considered things for a moment then walked backwards, towards the door, withdrawing back into the shadows.

'I look forward to working with you,' he hissed, before silently leaving the room.

Sulk slumped on the bench by his locker. He was physically and mentally exhausted and so unprepared for his next visitors.

The Kobassis entered mere minutes after the chamberlain's silent departure. They looked to be in a good spirits.

'Dat was a close one, Sulk,' said one. 'I like wot yoo did wiv dat deathroller. Could 'ave gone wrong though. We'd be 'avin' a very different discussion if it had.'

'Speakin' of which,' said the other Kobassi, 'how did it go wiv da chamberlain?'

Sulk was instantly afraid. He glanced around for an escape route, but the ogres were blocking him. He decided on bravado instead.

'It went well, he's keen for me to remain in your employ…' he chanced.

'Good, dat's good,' said the first Kobassi. 'We've always valued yer relationship with da Eyes.'

Sulk wiped sweat from his head with a shaking hand. Thank Nuffle the toilets were close.

The Kobassis picked up on Sulk's confusion. 'How else do you think we feed the chamberlain false information?

It keeps hiz cronies away from our real operationz,' one of them explained.

'We hate grasserz,' said the other. 'Unless it suits our purposes.' With that, the closest Kobassi clapped Sulk a friendly slap on the back. It was the hardest he'd been hit all day. 'Get yerself cleaned up. We'll see yer tomorrow.' The ogres left.

Sulk washed and changed and walked out the stadium, not caring if he ever set foot on a Blood Bowl field again. He had a suspicion he might have to, but that was a worry for another day. For now he could focus on his true passion. He wasn't sure what he was going to call it – he toyed with the Reikland Society for the Protection of Clobbered Animals, but he thought that would need shortening somehow. Still, he knew what he had to do next; the Gouged Eye had already threatened to kill the Dwarf Giants' team mascot. Sulk had to get there first – he had to save a terrier called Rolf!

HOPPO'S PIES

GUY HALEY

The glory days of the Grotty Stealers were far behind. Coach Diglit swung his legs despondently on the subs bench as the shower of snottle piddle the club's owner liked to call 'players' tried their best to get every rule of the game wrong.

There are not a great many rules in Bloodbowl, so they were very close to achieving their goal.

The Stealers were practising their chuck play – very, very badly. Captain Snirbad 'The Cobbler' Greenguts was bossing the team about, making things worse. Diglit's catchers Gufberk and Fugwit invariably ran the wrong way as soon as snotling Ned was tossed down the field, if Ned even left the giant, scaly claws of Ozbog the troll. They were on Ned Five, or maybe Ned Six, that day. Diglit counted better than most goblins, but it had been a struggle getting over five since the accident. Within the iron sleeve of his prosthetic claw, the stump of his left arm twinged at the memory. The worst time to fumble a catch was when the ball had been replaced with a juvenile cave squig.

Mork and Gork, his head hurt. It could have been the fungus brew he drowned his sorrows in or the high level of job stress, but it was probably both. He had loved being a player and hated his career change. The coach's cap weighed on his head like a stone troll's bottom.

'Nah! Over there, stupid!' shouted Snirbad.

The squealing of a lineman cut through his brain. The team's sole orc, Nork the Dork, was laughing like a drain. Diglit shuddered and hunkered down, his long ears drooping sorrowfully.

The play was too painful to watch. His eyes were drawn to the balding pitch, then to the bench he sat upon. The paint was flaking off; the wood beneath was grey and rotten. The stadium was in a sorry state. The west stand had burned down five years ago, and was now a pile of weed-choked, fire-blackened timbers. The east stand had more holes in its roof than tiles and every rail of the spiked iron fence he'd put in to keep the opposing fans apart was bent. The turnstiles were crooked, the ticket booth boarded up for want of money to buy new glass after the last riot.

It had not always been like this. Diglit remembered the stadium when it was packed with goblins of all types, stamping and singing as he, Diglit, caught the ball and raced away towards another touchdown. The ghostly wailing of squig pipes echoed from some far away place. The remembered roar of the crowd was a torment. All that had been before he had lost his arm. The crowds these days were thin.

Diglit blinked. Movement caught his attention at the corner of the field. Not the furtive movement of goblins, but the confident swagger of... a dwarf?!

Diglit's gripped the bench. Splinters dug into his remaining hand. The pincer of his claw crunched through the wood.

'Oi!' he shouted, shooting upright. 'Oi!'

He marched across the patchy turf, kicking an errant squig out of the way in anger.

'What you doing here, stunty?' he shouted.

The dwarf was wearing a riveted construction helmet polished to a high shine, and a fine set of armour. A human came out of the ruins of the west stand as Diglit approached. He slowed, his natural goblin cowardice triumphing over his indignation. Hope tacked itself onto this quick emotional switch. The duo were builders of some sort, that much was clear from their clipboards, helms and interesting collections of coloured quills tucked into their top pockets. For the tiniest sliver of a second, Diglit thought that maybe, just maybe, Boss Grobblehod had sent them to rebuild the west stand.

Of course, life didn't work out like that. Especially Diglit's life.

'Ah, er, well well!' said the man, who sweated nervously in the goblin's direction. 'Coach Doglet is it?'

'Diglit,' said Diglit, grinding his pointy teeth together. The man was twice his weight, but seemed worried about something.

'Quite,' the man checked his clipboard. His face did the little, complex dance of a man engaged in an internal monologue he is unwilling to share. The dwarf glared at Diglit without blinking. Eventually, the human looked up. 'Weren't you informed?' he said sheepishly.

'Of what?' said Diglit. He folded his arms over his grubby Stealers jersey. His prosthetic claw dug into his armpit.

'Of the survey,' said the man. 'We're here to look the stadium over. Boss Grobblehod is selling it off, didn't you hear?'

'What?'

'No wins, no team,' said the dwarf. He smiled, displaying

two rows of gold teeth. His voice was so deep it hurt the goblin's ears. 'Boss Grobblehod isn't pleased with you, little greeny. Prime land, this. Make an excellent place for real estate. Actually,' said the dwarf with an expression of mock realisation, 'he might have bought your hopeless band only to get his hands on your stadium. Can you imagine that?'

'What?' said Diglit.

'Not for goblins. No,' said the dwarf, answering a question Diglit hadn't asked. His smile grew, making his black beard bristle. 'Filthy things. All this is going to be tree house condominiums for elves.' He whipped out a leaflet from his back pocket. *Leafy Heights,* it read. *Arboreal Life for the Discerning Fey.* 'They don't smell. And they pay their bills.'

'Mr Hoffsonsson,' admonished the man. 'There is no need to be so… racist.'

Hoffsonsson mumbled something under his breath, his psychotic smile still plastered over his face.

'What?' said Diglit again, but it came out as a pathetic squeak this time.

'It's all here, I'm afraid,' said the human, holding out his clipboard. A sheet of paper dense with words was thrust into Diglit's face. He had time to read precisely none of it before it was snatched away. 'If that's not good enough for you, you can speak with the boss himself…?'

The man let his question hang. Diglit had no wish to see Boss Grobblehod.

He looked from the feigned sympathy of the human to the undisguised hatred of the dwarf. His temper snapped.

'I remember this place when it was full of goblins, cheering us all the way to the touchline,' he said. 'We's just in a rough patch, is all. I'll make the Stealers great again, you'll see! We's got a match tomorrow, and we is gonna win!'

A horrible scream echoed around the dilapidated stadium. It didn't seem physically possible, but Mr Hoffsonsson's grin got even bigger as he stared past Diglit at the players.

'Good luck with that, greeny.'

Diglit spun around. Goblins were running in every direction. Ozbog the troll was scratching his behind with one hand. In the other, he held half of Ned. His eyes stared off into that distant realm only the truly moronic can see. His jaw worked round and round on a tricky piece of grub. Ned's head, for sure.

'No no no no no no no no!' said Diglit. 'You two, wait here!' Then he took off, sprinting back through careening greenskins to the centre of the pitch.

Only Snirbad and Nork the Dork were still in place. Snirbad was kicking a linesman in the head; Nork the Dork was bent double, laughing at the violence so hard his drool spattered the field.

The snotling's skull cracked noisily in Ozbog's mouth.

'No! No! Bad Ozbog, bad!' shrieked Diglit, waving his hands up at the troll. 'You's not supposed to *eat* 'em, you's supposed to *throw* 'em!'

Ozbog's eyes slid around to look at the coach, then at the tattered remains of the snotling. He sighed deeply, and with a nonchalant heave pitched the remains of the dead snotling all the way down the field. It hit the rotten pitch siding with a wet bang.

Diglit snatched his cap off and jumped up and down on the spot. 'Not now! While he's still alive! With the ball!'

Nork hooted all the louder.

'Don't know why you's laughing, orc boy,' snarled Diglit. 'You's so stupid you can't tell your feet from your hands.'

Nork's craggy forehead wrinkled. 'I does,' he said slowly.

He held up his hand. 'This is my, um, and this is...' He stopped, confounded. 'Er.'

Diglit blew his whistle. The shrill noise stopped the fleeing greenskins in their tracks. 'Everyone back here!' he shouted. 'You!' he stabbed his claw at Ozbog. 'Stay here!'

Ozbog belched.

'Nork, stop laughing. Snirbad, stop kicking Buksnag in the head.' Diglit tugged his dirty trousers up. 'You's pathetic. You's rubbish. I'm getting another snotling, and then we's going to do this properly, right?'

Diglit stomped off towards the facilities under the east stand.

'The Cobbler,' he muttered to himself. 'Be all right if we called him that for some Mork brilliant game reason, like, like if he nailed people's feet to the ground. Stupid. It's only his day job, innit? Zogging Snirbad.'

It was true. The Stealers couldn't afford full-time pro players any more. His captain was a shoemaker. The rest of them Diglit had drugged, kidnapped, blackmailed or told outrageous lies to in order to get them in the squad. Of the sixteen potential players he could choose from – not counting the snotties of course, there were always hundreds of them – Ozbog and Nork alone were pros, and they were both rubbish.

He ambled through the tunnel towards the changing rooms, feet splashing through an inch of dirty water. Rippling, reflected light shone on the ceiling. A strong smell tickled his nostrils, a sort of nauseating combination of ancient, unwashed gym socks, mushrooms and snotling droppings. It only got stronger the closer he got to the changing rooms. Not that they used them to actually change in any more, not since the snotlings had escaped from their cages and overrun the place.

He reached the door. The water was up to his ankles.

Taking a deep breath he instantly regretted, Diglit lifted up the rusty weight they kept by the door to keep the snotlings in and pushed his way into the dark, dank room.

A dark, noisome space greeted him. Water ran from the broken shower pipes, staining the tiles yellow. The players' lockers had been pushed over. Heaped on everything were rancid piles of snot mess. From this soft and treacherous landscape, tall mushrooms reached upwards, glowing greenly. Diglit had a nice sideline in selling those. Maybe he'd throw in the towel and become a mushroom farmer. That would be lovely.

'Here, snotties!' he called. His voice echoed from vaulted stone and water. 'Got something for you!' He fished about in his pocket and drew out a bar of Lustrian Delight he'd sat on. 'Here, snotty snotty snotty!' he called. Keeping his guard up – snotlings could be vicious – he peeled the wrapper from the bar. Melted xokolat oozed onto his fingers.

'Snotties! Snack time!'

There was no reply.

'That's strange.' Frowning, he hunted about under overturned footlockers for the snotlings. Normally the place was alive with irritating tittering and the patter of snotty feet. It was suspiciously silent.

'Snotties? Come out! I's got a lovely bit of Lustrian Delight for you!'

Still no reply. Diglit went deeper into the room. Still no snotlings. He stopped and scratched his head.

'The only time they all hide is when they is scared,' he said quietly. 'And that means...'

A dark and rumbling voice cut through the gloom. 'Hello, Diglit,' it said.

Diglit whirled about. Looming over him was the coal-eyed silhouette of an orc. A soft splashing announced the arrival of a second. Both were huge, and dressed in identical suits.

'Gitthrog, Throggit!' he yelped. 'This is a nice surprise.'

'No it ain't,' said the first. Gitthrog, Diglit thought. The two were harder to tell apart than Gork and Mork.

'And it's *Mister* Throggit to you, runt,' said the other.

'You've let this place go, runt,' said Gitthrog, lifting up a foot. 'You've wrecked me boots with all this poop.'

'Mine too!' said Throggit, seeming affronted Gitthrog hadn't included his boots in the complaint. 'And I ain't happy about that.'

Diglit managed to open his mouth to speak. He got as far as 'Gk!' before a giant green fist the size of a meteor put him into an unwelcome sleep.

A strange rocking soothed Diglit. It almost made the horrible pain in his head bearable.

'Diglit,' said a voice.

'Go away,' he muttered. 'Sleepy.'

Something hard drove into his ribs. Diglit's lungs deflated like a burst squig, and he came awake.

Diglit was lying bound on the thick purple rug of a carriage. Hooves rattled off cobbles. Wheels clattered. Every few seconds, the carriage bounced painfully. Tight bonds dug into his wrist and ankles, looped about his iron claw and drawn in cruelly so they pressed into his back.

Three unkind faces stared down at him: Throggit, Gitthrog, and their employer, Wicked Boris.

Boris was an odd name for a dark elf. Diglit had always thought so. He had no idea why he was called Boris. The reasons for the 'Wicked' appended to the front, however, were widely known. There were lots and lots of reasons, but most involved sharp objects, long, final nights in this life and considerable amounts of pain.

Diglit's guts turned to water as Boris pulled off his velvet gloves one finger at a time and took out a leather case from inside his fur jacket. From this he retrieved a folded device of metal and glass, which he began to carefully unfold.

Diglit's eyes goggled in fear.

'I ain't got the money!' he shrieked. 'Don't hurt me!'

The orc twins guffawed. Wicked Boris held up one wicked hand.

'Silence!' Wicked Boris said. He stared coldly – Diglit might even had said wickedly – from under his shock of bone-white hair. The orcs, though each was four times the elf's weight, muttered their apologies and looked at their feet.

The elf finished his unfolding. In his hands were a pair of rose-tinted spectacles, which he placed on his delicate nose. Diglit whimpered with relief.

'You. You told me that you would pay me by last Backer-stag. What day is it now, Diglit?'

'Er…'

'It is now Wellentag.'

'I'll get the money!' said Diglit.

'I've given you an extra five days, Diglit. You didn't come to me and tell me you were going to be late. You haven't said thank you that I have not yet peeled your head like a little green grape for being late. You thought I'd forgotten, didn't you, Diglit?'

'No!' protested Diglit.

He *had* hoped the elf had forgotten.

Wicked Boris stared out of the window. 'I suppose you should be commended for your loyalty to that pathetic team of yours. Only a fool bets on an obvious band of losers – only a real fool would borrow the money from someone like me to do so.' He smiled distantly. 'You are at least a loyal fool.'

'It was a sure thing! I was robbed.' What he meant was, the drugs he had put into the Averheim Eagles' mid-match beer had been fake and had done nothing to help win the game.

'You said that the last five times,' Boris said. 'I don't care for loyalty. I like money. I want my money. You have a match coming up. You better win the money – my money – back. Next time I see you, either give me the money, or–' he made scissors of his fingers and worked them quickly. 'Snip snip snip! Grape time.'

'Thanks, thank you, er, sir. Yes. Thanks!' said Diglit.

'Do not thank me. Gentlemen, show Diglit we mean business.'

Throggit and Gitthrog looked at each other.

'Oh, for the love of Khaine! Hit him!' said Boris, tossing his hand up in frustration. The scent of lavender accompanied the gesture.

'Nice,' said Diglit appreciatively. It was better than the stink of snotling droppings coming off the orcs' feet, anyway.

The orcs hit him. Plenty of times. The carriage rocked madly as they meted out clumsy orcish violence to his person.

'Enough!' said Wicked Boris.

'Thanks,' said Diglit weakly. He spat out a tooth.

'Toss him out!' said Boris.

'Oh no,' said Diglit.

The door creaked open, and he was lofted through the air.

Diglit had spent his early years as a player being hurled the length of the field by careless ogres. He had learnt how to land properly. Even tied hand and foot he managed to put enough roll into his impact to prevent his neck breaking. But without his arms free, he could not stop the bone-rattling bouncing across the cobbles, or the skin-abrading slide, or the terrible crash into the refuse cans that finally halted him.

'Owwwwww,' groaned Diglit. Rubbish fell onto his head with a soft, stinking thump.

Wicked Boris' carriage thundered away into the night.

The rope had been loosened by his skid across the cobbles. With some difficulty, he got his arm into a position where a sharp twist of his iron claw could snap it. His arms freed, he snipped through the bonds round his feet. Groaning profusely, the little goblin struggled upright.

He had come to rest by a boarded-up factory. Clusters of dirty tenements lined a cobbled road. Washing hung limply between them. Although the highway was broad, the district had seen better days. The wood covering the factory windows was pasted over with dozens of last season's Cabalvision posters, washed white by the rain.

He had no idea where he was. There was no one about. He couldn't even tell what manner of creatures lived in the buildings. Lights burned in only a few of the windows.

Joints popping, Diglit hobbled off the road, past the rubbish. Wincing, he came to a filthy, buckled pavement running alongside the factory, and rested his head against the wall until the pins and needles in his extremities subsided, then set off home.

Now, it is said that certain kinds of goblin have an uncommonly good sense of direction. This is propounded by that kindly, though terribly misguided, school of thought that assumes everyone has to be good at something. Although there are sorts of goblin that can find their way out of a deep cave system or through the thickets of a spider-haunted forest, Diglit wasn't one of them.

Within a minute, give or take, Diglit was hopelessly lost.

* * *

He stumbled on through the night, becoming colder and more miserable with every step. The few gas lamps that hadn't been smashed hissed sinisterly. Luminous things flew overhead through the thin mist, making him dive for cover.

It was while hiding from one of these spectres that the most delicious smell hit his sensitive nose. His nostrils twitched. His stomach grumbled. Before he knew it, he was limping towards the source. A dark alleyway opened between two dirty buildings. Squinting, he saw a small caravan lit by a single small lantern. A fat pony wearing a nosebag was yoked to the front. The caravan was brightly coloured, the red-trimmed blue panels decorated with pictures of pies.

'A pie wagon!' Diglit whispered. Seeing such a gaudily painted vehicle in a run down neighbourhood should have set off all Diglit's well-tuned survival instincts, but his stomach was entirely in charge. His nose prickled. His mouth flooded with saliva. He crept nearer.

Someone in the caravan was whistling loudly. Smoke fragrant with glorious pie scent poured from a crooked stovepipe poking out of the curved roof. The caravan rocked, and a door clicked shut on the far side. The baker was talking softly to the pony. Diglit crept around the caravan, his good left hand lightly trailing along the glossy paint. Reaching the end, he popped his head around, coming face to face with a fat halfling.

'Good morning, my friend!' said the halfling.

Diglit jumped out of his skin. 'Aiee!' he shrieked, and fell over.

The pony snorted. 'Shh, shhh, Dennis,' said the halfling. He walked around to where Diglit lay sprawled on the floor.

'Well, well, and what happened to you?'

'What? Me face, it's always been like that. I'm not a halfling.'

'I didn't mean to say you were!' said the baker cheerily. 'It is plain as fried eggs that you're a goblin. I meant you are all beat up.' The baker held out a pudgy, floury hand. Diglit looked at it.

'Ain't you afraid of me?'

'Should I be?' said the halfling. 'Always give people the benefit of the doubt, is what my old man said.'

'Oh? Do him any good?'

'Nope, he was eaten by the ogres he was cooking for when he forgot to order enough bacon, but it's a good principle.' The halfling held his hand out further.

Diglit hesitantly took it. The halfling hauled him to his feet.

'You look to be in need of a pie,' said the halfling. 'The name's Hoppo Longfoot, and this is my Pies O'Mystery van.'

He rapped on the caravan with fat knuckles.

'I smelled 'em,' said Diglit. 'Thought I'd come and buy one.'

'And not steal?' chuckled the halfling.

'Nah!' said Diglit, though he would have stolen one if he could. 'I got money.'

'Well, you're in luck – I have just finished baking today's pies this very minute. I sell them at matches, you know. Everyone loves the pie van.' He looked the goblin up and down. 'Are you in the game?'

'Coach,' said Diglit. 'Grotty Stealers. You won't have heard of 'em. They's rubbish.'

'Oh, but I have heard of them!' said Hoppo. 'Go Stealers!' He made a half-hearted attempt at the supporter's jig. 'Yes? If you're all the way down here, you must have had a bad night.'

'Bad life, more like.' Diglit clacked the nippers on his claw together disconsolately. 'Squig ball. From best greenskin catcher three years running to worst coach in one bite.'

'Ah, a terrible tale.' Hoppo made a moue of sympathy. 'A pie will cheer you up. Come on!'

Hoppo patted Dennis on the way past, and went back into his van. A second later, the serving flap opened up. Hanging from chains, it made a broad counter. Warm yellow light spilled into the alley and with it a flood of mouth-watering aromas. Hoppo looked down from on high benignly.

'What can I get you, sir?'

Diglit's wide eyes took in the illustrations of delicious pies covering a board over the rows of warming boxes behind Hoppo. A surprisingly large oven took up the front of the cart. There wasn't much room for the halfling in there. What was within the pie van was mostly pies.

'What's the most bestest, special-est pie you got?' whispered Diglit. His pains were forgotten. He wanted a pie more than anything else in the world.

Hoppo smiled broadly and counted off his wares on his chubby fingers. 'Well, I have squig and bacon, and chicken, beef, goat, vegetables too, for the elves. You know how they are.'

Diglit didn't like the idea of vegetables. 'More special than that! What's that one I can smell?'

Hoppo frowned. 'Oh, that's the last sort of pie I cook at night. The oven needs cleaning after, you see. With sanctified scouring powder,' he confided.

'Want that one. Smells yummy.'

'It does, it is true, but it's not a good idea.'

'Want it!' whined Diglit.

Hoppo sighed. 'I don't know…'

'Please!' said Diglit, and for the first time in his life really meant it. 'I's never smelled anything so delicious ever in my whole life.'

'Well, well.' Hoppo looked pained. 'Oh, all right then. I don't suppose one could hurt...' He picked up a pair of flowery oven gloves and then, after a thought, laid them aside in favour of a pair shot through with metal thread. 'Lead. Only way to be sure,' he said with a wink. He opened the oven. There were eight racks, each with eight pies upon it.

Diglit couldn't see why Hoppo had made such a fuss. They didn't look dangerous; they were golden-crusted, yummy smelling, lovely pies, but still just pies for all that. 'These are ready for the warming boxes. You're lucky to have it right out of the oven.'

'Yeah, yeah! One of those!' said Diglit jumping up and down. 'How much?'

'Fifty pfennigs.'

'How much?' squeaked Diglit. 'I could buy ten mushroom patties from Burgher Kings for that!'

Very carefully, Hoppo set the pie on the counter. 'There are certain... ingredients in this here pie that cost a great deal. But I promise you will never taste its like again. And I mean it,' he chortled awkwardly. 'It's not safe to have more than one.'

'Gimme!' said Diglit. He took out his purse and upended it. Forty pfennigs, three buttons, a centipede and a startled pocket squig fell onto the counter.

'Got forty,' said Diglit. He made his eyes as big as he could. 'I'm only ten short.'

'I'll let you off – you look like you need it.' With evident pride, Hoppo wrapped the pie in a little napkin embroidered with the legend 'Hoppo's Pies O'Mystery'.

Diglit ripped off the napkin. Trembling in anticipation, he raised the pie to his mouth and took a good long sniff. Delicious steam tickled his nose. He took one tentative bite.

The flavour was indescribable, like the tastiest squig pasty he had ever had, but with extra savour, and a whole bucket of added zing. It tingled in his mouth, and fizzled all the way down to his belly.

The effect didn't stop there. Little bursts of pleasure wriggled all the way to the ends of his fingers and down to the tips of his toes. His stump, which was always sore, was soothed. His headache lessened. Energy filled his every fibre. His eyesight became keener, his hearing sharper. He felt the need to run and shout. He felt *strong*.

'Wow,' he said with his mouth full. 'Wow!'

'Good, eh?' said Hoppo, beaming with pride.

Diglit opened his mouth as wide as he could and stuffed more of the pie into his face. He wolfed it down. The sensation of wellbeing increased. He reached his hands to his mouth only to find them empty. Disappointed, he let them drop to his side. Hoppo pushed the buttons, pocket squig and centipede back towards Diglit.

'A pleasure doing business with you,' he said.

'Want another,' Diglit said. 'Now.'

'Apologies, my friend,' said Hoppo. 'Sorry. One is quite enough.'

His voice grew quieter at the look on Diglit's face.

'More!'

'You haven't got enough money,' said Hoppo.

Diglit leapt onto the counter, making the caravan rock, and launched himself at the halfling. There followed a brief tussle, in which Hoppo found himself overpowered and tied up with his own apron strings, with a bunch of his own embroidered napkins shoved into his mouth.

'Mmmph!' he said, struggling.

Diglit wasn't listening. He held up his hand and flexed

his fingers before his wondering face. 'That was too easy. That pie's done something to me.' He looked at the halfling. 'What's in it?'

'Mmmphthone!' said Hoppo.

'What?'

'Mmmphthone!' said Hoppo urgently.

'Not a clue what you is saying. Never mind,' said Diglit. A cunning look passed over his face. 'I's got an idea.' He went to the oven. 'But first, one for the road.'

He gobbled another pie before stealing the caravan: pies, pony, halfling and all.

Diglit held the pre-match briefing in a dirty tent. It was cramped, and smelt like a small space crammed with goblins, which is to say, very bad indeed. So bad, it masked the smell of the delicious tray of pies hidden under a cloth in the corner.

Diglit buzzed with energy. His entire being tingled. There was a pleasant, strange feeling in his stump. He hadn't felt this good in years.

He was speaking fast. He had to; he had a difficult match to sell.

'They only has sixteen players to choose from, same as us,' he soothed. 'It'll be fine.'

'Sixteen minotaurs, you git!' shouted Snirbad. 'Sixteen ten-foot-high, bull-headed, muscle-bound cowmen! Against us!' He held out his hand towards the rest of the team, smacking Gufberk in the face by accident. Ozbog waved cheerily through the tent flap. Everyone else looked terrified. Even Nork was unusually subdued.

'Nork not happy,' said Nork. He was still looking from his hands to his feet in bewilderment.

'Why didn't you tell us we'd be facing the Bovine Brawlers?' said Snirbad. 'We'll be massacred! I'm a zogging cobbler for Gork's sake, not a black orc!'

Fine time you took to come to that realisation, thought Diglit. Snirbad wasn't particularly bright, but even he had begun to get suspicious when the stadium had filled with drunken beastmen. Now the stands heaved with goat-faced fans, and the rickety grounds echoed to a tuneless rendition of that traditional beastfolk classic 'Baa-baa-ba-ram'.

'Look, lads, I know things look hopeless, but I's got something that will pep you all right up.'

With a flourish, he whipped off the cloth from the pie tray.

'Oooh, pies!' said Nork.

'We're going to be stamped flat, and you offer us a snack?' said Snirbad.

'Not a snack,' said Diglit.

'A meal?' said Fugwit.

'That's not a meal,' said Zogbod. 'A meal needs some chips.'

'Neither snack nor meal!' declaimed Diglit. 'Better than that. They's pies, they's delicious.' He leaned forward to whisper. 'And they's magic!'

'Magic pies?' said Gufberk in awe.

'They'll make you run faster, think better, fight harder and throw further. These pies,' said Diglit, 'will make you *win*!'

And I'll be able to pay off Boris, and Grobblehod will think twice before selling off the stadium, he added to himself.

'Magic pies!' said Gufberk.

As one, the team surged forward. Diglit shoved them all back. They stared at him in amazement.

'You're stronger! Have you had one?' asked Snirbad suspiciously.

'I's had two!' said Diglit, holding up the requisite number of digits.

This time, Diglit was floored as the entire team rushed at the pies, grasping hands out to grab them.

Diglit crawled out from under the tent skirts as a brawl broke out inside. That was fine by him, just as long as everyone got a pie. The tent fell down, its fabric writhing with goblin shapes as they fought. Soon enough, the sounds of bickering subsided into eager chomping and coos of delight.

Ten minutes later, Diglit was on the field surrounded by goblins with gleaming eyes. They looked upon their minotaur foes without a shred of fear.

'This is better than fungus brew!' said Snirbad.

'I feel brilliant,' said Gufberk, dancing from foot to foot. 'I could run for miles!'

'I had six,' said Fugwit.

'Well I had ten,' said Snirbad smugly.

'I didn't get none,' said someone sadly. Nobody cared.

'See?' said Diglit. 'But don't go getting crazy – this has to be a running, catching game. You's all magicked up, but, well, they is still minotaurs and we is still goblins. Don't try fighting. Run. Dodge. Catch! Just like we practised.' He thought a moment. 'Well, not just like we practised – *better* than we practised.'

'Yeah!' said his team. Even Ozbog was paying attention.

The ref, a tired looking Tilean with a red nose, blew his whistle to signal the start of the match.

The minotaurs' huddle broke apart, revealing the diminutive figure of their ungor coach. Diglit stuck his tongue out at him. The ungor responded with a two-fingered salute.

As his team went to the centreline for the coin-toss, Diglit drew out his last pie from inside his jacket and munched thoughtfully on it. His stump tingled as he ate. His claw felt oddly uncomfortable, and he had to pull it out from his sleeve a good inch before it started to feel comfortable again.

The coin was tossed. The Stealers got to pick, and wisely chose to receive. Diglit went to his bench to watch. With the peep of a whistle, the match began.

The minotaurs' star player booted the ball hard enough to flatten a giant, but Diglit's team were operating far beyond normal capacity. Gufberk smoothly caught the ball. Without looking to see where it was going, he lofted it backwards to Ozbog. And, amazement beyond amazement, Ozbog caught it!

Minotaurs came thundering down the pitch, mooing loudly, heads down, in a bid to simply trample the goblins dead. The Stealers could not be caught: they capered, switching direction rapidly, leading the minotaurs on a merry dance. The goblins in the stand laughed. The beastmen bleated angrily. The ungor coach was jumping up and down like a goat on a mountain, shouting to his players, but they paid no heed. They were so intent on flattening the maddening gobbos that they didn't notice Ozbog fish out a snotling from a bag and press the ball into its scrawny arms. With poise Diglit thought impossible, Ozbog drew back his arm and hurled the snotling down the length of the pitch.

A tear came to Diglit's eye. It was beautiful. Ozbog's throw arced perfectly. The snotling and ball bounced across the bald turf. The little greenskin got to its feet, shook out its ears and looked around. The entirety of the Bovine Brawlers were charging around the greenskin half of the pitch, the goblins leading them on like so many Estalian matadors.

'Go on! Go on!' bawled Diglit, spraying pie everywhere. 'Go on!'

With great effort, the snotling hefted the ball, tottered forward, and fell over the touchline.

Wheeeeeeep! went the ref's whistle. 'Touchdown!' he bellowed.

The crowd went wild. There were nowhere near as many goblins in the stadium as there used to be in the old days, but they made more than enough noise to make up for it. Squig pipes blared. For the first time in years, cheers rang in Diglit's ears. A minotaur had caught one of the goblin linemen and was pawing it angrily into the ground with its hooves, but that was a price worth paying.

Play was set up again. This time, the goblins kicked. The ball went hurtling towards the Bovine Brawlers blitzer, a massive, jet-black bull of a thing. He held out sure hands to receive the ball, but incredibly, it was snatched from the air by Gufberk at the apex of a twenty foot leap. He hit the ground running, a green blur whizzing down the outside field. The minotaurs were so surprised they could only swipe at the runner as he rushed past.

'Touchdown!' yelled the ref.

Diglit got up and did a little cackling dance. He stopped. He burped. He was feeling funny. He shook his head. His players were also behaving strangely. Gufberk was running a victory lap when, quite unexpectedly, his left leg fell off. His right foot ballooned in size; his remaining leg thickened. He shrieked in terror, but couldn't stop. His sprint became a bounding hop.

He wasn't the only one to suffer unscheduled mutation. Nork stood still, shivering, as long green hair sprouted from all over his body. Fugwit had split into two half-sized versions of himself, which were engaged in a violent argument with each other. Snirbad appeared to be melting into the grass, while Ozbog had grown a second head.

Diglit watched in horror as half of his players spontaneously mutated.

He looked at the pie in his hand. It wasn't going to happen to him, was it? He'd only had two and a half – well, two and three-quarters. That three-quarters couldn't matter, could it? Snirbad had eaten ten!

No such luck. The writhing feeling in Diglit's stump intensified. His claw dropped to the ground. Before his eyes, a pair of new-formed, taloned hands sprouted from underneath his jersey, worming their way towards the light on the growing stump of his arm. All a deeply violent pink.

'Aieee!' shrieked Diglit.

The minotaurs bellowed their anger. The ungor ran to and fro along the pitch boundary shouting, 'It's a fix! It's a fix!'

'Cheeeeeaaaaaatsssss!' bleated something in the beast-crowd. Outraged, the herd in the stand rushed forwards. The barriers gave way with a series of rotten cracks. The beast-men spilled onto the pitch and into the goblin section of the stand. Shouts and screams and snatches of merry song rent the air as the entire stadium exploded into violence. Within seconds everyone was fighting everyone else. Minotaurs battled the heaving monstrosities the Grotty Stealers had become. Beastmen fought goblins. Goblins fought each other.

'Nooo!' wailed Diglit. The tingling sensation moved to his head. He felt things bursting from his scalp. All of a sudden his view of the world changed as eyes opened on the newly sprouted thatch of stalks crowning him.

Behind him – the sensation of being able to look in every direction at once made Diglit nauseous – Hoppo the halfling was staggering through a gap in the fence of the grounds. He was aghast, wringing his fat hands together. 'I'm too late!' he wailed. Spying Diglit, he came trotting over, dodging piles of snotlings enthusiastically emulating their biggers and betters by punching each other in the face.

'What has you done to me!' shrieked Diglit.

'I told you to eat only one. There's warpstone pepper in that pie! I sell to everyone, you see, even the skaven!'

'What? Why hasn't it done this to you?' wailed Diglit.

'I'm a halfling, aren't I? Warpstone doesn't have much effect on us. But even I have to take precautions. It's dangerous stuff. I mean, what I do isn't exactly legal. Why do you think I was baking in an alleyway at three o'clock in the morning?'

'So why did you give me one?'

'Because you looked sad,' said Hoppo. 'And they are damned tasty.'

Diglit slumped. This was a disaster. Then, from the corner of his many new eyes, he saw the ball lying, ignored, in a tussock of grass at the edge of the pitch.

Maybe not a disaster. Maybe not at all. He stood taller. He could see *everything*. He flexed his new limb. Catching the ball wouldn't be a problem any more, because Diglit had gone from having one too few hands to one too many.

With a sudden whoop, Diglit ran for the ball. He'd never lost the knack of running. He was a goblin, after all. It paid to be able to run away. The bending of this instinct so that they ran towards things rather than away is the most remarkable thing about goblin players, but is sadly overlooked.

Diglit ignored Hoppo's shouts to return and scooped up the ball with his new pair of hands. As he legged it towards the Bovine Brawlers' end zone, his head filled with possibilities.

The touchdown he scored a moment later was the first realised, but Diglit was thinking bigger.

Chaos teams won the major leagues frequently, and they had plenty of mutants in their squads.

THE FREELANCER

ROBERT RATH

Mort D'Arthur wiped the blood off his knuckles and wished they'd come to a different pub.

Not that the others had been any better. This was the sixth sports tavern they'd been to. All of them were the same: tombs of fandom stuffed with dusty leather balls, tattered jerseys, a rack of amateur trophies and yellowing *Spike!* articles trumpeting years-old upsets.

In four out of those six taverns, he'd had to put a guy on the floor. All four of them red-faced drunk. All wearing Nuln Gunners jerseys. Each with a bone to pick about how a missed pass or the recent three-game suspension had cost them a wager.

This guy came at the talent with a bottle. Mort pushed his charge towards the VIP room and laid the drunk out with an efficient takedown. Kick to the knee, fist to the head. Nothing excessive or flashy, just the workmanlike beatdown of professional muscle.

Because whatever else he might be, Mort was a professional.

He didn't mind the shouts and jeers. Or even occasional bricks and bottles. He'd put in seven years as a league referee, a job that required him to keep composure while taking abuse from bigger, better men than these. But those days were over. Now, this was his career. The bastard work that kept the league running, that made sure the players showed up and fans were there to cheer them. Mort lived in the shadowy realm that lurked just beyond the edges of the Cabalvision camras, a place that would always value men who knew the rules of the game, and how to subvert them.

And everyone knew that if you needed to buy silence, rig a draft pick, or seal a contract negotiation by bouncing a player off a few lockers – Mort D'Arthur was your guy.

Back home, knights that fought for anyone were known as free lances. And that's what Mort was – a freelancer. A role tailor-made for a disgraced referee.

Drunk dispatched, he trudged up a narrow staircase to the VIP room.

'I could've taken him,' said Hoozier, rolling his shoulders back into the room's tiger-skin booth. His arms, bulging like the Worlds Edge Mountains, rested on the back of the feline upholstery. 'Guy like me doesn't need a bodyguard.'

'Game tomorrow, *Monsieur* Hoozier,' said Mort. 'We're not taking chances.'

The VIP room – called the MVP room in deference to the tavern's theme – was no larger than the pig pen on Mort's family farm back in Bretonnia. Dented breastplates crowded the walls, each painted with the face of a man who'd won Nuln's Most Violent Player award. And in the very centre, the paint still fresh on the steel, hung a portrait of Kaspar Hoozier.

Hoozier sat directly under it, of course.

'I'm humble,' said Hoozier with a shrug. 'Approachable-like. If a fan has a problem, I crump 'em myself.'

'If you break a finger on some drunk fan's skull, the Gunners won't make the playoffs, *n'est-ce pas*?' Mort retorted.

Hoozier flashed the square-jawed grin that radiated out from magazines, scandal rags and boxes of McMurty's Breakfast Oats. It was fake as a freak show mermaid.

'Fine, you're a *consultant*, that's what Cherbourg called you,' Hoozier purred. 'So go consult about getting me a drink. Then we'll hit the dance halls.'

'*Non*. We agreed no dance halls,' said Mort, tired of this conversation. 'No one sells that goblin junk at sports taverns.'

'It helps me throw better,' Hoozier growled. Then, hearing his own desperation, he leaned back as if it were no big deal. 'Slows things down, is all. Shows me the angles. How the squigskin is gonna fly.'

'It's dangerous, brewed in filthy caves, and they'll find it during pregame substance inspection.'

Hoozier rose, filling the small room with the threat of violence. 'What does a defrocked zebra know about what a player needs? Eh? They've got clean stuff now, good stuff wizards can't detec–'

'Drinks, drinks I can do,' said Mort. 'What do you want, Bloodweiser, or Blood Light?'

The question threw the player off balance, as Mort knew it would. Due to endorsements, Hoozier could only drink Bloodweiser products, so a drink order was a minefield. He finally waved.

'Whatever. Just have the girl bring it up. The one with purple hair.'

Mort slid down the narrow stairs before the player's mood

changed, leaving Hoozier to stew in the tiger-skin booth. He hoped he wouldn't have to fight again.

Because Mort wasn't a bodyguard.

Bodyguards were supposed to protect you from other people.

Mort, on the other hand, had been hired to protect Hoozier from himself.

OFFICE OF FETWIN CHERBOURG, GUNNERS FIELD
ONE WEEK BEFORE KICK-OFF

'Kid's costing us a fortune in insurance, Mort. He's a scandal machine.'

Mort took the good Bretonnian red Cherbourg offered, locked eyes, clinked glasses.

Most team owners were boring, fat burghers with a sports hobby. Cherbourg was none of those things. Smart. Suave. Fleets of giant squid had died to keep his hair that perfect shade of black. The Nuln Gunners were an investment he managed down to the smallest detail, and his office reflected that. He'd hijacked a private box at Gunners Field, its glass walls overlooking the pitch.

It felt good to be back in a stadium.

Below, the Gunners were clobbering a Lustrian team. Game day and Cherbourg was still working.

'You don't want to watch this?' asked Mort. On the field, Hoozier ran sideways to evade a saurus and drilled a pass, cannonball straight, between two skink defenders and right to a receiver. Lady, the man was good.

'It's a friendly,' Cherbourg said, waving in dismissal. 'Doesn't affect rankings. Point is, Hoozier's draining serious crowns with these three-game suspensions, Mort. It's not the old days. Wizards conduct pregame doping screenings now. If Hoozier gulps down a phial of Madcap mushroom, you can't just shove him under a cold shower and slap him until he stops hallucinating. League says if he tests dirty again, it's a lifetime ban. But the kid doesn't treat it seriously. He thinks he's too high-profile for the league to expel.'

The stadium roared. Touchdown Nuln.

On the Lustrian sideline their coach – a bulbous slann mage-priest sitting cross-legged on a floating platform – unleashed a torrent of sacred profanity. To calm him, a skink assistant tossed a fist-sized insect in the air. The coach, momentarily distracted, sniped it mid-flight with his whip-like tongue.

Mort turned back towards the desk. 'If Hoozier's a problem child, cut him.'

'I built our offence around that kid,' said Cherbourg. 'I've got twenty thousand jerseys with his number printed on them. If he gets clipped for Madcap, I might as well give them to the lizardmen down there, let them hand the things out to little skink orphans in Lustria. And next week's the semi-final.'

'So what do you need?'

Cherbourg came around the desk, faced him at the window square-on. 'I've been keeping him locked up at the training facility, but his contract gives him a day of leave before games. I want you to escort him. Let him party, but keep him out of the dance halls where cap-heads hang out. Hit clean places – maybe sports taverns, he likes attention – and deliver him on his feet, with a clear system and ready to play.'

'I'm not a talent handler, I don't do flattery.'

'I don't want you to flatter.' Cherbourg smiled. 'I want you to lay down the rules, keep him from going out of bounds. Blow the whistle every now and then. It's what you're good at, right? You used to be.'

That stung. Hurt so much Mort wanted to say no.

But two days earlier, the league's collection ogre, Grauf, had come knocking.

Grauf was the friendliest enforcer in the league. After dislocating Mort's shoulder, he kindly offered to pop it back in place. But that geniality didn't obscure the message. If Mort came up empty on his league fines again, Grauf would break both knees and a few fingers as interest.

So Mort swallowed his pride. 'How much?'

'I'll give you the team marker to cover expenses. Deliver him to the game uninjured with a clean system – and it's worth two thousand.'

Mort said yes.

'And Mort?' added Cherbourg. 'That scandal columnist Skellig Queem is sniffing around. Fair warning.'

Mort's jaw clenched. Of course, Cherbourg had held that back until after he'd agreed.

Down on the field, a skink doctor was using the slann's distended belly as a trampoline. The amphibian had fallen from his perch on the floating plinth. He gasped, pink tongue lolling out of his mouth like a ship's cable.

The fat frog had swallowed a sideline pass.

BOOT & BALL TAVERN, STADIUM DISTRICT
LESS THAN FOUR HOURS BEFORE KICK-OFF

Mort bellied up to the bar, plotting his next move.

Hoozier wasn't making this easy. Whined all night, even

tried to escape. But now Mort had him pinned in the back. He'd scouted this place out. The MVP was up a little staircase at the back, and Mort could sit at the end of the bar, blocking passage in and out. The tavern had a cellar door if they needed to run.

It was four in the morning. He might pull this off.

Provided he could get Hoozier to stay where he was until he tired out.

He caught sight of the server. Corkscrew purple hair cascaded from her scalp like the boughs of a weeping willow. Her black gown, cut short, was clearly tailored to encourage tips. Mort waved her over; she held up a finger.

Mort waited. Scanned the articles tacked behind the bar. As was traditional in sports taverns, the tavernkeeper had decided to leave them up until they fell apart.

Then he saw it.

BRETONNIAN GONE BAD

Blood Bowl's 'Cleanest Official' Runs Unprecedented Web of Corruption – A *Spike!* investigation by Skellig Queem

A year later, it still put a bad taste in his mouth, like the time he'd tried chewing tobacco-squig.

Skellig Queem.

The muckraker who'd got him thrown off the pitch. Queem, the reason Mort had the largest fine in league history hanging over his head. The rat bastard who'd ruined Mort's side venture by knocking on a few doors.

'Get you something, love?' said the server. Mort nodded.

'A Bloodweiser for the MVP.' He flashed the team marker, a palm-sized medallion stamped with the Gunners' cannon logo. It was a roving expense account, as good as cash anywhere in the city.

She leaned in, raised an eyebrow. 'Just came on shift. Is it true Kaspar Hoozier's upstairs?'

Mort spotted a Gunners shield tattooed on her left forearm. She was pretty, looked clever. And he needed Hoozier distracted.

'He asked you to deliver it personally.'

She gave a knowing, conspiratorial smile. Ordered two beers pulled from the tap. Went up carrying both by hand, no tray.

Thank the Lady. If those two went at each other like a couple of face-eater squigs, Hoozier wouldn't be so eager to hit the clubs. This might just work out.

As long as there were no surprises.

Someone bellied up to the bar next to him – or rather, chested up to the bar. At the hint of musk, Mort clenched the team marker so hard he nearly bent the medallion in half.

'Well, this will make a great lead,' the thing said. 'Mort D'Arthur, defrocked referee and dirty-work freelancer has a new job – babysitting. A filthy guardian angel, hired to watch over the league's scandal children and cap-fiends.' Out the corner of his eye, Mort saw the inhuman thing sketch a hammer in the air with two fingers, like a priest. 'Editor might trim it, seems a little purple.'

'Get out of here before I beat you to a paste.'

He only half believed it was really him. But yes, there he was. The rat-faced bastard himself, beady black eyes staring at him through rectangular, green-tinted glasses.

Spike!'s scandal columnist. A character assassin with enough victims to make Clan Eshin proud. The Plague Monk of Paparazzi and Seerlord of Sleaze.

Skellig Queem.

'Beat me to a paste?' Queem recoiled, claw to his chest,

miming shock. 'And make this a *real* scandal? You're too smart for that.'

'Maybe *oui*, maybe *non*,' Mort said. 'You ruined my life.'

Queem raised a finger. 'Actually, *you* ruined your life... I just documented it.'

There was something about Queem that made Mort's skin crawl. It wasn't that he was a skaven – he'd dealt with rat-men on the field. What was so disturbing about Queem was how normal he acted. He still talked fast as a ratling gun, sure, but he barely repeated words. He communicated with mimicked facial expressions rather than musk, and slicked his fur with pomade. He was somewhere halfway between human and rat, and that made him much creepier.

Plus, he was a tabloid journalist.

'Nothing to see,' said Mort. 'Just a broken-down zebra having a drink.'

'Oh my no, much, much more to see here.' Queem said it without looking at him. Instead, he flicked his finger over some kind of slate, cocked an eyebrow. 'Kaspar Hoozier, for one.'

'*Quoi*? What makes you think he's here?'

'A tip,' said Queem, waving the slate. It was some kind of magic mirror. Emerald runes danced across its face. 'Smart-squeaker. Next big thing. I have fifteen thousand acolytes on Skitter.'

'You shouldn't use that thing, it'll give you warp poisoning,' said Mort, deeply hoping Queem would get warp poisoning. 'Besides, why would a professional risk his career by going out the night before a major game?'

'Because he's thick.' Queem waved a dismissive claw, eyes on his mirror, flicking it with his thumb. 'The more interesting question is why *you're* here. Why's a broken-down zebra – your words – bodyguarding for Nuln's golden boy and paying his tab with a team marker?'

'I'm sure you have a theory.'

Mort had never made full eye contact with a skaven before. He didn't like it much. There was a flicker of green fire in those eyes that didn't come from the warpstone-tinted glasses.

'I think Cherbourg hired you to follow his cap-head player around and slap the mushroom juice out of his mouth. Been follow-stalking Hoozier for months. He's my next big kill. Rumour is he's going to test dirty tomorrow. Not just dirty, but Madcap dirty. But now I foresee a two-birds, one-stone hit piece. Fallen ref and junkie player. Compelling hook, right?' He poked Mort in the chest, felt something metal hanging under his shirt on a thread. 'Is that what I think–?'

Mort grabbed Queem behind the ear, slammed his face into the bar so fast the rat's mirror fell from nerveless fingers. Queem wriggled like a speared kraken.

People were looking. Mort's hand itched just touching the journalist's pomaded grey fur. He didn't care.

Queem, seeing no progress, went defensively limp.

'If you're so fixated on nailing Hoozier,' Mort said, 'why the hell are you talking to me?'

'I'm just giving it time to take hold-effect,' said Queem. He still managed to sound arrogant, even with his face in a puddle of ale.

'Giving *what* time?'

'The Madcap, you dolt. You're far too innocent for this job, Mortimer. Eyeball the signs. Black dress? Skull earring? Purple hair? Classic cap-head if ever I saw one.'

Mort's mouth worked noiselessly, trying to absorb the information.

Queem rolled his eyes. 'The server's a dealer, stupid. Why do you think Hoozier wanted her?'

Mort was already gone. On his feet, up the stairs. The door to the MVP was shut but that didn't stop him. He threw his shoulder into it just above the brass knob, busting the frame.

There were so many possibilities of what he might find in there. Hoozier dead, purple from overdose. Hoozier and the girl minus clothes. A hulking Blood Bowl player in the blind depths of cap-rage.

What he discovered was so unexpected, it stopped him cold.

Hoozier sat cross-legged on the tiger-skin couch, placid as a monk. The girl knelt in front of him, an arm's reach away, looking up at the player. Nothing violent, nothing bizarre.

That was good.

'Blorp. Blorp,' said Hoozier, flicking his tongue into the air first left, then right. 'What vassal approaches? Brought you a sacrifice?'

That was bad.

Mort's training kicked in. *Read the details, assess the situation, make the call.*

There was a black glass phial in Hoozier's hand. Rough and bulbous. Goblin-made.

'How much did he take?' asked Mort.

'He said he could handle it,' she whispered, fascinated. 'You should kneel. It upsets him if you don't kneel.'

Mort pressed money into the girl's hand while pulling her up and towards the door. Moving fast, talking faster. 'Say nothing. You brought him a drink, then left. If anyone offers money for an interview, come to me first and I'll pay more, *comprenez*?'

She paused as he tried to hustle her out, staring. 'What's *that*?'

'Your first offer,' waved Queem, leaning against the busted door frame.

'Out.' Mort shoved both onto the stairs and slammed the broken door.

'Blorp!' said Hoozier. 'I hunger, scaly minion! Pay homage or you will feel the numinous lash of my tongue.'

It clicked into place: the Lustrian mage-priest from last week. Lady protect us.

The important thing was to keep him calm. Madcap was, strictly speaking, made for goblins. In humans it caused hallucinations at low heart rates. But if Hoozier's adrenaline cranked, he'd go into cap-rage.

'My lord,' said Mort. He bent, a bow low enough to mollify any noble. As a Bretonnian, Mort had long experience avoiding beatings via deference. 'She displeased you, so I removed her.'

'She... she did?'

'Yes,' said Mort. He heard a squeak of hinges – Queem – and threw one foot back to pin the door shut. 'Yes, mage-lord, she betrayed the location of this temple. I have sent her for sacrifice.'

Sharp knuckles rapping the door. Mort forced his foot back.

'What kind of sacrifice?'

'Aaah. Ritualistic mangling?'

Hoozier nodded, flicked his tongue out at an invisible insect. 'Blorp! It is so.'

'But here's the thing, sacred one, there is a journalist outside.'

'A journalist?'

'Yes, and… to fool him, you must cloak yourself in illusion.' Mort wiggled his fingers. 'Disguise yourself as Kaspar Hoozier, star thrower for the Nuln Gunners.'

'That seems difficult. Blorp.'

'You'll find it quite natural.'

Queem's muffled voice. 'I'm not going away.'

'He's not going away,' repeated Mort.

'Very well.' Hoozier inhaled, as if sucking in the very breath of the cosmos. His feet came to the floor, his hands to his lap. He flashed the Hoozier smile. 'Let him enter.'

Mort opened the door a crack. A snout poked through, followed by a pair of rectangular glasses.

'Hello, Kaspar,' said Queem.

'Hello, sir,' said Hoozier. 'I am Capstar Whozeer. Human thrower of the Guln Nunners.'

'Right,' said Queem.

'My skin is pink and soft,' insisted Hoozier.

'Really?' said Queem.

'I am covered by downy hair, and my reproductive organs…'

'Interview over,' said Mort, stuffing Queem's head back into the gap, meeting resistance as he tried to close the door. 'Big game tomorrow, and Monsieur Hoozier–'

'Whozeer,' corrected Hoozier. 'Blorp, blorp.'

Mort twisted. 'Shut up, you spoi–'

Funny thing about rats – they can squeeze through the narrowest gaps.

Queem popped into the room like a champagne cork. 'How much did you take, Kaspar?' He reached into his robes. 'Was it Madcap or something more… exotic?'

Mort saw the warpstone camra emerge from Queem's sleeve. He grabbed the device, wrestled the lens upwards. A flashbulb crystal popped, illuminating the ceiling in a burst of green heat lightning.

'Magic!' screeched Hoozier.

'Give me the camra, you little skaven–'

'Skaven?! Skaven in the temple?' Hoozier surged to his feet, frame bulging. Corded muscles swelled like thunderheads barrelling towards land. Engorged veins ran purple, rivers swollen in a storm.

Full-on cap-rage. *Fantastique.*

Read the details, assess the situation, make the call.

Hoozier went for Queem, violence in his eyes. Mort had already failed, but he could at least prevent total disaster. After all, *Madcap Scandal Ends Nuln Cup Bid* was a much better headline than *Nuln Player Murders Rat-Bastard Writer, Tabloid Scum Mourn.*

So Mort put his body between a charging Blood Bowl player and the being he hated most in creation.

Then he punched Hoozier in the man's tree-trunk throat.

The thrower staggered backwards, coughing. He looked at Mort with big hurt eyes, like a kicked snotling.

'Well,' said Queem. He stepped back outside and shut the door.

Hoozier launched himself forward.

Mort was big, but he wasn't Blood Bowl big. In the league, teams wouldn't even sign a thrower who weighed less than two hundred and twenty pounds. You needed that kind of weight to keep all your bones in place when a black orc took you to the astrogranite.

But a good referee could read when trouble was coming, and get the hell out of the way. Refs who didn't know how to dodge got weeded out by attrition. And if they couldn't avoid getting hit, they had a little magic to help them out.

Hoozier swung high. Mort dived low, ducking under the right hook. Behind him, he heard a splintering crash and an alarmed squeak as the thrower punched through the flimsy door. Hoozier yanked at the shattered wood, stuck.

It gave Mort the moment he needed. He snatched the breastplate with Hoozier's face on it off the wall. Plunged a hand into his shirt and found the metal object swinging from his neck by a cord. Brought it clear and pressed it to his lips, tasting pure silver.

Hoozier screamed in rage, started forward.

Mort blew.

A whistle, clear and pure, pierced the air. Hoozier froze mid-step, one foot forward, fist wound back. Blinking.

Stun spell. It had saved more than a few zebras in a pinch.

Mort brought the breastplate down on Hoozier's forehead with both hands. It made a gong sound when it hit. The big man dropped like a disenchanted zombie.

Mort stood there, breath heaving, whistle still to his lips, picture frame smeared with Hoozier's blood.

Pop.

Warpstone flash bathed the room. Queem, standing in the door with his camra. Then the rat turned to go.

Mort could feel it all disappearing. His fee. His sideline as a fixer-enforcer. His poor kneecaps. What remained of his honour.

Mort's ancestors had been men-at-arms for centuries. As knights rode by in gilded armour, blessed by the Lady, the D'Arthurs held abominations at bay with nothing but a wooden shield, a hand-me-down helmet and a billhook. It was a noble life. A hard-working life. A life Mort had fled at the first hint of money and fame.

He was too smart to get disembowelled on behalf of some knight, he thought. If he was going to risk his life, he wanted to do it for big money in front of roaring crowds. But the past was the past. This foul job was all he had left. And though he was no man-at-arms, he was still a D'Arthur. A family that did foul, thankless work, and did it well.

Mort was a professional, and professionals don't quit when things go sideways.

He grabbed Queem's tail, yanked him back inside.

'Where do you think you're going?'

'To get the type set,' answered Queem, in manic glee. 'With luck-fortune, I can scoop Cabalvision.'

'And ruin your career?'

Queem adjusted his glasses and looked at Mort sidelong. No one could look sidelong *quite* like a skaven. 'Excuse-pardon, but this?' – he indicated the room – 'This is a masterpiece. Cap-head player. Seedy tavern. Disgraced zebra. Madcap overdose. Brawl. Stolen whistle. Things of this nature are why the Horned Rat invented the REALLY BIG headline font.'

'File this article, and you'll look foolish when Hoozier turns up to play tomorrow.'

Queem snickered. *'Turns up to play*? Even if you get him to the game alive, he'll never pass substance screening.'

'He will.'

'My dear friend-tool, the game's in four hours. I've never met someone so full of crap – and I was born in a sewer.'

'Stick around and keep his name out, and I'll show you how a player can pass inspection, even this far gone.' Mort knelt, put an ear to Hoozier's chest. 'Heart's still beating. It's enough to work with.'

One of Queem's notched ears twitched. He sniffed. 'Constables down the street. Girl must've talk-blabbed. We have two minutes, maybe.'

'Decision time,' said Mort. 'Keep Hoozier out of it and I'll show you how fixers like me get players cleaned out.'

'That'd be a gross violation of journalistic integrity,' said Queem. 'Throw in an interview with Cherbourg and it's a deal.'

'Done. Now help me get him up. There's a cellar exit.'

Mort and Queem hoisted the unconscious thrower to his feet, one on each side. Mort had to hunch to equalise their height.

'Are you certain-sure you can fix this?'

'Oh *oui*, *oui*.' Mort guided the stumbling trio down the stairs. At the bottom, they hung a left down to the cellar. 'We just need to get him to Doctor Cleanblood.'

'Doctor Cleanblood?' Queem whispered. The stamp of armoured boots hammered through the tavern floor above them. 'I love this article already.'

They hit the street. Nuln rose around them, glorious and grimy. Fog clung to gable roofs and street corners – locals tried to pass it off as romantic mist, but it was coal smoke from the armoury forges.

'Ugh,' said Mort. 'It's bad tonight. I can taste it.'

Queem breathed deep, smacked his tongue against his palate. 'Woody, with a chalky coal body and a splash of molten iron. Smooth dung finish. Add in some warpstone, and it's almost Skavenblight.'

'Were you really born in a sewer?' asked Mort.

'With eighty brothers and sisters.'

'Big family.'

'Not really.' He grinned. 'I ate them!'

Mort tried not to think about that. 'So, hypothetically, if someone was carrying a half-conscious celebrity and wanted to avoid the city watch...'

'I'll find a grate.'

WESTEN DISTRICT

TWO HOURS BEFORE KICK-OFF

Eighty stinking, disturbingly sticky minutes later they were in an alley, knocking on an unmarked door. The narrow passage stood right on the dividing line where the merchant residences of Westen District met Shantytown, money on one side, desperation on the other.

Hoozier groaned.

Mort checked the player's pulse. 'I'm not sure that was good for him.'

'We only dropped him twice,' said Queem. 'And the effluvia-filth was shallower than usual.'

'This whole city needs a doctor,' grumbled Mort. He knocked again. 'Piotr, open up.'

The door opened and a head peeked out.

Queem seemed disappointed. Whatever he'd expected, it wasn't this little wild-haired man in his lank undertaker's outfit.

'It's almost sunrise,' said Piotr.

'Emergency.'

'Mortimer, you know I don't work between sunrise and four. That's my personal time. For personal things. Come back tomorrow.'

'*Naturellement*,' said Mort. 'Shall I just dump Monsieur Hoozier out here then?'

Piotr's eyes dodged between Mort and Queem. He lifted

Hoozier's lolling head up then jumped back with a shriek. 'That's Kaspar Hoozier.'

Mort flashed the Nuln marker.

'Well don't stand out in the alley. Bring him in! Bring him in!'

They shuffled inside, threw Hoozier on a table. Mort bent, stretched his aching back.

Queem scuttled up to Piotr, notebook open.

'So is Doctor Cleanblood spelled with a C or a K?'

'I don't like that name,' said Doctor Piotr Klenblüd. 'Mortimer, tell him I don't like that name.'

'He doesn't like that name.'

Queem's pen danced across paper. 'And you're a vampire?'

'What of it?'

'You just don't... look...' Queem rolled his wrist as if to say, *you know*.

'Oh, I see. Well I'm very sorry,' said Piotr. 'Were you expecting aquiline good looks? Slicked-back hair? Someone taller than a thirteen-year-old?' Piotr ran a hand through his wild, electric-shock frizz and sneered.

One of his fangs had grown in diagonally.

Queem shrugged.

'Stereotype and media culture! Those vampires in magazines, they're always gorgeous, but–'

'Piotr,' said Mort. 'The game's in two hours.'

'I'll get my things.'

Piotr opened a cracked leather apothecary's bag, rummaged inside, and emerged with two semi-opaque coils of tubing. Each one ended in a cork with a needle embedded in it – a big needle.

Queem leaned in, staring.

'Squig intestine,' Piotr said, offhand. 'Very durable, always returns to its original shape.' He fitted one tube to his right fang, the other to his left.

'Is he,' stuttered Queem. 'Is he going to...' Then he noticed the tubes had faded yellow labels.

One read IN. The other read OUT.

'Hold him down, please,' said Piotr. 'I need quiet. If I lose focus, I sneeze – and nobody wants that.'

With impossibly fast hands, he punched the IN needle into one side of Hoozier's neck, and the OUT needle into the other.

Then he closed his eyes and tilted his head back. A conductor enraptured by an exquisite crescendo.

Blood crept up the IN tube, met the crooked fang, and after a moment, dribbled down the OUT tube. It came slow at first, then steadily, with the whooshing, spurting hiss of a bilge pump.

Piotr's ash-grey face bloomed pink.

'He's laundering the blood,' whispered Mort. 'Vampires are unaffected by intoxicants. He takes the blood out, neutralises it and pumps it back in.'

They watched for one minute, two.

'How long does it ta–'

Hoozier moaned, head rolling to one side. His eyes flickered under closed lids, deep in dream.

'Hold on, Queem.' Mort leaned on Hoozier's wrist. 'Tight.'

Hoozier's eyes snapped open. Sober. Alert. Bulging. Questing around to take in the blood tubes, the rat holding him down, the vampire.

Then he screamed. Not a manly scream, but one like a very small girl falling off a very tall building.

'Kaspar!' Mort said, forceful but steady. 'Easy. Easy. We're helping you.'

Hoozier fought. Mort put his whole weight on the arm, but it lifted anyway. Queem came right off the floor, wrapped his tail around a table leg to shackle himself down. The long scream turned into a series of repeating screeches.

'Mort,' said Queem.

'What?' Mort grunted.

'Do vampires turn purple?'

'Don't be…' Mort looked up. Piotr was snuffling, snorting and turning mauve. '*Merde.*'

'I thought–'

'Piotr,' said Mort. 'Piotr, you can stop now. Piotr!'

Mauve veins bulged in Piotr's neck. His eyes showed jewel red. Furious hunger on his features.

Cap-rage mixed with bloodlust.

So Madcap *could* affect vampires – if they took enough.

Piotr made a hideous slurping sound. Inside the tubes, the blood slowed and reversed. Instead of IN and OUT, they were OUT and OUT. Two big straws sucking Hoozier dry.

Mort grabbed the tubes, ripped them free. Drops of red stained Hoozier's befouled jersey. The thrower scuttled off the table backwards, away from the bloodsucking horror. Crab-walked until he nestled in a corner.

Piotr leapt onto the table, crouched and hissing, tubes dangling from his fangs like catfish whiskers. He sprung for Mort's throat.

Mort got his arm up. The little vampire clamped down on his forearm, the durable tubes saving Mort from the fangs. Piotr snarled, shook him the way a dog shakes a rabbit. Mort felt his boot heels clip the ceiling before Piotr slammed him down on his arse and went for the jugular. Mort grabbed handfuls of frizzy hair, felt a cool tongue lap his neck.

Pop.

The green heat-lightning flash of a warpstone crystal lit the room.

'Really?' Mort snapped. 'Now?'

But the vampire let go, hissing, shielding his face with his hands.

Queem worked the action of his camra, plugged another crystal in the flash dish, let off another burst at the retreating vampire. 'Stab him!' he shouted. 'Use your murder-knife!'

'My *what* knife?' yelled Mort.

Piotr moved whip-fast. One second he was cowering, the next he'd backhanded Queem's camra into the ceiling. Lenses and focus rings rained down on the floorboards. Then he came at Mort on all fours, scuttling across the floorboards like a lizard, clawing up towards his neck.

Queem hit the vampire sideways, leaping on his back with a grace that seemed foreign to his hunched posture. Piotr tried to reach the scratching, chewing thing riding him, but Queem sank his teeth into the vampire's shoulder and hung on. Two hyperactive monsters locked in a cyclone of hissing and clawing.

Then Mort saw Queem's knife. Really, it was less a large knife than a small scimitar. The skaven pulled it from his robes, paused to seek his target, then stabbed down.

Piotr stumbled, blinked. His eyes cleared, the crimson rolling back to reveal a puzzled expression, as if trying to identify what was wrong.

Answer: there was a knife embedded in his head, diagonally, at the same angle as his crooked fang.

His eyes rolled up and he dropped forward. Queem rode him all the way to the floor.

'*Saint Graal*,' Mort breathed.

Queem yanked the blade free, turned, pointed at the gory steel, incredulous. 'Who doesn't carry a murder-knife?'

'I… don't?'

'Lucky-fortunate I was here, then.'

'You…' Mort took stock. 'Thank you.'

'Well,' Queem sniffed, twitched his whiskers. 'I figure you've got a few more stories in you. Feature stuff, you know. Headline-worthy. Be a waste if you died.'

'Poor Piotr.'

'Vampire.' Queem rolled his eyes. 'Immortal.'

'*Oui*. Suppose he'll be fine if we pack him in a coffin before sunrise–' Mort's eyes snapped wide. 'Sunrise!'

Queem straightened. 'Let's go.'

Hoozier was nestled with his back to the corner, knees drawn to his chest, eyes haunted. It didn't help that a bloody, filth-stained Bretonnian and an abominable rodent were trying to coax him out.

'Game day, Kaspar,' said Mort. 'One hour before final check-in, two until kick-off.'

'Greetings,' said Queem, shaking his limp hand. 'Skellig Queem, *Spike!* Scandalmonger of Skavenblight, Clanrat Columnist, etcetera. Big fan. Been follow-stalking you for a while now.'

'Stadium's three districts away. You ready to run, Kaspar?' Mort asked.

'F-forgot how.'

'You'll remember on the way,' said Queem.

In fact, they had a hard time keeping up. Hoozier's system was whistle-clean. Probably for the first time in years.

'This feels great!' Hoozier said, jogging backwards. 'Does sobriety feel like this all the time?'

'Pretty much,' Mort huffed.

Hoozier shook his head, smiling at the wonder of it, and pulled further away.

They heard the chanting as they approached the stadium.

'Hoo-zier! Hoo-zier! Hoo-zier!'

'They're about to get what they want,' Hoozier grinned. He grabbed a street light, swung around the last corner, threw his arms out to accept the crowd's love as he jogged into the home team's staff entrance.

Mort turned the corner, grabbed the back of the player's jersey. 'Uh, Kaspar.'

A hundred sets of painted faces turned towards Hoozier. They were painted the wrong colour.

Not fans, a mob.

'Get him!' someone screamed.

Hoozier crouched low, Queem drew the murder-knife.

'Go on the whistle?' Mort offered.

He blew it.

The crowd didn't have a chance. The trio bored though the stupefied mob like a musket ball, Hoozier blitzing like he was on the field. Within thirty seconds, they were through, past the phalanx of security protecting the entrance with siege shields.

Hoozier made check-in with two minutes to spare. Breezed through substance inspection. Some anomalies, sure – a hint of undead, but that was probably from the mob blood on his shirt. He had just enough time to gear up before the coin toss.

Mort had done it. Despite everything, he'd got Hoozier here and ready to play. He walked the sideline in a borrowed Nuln staff shirt, letting the glow of the stadium wash over him. The buzz of the crowd, the smell of blood on grass.

The JumboBall, levitating precariously over the field, replaying the last catch.

He saw a knot of referees discussing a call and waved. They turned their backs.

'Screw 'em,' said Queem, sliding up beside him. 'They couldn't do what you did last night.'

'Yeah... screw 'em,' Mort agreed. 'I fulfilled the contract. Kept my honour for today.'

Hoozier scored a touchdown. Announcers howled. Cannons shot confetti into the stands. A cheerleader tossed her purple hair.

Purple hair.

'I need to see Cherbourg,' said Mort.

Cherbourg's office had the curtains drawn. Heavy velvet muffling the cacophony of game day.

Mort laid the team marker on the desk. 'Hoozier, delivered as agreed.'

'Your fee.' Cherbourg tossed a heavy purse on the desktop. It landed hard. 'I have a meeting. You know the way out.'

No glass of wine this time, Mort noticed.

Mort gestured towards the curtained windows. 'Hoozier's having the game of his life. Gunners up by three. Congratulations, you're in the finals.'

'We'll sell a lot of jerseys,' Cherbourg said, sour.

'It was a strange night,' Mort chuckled, sitting on a corner of Cherbourg's desk. 'Queem showed up on an anonymous tip. Had to promise him an exclusive to buy him off. A bartender passed Hoozier some Madcap. Then the watch raids the place, which is odd... Usually they're so slow.'

'Better if I don't know details,' Cherbourg said, suddenly very interested in his desk drawer.

'Then we get to the stadium, and there's a mob. Turns out...' Mort drew a flyer from his pocket. 'Someone put a bounty on him. Death or serious injury.'

Cherbourg said nothing.

'And strangely... the waitress who passed him Madcap – she's on the cheer squad today.'

'Had to keep her quiet, somehow.' Cherbourg pulled a long-barrelled pistol from the drawer. 'The question is, how do I keep *you* quiet?'

'Money is traditional.' Mort shrugged. 'But your accounts are a little short. You'd planned to get Hoozier arrested or killed, *non*? Then use his insurance policy to bail out the club? I was there to steer him to the right places, be a witness for the claim.'

'And attract Queem,' Cherbourg said. 'Once I tipped the rat-bastard off that you were there, he couldn't resist. And when his article smears Hoozier out of the league, I'll still get the insurance claim. In fact, you promised the little vermin an exclusive? I'll give him a quote for your obituary.' He smiled. 'Mort D'Arthur, disgruntled ex-referee, came at me in my office over a botched contract. Self-defence. No one would question it.'

'Well, they might,' said Mort. He drew back the curtain.

Cherbourg's mouth opened in a silent *no*. Staring back through the window was his own face, ten feet tall. A mirror of the scene inside his office – the owner pointing a pistol at Mort – floated outside.

For the first time in sports history, the Nuln JumboBall wasn't tuned to Cabalvision – it was a live feed from *Spike!*.

Queem stepped out from behind the curtain, a camra rig on his shoulder. 'Any comments on your new management style, Mister Cherbourg?'

Mort shrugged. 'I promised him an exclusive. And professionals keep their promises.'

DISMEMBER THE TITANS

GRAEME LYON

Blood soaked the astrogranite of the Light's Hope Stadium.

This in itself wasn't unusual. Nuffle knows I've spilled plenty myself in the course of countless Blood Bowl matches – both mine and various opponents'. But this was a little different. For a start, it wasn't match day. The stadium wasn't filled with the noise (and smell) of cheering fans, and I wasn't wearing my crimson and white Talabheim Titans kit and facing off against whoever hoped to take the team down a peg or two this week.

And usually, when Blood Bowl players were left with missing limbs, it was obvious why, and who had torn the offending extremity off.

The corpse of Hans Kniezehen had been carefully laid on the field in the spot he usually occupied at the start of a game. It was deliberate and provocative. And in the case of Johann Walsh, star Catcher and my best friend, what it provoked was a seemingly never-ending stream of vomit.

Though, to be fair, that was probably because of the missing limbs and the fact that most of Hans' innards were spread in a six-feet radius around him.

The stench was terrible – the rich copper tang of blood mixed with the unmistakable smell of voided bowels. It was like being downwind of a beastman just before laundry day. Most of the team, and our head coach Gerritt Vanderwald, were staying as far away as possible from the scene of the crime.

At least, I assumed it was a crime, because it seemed *quite* unlikely that Hans had accidentally disembowelled himself and removed his own arms and legs.

Ghurg the ogre was standing protectively over Johann as he emptied his stomach onto the pitch, and Gerhardt, the team's water boy and unofficial mascot, had been sent to the nearest watchhouse to get someone to come and look at the scene.

I wasn't holding out much hope that they would come. They hadn't for the previous two disturbingly similar deaths. The murder of relatively wealthy Blood Bowl players didn't tend to bother the watch much, and it really didn't help that the local watch commander was a diehard fan of our local rivals, the Talabec Taleutens. After the last death, I'd had a blazing row with him when he shrugged and said it would just make the next Titans–Taleutens game an easier win for his boys. If Ghurg hadn't picked me up and carried me away, I'd have committed murder myself. Bet *that* one would have led to an arrest.

I was as near to the corpse as I could bear to go, a handker-chief over my nose and mouth in a vain attempt to smother the smell.

'Find anything, Juliana?' I turned to see a chalk-white

Johann walking towards me, Ghurg behind him like a huge and imposing bodyguard. A diminutive goblin sat atop the ogre's shoulders. How we'd adopted the goblin was a long story, but he was useful on occasion. Just now he was leaning down to rub Johann's shoulders. It would have made me laugh if I hadn't been standing almost in the guts of a fellow player.

'Looks the same as the others to me. Arms and legs missing, intestines…' I trailed off as I saw Johann gag. 'Well, you know. Nothing obviously different. Nothing that hints who it might be.'

'Three,' Johann said, pain in his voice. 'Three of our friends dead, and we have no idea who's doing it or why. Who could be this cruel?'

I considered reeling off a list, starting with at least a dozen Blood Bowl players I could think of, some of them standing not thirty feet away, but I bit my tongue. This went beyond the usual casual violence of the game. There was something almost ritual and occult about it. Something disturbing.

'Someone who hates us, I would guess,' I said. 'Someone who knows their way around a knife. Someone with a strong stomach as well.'

I sighed in frustration. 'We still don't even know why the killer chose those three, how he found them, how he incapacitated them… It's not like any of them are pushovers.'

I gestured over to a pair of the team's cleaning crew who'd been hanging around since they found the body. They both seemed fine – but then, our cleaners had to have strong stomachs, especially for cleaning out the privy when we hosted a dwarf team. All that ale did funny things to their bodies.

'There's not much point in waiting,' I told them. 'Get the body down to the infirmary.'

They started loading the corpse onto a stretcher, trying hard not to step in the spread innards and fluids, and failing miserably. After a minute or two, they were joined by a stooped, gaunt man in a white coat, who kept glancing over at us as he issued them with commands.

'We do have one small advantage on our side this time,' I said with false cheer.

'What's that?' asked Johann miserably, trying not to look in the direction of the corpse.

'Our new team apothecary,' I said, pointing over at the white-coated figure. 'I think he used to work in a morgue somewhere down south. Maybe he can find some clues on the body.'

Johann looked at me warily. 'Please tell me you don't want to be there while he… does whatever he does with it.'

'You know me, Johann,' I replied. 'I never turn down a chance to watch an expert at work.'

Johann did know me, better than anyone, just as I knew him. That had been the case for nearly two years, ever since the body-swapping incident. I'd been a cheerleader then, dreaming of being on the pitch tackling orcs rather than by the side shouting vapid slogans and being leered at by half the crowd.

I'd had my chance when an incompetent wizard had cast a spell that swapped my mind into Johann's body and vice versa. I'd scored a winning touchdown and once the mess had been sorted out and I was back in my own skin, I was quickly signed up by an Amazon coach who'd been watching the game.

I spent a season over the sea in the Lustria League learning how to be a blitzer from some of the best in the business, but the warm climate didn't agree with me and I returned to Talabheim, where Johann convinced the Titans' owners to take a risk on a female player – one of the very few in the Old World. I still didn't know quite what he'd done to get me on the team – he'd never told me, no matter how many times I'd asked – but I remained grateful.

The owners were grateful now too – the combination of my blitzing ability (and the surprise a lot of players felt seeing a small human woman barrelling towards them) and Johann's well-honed catching skills had made us a formidable pair. The fact that we could often get a sense of what the other was thinking helped a lot. Commentators had started referring to us as a pair more often than not, and we'd even had a few sponsorship deals as a double act – though the number of McMurty's spamburgers we'd had to eat for a Cabalvision advert had put us both off endorsements for a while.

That aside, we worked well together and with us leading the squad, the Titans were in serious danger of becoming a team people outside Talabheim paid attention to. Another season like this one and we might even make a dent in one of the major tournaments.

If we had any players left, that was. With three dead in two weeks – and none of them on the gridiron – things were looking distinctly shaky.

The infirmary was in the basement beneath the stadium, through a winding series of service corridors. It sat directly below the home team dugout, with a trapdoor and elevator that could be used to lower injured players for treatment. When they were beyond help, or if the player was particularly unpopular with the rest of the team, the elevator stayed at the bottom and the body was just pushed down through the trapdoor.

'I hate it down here,' muttered Johann. 'It twists and turns so much you could play Dungeonbowl in it.'

'That's not a bad idea, actually,' I said. 'It would be something a bit different for the fans. Maybe a bit tight for the camra wizards though. They'd be right in the thick of the action, and you know how they hate getting their robes dirty.'

'That was one time,' said Johann. 'And I paid for a new set when the blood wouldn't wash out.'

I glanced at him and saw a thin, slightly pained smile on his face. I knew he appreciated my attempts to keep the mood light even in the face of tragedy.

We reached the open door of the infirmary and I stopped, giving a tentative knock on the frame. Inside, a thin, reedy voice said, 'Come in.' I glanced back at Johann, and he nodded and stepped inside.

The smell of the open corpse on the metal table in the room's centre was almost masked by the exotic scent emanating from a dozen or so censers that had been strung around the walls. Each had a burning candle hanging beneath it, and was stuffed with herbs. I moved to the closest and sniffed it curiously. I couldn't place the smell.

'Ah, interested in my counter-microbials, are you? Trade secret recipe, I'm afraid. The Guild of Morticians would be most upset if I gave that away.'

I turned to face the new apothecary. Close up, he seemed quite short, possibly because he walked with a hunch, and he was very slender, to the point of being gaunt. His pinched, pointed face gave him a vaguely sinister look, and though he was well-dressed in clothes that were clearly very expensive given their cut, there was something about him that gave me the strangest sense of shabbiness.

'I am Doctor Werner von Blaustein,' he said, bowing slightly.

'And you need no introductions, of course. Johann Walsh and Juliana Tainer. "Beauty and the Beast", *Spike! Magazine* calls you, I believe.'

'Only because Johann's so pretty,' I said.

'And because of the way you broke their reporter's wrist when he grabbed your bum,' Johann added.

'I gave him a warning first. He chose not to listen.'

The apothecary laughed hollowly. 'I see your reputation as a double act off the field as well as on is well earned. I don't want to appear prurient, but tell me, is there more than mere friendship here, hmm?'

'Yes,' said Johann sharply. 'Juliana is like my *sister*.' He emphasised the last word strongly. We were both sick of getting that question from, well, pretty much everyone. Not to mention being splashed on the sports pages whenever we were out in public together, as if that was at all relevant to the game.

Von Blaustein got the hint. He coughed. 'I used to have a sister,' he said, then, as an awkward silence fell, he moved on to business. 'I've had a preliminary look at the body of your erstwhile comrade,' he said. 'I'd say he's been dead for about six hours, and that he died from exsanguination as a result of the dissection of his torso and removal of his limbs.'

It took me a moment to translate the medical terms – I'd never been much for biology – and I'm sure my face must have mirrored Johann's as he did the same and paled.

'You mean he was alive when he was cut up?' I asked in horror.

'Oh, absolutely,' said the apothecary.

'What kind of person could do that?' asked Johann.

Von Blaustein answered the rhetorical question as he bent over the body and examined it more closely. I saw Johann turn away and study the wall. 'One with training and some considerable skill. The cuts are clean and made in strategic places, such as they would be in a limb for transplant. The removal of the intestines was performed by a practised hand. All in all, I'd say that you're looking for a surgeon. In fact, looking more closely, I would say...'

He paused, raised a finger and stepped over to a door on the other side of the infirmary that I recalled led to his office. He emerged a moment later carrying a large wooden box. 'What do you know of surgical knives?' he asked.

'Nothing,' I answered.

He nodded. 'Anyone who practices surgery, on the living or dead, will have a highly prized set of knives and scalpels. These are mine.' He opened the box and I peered inside at a set of a dozen pristine blades of various shapes and sizes, some of them frankly terrifying. He pulled a couple out and bent over the corpse again. He seemed to be comparing the blades to the cuts on the torso and where arms and legs had once been.

'What are you doing?' I asked.

'Applying scientific method,' he said. 'I have a theory, and I'm gathering evidence. And I'm pleased – or perhaps that's not quite the right word – to say that I am quite certain the cuts were applied with blades very much like these. In fact, they may have been exactly these blades. I don't suppose my predecessor had a grudge against the team at all?'

I laughed. 'He didn't last here long enough. The last three have all upped sticks and gone within a few weeks of starting. No idea where. They just cleared their desks and vanished in the middle of the night.'

Von Blaustein raised a narrow eyebrow. 'How intriguing. I hope I last a little longer than them.' He looked thoughtful for a second. 'You intend to investigate these crimes?' he asked. I nodded. 'In that case, I'd look at people who have reason to hate the Talabheim Titans. I assume your security team keeps any threatening letters the team has received, hmm?'

Going through the hate mail was a worryingly long and tedious task. We drafted in Gerhardt to help, and Doctor von Blaustein hung around as well after he'd finished whatever he was doing with Hans' body. It turned out that for every fan who loved the Titans there was another who would happily stab half the team to death for extremely spurious reasons. We'd been there for hours before we had any sort of a breakthrough.

'Here's one for Hans,' said Johann, waving a piece of parchment. 'Says he should die because he missed with that pass in the Nuln Oilers game a few months back and bruised Karolina's face with the ball. I guess this guy is a big fan of hers.'

I glanced at the signature and rolled my eyes. 'Yeah, I know that one. He's gone through an obsession with every cheerleader on the squad, myself included. He's harmless though. Also definitely doesn't have the skills we're looking for. He can barely dress himself.'

'What about this one?' piped up Gerhardt from the corner of the room, where he was cross-legged on the floor surrounded by parchment next to the apothecary, who seemed sound asleep. 'I know the name. He's a barber in the old town who also does surgery. He took out my uncle's tooth a year or two back. Took half his jaw with it too.'

Johann leaned over and grabbed the parchment from Gerhardt's hand. He gave it a scan and nodded. 'Looks promising,' he said. 'Some very… vivid imagery in here. Including disembowelling. One to check out, I think.'

'Does he threaten anyone in particular?' I asked.

'The whole team in general. Seems to think we're responsible for a reduction in his business for reasons he doesn't really make clear. Seems a bit mad, to be honest.'

'Old town, you say?' I asked Gerhardt. The boy nodded.

'Yeah. Down by the big warehouses. He converted one into his shop and surgery.'

'Should we pay him a visit?' I asked Johann. He thought for a moment and shook his head.

'Could be dangerous. I think we need to keep an eye on him instead. Watch his shop and see if we can catch him leaving and follow him.'

I'm not entirely sure what I expected from a stakeout. The word conjured scenes of sitting in a coach – borrowed from the stadium for the night, with a quick covering of mud obscuring the team logo on the side and the horse sent back with Gerhardt so it wouldn't draw attention – trading wisecracks with Johann and keeping an eagle eye for anything going on in the barber's shop. Johann wasn't convinced it would be quite as exciting.

'I think you've been watching too much of *Zavant Konniger's Mystery Hour* on Cabalvision,' he grumbled.

He was right.

The first hour was reasonably good fun. Johann brought snacks, and it was a bit like a two-person party in a cramped and smelly carriage. We peered out the windows through the rain towards the dark barber shop and gossiped about the latest ridiculous rumours we'd heard. The novelty soon wore off though. Perching on the uncomfortable bench in the back to see out the window put my leg to sleep.

We spent a while working out a new way of communicating on the field – a system of taps on our armour that the other could see, with different plays and suggestions for different combinations of taps. That took up a good while, but as the hours wore on, my eyes started to close – but I couldn't let myself drift off, not least because Johann was already out for the count, having fallen asleep shortly after we came up with the tap for buying the other time for a risky play.

At some point, sleep overcame me. I woke to find light piercing the clouds. The rain had stopped during the night, and the grimy old district of the city looked almost pretty in the morning sunshine. My head was also cloudy, so it took me an embarrassingly long time to figure out why I was in a carriage on the street with Johann snoring beside me. When it hit me, I sat bolt upright, hitting my head on the carriage ceiling, which made me swear loudly.

'Not the pliers!' shouted Johann as he was shocked from his slumber. He shook his head and looked around. 'Juliana? What are we– oh! The stakeout. What time is it?'

I wasn't quite sure, but one thing seemed certain – it was late enough that the barber shop should have opened, but it was still dark inside. I swore again and opened the doors of the coach, hopping out. Johann followed, blinking blearily up at the sun.

I marched over to the door of the barber shop, the expression on my face obviously enough to stop the people on the street from getting in my way. I banged hard on the door, which yawned open. Inside was a small room with a couple of chairs in front of mirrors, and a door at the back. I moved cautiously towards that, and tentatively pushed it open. A smell hit me, a rich metallic stench that was becoming all too familiar, with another undercurrent that I couldn't quite place. It was almost like spoiled fruit.

Cautiously, I stepped inside, Johann following behind. 'Not another one,' he said in a low voice. 'Who do you think it is this time?'

I didn't answer. The inside of the back room was large and wreathed in shadows. In the light from the door, I could see a dentist's chair with its back to us. Blood soaked the ground around it, and I thought I could see intestines snaking down from the seat. I pulled up my top, over my mouth and nose, moved towards the chair and slowly turned it around, bracing myself for the sight of another one of my teammates with his insides in the wrong place.

I got half of what I expected.

In front of me was another eviscerated corpse, with arms and legs missing, but it neither wore the crimson and white of the Talabheim Titans, nor did it have a face I recognised. It was a heavy-set man, past the prime of his life (well, obviously, but even before he died, he was getting on a bit) with a full greying beard and shaved head. He'd clearly been well muscled once, but it had gone to fat.

'Who is that?' asked Johann, the mystery obviously overwhelming his usual physical reaction.

'I think,' I said slowly, 'that it's our suspect.'

'Ah. That's awkward. Unless you think he cut himself open.'

'I've seen stranger things,' I mused. 'But I think we can probably rule that out, unless he somehow hid his arms and legs before he bled to death.' I looked back into the shop and saw an oil lantern sitting on a low bench beneath the window, and pointed to it. 'Light that, will you? I want a closer look at this.'

'Why do you always want a closer look?' he asked, as he grabbed the lamp and a long match from the box next to it, and lit it with shaky hands. He held it up and the light illuminated more of the shop… including something in the now receding shadows. Something that moved.

I jumped, and bumped the chair. The remnants of the corpse fell forward and slumped to the ground. Innards scattered over the floor, blood and other bodily fluids sloshing onto – and into – my shoes. A pair of expensive Orcidas, limited edition, ruined. And whatever was in the shadows started to come towards us.

A low moan echoed through the space, and a figure emerged, arms outstretched. It was followed by another, and then more. They were slow and shambling. I suddenly realised what that other scent was that I'd been unable to place: the sickly sweet smell of rotting flesh that I'd experienced playing Blood Bowl against undead teams. The figures were zombies.

As they came closer to the light, I saw that they were unlike the zombies I'd seen on the field. Those had clearly been humans who had died and been resurrected through dark magic. Flesh sloughing from bone and rotting teeth peering from behind peeled-back lips had been hideous enough, but what was in front of us now was an order of magnitude worse.

Each of these creatures seemed to have been constructed – there was no other word for it – from a variety of different corpses. Mismatched limbs had been neatly stitched to torsos in a fusion of magic and mad science that I'd only witnessed before in some of the creations that unscrupulous skaven teams tried to sneak onto the pitch.

Horror froze me in place, and I guessed it was the same for Johann – even the shaking of the lantern light had stopped. The exit was behind us, but we couldn't just leave and let the stitched-together zombies escape onto the street. There would be carnage. As I tried to formulate a plan, instinct took over. This was just like a game of Blood Bowl, and we could win it, Johann and I.

'Johann, long pass!' I yelled before barrelling forward. I don't think I took the zombies by surprise, exactly – that feeling was probably beyond them now – but they certainly didn't have a chance to grab me as I pushed them aside. One grasping arm came close, and I noted a faded word emblazoned on it that seemed familiar, but that thought could wait. When I reached the far wall, I turned and shouted, 'Now!'

Johann was a Catcher, not a Thrower, but he made the pass of his life with that lantern. It arced over the heads of the zombies, trailing sparks, and I caught it out of the air by the handle, and swung it into the body of the nearest creature. It smashed and splashed the zombie with burning oil. The patchwork undead monster went up in flames like dry tinder. The fire spread quickly, and I went low, dodging between their legs and grabbing Johann as I passed him. We sprinted through the door and Johann slammed it shut behind us. We quickly exited the shop, watching through the dirty window as the zombies burst through the back door, setting the fixtures and fittings aflame. In short order, the entire building was ablaze, and it looked like the fire might spread to adjacent structures.

I looked at Johann, who tore his eyes away from the conflagration and fixed them on mine.

'After my job, are you?' he asked. 'That was a hell of a catch.'

I smiled, but only briefly. 'We should get out of here before we're blamed for this fire,' I said, and headed away from the scene. We were being ignored for now as people ran for water, ran for help or just ran around in a panic, but that wouldn't last. The very last thing we needed just now was another mention in the gossip columns. We left the carriage. Without the horse, we had no way to get it back, and it would just draw attention.

As we walked back in the direction of the stadium, the adrenaline high subsided and I remembered what I'd seen on the arm of one of the zombies.

'Johann?'

'Yeah?'

'Hans had a tattoo on his arm, didn't he?'

Johann let out a little laugh. 'Yeah. He got it on a drunken night out after we beat the Barak Varr Pirates. He asked for "Mother", but he was slurring, and he'd lost some teeth during the game when a Trollslayer hit him, so the tattooist didn't understand what he was saying.'

'That's what I thought,' I said.

'Why do you ask?'

I paused for a moment before I answered. 'Because I really don't think there's likely to be more than one arm in Talabheim with "Muffer" tattooed on it.'

'You're sure it was that tattoo?' Johann asked for roughly the hundredth time as we entered the Light's Hope Stadium and started navigating the corridors towards the Titans' dugout.

'Unmistakably, and if you ask me again, you'll be getting a broken kneecap,' I said firmly.

'What's that about a broken kneecap?' Doctor von Blaustein asked, emerging from a corner in front of us. I thought I saw him quickly stuff something into his pocket, but I paid it no mind.

'Just a hypothetical break,' Johann told him as we continued walking and he fell into step with us.

Von Blaustein smiled a thin-lipped smile. 'Not much I can do about hypothetical injuries, I suppose. How did your surveillance go?'

I shook my head. 'Not well. The barber wasn't the killer.'

'Oh, and how do you know?'

'He was dead and missing–'

The last words were knocked from me as we came up through the dugout and stepped onto the field... where another Titans player was dead.

'He looked a lot like that, actually,' said Johann, his voice devoid of any humour whatsoever.

Von Blaustein ordered us down to his office while he arranged for the body to be brought to what I could only think of now as the morgue. He arrived a short while later and bustled around the small space making tea. I peered at the walls, which were filled with hand-drawn anatomical diagrams, many of them painted with delicate watercolours. The apothecary must have seen my interest.

'I did those myself during my studies,' he said. 'The human body is a fascinating thing, and the bodies of other races even more so.' He pointed to the wall behind me, where cross-sections of an orc, a skaven and a beastman were displayed. 'Never been able to get permission to autopsy an elf or dwarf,' he mused. 'And I'd love to see what a lizardman is like inside.'

'Mushy, in my experience,' I said absent-mindedly, thinking back to my time in the Lustria League.

'It's astonishing how many similarities there are between the various species under the skin,' von Blaustein said, handing me a large mug of steaming tea, and then passing another to Johann. 'It's curious, isn't it, that despite the similarities only humans seem to take to being raised as undead?'

'Undead?' Johann asked, glancing at me. What had brought on this abrupt turn in the conversation?

'Yes,' the apothecary said. 'You only ever see human zombies and skeletons in Blood Bowl teams, don't you? And have you ever met a dwarf vampire or orc werewolf?'

I relaxed and took a long sip of my tea. It was much sweeter than I liked, and had a herbal flavour I didn't recognise, but I was hardly a tea connoisseur. I sat back and looked at Johann as he swallowed half his mug of tea in one long gulp, only half listening as von Blaustein continued.

'I'd imagine all the patchwork zombies you encountered in that barber shop were made entirely with human parts as well, weren't they?'

It took a minute for what he'd said to filter through. Johann was quicker than me. He sat up sharply, spilling some of the remnants of his tea and wincing as it scalded his hand. 'How do you know there were zombies?' he asked cautiously, setting the mug on the desk.

'I heard you mention them when we met in the corridors,' the apothecary said. I thought back. It was possible – it had been a long morning so far, and my memory of exactly what had been said was hazy. But Johann was staring at von Blaustein now.

'No,' he said firmly. 'We haven't used the word "zombie" anywhere near you. And we certainly never mentioned that they were made up of different parts.'

Von Blaustein smiled again, though he seemed very far away now, as if I were watching him through a long, dark tunnel. He straightened himself up, and I realised for the first time that he was quite tall when he wasn't hunching over.

'Hunching is a funny word,' I slurred, though I wasn't sure why.

Johann looked at me in alarm. 'Juliana, what's wrong?'

'I think I'm drunked,' I grinned at him. 'Nonono. Not drunked. Drugged.'

I felt like I needed a little sleep now, and my body seemed to agree, because I was lying on the floor, and I didn't remember telling it to go there. I looked up at Johann, who had launched himself out of his chair, but he seemed to be falling like a treeman after a hard block, verrrrrrrrrrrrrry slowly and at a funny angle. Or maybe I was at a funny angle. It was hard to tell, and then Johann had fallen on top of me and his body was warm and everything went dark.

I opened my eyes, and it was still dark.

I blinked several times, and my eyes started to adjust to the gloom. My brain took longer to get into gear. I felt fuzzy. How much had I had to drink? I couldn't even remember being anywhere near an inn, let alone drinking anything with a little umbrella in it. I remembered... a cup of sweet tea. In an office. With... a serial killer. I swore loudly and repeatedly and tried to sit up, but realised that something was holding my wrists and ankles tightly. Something cold, dry and papery. Something that smelled dangerously familiar. I blinked again and looked around. And screamed.

I was lying on a long stone table, and my arms and legs were being held in literal death grips – by patchwork zombies.

'You're awake then,' came Johann's voice from nearby. Relief flooded through me.

'Johann, where are we?' I asked.

'Best I can tell, Doctor von Blaustein's murder den. He's been in and out, muttering to himself.'

'Do you have a plan to get out?'

'Maybe. I–'

The banging of a door somewhere above us cut Johann

off, and I looked up to see the light of a lantern, a hooded figure carrying it. I heard booted footsteps banging down rickety wooden stairs, and a moment later the traitorous apothecary stood before us, bathed in the lantern light. He had swapped his white coat for a long black robe, and with his gaunt features and stooped gait, he looked every inch the necromancer I now knew him to be.

'I thought I heard you talking,' he said. 'I'm so sorry to have kept you waiting.'

'If you're sorry, you can let us go,' snapped Johann.

'Not that sorry, dear boy,' he laughed. 'I'm afraid you'll both have to die tonight. On the plus side, you'll both provide excellent parts for my players.'

'Your *players*?' I asked. 'What are you talking about?'

'Allow me to explain,' he said. 'It all began some twenty years ago, right here in Talabheim. I grew up in the city, you see – in this very house, in fact. The middle child and youngest son of the venerable von Blaustein family. And I was immensely talented. My tutors couldn't keep up with me, I outclassed great thinkers at my family's banquets. I was, even if I say so myself, a prodigy. But I wanted only one thing. Can you guess what, hmm?'

'To be a murdering psychopath?' Johann growled.

'I'm no psychopath, young Johann. I kill only in service to my greater goal. That I enjoy it is just an added bonus. No, I wanted only to play Blood Bowl for my favourite team. The mighty Talabheim Titans. This was back in the glory days of the NAF, you understand, when the Titans were a truly world-class team. Not the rabble we have now.'

I bristled at the insult and tried to pull my arms away from their restraints, but the gripping hands were too firm.

'I had every piece of merchandise the team sold. I attended

every game, home and away. I donated huge amounts of my father's money to the team's coffers. So when open tryouts came up, I was sure that my contributions would be enough to get my foot in the door. I went along, in the finest gear money could buy…'

He trailed off and went silent. I had a funny feeling that I knew what was coming next.

'And you were totally humiliated, weren't you? Failed miserably, I'm guessing?'

Von Blaustein slammed his fist down on the stone slab I was held against. 'My name should have been enough. My money. But I was told none of that mattered. Only skill! I could have learned the skills. I just needed the opportunity, and I should have been given it! Instead I was laughed off the pitch. It was clear what I needed to do.'

'Practise and become a better player?' said Johann.

'After such a humiliation? No,' spat the necromancer. 'I had to get my *revenge*. No one could be allowed to get away with treating me like that. No one. So I planned. I planned so carefully. I would bring the Titans down and replace them with my own team – made up of parts of their players. The ultimate vengeance!'

Silence fell. I was too stunned to know what to say. He continued: 'So I went away and studied medicine, learning all the intricacies of the human body so that when the time came, I could take them apart and put them back together again. And then I turned my attentions to a darker art. You may have heard that I studied and worked in the south, hmm? But perhaps not exactly where…'

'Stirland, I heard,' I said.

'Technically, yes. After all, Sylvania *is* nominally a province of Stirland.'

Sylvania – realm of the undead. Ruled by the vampire counts, it was renowned as a mist-shrouded land where horror lurked in every shadow. Clearly von Blaustein had learned the dark arts there.

'I returned to Talabheim and decided the best way to get my hands on Titans players was to join the team as its apothecary. I got rid of the last few until I was the best person left for the job. And in the meantime, I started working on the players. The first I followed to an alehouse and drugged his drink, just enough that he'd fall unconscious when he got home. The second…'

I ignored his droning explanation and focused on another sound in the basement. Beside me, Johann was tapping his fingers against his stone slab, in a pattern that it took me a moment to recognise – it was the system we'd worked out in the carriage what seemed like months ago, but was only the previous evening. Johann was asking me to buy time for him to enact a risky play. I had no idea what he was planning, but it was going to be our only chance. I tried to grab and keep von Blaustein's attention.

'You said you grew up in this house?' I asked him. 'Where are your family? Your servants? I assume there are servants. Rich types like you always have them.'

'They're around you,' he said. 'Some of my first experiments when I returned home after learning how to raise the dead. Oh, I learned so much, but I took it further. Fusing magic and medical science – just like with the censers in my infirmary – which helped keep bodies fresh for me to work with. The wonders I'll be able to perform when I can start working on other races. I will truly push the boundaries of necromancy!'

'I would ask if you're insane, but I think that's blatantly obvious at this point,' I said.

'Insane? Dear me, no,' he laughed. 'If I were insane, I'd never have been able to make such a daring plan work. But work it has. With you two out of the way, there will be no more real threats from your fellow players. I'll be able to kill them all one by one and replace them with my perfect creations, my very own Talabheim Titans! But first I have to kill you. And I'm afraid it's going to be a long, slow process. I am, you see, a very, *very* good apothecary, and I can keep you alive through the entire process. It makes it easier to reattach your parts to other bodies. It will hurt rather a lot though.'

He had moved closer as he spoke and was now much nearer to me than I was comfortable with, and had one of his very sharp knives in his hand. I breathed a sigh of relief as he stepped away again and set the lantern down, but that relief vanished when I saw the spark of a match being lit. Von Blaustein, eerily illuminated by the flickering glow, used it to light some sort of burner on a workbench that ran across one wall beneath racks of what looked like body parts suspended in liquid.

The burner hissed as gas escaped it, and the match found the gas and erupted into a spear of flame. The apothecary held the knife into the fire.

'Heating the scalpel leads to cleaner cuts that cauterise to slow blood loss,' he said. 'It hurts more as well, I understand.'

I hoped that whatever Johann was going to do was going to happen soon.

Even as I had the thought, Johann snapped into action. There was a loud cracking sound from my left, and somehow, amazingly, he was moving. I craned my neck to see and watched him punch the patchwork zombie holding his left arm, somehow having freed his right. It reeled back, and Johann pushed himself forward, kicking the two creatures gripping his legs to the ground. Then he was free and attacking the zombies holding me.

The pressure on my left arm lifted and I reached up to see the necromancer above me. I grabbed his wrist as he brought the knife down. He pushed harder, but he was no match for my Blood Bowl-honed muscles.

'You really should have just worked on your physical skills and tried again to join the team,' I told him. 'Brains are all very well, but you can't beat a bit of strength in Blood Bowl.'

I pushed his arm to the side and the blade cut into the zombie holding my other arm – it reeled back with a distressingly human-sounding scream.

Johann quickly freed my legs and I swung around and kicked von Blaustein in the chest. He fell into the workbench, where the burner was still blasting out flaming gas. The necromancer screamed and flailed, hitting the shelves. Several jars shattered, spilling thick liquid onto him and the floor around him. The fluid accelerated the fire as it doused von Blaustein.

I glanced at Johann, then up at the stairs, which were in serious danger of being set alight. He nodded, and without a word, we ran for it.

We made it up through the sprawling mansion and outside. We collapsed onto the lawn and watched as the flames spread and consumed the ancient building.

'We really need to stop setting fire to things,' Johann said at length.

'I'll get right on that as soon as people stop attacking us with flammable undead things,' I replied.

'Fair point.'

'How did you break free back there?' I asked.

'One of the things holding me had Hans' other arm. I

recognised it from that other tattoo he had. The one that was even worse than "Muffer". He broke that wrist in a training accident a few years ago, and it's been weak ever since. I used that to my advantage.'

'Good old Hans. A solid team player, even in death.'

We lapsed into silence and watched the mansion burn until it collapsed in on itself.

'You know,' I said eventually, 'we're going to need to recruit some new talent. I wonder if the coach will go for open tryouts…'

The look Johann gave me was indescribable, and utterly priceless.

ABOUT THE AUTHORS

Josh Reynolds' extensive Black Library back catalogue includes the Horus Heresy Primarchs novel *Fulgrim: The Palatine Phoenix*, and three Horus Heresy audio dramas featuring the Blackshields. His Warhammer 40,000 work includes the Space Marine Conquests novel *Apocalypse, Lukas the Trickster* and the *Fabius Bile* novels. He has written many stories set in the Age of Sigmar, including the novels *Shadespire: The Mirrored City, Soul Wars, Eight Lamentations: Spear of Shadows*, the Hallowed Knights novels *Plague Garden* and *Black Pyramid*, and *Nagash: The Undying King*. He has written the Warhammer Horror novel *Dark Harvest*, and novella 'The Beast in the Trenches', featured in the portmanteau novel *The Wicked and the Damned*. He has recently penned the Necromunda novel *Kal Jerico: Sinner's Bounty*. He lives and works in Sheffield.

Robbie MacNiven is a Highlands-born History graduate from the University of Edinburgh. He has written the Warhammer Age of Sigmar novel *Scourge of Fate* and the novella *The Bone Desert*, as well as the Warhammer 40,000 novels *Blood of Iax*, *The Last Hunt*, *Carcharodons: Red Tithe*, *Carcharodons: Outer Dark* and *Legacy of Russ*. His short stories include 'Redblade', 'A Song for the Lost' and 'Blood and Iron'. His hobbies include re-enacting, football and obsessing over Warhammer 40,000.

Andy Hall is a professional writer with many years in the games industry. After a stint working for Games Workshop's magazines *White Dwarf* and *Fanatic*, he is currently lead writer for the PC strategy game *Total War: Warhammer*.

Matt Forbeck is the author of the Black Library novels *Blood Bowl, Dead Ball, Death Match* and *Rumble in the Jungle*, based on the Blood Bowl boardgame. He is a prolific author of science fiction and fantasy based in Beloit, Wisconsin.

Graeme Lyon is the author of the Age of Sigmar novella *Code of the Skies* and the audio drama *Sons of Behemat*, as well as the Space Marine Battles novella *Armour of Faith*. He has also written a host of Warhammer 40,000, Warhammer Age of Sigmar and Warhammer short stories including 'The Carnac Campaign: Sky Hunter', 'Kor'sarro Khan: Huntmaster', 'Black Iron', 'The Eighth Victory', 'The Sacrifice' and 'Bride of Khaine'. He hails from East Kilbride in Scotland.

Alec Worley is a well-known comics and science fiction and fantasy author, with numerous publications to his name. He is an avid fan of Warhammer 40,000 and has written many short stories for Black Library including 'Stormseeker', 'Whispers' and 'Repentia'. He lives and works in London.

David Annandale is the author of the Warhammer Horror novel *The House of Night and Chain* and the novella 'The Faith and the Flesh', which features in the portmanteau *The Wicked and the Damned*. His work for the Horus Heresy series includes the novels *Ruinstorm* and *The Damnation of Pythos*, and the Primarchs novels *Roboute Guilliman: Lord of Ultramar* and *Vulkan: Lord of Drakes*. For Warhammer 40,000 he has written *Ephrael Stern: The Heretic Saint*, *Warlord: Fury of the God-Machine*, the Yarrick series, and several stories involving the Grey Knights, as well as titles for The Beast Arises and the Space Marine Battles series. For Warhammer Age of Sigmar he has written *Neferata: Mortarch of Blood* and *Neferata: The Dominion of Bones*. David lectures at a Canadian university, on subjects ranging from English literature to horror films and video games.

Gav Thorpe is the author of the Horus Heresy novels *The First Wall*, *Deliverance Lost*, *Angels of Caliban* and *Corax*, as well as the novella *The Lion*, which formed part of the *New York Times* bestselling collection *The Primarchs*, and several audio dramas. He has written many novels for Warhammer 40,000, including *Indomitus*, *Ashes of Prospero*, *Imperator: Wrath of the Omnissiah* and the Rise of the Ynnari novels *Ghost Warrior* and *Wild Rider*. He also wrote the *Path of the Eldar* and *Legacy of Caliban* trilogies, and two volumes in The Beast Arises series. For Warhammer, Gav has penned the End Times novel *The Curse of Khaine*, the Warhammer Chronicles omnibus *The Sundering*, and recently wrote the Age of Sigmar novel *The Red Feast*. In 2017, Gav won the David Gemmell Legend Award for his Age of Sigmar novel *Warbeast*. He lives and works in Nottingham.

David Guymer's work for Warhammer Age of Sigmar includes the novels *Hamilcar: Champion of the Gods* and *The Court of the Blind King*, the audio dramas *The Beasts of Cartha, Fist of Mork, Fist of Gork, Great Red* and *Only the Faithful*. He is also the author of the Gotrek & Felix novels *Slayer, Kinslayer* and *City of the Damned* and the Gotrek audio dramas *Realmslayer* and *Realmslayer: Blood of the Old World*. For The Horus Heresy he has written the novella *Dreadwing*, and the Primarchs novels *Ferrus Manus: Gorgon of Medusa* and *Lion El'Jonson: Lord of the First*. For Warhammer 40,000 he has written *The Eye of Medusa, The Voice of Mars* and the two Beast Arises novels *Echoes of the Long War* and *The Last Son of Dorn*. He is a freelance writer and occasional scientist based in the East Riding, and was a finalist in the 2014 David Gemmell Awards for his novel *Headtaker*.

Guy Haley is the author of the Siege of Terra novel *The Lost and the Damned*, as well as the Horus Heresy novels *Titandeath*, *Wolfsbane* and *Pharos*, and the Primarchs novels *Konrad Curze: The Night Haunter*, *Corax: Lord of Shadows* and *Perturabo: The Hammer of Olympia*. He has also written many Warhammer 40,000 novels, including the first book in the Dawn of Fire series, *Avenging Son*, as well as *Belisarius Cawl: The Great Work*, *Dark Imperium*, *Dark Imperium: Plague War*, *The Devastation of Baal*, *Dante*, *Darkness in the Blood* and *Astorath: Angel of Mercy*. He has also written stories set in the Age of Sigmar, included in *War Storm*, *Ghal Maraz* and *Call of Archaon*. He lives in Yorkshire with his wife and son.

Robert Rath is a freelance writer from Honolulu who is currently based in Hong Kong. Though mostly known for writing the YouTube series *Extra History*, his credits also include numerous articles and a book for the U.S. State Department. He is the author of the Black Library novel *The Infinite and the Divine*, and the short stories 'The Garden of Mortal Delights' and 'War in the Museum'.

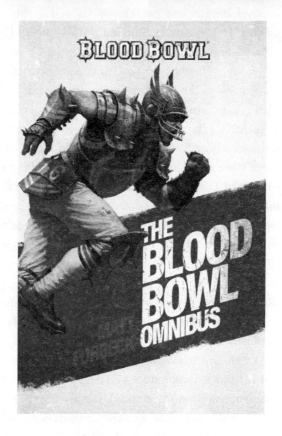

An extract from
The Blood Bowl Omnibus
by Matt Forbeck

From where he stood at the edge of the field, Pegleg looked at his bench. His gaze sliced through each of the players, evaluating them one by one.

Dunk felt Pegleg consider him for a moment and then move on, and he couldn't tell if he was relieved or disappointed. The other scrubs sat frozen stiff, afraid to attract their coach's attention with the slightest movement. Beside him, Dunk could hear Simon whispering a mantra over and over again: 'Don't pick me. Don't pick me. Don't pick me.'

Dunk looked up at Pegleg and saw the coach glaring down at him, a pitiless smile on his face. 'Mr. Hoffnung,' Pegleg said, pointing his hook at the rookie. 'You're in.'

Dunk surprised himself by leaping up and darting out of the dugout to stand next to Pegleg. 'Who am I in for, coach?' he asked.

Pegleg lowered his head and rubbed his eyes with his good hand. A low moan emanated from the other side of the dugout where an apothecary, a tall thin man wearing a grimy, once-white coat and a pair of magnifying glasses over his eyes, was working on Karsten.

'No leeches!' the lineman screamed. 'No leeches!'

'It's that or the bone drill,' the apothecary wheezed. As he spoke, he put down the slimy green things flopping about in his fists and picked up a vicious-shaped metal device. As he spun its handle, the blood-caked tip whirred and clacked. Dunk had never heard such a horrible threat.

'Leeches!' Karsten said. 'By Nuffle's dirty cleats, I'll take my chances with the leeches!'

'But Karsten's a lineman,' Dunk said. 'I'm a thrower. What about Guillermo?' The rookie looked back over his shoulder to see the new lineman drawing a finger under his throat at Dunk. He wasn't sure if Guillermo meant for him to be quiet or that the lineman wanted to kill him. Maybe both.

'You're my man, Mr. Hoffnung,' Pegleg said. 'Don't question my judgment – ever.'

'Aye, coach,' Dunk said with a snappy salute.

Pegleg glared at the rookie as if he couldn't tell if the salute was in mockery or earnest. Then he looked out at the field and said, 'No matter. Make your peace with Nuffle, Mr. Hoffnung, and welcome to your first game of Blood Bowl.'

Armed with some hurried instructions from his coach, Dunk strapped on his helmet and charged out on to the field. The crowd cheered as he raced toward his designated spot, right near the midfield line. Dunk raised his hands in the air to encourage them.

'What do you think you're doing?' Dirk said, standing opposite from Dunk across the line.

'Working the crowd!' Dunk said. 'Blood Bowl's a game that's larger than life. I'm giving them what they want.' He raised his arms again, and the cheering grew.

'Listen to them go!' Dunk said. As he spoke, he spotted Spinne standing several yards back and caught her eye. She smiled at him and blew him a kiss. He caught it in both hands and raised it into the air like a trophy before bringing it back down to stuff into his mouth. The crowed loved it.

'Do you hear what they're saying?' Dirk asked.

Dunk stopped pandering to the stands for a moment and listened carefully. It took him a moment, but he managed to pick some words out of the roar, two words that the fans kept chanting. When he realised what they were, he blanched.

'Fresh meat! Fresh meat! Fresh meat!'

Then the crowd began its collective low groan again, signifying the upcoming kick-off. As the sound grew louder and higher, Dirk beckoned Dunk with a crooked finger, saying something.

'What's that again?' Dunk asked as he leaned forward, cocking his head toward his brother.

The screaming of the crowd reached a crescendo as Dirk shouted at Dunk. 'Remember when you knocked me out of that window when we were kids?'

Dunk nodded. He'd been ashamed of that incident since the day it had happened. Dirk had fallen from the keep's east tower and nearly been killed. Only the intercession of the best apothecary in town had saved the young boy's life. It had been an accident, but the blame for it fell squarely on Dunk's shoulders.

Dirk flashed Dunk an evil grin, then lowered his shoulder and slammed his spiked pad into Dunk, knocking him flying backward to the ground. Dunk's head hit the ground, and stars zoomed past his eyes. The next thing he knew, he felt Dirk's boots stomp on his chest as the Reaver blitzer literally ran right over him.

'Now we're even!' Dirk shouted back as he charged down the field, after the ball.

Dunk crawled to his feet and shook his head. It felt like his brain was loose. The world swam around him, threatening to pitch him off its edge.

The rookie clung to what Pegleg had told him, and he started running toward the end zone.

'Your brother is going to knock you flat,' Pegleg had said.

'No he won't, coach,' Dunk had said, bouncing up and down as he surveyed the field. 'I can take him.'

Pegleg had grabbed the faceguard on Dunk's helmet and wrenched the rookie's head around until they were looking eye to eye. It had hurt, but Dunk hadn't said a word, his tongue catching in his mouth.

'You're going to let him,' Pegleg had said. 'Then you're going to get up and run for the end zone for all you're worth.'

'Which one?'

'Theirs,' Pegleg had said, pointing in the direction the rest of the Hackers were already facing.

'Got it, coach. See, I always get those mixed up, whose end zone is whose. Is yours the one you're defending or the one you're attacking. I can never–'

'Go. That. Way.' Pegleg stabbed his hook toward the Reavers' end zone to punctuate each word. Then he brought the hook around to come up under the chin trap of Dunk's helmet. The sharp tip had caught Dunk right in the fleshy part of his neck there. A single sharp jab could have shoved the hook up into Dunk's mouth so that Pegleg could lead him around by his jawbone.

'Don't disappoint me,' Pegleg had said. Although he'd only whispered, Dunk had heard him as clearly as if everyone else in the stadium had been struck dumb.

All this in mind, Dunk sprinted as hard as he could toward the Reavers' end zone, struggling to clear his head as he ran.

'This time, Kur Ritternacht fields the ball directly,' Bob's voice said. 'He gets some good blocking from the Hackers' linemen and moves the ball forward. K'Thragsh, the only nonhuman player on the field, opens up a hole for him, and he dashes through it.'

'Yes!' said Jim's voice. '"Monster" M'Grash K'Thragsh was one of the Hackers' standouts last year, and a play like that really shows you why. That's the sort of player you can build a team around – or destroy another team with!'

As Dunk ran, he heard someone else pounding after him. He glanced over his shoulder and saw Spinne racing towards him. He had the angle on her to the end zone and he knew he'd get there first. He winked at her, then looked up past her toward the sky.

There, hovering in the air like some great bird of prey, hung the football. It paused for a moment at the top of its arc, then came plummeting back to earth. As it approached, it seemed to move faster, and Dunk realised he'd have to run as fast as he could to catch it.

His eyes still on the ball, Dunk sprinted for the end zone and a date with the ball for which he could not be late. As the ball closed the last few yards toward their mutual meeting spot, he stretched out his arms as far as they could go. The ball landed hard in his fingertips, hard enough to break them, or so it felt. He grabbed at the ball as it were life itself and pulled it in hard to his chest, where he cradled it like an infant.

Dunk hit the ground and rolled hard, keeping himself wrapped around the ball, protecting it from the Astrogranite, which was not as forgiving as he'd hoped. As his momentum faded, he rolled neatly out of his tuck and to his feet. He held the ball high over his head in a moment of pure triumph, and roared along with the crowd.

'Amazing!' Bob's voice said. 'Hoffnung, the rookie phenom from Altdorf, scores a touchdown in his first minute of play!'

The moment was cut short, though, when someone hit Dunk from behind and drove him into the stands.

'Ooh!' said Jim's voice. 'Apparently Dunk's not as much of a lover as a fighter. Lady Schönheit there just made him pay so much for his score that he'll be making equal monthly instalments for the next three years!'

The fans, some of who were more frightening than the players, grabbed Dunk with their meaty paws and greasy claws and passed him bodily up toward the top of the arena. Someone ripped the ball from his hand and bit it in half with his frothing teeth; a rabid dwarf, from the look of him, with a chain that hung between his pierced ear and nose. His face and the shaved sides of his head were tattooed, except where a thin dorsal fin of hair stabbed up from the top, dyed a glaring orange.

Dunk was just happy the dwarf had gone for the football instead of his arm. He looked back down to where he'd come from and saw Spinne waving at him and blowing a good-bye kiss.

'I'll be right back!' he shouted down at her.